DEAD BY THE DOZEN

A MYSTERY THRILLER

JOHN CORWIN

OVERWORLD PUBLISHING

— • —

VENGEANCE COMES

Carver goes to El Fuerte to visit his friend, Joe Donelly, only to find out he's dead.

Joe bred prize-winning horses. One of those horses supposedly kicked him to death. Carver doesn't buy that for a minute.

For one thing, Joe was a former Navy SEAL. He taught Carver everything he knew. He was a careful man. Skilled. Quick on his feet. A pro at handling horses.

Carver quickly discovers there were plenty of reasons for someone to want Joe dead. For one thing, he was running for mayor of El Fuerte, and the sitting mayor is as crooked as they come. Joe wasn't big on politics, but the city was threatening to annex his property and he ran for office just to stop it.

The mayor of El Fuerte is also apparently in league with gangs. She runs the city like she owns it. She spends the city's money like it's her own.

She uses gang members to threaten anyone who gets in her way. And the police do everything she says. She owns them lock, stock and barrel.

The more acquainted Carver becomes with the locals, the more convinced he is that one of them killed Joe. But who did it and why?

The guilty might not be a single person. There might be several people who had a hand in Joe's death. And if that's true, it doesn't matter to Carver. He'll send them all to meet their maker.

Even if he has to kill them by the dozen.

BOOKS BY JOHN CORWIN

Books by John Corwin
Want more? Never miss an update by joining my email list and following me on social media!
Join my Facebook group at https://www.facebook.com/groups/overworldconclave
Join my email list: www.johncorwin.net
Fan page: https://www.facebook.com/johncorwinauthor

PSYCHOLOGICAL THRILLERS
The Family Business
AMOS CARVER THRILLERS
Dead Before Dawn
Dead List
Dead and Buried
Dead Man Walking
Dead By The Dozen
Dead Run
Dead Weather Days
Dead to Rights
Dead but not Forgotten
CHRONICLES OF CAIN
To Kill a Unicorn
Enter Oblivion
Throne of Lies
At The Forest of Madness
The Dead Never Die
Shadow of Cthulhu
Cabal of Chaos
Monster Squad

JOHN CORWIN

CHAPTER 1

Joe Donnely was enjoying his last morning alive.

He had a fresh cup of coffee. Black and a little bitter. Just how he liked it. He was sitting on his front deck, staring out at the mountains. They were green this time of year. The rocky soil was covered in scrub brush and wildflowers.

The morning temperature was nice and cool. Just perfect for sitting outside with a hot cup of coffee in hand. That would change quickly with the rising sun. By the middle of the day, it would be in the mid-eighties.

Andrea came out of the front door carrying a to-go mug. She leaned over. Kissed his forehead. "I'll see you in town for lunch?"

He took her hand. Kissed it gently. "Sit down and enjoy the sunrise with me." He pulled her into his lap.

She laughed. Nearly dropped her coffee mug. She set it on the table next to his chair. Kissed his cheeks. Hugged him. "Amor, I'm so sorry I can't this morning. I can't be late for my appointment."

"I know. I'm just teasing you, baby." Joe kissed her long and hard. "I'm going to take Sunshine out for a ride. Probably take him down the valley and around the mountain."

Her eyes flared with concern. "Is he broken enough for that? I thought he was still giving you trouble." Her Spanish accent grew stronger with her concern.

"He's almost there." Joe's eyes went distant like they always did when he talked about a challenge. "By the end of the week, he'll be good as gold."

Andrea took off his wide brimmed hat. Smoothed his hair back. "I hope he's as good a breeder as you think."

"Oh, he's going to be good all right. Might even give Champ a run for his money."

Andrea kissed Joe on the forehead. Stood and took her coffee. "Okay, amor. Be careful." She leaned over and kissed him hard on the lips. "I love you so much."

He stood and gripped her in a long hug. "I love you, too. I'll see you for lunch."

Andrea walked down the front steps. She followed the covered walkway to the carriage house. It was a quaint two-story garage that looked like a house. She entered the side door. The front garage door rolled up a moment later and her black Range Rover pulled out.

The garage door rolled closed. The Range Rover drove off the concrete pad and onto the gravel road. Dust trailed behind it until it vanished around the curve.

Joe leaned back and sipped his coffee. He envisioned his ride on Sunshine. Envisioned how he was going to keep control of the stallion. Bend it to his will. Turn it into the horse he always knew it could be.

It had been pure luck to come across a prize thoroughbred like him. An eccentric Silicon Valley millionaire had purchased dozens of thoroughbreds and built a horse breeding ranch further up the valley.

He'd been obsessed with creating a super racehorse and winning the Kentucky Derby. Then his company failed. Gone bankrupt. The horse ranch was liquidated along with everything else. A random rancher purchased a handful of horses at auction.

The rancher continued breeding them. Not for racing. Just because he and his wife loved horses. They made their money from horse tourism. In other words, people paid them to ride their horses. Joe's friend, Rick, had taken his family there on their way down to San Diego for their annual visit with family.

As was customary, Rick stopped by to see Joe. They'd served in the Navy together. Become lifelong friends. Rick told Joe all about the horses. Told him about the horses the owner hadn't been able to break.

Joe had gone to see for himself. He'd seen some amazing horses running wild in the fields. But the one that caught his eye immediately was the golden chestnut standing sentinel on the hill. His hair coat gleamed in the sun despite not having been recently cleaned.

After lengthy haggling and written promises to treat the horse with dignity, the rancher had sold Sunshine to Joe. Told him he didn't think it was possible to break the horse. That it had run wild for too long.

But Sunshine was still a youngster. Joe believed he could still be taught. And he'd made a lot of progress over the past few weeks. Maybe this week would be the week. Maybe today, even. He'd know for sure in a few minutes.

Joe finished his coffee. Took the cup inside. He put sunscreen on his face. Got his water bag. His rifle. Just in case he ran into a mountain lion or other hazardous wildlife.

He went out to the horse stable. Slid open the door. Cool air drifted out. It might be a glorified barn, but he kept it climate controlled. Made sure all his prized horses were comfortable even on the hottest days.

His helpers would arrive in an hour to take the horses out to graze. They'd bring them back in. Brush down their coats. Pamper them like the royalty they were.

Joe stopped at the first stall. "Hey Belinda." He rubbed the mare's nose. She snorted gently. Bobbed her head in greeting. He worked his way down the stalls. Said hello to everyone.

Then he reached the last one.

Sunshine stared out at him. Didn't bob his head. Didn't snort. But he also didn't bare his teeth or buck wildly. That was progress.

Joe reached a hand over the gate. Touched Sunshine's nose. The horse whickered. Kept staring at him out of one eye.

"Are we friends now?" Joe petted Sunshine's nose. "I feel like we're becoming friends."

Sunshine whickered again.

Joe picked up the bridle. The next test was opening the gate. Joe unlatched it. Swung it out slowly. He slipped inside the stall. It was one of the smaller stalls by design. There was still plenty of room for a horse, but the horse would always be in reach.

That made it easier to put the reins on over the gate if he had to. Sunshine was calm enough now that Joe could go inside the stall and do it without fear of being crushed.

He put his thumb in the back of the horse's mouth. Sunshine's teeth parted. He slid the metal bit between the teeth. Lodged it in the gap behind the teeth at the back of the mouth. He slid the straps over the ears. Buckled the strap under the chin.

There was a faint clatter. Like a door being shut. It sounded like Angel and Ron might have arrived early. Joe poked his head over the gate. Looked toward the front door. No one was there.

"Angel?" Joe stepped out of the stall. He closed the gate behind him. "Ron?"

No one answered. He walked down the stalls. Walked to the front door. Slid it open. He looked outside. No one was there. Ron's old Chevy pickup wasn't parked in its usual spot. Angel's new Dodge Ram wasn't there either.

He went back inside the stable. Picked up the rifle. Snapped in the magazine. Rocked a round into the chamber. If it hadn't been his helpers, then that meant it was something else. Something dangerous.

Probably a bear. But it wouldn't be the first time a mountain lion got brave enough to sneak onto the property. The predators sometimes came after the horse when they were grazing. They didn't stand a prayer of catching them. Not unless they sneaked through the tall grass.

There was plenty of scrub and tall grass to hide in around the house. Joe didn't even bother maintaining a lawn. Not in this climate. It was easier to just let nature run its course and put gravel around the house to keep it from growing too close.

The price for letting nature encroach was letting wildlife do the same. Racoons, foxes, and coyotes weren't shy about coming close to human habitats. They were content finding food in the garbage, if nothing else.

Coyotes were notorious for eating pets. Dogs and cats weren't safe outside. That wasn't why Joe didn't have a dog. He wasn't worried about coyotes eating it. He just preferred horses. And Andrea didn't want an inside pet anyway.

Bears were the biggest worry. They were curious. They liked digging through the garbage. They liked trying to dig under the house. They'd pulled the vapor barrier plastic out of the crawlspace more times than he could count.

He didn't know why they did it. He didn't understand what even attracted them to it. Maybe it was the crinkling sound it made. Maybe they did it for fun. He'd finally had a reinforced door installed to keep them out.

Joe prowled around the perimeter of the stable. Kept his rifle at the ready. It was a Colt M4. It was overkill for most things. It was just about right for putting down a bear if it came to it. Not that he wanted to kill a bear or any wildlife.

Not if he could help it, anyway.

Conservationists wouldn't like it. The state government wouldn't like it. He'd have to have a good reason for shooting a bear or even a mountain lion. Coyotes and racoons didn't matter quite as much.

Then of course, there'd be the local fallout. The talk around town. Certain groups would use the incident to smear his name. He couldn't afford to deal with that right now.

If he saw a bear, he'd try to scare it off. Yell at it. Make himself look big. Fire a shot in the air if he had to. That worked most of the time. The black bears in these parts weren't too big. If a human challenged them, they'd usually run.

Unless it was a momma bear with cubs. Then you'd have trouble. The bears might not be big, but they were powerful. No man could tussle with a bear and come out the victor. He knew of exactly one guy who could probably do it, but it wouldn't be with his bare hands.

Joe kept prowling. Kept his footsteps quiet. Kept the rifle at the ready. On the off chance it was a mountain lion, he wanted to be ready. Unlike bears, they could pounce you before you even saw them.

He finished a circuit around the stable. No sign of bears. No sign of anything. Maybe it had just been the wind. Maybe it had been one of the other horses. He didn't regret taking the time to check.

If a mountain lion or other wild animal got into the horse stable, that would be bad. Real bad. Because the horses couldn't run. Their stalls were big. Maybe big enough to give them a chance to kick a predator in the head. But he didn't want to find out.

He walked to the carriage house. Walked around it. All the doors were closed. No sign of wildlife. He did the same for the house. It was possible a bear had walked past the stable and gone to check out the trash.

Joe kept the trash secured in a metal dumpster. It was a small dumpster that was picked up once a week by a private service. He was just outside the city limits so public trash pickup wasn't an option.

The area around the house was clear too. He didn't see any bear tracks in the dusty soil. If it was a mountain lion, then it was doing a good job of remaining concealed. He'd only ever seen one roaming on his property. It had been after a rabbit.

Joe went back inside the stable. Rocked the magazine out of the Colt. Cleared the chamber. Thumbed the bullet back into the magazine. It was an old habit. Came to him as naturally as breathing.

Joe put the rifle against the wall. He slid the stable door closed. Stayed still for a moment and listened. He heard horses walking in their stalls. Heard a hoof stomp. Heard a horse snort. All the usual sounds in a horse stable.

He stayed there for another minute. Kept listening for anything out of the ordinary. The sounds of an animal digging. Of a bear raking its claws on the wood siding. All he heard was the wind and horse noises.

Joe went back to Sunshine's stall. He reintroduced himself. Put his hand out for a smell. Rubbed the horse's nose. Made sure he was as calm now as he had been a few minutes ago.

Sunshine stared at him. Nostrils flared. He whickered. Same as last time. No aggression. No fear. Not yet, anyway. That could change at a moment's notice.

Joe let himself back inside the stall. Sunshine's coat was shiny as ever, but he brushed him down real quick anyway. Sunshine whickered. His head bobbed up and down. Nostrils flared. He bucked. A ton of horseflesh pushed Joe to the side.

Joe backed into the corner. Rubbed Sunshine's hide. "What is it, boy? What got you riled up all of a sudden?" He pulled on the bridle. "Calm down, boy. Calm down."

The horse went silent for a moment. Nostrils flaring. Ears flicking. It wasn't his usual misbehavior. It was like something was spooking him.

Wood rattled. Like another horse was pressing against the stall door. Joe was backed into a corner. He couldn't get to the stall door with Sunshine in his way. Maybe there was something outside. A bear or something was spooking Sunshine and the other horses.

Sunshine reared up. Stomped his hooves down. He neighed. Shook his head like he was trying to buck.

"Calm down, boy." Joe kept his voice calm, but firm. He pulled down on the bridle. Stroked the horse's neck. Horseflesh pressed him into the corner again. He pushed back. Pulled more firmly on the bridle. "Nothing is out there, boy. I checked."

Joe opened the gate. Sunshine tried to rear up. Tried to buck. Joe kept a firm hand on the bridle. Sunshine's behavior wasn't as bad as the first time Joe had tried to coax the horse out of the stall, but it definitely seemed to have regressed.

Something was causing this behavior. A wild animal maybe. A scent in the air. Sunshine hadn't suddenly reverted back to his wild self. Not after all this time and effort.

"Do you smell something, boy?" Joe tried to slip past Sunshine and out of the stall. The horse bucked sideways. Knocked Joe good. He stumbled. Fell against the gate. It swung outward.

Joe put his shoulder into Sunshine's side to keep him from rotating. He pulled himself upright. "I guess today wasn't the day."

He pulled Sunshine out of the stall. Figured maybe the horse needed some breathing room. Sunshine was just out of the gate when he reared and bucked. His hind end twisted around and caught Joe in the chest.

Joe stumbled back. Movement caught his eye. He looked left. Just in time to see a flash of metal. A horseshoe coming straight at him. His last thoughts were, *That's impossible.* The horseshoe hit his forehead. He went down hard on his back.

The world was a blur. Consciousness faded to darkness. There was a muffled sound. He was too out of it to make sense of it. And then something crashed down on his head and the lights went out.

Joe's final morning was over.

CHAPTER 2

Amos Carver was watching a one-sided argument.

A tall man towered over a much shorter, older woman. She was bending slightly backwards. Neck craned up just so she could look the man in the face. She was holding her phone down at her side.

A moment earlier, she'd been recording with it. Specifically, she'd been recording a group of women who were walking through the park. One of the women had talked to the big guy. Pointed at the older woman.

The big man had nodded. Grinned. Walked over to the older woman. Started talking. At first, the older woman looked like she couldn't believe what was happening. Then the hand holding the phone had dropped to her side.

Her expression went from confused to frightened. It had all happened in an instant. Like prey suddenly realizing it was being hunted. Carver had seen it countless times before. Usually right before he killed or captured a target.

But that had been during his military life. This was out in the regular world. The civilized world, as they liked to call it. Far away from warfare. Far from those who would kill you if they thought you weren't a loyalist.

Carver was here because it was the closest bus stop to his destination. It was a small town. Population thirty-two thousand, according to the sign at the city limits. But it wasn't all that far from a much larger city.

Los Angeles was only forty minutes away, give or take. That was a forty-minute drive he didn't plan on taking. Not after the welcome the last big city had given him. Things were nicer out here in the small towns.

Or at least they'd seemed that way at first. The big man was still talking to the older woman. He kept his voice low. Kept a mean smirk on his face. He wasn't touching her, but his body language was aggressive.

The woman seemed frozen in place. She had to be. Otherwise, she would have backed off or turned and run. Maybe she wasn't frozen. Maybe she was brave. The look on her face told Carver she was in shock.

Carver had already looked over the big man. He saw the usual signs. The teardrop tattoos under the eyes. The tattoos on the arms. The proverbial writing on the wall. Except the writing wasn't on a wall. It was on the skin.

A letter and a number were on the man's neck and both forearms. *S8*. It didn't seem likely anyone would get the same tattoo in three places unless it was important to them. Maybe the name of their gang.

Carver might be wrong. It might stand for something else entirely. But he didn't need to see those tattoos to know the big man wasn't your ordinary run of the mill citizen. He was cocky. Dead sure of himself. Like he had full authority to be towering over this woman.

The woman finally said something. The man bumped her with his stomach. He was taller, so his stomach hit her on the chest. She stumbled backwards. Dropped her phone. Landed on her butt.

Getting involved in arguments between two private individuals wasn't something Carver usually did. But there was something about seeing a large young man pushing around an older woman that just didn't sit right with him.

Carver got up. Helped the woman to her feet. The big man was bending over to get her phone. Carver scooped it up first. Handed it to her.

The woman seemed surprised. She'd been on the ground. Suddenly she was back on her feet. A stranger was holding her phone out to her.

"Hey gringo, hand that phone over to me." The big man held out his hand.

He was half a head taller than Carver. Bigger than Carver. But not in the ways that mattered. His midsection was big and round. He wasn't obese, but he wasn't slim either. His chest looked practically concave compared to his belly.

His arms were thick. But they weren't muscular. They didn't have muscle tone. Judging from how loose the sleeves were, his biceps didn't have much going for them either.

Carver had learned the hard way that sometimes none of that mattered. Some people were just naturally stronger than others. People who did hard labor were usually stronger than they looked.

Construction workers, iron workers, oil riggers, and roughnecks usually didn't look like much on the outside. But their work drilled strength deep into their bones. They had handshakes of steel.

Carver had grown up doing hard manual labor. It had been a daily part of life around the Carver household even when he was just a kid. And after his parents died, he'd kept doing hard, dirty jobs.

He figured it was because his dad wanted to prepare him for a life in the military. If that was his goal, it had worked. Basic training had seemed easy in comparison to most jobs he'd had.

Maybe this big guy was stronger than he looked. Maybe gang life made him someone to be reckoned with. Carver didn't really want to find out. Picking a fight in the middle of a park while they were holding a festival wasn't a smart move.

The big man backed up a step so he could glare down at Carver. "I told you to give me that phone, gringo."

"It's not your phone, though, is it?" Carver stayed in place. "I think you should apologize to the lady and go about your day."

"Apologize?" The man laughed. "Do you know who I am, gringo?"

"An asshole?"

The man's face reddened. He held out his forearm. Probably to show the S8 tattoo there. "You know what that means?"

"That you're in a club?" Carver shrugged. "I was in a club once too, but I didn't get a tattoo for it."

"Section Eight, gringo. We run El Fuerte. We own everything and everyone in it. Including you."

Carver kept looking at him. Kept a neutral expression. "Isn't it kind of strange saying that name?"

"What name?" He looked confused. "Section Eight?"

"El Fuerte. It means the fort in Spanish."

"I know what it means."

"Strange, right? Who named the town? English speakers or Spanish speakers?"

The big man looked confused. "What are you talking about, gringo?"

Carver switched gears. "What's your name, big man?"

"I'm Hugo." He jabbed a thumb at his chest as if to emphasize the point. "Now, shut your mouth and give me the phone!"

Carver said nothing.

"Give me the phone!"

Carver kept looking at him. He said nothing.

Hugo stepped closer. Pressed himself right against Carver. "Give me the phone, or you're not leaving here in one piece."

Carver's first instinct was to break the other man's knee. To put him on the ground and finish him off with a savage kick to the throat. It was an instinct honed from years of surviving dangerous situations in dangerous parts of the world.

El Fuerte shouldn't be a dangerous part of the world. It was on American soil. It was a city. Filled with ordinary people. Also, apparently, with gang members.

Carver resisted the urge to put the man down. He decided to give the man a choice. "Back away from me."

"Or what?"

"I'll probably break your leg for starters. Then I'll see how I feel and go from there."

Hugo laughed. He nudged closer. "I'd like to see you try it, little gringo."

"Please, don't worry about it." The woman tugged on Carver's arm. "He can have the phone."

Carver shook his head. "No, he's going to apologize and walk away. Everyone gets to have a pleasant rest of their day."

"Not going to happen, little gringo."

"Second warning." Carver kept staring calmly at him. "There won't be a third."

Hugo held up a fist. "And then what?"

"That's one of my favorite questions." Carver nodded in approval. "I like to ask people that to make sure they're thinking things through."

"Yeah?" Hugo punched his fist into his palm inches from Carver's face. "Are you thinking it through now?"

Carver shook his head. "No, I thought it through ten minutes ago when I was watching a big boy like you intimidate someone half his size."

"Please don't do anything," the woman said. "You don't understand!"

"Wouldn't be the first time I didn't understand something." Carver shrugged. "But I'll do you the courtesy of a third warning, Hugo."

"Aw, how nice." Hugo swung his fist. This time he wasn't punching his palm. This time he was punching Carver. At least, that seemed to be his plan.

Carver had already stepped back. Hugo had telegraphed the move a full two seconds before doing it. He was big. His arms were long. He didn't have much muscle moving those long limbs of his.

For him to swing a punch, he had to lift a long arm and cock it back. Way back. For him to do those things, other muscles had to get involved. Chest muscles, shoulder muscles, back muscles.

They all coordinated to allow a person to punch someone else. Hugo didn't have big muscles. His jersey hung loose on his shoulders. It only tightened at his belly then hung like curtains past that point.

The baggy clothing had shifted suddenly. Told Carver that Hugo was cocking back his arm. Carver had already planned to step back. He needed a little space to do what needed doing. Even if he hadn't already been moving back, he would have had plenty of time.

Hugo cocked back his right arm. Carver stepped back. Shifted to the side. By the time Hugo was punching thin air, Carver's foot was crashing down on the side of Hugo's right knee.

The spin from the punch turned Hugo's shoulders away from Carver. Hugo's weight shifted from his right leg to his left. Which made Carver's leg strike even more devastating.

His leg folded sideways. There was a loud crunch. A loud scream. Hugo went down like a rag doll. Arms flailing. Legs folding under him like they were turned to gelatin.

Carver wanted to finish him off. At the very least break some ribs to keep Hugo down and out for a few weeks. Give him something to think about while he recovered. But the scream of pain attracted a lot of attention. Some people had been watching from afar. Recording the altercation.

The best thing to do was leave.

He turned to the woman. "Can you give me a lift?"

She stared at Hugo writhing on the ground. She blinked. Seemed to realize Carver had asked a question. "A what?"

"A lift. A ride."

"Yes." She nodded. "Let's go right now or there will be big trouble."

"Okay." Carver picked up his bags. He was down to just a duffel bag and a backpack these days. After he and Leon had spent a few weeks camping in the mountains, they'd gone their separate ways.

Carver didn't have a car. He hadn't wanted to buy one either. Not after what happened with his Dodge Ramcharger. He'd left his weapons bag in Leon's stolen van. Kept some essentials and left the rest.

"This way." The woman hurried away. She walked pretty fast for a short woman.

Carver paced behind her. She reached a Toyota SUV parallel parked on the road. Hopped in. He put his stuff in the back seat. Dropped into the front seat. She backed out. Turned down Main Street and headed west.

There were large billboards atop several of the buildings. The same attractive woman was featured on each one.

Join Mayor Herrada's efforts to keep El Fuerte amazing!

Mayor Jessica Herrada—working for the people of El Fuerte!

Carver was willing to bet the woman on the billboards was the mayor.

The woman gasped. "I forgot to ask where you're going."

"North. I'm visiting a friend who lives nearby."

She shivered. "My god, everything happened so fast. I can't believe that bitch sicced a gang member on me!"

"Some kind of personal feud?" Carver asked. "Was that woman the gang member's girl or something?"

The woman laughed. "Hell no."

Carver leaned back in his seat. "What's your name, anyway?"

"Oh, I'm Gloria." She laughed again. "I'm still shaking. I can't believe what just happened. And now you're going to be in the crosshairs."

"Not for long." Carver leaned his seat back a little. "I won't be around town for long."

Gloria slammed her palm on the steering wheel. "That bitch!"

"What's the story with you two?"

"You wouldn't believe me if I told you." She laughed mirthlessly. "I can hardly believe it's come to this." She blew out a breath. "What's your friend's address?"

Carver gave it to her.

She frowned. "The Donnely ranch?"

"That's the one." Carver looked at the map. The ranch was right near the northern edge of the city. There wasn't anything except miles of mountains and national forest further north.

Gloria gave him a look. "You're friends with Joe Donnely?"

"Yeah. Why?"

She laughed like she couldn't believe it. "Wow, you really should just leave town. Immediately."

"I plan to. I'm just visiting for a couple of days."

"Okay, well, don't go into town, whatever you do. If anyone asks, I'll tell them I dropped you at the bus station."

"Sounds good to me." Carver shrugged. "But what are they going to do if I go back to town? It was self-defense."

"Self-defense is a crime in these parts. Especially in El Fuerte. Especially against people like Hugo."

"I should be surprised they let self-proclaimed gang members wander the streets freely threatening people, but I've seen it plenty of times before." Carver shrugged. "It's nothing I can't handle."

"If you go back to town, you'll end up in jail or worse." Gloria put her hand on his. "Don't go back."

"Does the gang really run that town?"

"No. Section Eight isn't even the biggest gang in El Fuerte. There are at least three gangs in town."

"That's a lot of gangs for such a small place."

"There used to be more, but the FBI cleaned house about ten years ago." She sighed. "Now it's worse than ever. Not because of the gangs, but because of the mayor, the police, and the gangs."

Carver frowned. "You're talking like they're all in bed with each other."

"That woman who sent Hugo after me isn't just some random woman." Gloria shivered. "She's not just some woman I had a disagreement with." She took a deep breath. Released it slowly. "That woman is the mayor of El Fuerte."

"The woman on the billboards?"

Gloria laughed without humor. "Yep. She uses taxpayer money to promote herself."

Carver should have been surprised but he wasn't. It seemed like even the small cities were having big city problems these days. All thanks to Enigma, the shadow organization that was running the show in places like Portland and San Francisco.

Despite dealing with their local cells, Carver didn't know much about Enigma. And he didn't plan to. Leon had begged Carver to help him clean house. To help him hunt down the people behind Enigma and kill them. But that was an awful lot of work when Carver could just be chilling on a beach.

So, he'd said no. Told Leon to relax and enjoy life. They weren't overseas killing people for the government anymore. They were home. Forced into retirement.

It wasn't surprising to hear that the rot had worked its way all the way down here. It didn't matter. He wouldn't be in the area for long.

One thing did puzzle him, though. "Why did you laugh when I mentioned Joe? Is he tied up in this somehow?"

"Tied up?" Gloria snorted. "He's public enemy number one, according to Mayor Jessica Herrada."

"How so?"

"Because he's running against her in the election this year. And he's way ahead in the polls."

Carver couldn't believe it. Joe was anti-political. He liked to stay far away from that kind of nonsense. He was like Carver in that regard. He just wanted to do his own thing without interference.

Something had changed his mind. Something big. Because Joe Donnely wasn't the kind of guy to make such a decision lightly. He never jumped headfirst into anything. He was the kind of guy who always looked where he was leaping.

In fact, he studied where he was leaping until he knew exactly where he was going to land and what he was going to do the instant he landed. Which meant he'd done the same in this situation. Carver still couldn't believe it.

And he couldn't wait to ask Joe what in the hell changed his mind.

CHAPTER 3

Monty knelt next to the body.

"Damn it, Joe. How could you be so stupid?" He studied the markings on the dead man's face. Compared them to the bloody horse tracks. The stable floor was concrete. Not dirt like most.

There was a layer of gray sealant on top of the concrete. It was slick to the touch. Made it easier to clean the floor. There were drains in front of each of the horse stalls. Hose bibbs and hoses too.

One of those hoses would eventually be used to clean up the pool of blood under Joe's head. But not now. Not until Monty had a clearer idea of what happened here.

The two helpers, Ron and Angel, stood a few feet away. Faces white with shock. Mouths open in disbelief. They'd called the police department. Dispatch tried to transfer it to the golden boy, Detective Brent Landry, but he'd been out on vacation for almost a month.

Monty stood. Ran a hand across his balding pate. He knew Joe pretty well. Had known him, at least. Not so much as a friend, but as a fellow horse enthusiast. Monty was more on the gambling side and not at all on the breeding side.

His ex-wife viewed it as a big problem. He viewed it as entertainment. Nothing more. So what if it chewed up half of his disposable income every month? When he won, he won big. He'd learned early on to put his money on Joe's horses.

Hell, Joe's horse, Canter, had helped Monty clear a profit last year. It hadn't been enough to entice his ex to come back, but it gave him extra time at the track. It had also been enough to pay back his bookie.

Besides, his ex-wife had plenty of other reasons to never come back.

Monty turned to the helpers. "Who found him?"

"Me." Angel wiped a tear off his cheek. "He's been working with Sunshine for weeks. The horse was responding so well. I don't understand how this is possible."

"It's not possible," Ron said. He shook his head. "Ain't no way Joe would get behind Sunshine. Ain't no way Sunshine would be kicking."

Monty nodded. "You get bears and coyotes around here, don't you?"

"Yeah. We get raccoons and harmless critters too," Ron said. "If you're trying to imply something spooked the horse, I'm here to tell you that it wouldn't matter."

"How so?"

"Sunshine was bucking mad when Joe brought him home. He was probably the most feral horse I'd seen in a long time." Ron spat into a nearby drain. "Joe handled him easily. No problem. He knew how to handle even the wildest horses. He knew to never let his guard down in case something spooked a horse too."

Angel nodded. "It's true. He broke two wild broncos just for fun. I never saw a hoof come close to hitting him. Besides, Sunshine wasn't a kicker."

Monty raised an eyebrow. "Don't all horses kick?"

"Most do, but some don't. They buck and twist which is different."

"But he thought this horse was almost broken, right?" Monty wrote down the bullet points on a notepad. "Maybe he let his guard down just for a second. Something spooked the horse. The horse kicked and it hit him just right."

Angel looked at the body. His eyes locked onto Joe's blood-crusted face. He shook his head. "It's not possible."

"And yet, here we are." Monty kept writing. "I agree, though. Something isn't right with this."

He looked up from his notepad. "You have ice or a cooler?"

Angel nodded. "Yeah, we have a fridge where we keep antibiotics and stuff."

"Good. I'll be right back." Monty went out to his car. Got his forensics kit. It was basic, but it was enough to do the job. He went back inside. He used a syringe to draw blood from different parts of the body.

He filled three vials. Without a beating heart, it was harder than usual. But he'd drawn blood from plenty of dead bodies.

"Why are you doing that?" Ron asked.

"Normal procedure." He held up the vials. "Where's the fridge?"

"Back here." Ron took him toward the back of the stable. He turned between two stalls. There was a small area with an exit door and an old white refrigerator.

Monty opened the freezer door. Put the vials inside. Closed the door. "Thanks."

Ron nodded. "What now?"

"I need to examine the area better." He went back to the body. Knelt and sighed again.

"Monty, what in the blazes are you doing out here?" A middle-aged Hispanic man was standing just inside the stable door. Not just any man. It was Captain Lucas Hernandez from the local Sheriff's station. "You're a long way from the horse track."

Monty flinched. "I'm sorry, what was that?"

"You heard me." Lucas tilted his head slightly. "And what are you doing in my jurisdiction?"

"The call came through the emergency call center." Monty dialed down his anger. It was no secret that he spent a lot of time at the track. "Besides, this is as good as city jurisdiction now."

"That's a load of horse pucky. The annexation was delayed."

"Not delayed unless the county court agrees." Monty lowered his notepad. "I had word they were going to turn down the injunction. The annexation is going to go into effect on schedule."

"This is still county jurisdiction, detective." Lucas touched the Sheriff badge on his uniform. "I'd appreciate some respect until the annexation actually goes through."

"Sure, but what are you going to do?" Monty pointed at the body. "We have a dead body. Possible foul play."

"Foul play?" Lucas put his hat back on. Tucked away his handkerchief. Strode across the polished gray floor. He looked at Joe. Looked at the bloody hoofprints. "Looks like a clear-cut accidental death to me."

"It's not possible." Angel shook his head angrily. "Joe would never get caught off guard."

"Sure looks like he got caught off guard." Lucas walked around the body. Knelt next to the bloody hoofprints. He was a slim man. About six feet tall. Nearly a head taller than Monty. He exuded arrogance. Or maybe it was just confidence.

Monty had never liked him. The sheriff's department was always looking to claim jurisdiction over anything they could. All so their political leaders could claim credit. The Los Angeles County Sheriff's Department was a lot bigger than most city police departments.

That gave them clout. Gave them inroads with state government officials. Clout and inroads El Fuerte police department certainly didn't have.

The LASD was also huge. Arranged into stations around the county. Each station was run by a captain. Each captain was still beholden to local politics to one degree or another.

And this one was no different.

Angel was still talking. "It wasn't an accident! You know as well as anyone that the mayor had it out for Joe."

"You claiming this was a murder?" Lucas laughed. "That the mayor hired this horse to kill this man?"

"Sunshine didn't kill him!" Angel shouted. "I just know it."

"I've been working here for the better part of ten years." Ron shifted the tobacco in his lower lip. He spit into the drain. "Ain't no way Joe was killed by any damned horse."

Lucas was still kneeling next to the body. Studying the bloody mess of a face. He stood. Faced the two helpers. "First of all, how dare you accuse Mayor Herrada of murdering a political opponent? And second of all, you bend down and look at that face and tell me a horse didn't do that."

Angel stared at the face. He remained silent.

Ron shifted the tobacco around in his mouth. Spat again. "It looks like a horse did it, but it wasn't Sunshine."

Lucas shook his head. "Where's the horse?"

"In the stall." Ron pointed to the nearest stall.

Lucas turned to Monty. "You've been here longer than I have. Catch me up on the details."

Monty worked his jaw back and forth. He knew it was useless to argue. This was still county jurisdiction until the court denied the injunction. "Ron arrived to find Joe lying here. He ran over, checked for a pulse. There was no pulse. The subject's skin was cold to the touch. I tried to contact the wife, but she is not answering her cell phone."

Lucas nodded. Walked around the body and over to the stall. He looked inside. "Keep going."

"The horse, Sunshine, was standing near the body. His left hind hoof was covered in blood. Bits of bone and tissue were also on the hoof. The right hind hoof only had blood on the bottom."

Lucas was looking over the gate. "Blood on the left hind hoof goes all the way up to the hair. There's splatter too. No way that could've happened unless that hoof hit Joe's face."

"Or the horse just walked in the blood," Monty said.

"I'm telling you it ain't possible." Ron shook his head. "I can't prove it, but I know it all the way to the core of my being."

Lucas backed away from the stall. Gave Ron an understanding look. "I know you don't want it to be true. None of us do. Joe Donnely bred some amazing racehorses. Hell, most of his products are regular winners at the local track."

"Horses ain't products," Ron said. "They're animals."

"Living, breathing works of art," Angel said. "And now, the artist is dead."

"You two sure don't sound like normal ranch helpers." Lucas pressed his lips together.

"We're highly qualified at what we do." Ron scowled. "We don't just feed and brush down horses. We keep them happy and healthy."

"Are you qualified in equine husbandry?" Lucas asked.

Angel shook his head. "Joe used Beth Gatti for that."

Lucas took out a tablet and typed in the information. "She's a veterinarian?"

"Yeah." Angel stared at Joe's body again. "Equine Veterinary Services to the east of town."

"Are the CSI people coming?" Ron looked from Monty to Lucas. "Maybe someone drugged Joe and got the horse to kick him while he was down."

"My people are coming to photograph the body and remove it," Lucas said. "They'll do a tox screening and standard autopsy."

Ron nodded. "Okay. Good. Because I know this was foul play. No question about it."

"No offense, Ron, but you're not a detective." Lucas turned to Angel. "And neither are you."

Monty cleared his throat. "I am. And in my qualified opinion, I think something is strange about this. I also tend to trust Ron and Angel's expertise in regard to Joe's capabilities and the state of the horse, Sunshine."

"And I appreciate your opinion." Lucas took out his phone and tapped on the screen. "Now, I'd appreciate it if you cleared out, seeing as this is my jurisdiction. You can send me a copy of your notes as well. I'm sure they'll be helpful."

"I already told you everything." Monty shrugged. "Maybe you should've taken notes."

"You're right. It would probably be hard to read your notes anyway." Lucas looked him up and down. "Smells like you've already been hitting the bottle this morning."

Monty clenched a fist. Bit his tongue to keep the first words out of his mouth. "That's my aftershave, you arrogant son of a bitch."

"You wear tequila for aftershave?" Lucas chuckled. "I admit, it is quite aromatic."

Monty considered punching the captain. He considered letting Sunshine out of his stall and hoping the horse caved in Lucas's face for him. Instead, he forced a smile. "Well, I guess it makes me smell better than you."

"What the hell is wrong with you people?" Ron spat and missed the drain. "You're acting like kindergarteners while there's a good man lying dead at your feet."

"I'll stick around and make sure Lucas's people do a good job." Monty backed off. Walked to a wooden bench near the back door. He sat down and wrote a text to the police chief. *Lucas is claiming jurisdiction out here at the Donnely ranch.* He sent it, then called Joe's wife, Andrea again.

She answered this time. "Can't you people leave us alone? I'd report you all to the police if I thought it would make a difference."

Monty cleared his throat. "Um, Andrea, this is Monty."

"Monty?" She sounded confused. "The detective?"

"Yes." It was natural for her to be unsure. Monty had really only spoken to Joe. "I'm sorry, I should have identified myself better. I'm Detective Monty Ford with El Fuerte PD."

"What?" She sounded at a loss for words. "What is this regarding?"

"It's about Joe."

"Did the police finally track down the people making those threatening calls?" She sighed with relief. "God, I hope so. I had to change my cell number twice!"

"Ma'am, I'm sorry, but this isn't about that. Are you driving?"

There was a long pause. "What's happened. Is Joe okay? Did something happen to Joe?"

Monty took a deep breath. "Mrs. Donnely, I'm so sorry to tell you that Joe is dead."

The silence deepened. It ended in a long shuddering wail. "No! No! That can't be true! What are you talking about?"

"Mrs. Donnely, it looks like the horse, Sunshine, kicked him in the face. The kick was fatal."

"No!" She screamed and the call was cut off.

Monty had called plenty of people to tell them about the passing of a relative or loved one. He'd gone in person when he could. He'd seen all kinds of reactions. From cries of agony and sorrow to shouts of joy.

There were a lot of deaths in these parts. Lots of gang violence. Lots of crime. It had been bad when he was a kid, and it was even worse now. Or maybe it just felt worse because he was a cop who saw everything.

Monty stood. "What's the ETA on your people, Lucas?"

Lucas did a double-take. Gave him a confused look. "You're still here? I told you to go."

"I'm a detective. I have a right to be here."

"No, you don't." Lucas motioned toward the rear door. "Now, get out of here or I'll have some deputies escort you out."

Monty clenched his teeth to keep the words from spilling out. He turned the grimace into a grin. Turned and left through the side door. He walked around the backside of the stable. He noticed some fresh tracks on the ground outside.

He knew they were fresh because the sandy soil didn't hold footprints for long. At least not well-defined tracks like these. They were from boots. Not smooth-soled cowboy boots. These were from hiking boots.

They were the same kind of boots Joe was wearing. He'd taken pictures of the body with his cell phone. Pictures from all angles. He remembered the boots. The bottoms had traces of soil on them.

That was normal, of course. Joe probably got that just from walking to the stable. It looked like he'd been walking around the backside of the stable, too.

There was a thin ribbon of concrete around the outside of the stable. It was a continuation of the floor. It was about two feet wide. Wide enough to walk on, but it would be easier to walk on the ground.

Monty stayed on the concrete so he wouldn't disturb the tracks. He took pictures. Walked the perimeter. The tracks kept going around the stable, but another set went to and from the house.

Like any set of footprints, they varied according to the soil. The soil turned to gravel near the house. That was where the footprints ended. But Monty clearly saw another set of prints coming back from the house toward the stable.

The prints continued along the side of the stable and probably circled around to the front. He went to the other side of the stable. Found the prints there as well. Not as many since there was more grass on that side.

He didn't see any other footprints. Just Joe's. They were firm imprints. Clear as day in places. Like Joe had paused to stand there for a moment. Like he'd turned from side to side. Searching his surroundings.

Monty formed a mental image. Joe came outside. Walked slowly around the perimeter. That was why the tracks were so deep and clear. He'd paused at the corners. Studied his surroundings. Saw nothing and started moving again.

It wasn't hard to guess what he was doing. He'd heard something. Maybe the horse had been spooked. He'd come outside to see if something was there. Monty had noted the rifle and supplies near the front of the stable.

He hadn't had a chance to look inside the saddlebag, but he was sure there was a box of bullets and a loaded magazine inside. The rifle was a Colt M4. An expensive weapon. Probably just one weapon of many that Joe had on his property.

Joe had loaded the rifle. Brought it outside. Patrolled around the stable. Around the separate garage. Around the house. Monty retraced the entire route. He didn't see any sign of animal tracks. Didn't see any dead animals.

It didn't look like Joe found any threats. He'd returned to the stable. Unloaded his rifle. Leaned it against the wall. Gone back to the horse. There was already a bridle on the horse when Monty arrived.

It looked like Joe had put the bridle on and been ready to lead the horse out of the stall. Something spooked it. He searched the perimeter. Found nothing. Came back. Got kicked in the head and died.

Monty paused in the driveway. He didn't want to leave. His gut instinct told him something was rotten here. His phone buzzed. He checked it. The chief had texted him back.

What are you doing out there? That's LASD territory. Leave now.

Monty wasn't surprised. He heard gravel crunching under tires. Looked up. Saw a red Toyota SUV climbing up the long drive. It slowed and stopped just in front of the garage. The woman inside wasn't Andrea Donnely.

A big man climbed out of the passenger side. The woman got out. Looked at the black and white SUV with the sheriff badge on the side. Looked at Monty's unmarked sedan. Looked at Monty.

The big man seemed to be studying him. Dissecting him with his eyes. Right then and there Monty knew one thing for sure.

This man was trouble.

CHAPTER 4

Carver was in trouble.

Maybe he wasn't. He wasn't too sure just yet. There was an unmarked police car in Joe's driveway and a Sheriff's SUV parked near a big white stable. A thin guy in street clothes was standing in the driveway.

The man's clothes were wrinkled and unkempt. His patchy hair was about shoulder length. It looked tangled and oily. Like he hadn't cleaned it in a couple of days. His skin was pink. The cheeks were blotchy.

One thing seemed sure. The man was a heavy drinker. Another thing seemed sure too. The man was a detective. The unmarked car was his. The detective was looking at Carver and Gloria with a confused look.

Gloria walked up to the man. "Where is Joe?"

The detective replied with a question. "Who are you?"

Gloria asked him the same thing. "Who are you?"

The man produced a wallet with a badge. "Detective Monty Ford."

"Did the mayor send you out here to harass Joe?" Gloria's fists clenched. "Is intimidation the only tactic she knows?"

Ford looked at Carver. "Who are you?"

"A friend of Joe's. I'm in town to visit him."

"Let me see your ID."

Carver ignored the request. The stable door was open. A shadow was moving on the other side, but he couldn't see who was casting it. He walked toward it.

"Hey, you can't go in there." Ford hurried after Carver.

Carver reached the door. Looked inside. Saw blood. Saw a body. Saw a Hispanic man with a beige shirt, green pants, and a cowboy hat leaning against a pole inside. The star on the man's shirt identified him as a sheriff.

The man looked up from his phone. He frowned. "Who are you?"

"A friend of Joe's." Carver was already crossing the distance between him and the body. He looked down. Saw the face. The face looked like it had been stomped on, but it was still recognizable. It was Joe.

It was a shock seeing him laid out like this. He could have died a dozen different ways on a dozen different covert missions, but he hadn't. He'd made it back home. He'd been living his dream.

The dead man on the ground wasn't as big and muscular as he'd been all those years ago. Civilian life had made him a little softer around the edges. His arms weren't as big. His stomach was a little rounder.

Those were signs he'd been living the good life. A good life apparently ended by a horse. That didn't seem possible. It seemed like a load of horse shit.

"Hey!" The sheriff held out his arms to block Carver from getting closer. "You're contaminating the scene. If you don't leave right now, I'll charge you with obstruction."

Carver didn't budge. "You the sheriff in these parts?"

"I'm the captain of the local station." He put a hand on his holstered gun. "You've got ten seconds to clear out."

There was a gasp behind Carver. He glanced back and saw Gloria standing in the doorway. The detective was behind her.

"Damn it, Monty!" The captain unbuttoned his gun holster. "Did you let these people in here?"

"There's no tape. No perimeter." Carver took pictures of Joe with his burner phone. Then he walked toward the door. "If this is your crime scene, you didn't secure it properly."

"It's not a crime scene, and don't you tell me how to do my job, boy."

Carver kept walking. He went outside. Looked on the ground. The gravel wasn't ideal for showing footprints. But the dirt to the left was a little looser. He saw a couple of sets of prints. Both looked relatively fresh.

One set matched the treads on Joe's boots. He noticed Ford watching him. The detective was wearing black leather shoes. The kind with smooth bottoms. The rounded end of the shoes matched the second set of prints.

The smooth prints were to the right of the boot prints. Then they vanished altogether. Probably because the wearer had walked on the concrete lip around the edge. The wearer was Ford.

Ford had tracked the prints around the building, but he'd been careful not to disturb them. Carver followed the boot prints. Judging from the depth of the tracks, Joe had been walking slowly.

He'd been taking careful strides. Like he was hunting something. A wild animal? A human?

"You noticed them too?" Ford said.

Carver didn't look up from the prints. "Hard to miss them." He walked around the outside of the stable.

Ford trailed behind him. "They go around the house, too. Joe has a rifle in the stable. He probably heard something and thought it was a bobcat or bear."

"They're common in these parts?"

"Common enough." Ford hurried through the scrub brush to catch up. "We get bears on the outskirts of town all the time. Most of them are tagged. They raid trash cans. Stuff like that."

"Did you find any animal tracks?" Carver asked.

"No."

"Tire tracks?"

"Not in close proximity to the stable. It's not like they'd show up in the gravel or on the concrete driveway."

Carver stopped walking. He turned to face the detective. "Tell me everything you know."

"You're a civilian." Ford looked confused. "This isn't your concern."

"Joe was a friend. A brother in arms." Carver stepped closer to the shorter man. There was an odor drifting off him. It smelled like cigarettes and alcohol. The man's eyes were bloodshot. His nose was red. Veins were starting to show in the skin. Typical signs of a heavy drinker.

Ford backed up a step. "I'll tell you as a courtesy. Because I liked Joe."

"Were you going to vote for him?"

The detective blinked. "How do you know he was running for office? Are you from around here?"

"Gloria brought me up to speed." Carver turned to face east. The ground was flat around the stable. Then it angled up a rocky slope. The hills continued to the south and north. It put the house and the stable inside a bowl with a flat bottom.

The gravel road leading away from the house went downhill. It didn't seem like a great place to be during heavy rain. The water would wash down from the hills, past the house, and down the road.

Or maybe it didn't. The gravel road didn't show signs of erosion. Maybe the hills sheltered the land from the worst of inclement weather. Maybe weather wasn't much of a factor in these parts.

This was southern California. Maybe it didn't rain much in this area anyway.

Carver had been trained to look for these kinds of things. It was vital to choose a good spot if you were camping. A tent needed to be on high ground. You didn't want to get flooded out of your tent if there was heavy rain.

Terrain was also an important factor when choosing a safehouse. Rhodes always wanted a place with multiple exits. A place that couldn't be approached by anyone without being seen if it was outside a city.

It didn't look like any of that was a consideration here. Joe might have been a SEAL but that didn't mean he held onto old habits when he became a civilian. You were supposed to be safe as a citizen. Carver knew from experience that was no longer the case.

"What are you looking for?" Ford said.

Carver turned to him. "Were you going to vote for Joe?"

The detective sighed. "I couldn't vote for him."

"You're not a citizen of El Fuerte?"

"I am, but Joe technically wasn't. He lives—lived—outside the city limits. Which means he wasn't eligible to run."

"Gloria said he was going to run. That he was way ahead in the polls." Carver started walking uphill. It wasn't a steep hill or a particularly tall one. The roof of the stable was higher. But it would still be a decent vantage point.

Ford paced alongside him. "Joe was going to run. The city planned to annex the land east of the city all the way up to the national forest."

"Joe's ranch was part of that annexation?"

Ford nodded. "It was supposed to go through in October."

"And that would make Joe a citizen? Eligible to run?"

"Exactly."

"So why all the nonsense about him being ineligible?"

Ford slipped on loose gravel. Caught himself on a mesquite bush. "The city council delayed annexation until December."

"And elections are normally in November?"

Ford nodded. "Meaning Joe wouldn't be eligible."

"Smart move, I guess." Carver reached the top of the hill. The terrain was flat for a distance before turning mountainous. The land was shades of green and beige broken by gray rock. A volcanic upheaval billions of years ago had formed this landscape.

The mountains were covered in short shrubs, sage, and mesquite. The grass was thin and clumped. The trees were short. Barely taller than shrubs. It didn't look like the ideal terrain for bears, but he wasn't a wildlife expert.

Ford kept talking. "It was a smart move by the mayor. She probably pressured the city council into it."

"You know that for certain?" Carver walked along the ridge. Looked down at the ranch. "I'm a cop. We hear all about political drama."

The soil was sandy and beige. There was gravel, but not enough to mask any footprints. Carver didn't see any signs of animals. No hoofprints, no pawprints. The nearest mountain looked close enough to touch.

Flat terrain distorted distances. Made it seem like a mountain that was miles away was just a few minutes' walk. That mountain was probably three miles away at least.

"There's a stream not too far that way." Ford pointed at a clump of trees that were greener than the others. "It runs north to south, curves west, and crosses into town. It's not uncommon for wildlife to drink from it."

"What kinds of animals do you get in these parts?"

"Bobcats, bears, mountain lions, deer, coyotes." Ford pulled a leaf from a bush. Rolled it in his fingers. "Racoons, skunks, rattlesnakes, and so forth and so on."

"You think a wild animal spooked a horse and it kicked Joe in the face?"

"That's how it looks." Ford shook his head. "I shouldn't be discussing it with you."

"If it was an accident, does it matter?"

"You're not a relative. His wife doesn't even know how he died yet, man." Ford yanked another leaf from the bush. "You're just some stranger who showed up and said he's a friend of Joe's. Will his wife recognize you?"

"Yeah." Carver took out his phone. Looked at the pictures of Joe. He didn't know much about horses. The main thing he knew was always lesson number one. Never stand behind a horse.

Never stand behind any hoofed animal that can kick you. If something startled them, their instinct was to kick. That was how they defended themselves. It was how they killed predators.

Carver couldn't figure how a seasoned horse guy like Joe could make the most basic mistake. "Tell me everything you know."

"Okay, I'll tell you." Ford tossed the leaf into the wind. He stared at the mountain to the east. "Sunshine was wild. Joe got him a few weeks ago. Started breaking him in. According to his helpers, Ron and Angel, the horse was buck wild, but it was coming around. He was supposed to take it riding today."

Joe had talked about breeding horses every chance he'd gotten when they were in the service. He'd grown up on a ranch that raised horses for sale. But they were normal horses. Just bred for normal riders, not racing. Joe had wanted to take things a step further.

The house, the ranch, all of it was nice. Real nice. It looked like Joe had followed his dream and done well by it.

"So, he was saddling it, the horse got spooked and kicked him in the head?"

"That's what it looks like." Ford shook his head. "Doesn't seem possible for someone with Joe's skills to end up that way."

"He heard something. Thought it was an animal." Carver pointed a finger at the stable. Traced the route Joe had taken. "He looked around. Didn't find anything and went back into the stable."

"Then whatever it was spooked the horse good." Ford sighed. "Game over."

Carver took out his phone and pulled up the video app. He searched for kicking horses. There were all kinds of videos. Lots of stupid people playing stupid games and winning stupid prizes. Namely, a hoof to the body or the head.

Monty looked curiously at the videos. "What are you doing?"

"Familiarizing myself with horse kicks."

"Why?"

"So I know what's possible and what's not." Carver watched another video. It looked the same as the others.

Monty laughed. "Think you'll become an expert?"

"Expert enough to know one thing."

"Which is?"

"That a horse didn't do that to Joe." Carver showed Monty the video. It showed a dozen different people effing around and finding out with horses. "What's the one thing these people have in common?"

Monty frowned. "They all got kicked by horses?"

"They all got kicked by horses." Carver played another video. "And this one?"

Monty watched it halfway through before commenting. "They also all got kicked by horses."

"They also all got kicked by horses." Carver slowed the playback. A grinning man walked up behind a horse. He slapped it on the rump. The horse leaned forward on its front legs, lifted its hind legs, and kicked the man about mid mass. Right in the chest.

Monty held out his hands in a shrug. "What are you trying to tell me?"

"Joe is over six feet tall. Most of these horses kick about chest high, even on shorter people." Carver resumed normal speed playback. "It's like they aim for it. Unless it's a dog, then they aim low for the head."

"You think it wasn't possible for Sunshine to kick Joe twice in the head?" Monty shook his head. "It's possible. He might have been trying to inspect a horseshoe. He might have been kneeling."

"I've seen people inspect horseshoes." Carver searched and found a video of a man doing just that. "They stand like he does. See where he is? He's next to the horse, not behind it. Experienced people stand to the side and put the horse leg between their legs to brace it. Not a single one of them kneels directly behind the horse."

Monty looked at the video. "Yeah, you're right. But maybe Joe tripped behind the horse. Fell into its back end and got kicked."

"The way the horse has to lift its hind legs means it would hit him in the stomach or chest." Carver pulled up the picture of Joe's face. "He was kicked twice almost in the same place. In order for the horse to do that, Joe would have to be looking down or crouched. He would have to be braced against something because the first kick would have sent him sprawling."

Monty nodded. "For what it's worth, I don't see how it's possible. But the evidence all points to that being the case."

"If Joe was braced against something like a stall, there would be bruising or cuts on the back," Carver said. "An impact like that would slam you against the wall."

"Well, the sheriff's department is sending out their people to look things over. But Lucas seems convinced it was an accident with the horse." Monty sighed. "I don't think you'll have much luck convincing him otherwise."

Under other circumstances, Carver wouldn't take much convincing. But from what Gloria had told him, these weren't ordinary circumstances. He'd hardly been in the town half a day and was convinced the mayor was a scum ball.

If she'd sent a gang member after an older woman like Gloria, she wouldn't hesitate to send someone out to take care of Joe. Until someone convinced Carver otherwise, he believed Joe had been murdered.

And he was going to find out how.

Chapter 5

The mayor may have had Joe killed.

The mayoral campaign was reason enough. But if the annexation had been delayed and made Joe ineligible, then was it still a motive? Or had Joe pissed off someone else? Someone powerful who wasn't the mayor?

Maybe it was the mayor. Maybe it was someone else. Maybe it had just been a horse. Carver's gut feeling told him it wasn't a horse. It was a human. Maybe a human using a horse to kill a target.

It sounded crazy, but he'd seen all kinds of crazy during his time in the service. Assassins came up with clever ways to eliminate targets. Some could make anything look like an accident. It was possible a creative individual had staged this scene.

The sheriff certainly wasn't going to help. If anything, it sounded like he wanted to make this as open and shut as possible.

A cloud of dust rose to the south. A black Range Rover appeared on the gravel road. It was coming fast.

"That's Ms. Donnely," Monty said.

Carver didn't reply. He walked over toward the stable and waited.

The Range Rover bounced onto the concrete driveway. It screeched to a halt. Andrea Donnely slid out. Her eyes were red. Her face was streaked with tears. She saw the sheriff's vehicle parked outside the stable.

She saw Carver. "Carver?"

"Andrea."

She ran toward the stable. Ford blocked the door. "Ms. Donnely, you don't want to go in there."

Andrea stiffened. "Get out of my way."

Ford sighed. Stepped aside.

She went inside. "Joe! Oh my God, no!"

Carver went in after her.

The sheriff stood in her way, arms spread out. "Ms. Donnely, you can't go any closer!"

"Get out of my way!" she screamed. "That's my husband!"

"I can't let you contaminate the scene. I'm sorry."

She tried to shove her way past, but he gripped her arms. "I'm very sorry for your loss, but you can't get closer."

She took a deep shuddering breath. Turned to Carver. "What happened? Were you here?"

He shook his head. "It happened earlier. His helpers found him when they arrived."

She turned to Lucas. "What happened?"

He pointed to the horse. "Looks like Sunshine kicked him in the face."

Andrea shook her head. "Impossible. Joe would never put himself in a position to get kicked, much less in the face."

"He was clearly kicked," Lucas said. "My forensic techs will be here soon to catalogue everything."

She shivered. Started shaking uncontrollable. "It's impossible." Tears streamed down her face. "He can't be dead. Can't be."

"I'm so sorry, Andrea." Carver took her hand. "We need to go outside. Sit down."

She looked up at him. Tears filled her eyes. "I-I can't believe it. It's impossible." She gritted her teeth. Took a deep breath. Gripped Carver's hand tight and walked out of the stable, pulling him behind her.

Carver followed her without comment. He'd only met Andrea a couple of times. In the grand scheme of things, he didn't know her all that well. He knew she'd been in the Navy. That was where she met Joe.

She'd been a JAG. Basically, a military lawyer as far as Carver knew. He wasn't all that familiar with that branch. All he knew was that they'd met on a ship during an operation. They hadn't gotten together until some time after they'd left the service.

Andrea led him to the house. She released his hand. Unlocked the front door. Opened it and motioned him inside.

The house was new and modern. The floor was a dark slate. The walls were light gray. And the interior was wide open. The foyer, den, and kitchen were basically one big room. It looked nice and spacious, but there was no room for cover if someone kicked down the front door.

Andrea walked past a black leather couch. Took a left into a hallway. Carver followed her. She took a right turn into an office and stopped. Took a long shuddering breath. Then she sat down at the desk inside.

The desk was rustic and utilitarian. There was a dark stained slab of wood on the top. The legs were black metal. There wasn't much else to it. There was an open laptop on it and two framed pictures.

The pictures showed a smiling Joe and Andrea, their cheeks pressed together. Joe looked happy. Joe had always been quick with a joke or a smile in the service, but he'd never looked as happy as he did in these pictures.

There was also a box filled with political signs. Another box with metal frames used to stick the signs into the ground of front yards. Joe's smiling face was on all of them. It was surreal seeing him on political posters.

Joe was about fifteen years older than Carver. He'd been married once, but his wife couldn't handle the military life. She couldn't handle Joe being away for so long. So, she'd left him right before a mission.

He told her he was being deployed for two weeks. She told him she wouldn't be there when he came back. He tried to talk her out of it. Told her he would take early retirement if that would help.

She told him it was too late. It was over and done.

Despite that, Joe had been as rock steady as ever during the mission. He hadn't cracked. Hadn't taken out his anger. He'd calmly and cooly eliminated three targets and gotten his team safely home.

After retirement, he'd found his happiness. Carver had noticed the night and day difference the last time he'd visited. He'd always figured true love was a myth. Maybe Joe had found it. No, there was no maybe to it. Joe had found it.

And now it was over.

Andrea pulled the open laptop closer to her. She pressed a button. Put her finger on the mousepad, and the screen unlocked. She opened an app and a grid of video feeds appeared.

Andrea tapped a finger on the screen. "After Joe announced his run for office, our property was vandalized. The sheriff's office wouldn't do anything about it, so he set up cameras everywhere."

"Good idea." Carver saw Lucas on one of the video feeds. Joe's body was visible on another. "Are these saved somewhere?"

"Yes." Andrea clicked on the one with Joe's body. The image filled the screen. She gasped. Shivered. "This can't be real."

Carver didn't say anything. There wasn't anything he could say to make her feel better. To make her accept the reality on the screen.

She breathed out, nice and slow. Nodded to herself. She clicked a button and a series of images appeared. They were timestamped. She clicked on the ones from earlier. The lights in the stable flicked on.

Joe walked into frame a moment later. He walked along the stalls. Stopped in front of one. Started talking.

"That's Sunshine's stall." Andrea turned up the volume and Joe's words could be faintly heard.

"Are we friends now?" He petted Sunshine's nose. "I feel like we're becoming friends." She wiped tears from her eyes. Stared at the screen in forlorn disbelief.

Joe went into the stall. The camera angle was just enough to see inside. There was a faint noise. Joe called out the names of his helpers. He left the stall. Went to the door and opened it. Disappeared outside for a moment.

When he returned, he picked up a rifle near the door. Rocked a magazine inside. Left the stable. The image grew fuzzy. It went black. An error message appeared. *Connection Lost. Attempting to reconnect.*

Andrea rocked back. She closed the video. Opened the next one. Joe was dead on the floor. Sunshine stood nearby. "What?" She switched to an external camera. This one was watching the front of the stable.

Joe walked into the stable. The camera recorded for a few more seconds then cut off since there was no more motion. The next video clip was moments later when Joe went outside. He had his rifle with him.

He was looking around. Scanning the area for wildlife, probably. He went around the corner and the video ended seconds later since it didn't detect any motion. The next video had a later timestamp. It showed Angel and Ron arriving.

"This can't be right." Andrea switched to other camera feeds. Only one had recorded something around the same time as the others. It abruptly cut off with a connection lost error like the ones inside the stable.

None of them had captured the last moments of Joe's life.

Andrea went through all the camera feeds one by one. They'd all gone down at the same time. "I don't understand."

"The cameras use Wi-Fi to upload their footage," Carver said. "Looks like there was a connection issue. A very convenient one. Where's your internet router?"

"In the closet." Andrea pointed to a closet door on the left wall.

Carver opened the door. Inside was a small white box with several blinking lights. There were three blue lights and one green one. He picked up the device. Looked on the back and found a sticker.

The sticker had an IP address and a default login for the router. He went to the laptop. "Mind if I check something?"

She nodded. Backed away.

He entered the IP address. A login screen for the Wi-Fi router appeared. He clicked the username field, and a saved username and password populated the blanks. He clicked the login button and the control dashboard appeared.

The device was a fiber internet modem with wireless built in. The log showed that the wireless had turned off just moments before Joe's death. It hadn't turned back on until moments after his death.

It hadn't disconnected due to an error. The wireless had been turned off by the modem during a firmware update. It had taken just over fifteen minutes to perform the update. Then it had taken another two minutes to restart.

"Take a look at this." Carver highlighted that section of the log.

Andrea looked at it. Frowned. "That can't be coincidence. It just can't be."

"It's not." Carver shook his head. "I can't prove it. It's just a gut feeling. But the modem doing an update at that exact moment doesn't jibe."

She navigated the menus. "It's set to automatically update. It must get a notification that one is available and download it."

Carver read the settings on the page. "The updates are automatic, but they're set to occur after one in the morning."

Andrea browsed back to the logfile. She scrolled through it. Shook her head. "The update was downloaded this morning and ran automatically moments later. Maybe the schedule setting doesn't work."

"Maybe." Carver checked the download settings. There was no website or download address listed. The device was made by Comtech. It was a big company that made a wide range of networking and communication devices.

He went back to the closet. Looked at the sticker on the device. The local internet service provider was part of KalTel, also a large company. It was possible someone from one of the two companies could have caused the download and update to happen the way they did.

It was an effective way to take down wireless communications at a specific time. Carver had used other methods to achieve the same thing when he'd been working for Scion. Those methods usually involved gadgets that could interfere with wireless signals.

Out here in the civilian world, a world without access to those gadgets, forcing a firmware update was an interesting workaround. It required a high level of access, however. That made it impractical for most people.

Had someone bribed a person at the internet provider or the manufacturer to upload an update or force an update at a specific time? That seemed like the only way to make it happen.

Andrea joined him outside the closet. "What are you looking for?"

He showed her the manufacturer and internet service provider information. "I'm trying to figure out how the update appeared at just the right time."

"You think someone at one of these companies could have done it?"

He nodded. "As far as I know, that's the only way it could have happened."

"How would we find out?" She shook her head. "I wouldn't even know where to begin."

Carver didn't know either. Maybe there was a local office for the internet provider. Maybe it was a small office. Finding the culprit in a large company would be like searching for a needle in a haystack.

He set the modem down. Shook his head. "Did Joe get any threats?"

"Not that I know of. After his speech at the city council meeting, a lot of people told him they were thankful for what he was doing. They supported him."

"He gave a speech?" That didn't sound like Joe.

She laughed. "Unbelievable, I know. He went to the city council and told them that he and the others in this area voted against annexation. The votes were eighty percent against it. But the city went ahead and collected signatures. He told them that without validation, the signatures were worthless."

"How did the city respond to that?"

She frowned. "Mayor Herrada told him he had no right to speak at a council meeting because he wasn't a citizen. That he'd have to wait until after annexation before he could speak again."

Carver grinned. "I'll bet that went over well with Joe."

"Oh, it went over really well." Her voice was filled with sarcasm. "He tried to reply to her, but they cut off his mic. So, he just raised his voice and said that if they were so hellbent on annexing the land, then he was announcing his run for mayor. He said a few other choice things he probably shouldn't have said, but that was the crux of it."

"He cussed like a sailor?"

Andrea smiled fondly. "Yeah. Just like a Navy sailor." She sighed. "Security escorted him out. He went straight to the print shop. Ordered yard signs and posters for his campaign. He called the local news channels and was interviewed by two of them."

Carver tried to wrap his head around it. "Sounds like he cracked. This is a man who loves his privacy and doesn't care much for crowds."

"The proposed annexation concerned him and a lot of others out this way. Ever since the mayor was elected, crime has been out of control. Hell, everything has been out of control." Andrea looked out the window. "The mayor has been spending city money left and right. The city council members couldn't stop her if they tried. She locked them out of the financial software and even locked out regular employees. By the end of her first year, the city went from having a ten-million-dollar surplus to a five-million-dollar deficit."

Carver whistled. "She blew fifteen million in a year?"

"Apparently." She turned back to him. "She raised taxes and that wasn't enough, so she decided annexing more territory would bring in more taxpayers."

"And that would mean higher taxes for Joe?"

"Higher property taxes for sure. And there was a proposed tax on people with a net worth over a million dollars."

"That would include just about every homeowner in this area, wouldn't it?"

"Yeah." She laughed in disbelief. "You can hardly find a home for under five hundred thousand in this area. And this is a popular bedroom community for Los Angeles."

Carver nodded. "I can see why Joe would decide to run. He always took matters into his own hands if nobody else could fix a problem."

All the air seemed to leave Andrea. She walked around the desk and dropped into the chair. Tears pooled in her eyes. She squeezed her eyes shut and shook with quiet sobs. "It keeps hitting me in waves. Over and over again. He's dead. My Joe is dead. The man I love more than life itself."

Carver wasn't much of a hugger. He stayed on his side of the desk. But he reached over and put a hand on her shoulder. "Joe was like a big brother to me. He helped me keep my head on straight. He got me through some tough times."

She smiled through her tears. "He always had a word of advice for every occasion, didn't he?"

Carver smiled. "He did. And I promise you that if this was a hit, then I'll find everyone responsible and make them pay for it."

Andrea gripped his hand. Squeezed it tight. Ferocity lit her sad eyes. "Do it Carver." Her voice turned to a hiss. "Make them pay for what they've done."

Carver nodded gravely. "I will."

CHAPTER 6

Carver didn't know where to start.

There was no security footage. No concrete evidence of foul play. Just a string of events that seemed too coincidental to be coincidences.

"I need a drink." Andrea rose from the office chair. "You want something?"

Carver shook his head. "I'm going to look through the laptop. Maybe there's something on it that'll point me in the right direction."

"Make yourself at home. You can stay in the guest room across the hall." She gestured toward a door opposite the office door. "Feel free to use Joe's truck if you need to go anywhere." She swallowed hard. Took a deep, shuddering breath. Walked away.

Carver looked through the recently opened items on Joe's laptop. The email program was one. The others were various documents that looked related to running for mayor. There was an application to be put on the ballot and a financial disclosure form for public officials.

The financial disclosure was several pages long. Joe's annual income was listed. He had a meager retirement benefit from the military. The income from the ranch was anything but meager. He'd cleared over a million the previous year and the year before that, almost two million. The years before that he reported losses.

His expenses were also huge. They were almost fifty percent of revenue. The document didn't go into detail about what they were. It probably cost quite a bit to care for breeding horses. Joe's two helpers probably cost a pretty penny too.

Carver opened the email program. There were hundreds of unread emails. The ones that had been opened were about ranch business or official responses to his candidacy filing for mayor. There were a lot of invitations for Joe to speak at gatherings.

Joe had responded positively to most of them. There were also emails from citizens with complaints about the current government. They wanted Joe to promise to fix the issues if he was elected.

The one thing Carver didn't see was anything threatening. No emails from people promising violence if he didn't drop out.

The emails weren't all positive. Supporters of Herrada had emailed Joe. Told him he was an idiot. Told him he should drop out because Herrada was the greatest mayor of all time. The usual political garbage.

Carver ran two searches. One for KalTel and one for Comtech. There were none from Comtech, but there were several from KalTel. They were service emails. Warning about service outages and routine maintenance.

One from two weeks ago warned of an upcoming maintenance window. It said the internet service would be down for approximately one hour starting at two in the morning. There were two follow up emails.

The scheduled outage had been this morning. But it had happened hours before the outage that took down the Wi-Fi.

The last email had been sent early this morning. It said the maintenance outage had gone as planned. The modems had been rebooted and services were restored. There was a link for support if anyone had problems.

Carver clicked the link. A website opened. A chat box appeared with multiple choice options. He clicked options until he reached a live chat operator.

This is Toby with KalTel. How may I help you?

Carver typed back. *My modem went down at seven this morning. It had a firmware update. Was this part of the planned outage?*

I'll check on that and get right back to you. Please stand by.

Carver opened Joe's browser history. It was set to purge anything over a month old. The recent history consisted of news videos and instructional videos for mounting a political campaign.

The chat window chimed. Carver switched back to it and found a message from the support guy.

There's no record of a recent firmware update. The last update was three months ago. I checked your modem logs, and it looks like the maintenance reboot might have caused the modem to think there was a new update. The firmware version for your modem is correct, so it looks like it just downloaded the last update and installed it again.

Your modem seems to be operating properly and I don't detect any issues. Is there anything else I can help you with?

Carver's gut told him there was no accidental download. *Did this happen to anyone else or just me?*

I'll have to ask. Please wait.

Carver didn't like gathering information over text. He preferred hearing someone's voice on the other end. It helped him to know if someone was lying. Not that he thought this guy was lying.

KalTel was a big company. The tech support guy might not be local. Odds were he was overseas, and Toby wasn't his real name.

The wait this time was almost ten minutes before the chat box chimed again.

Sir, I'm sorry. I don't have access to that information.

Carver replied. *Let's say someone wanted to take down my internet for a specific window of time. Who at your company would be capable of uploading a fake update file to my modem?*

Ellipses formed in the chat window indicating the guy was typing a reply. But a full minute passed and nothing appeared in the chat window.

A response finally came. *I'm sorry, Mr. Donnely. Why do you think someone intentionally wanted to take down your internet?*

Carver didn't want to get into that. *I just need to know who at your company could do that. I'm running for a local political office and need to know if someone intentionally sabotaged my internet.*

You think someone at our company would do that? I don't think I'm authorized to talk about that. I can ask a supervisor.

That wasn't where this conversation needed to go. A supervisor would see the potential liability and shut down the conversation. Carver typed a reply. *I want to make it clear that I'm not holding the company liable for anything. I just need to know if someone locally could have done that on their own to sabotage my internet.*

Ellipses appeared in the chat bubble. Toby's response appeared after another delay. *Everything is controlled centrally from here. When a new update is available for any of the many hardware devices we support, it is uploaded to a specific site. Most devices autodetect the new file and download it. But that would affect everyone, not just one device like your modem.*

Carver replied. *That's why I asked if others besides my modem were affected.*

I'm actually intrigued by this, Toby replied. *I think I know how to check.* A couple of minutes later, he continued. *I checked other modems in your area. None of them had updates. They were only down for the maintenance window and didn't go offline again.*

Carver felt like he was finally getting somewhere. *Mine shows it went offline for the update, right?*

Yes, but yours was offline for a very long time. Most updates take less than ten minutes. Yours took twenty-two minutes. There are no records of local techs visiting the residence or anything else to indicate how the update file was uploaded to the modem.

Carver's gut feeling solidified into certainty. *Could a local tech make that happen? Is there some way they could isolate a modem without physically being here?*

Mr. Donnely, I think it's possible but I'm just an in-house tech reading scripts. I'll ask one of our outside line techs to get in touch with you. Can you provide a good number for someone to call you?

Carver gave him his burner number and a warning. *Whatever you do, don't ask someone local. Ask someone from as far away from El Fuerte as you can, because I don't want them getting wind of this.*

I was thinking the same thing, Mr. Donnely. I'll ask some other techs here too.

Carver thought back to the last guy who'd helped him. Jeremy in San Francisco. He was dead now. No sense in getting someone else killed. *Toby, I'm going to be completely honest. This situation might be dangerous, so don't ask too many questions. Just have someone contact me.*

Dangerous how? Toby replied.

I'm getting death threats.

Toby took a moment before replying. *Death threats? You should call the police! I'm sorry that's happening to you. I'll be careful and hopefully find someone who can help you.*

Thanks. Carver ended the chat.

It felt like he was on the right trail. The fake update was no accident. It was planned. Someone knew about the cameras. They wanted them offline. But how had they gotten the drop on Joe? How had they gotten the horse to kill him?

A tox screening might give answers and Carver didn't trust the sheriff's office to do it. He went back outside. A black Sprinter van was parked in front of the stable. Three people in green polos and jeans were standing in front of Lucas.

There was a side door in the stable. Carver angled around the garage so no one would see him. He slipped around the corner and entered the side door. It was positioned between the last two horse stalls.

He hustled to the end of the stall on his right. Looked around the corner. No one was inside. He went to Joe's body. Took closeup pictures. The surrounding floor was covered in a pool of blood.

The blood was dried and coagulated. He didn't know much about post-mortem toxicology screenings, but he knew this blood wouldn't cut it.

"I thought you might try something."

Carver turned. Saw Detective Ford standing in front of the stall near the side door. "I'm ensuring there's a proper autopsy and toxicology screening."

"I took blood samples before Lucas arrived."

"Why?" Carver approached him. "You just so happen to carry collection equipment with you?"

"I carry forensic equipment everywhere." Ford shrugged. "I'm a detective. Sometimes I have to gather evidence before the CSI crew arrives due to unforeseen circumstances."

"What makes you think you can trust your people any more than I can trust the sheriff's office?"

"That's a good question." Ford glanced at the front stable entrance. "They're coming."

Carver looked back and saw the main door sliding open. He slipped between the horse stalls. Went to the side door and exited. Ford followed him outside and closed the door behind them.

"We need someone independent," Carver said.

"I know a couple of people." Ford stepped around the back corner of the stable. "I can tell you the process isn't fast or cheap."

"I have money."

Ford nodded. "I can take you."

"You can give me the blood samples and I'll go myself."

"You'll need an introduction first." Ford shook his head. "Just come with me and it'll be smoother."

"Okay. When can we go?"

Ford shrugged. "Now?"

Carver nodded. "Now. Let me get my things first." He saw Gloria standing outside her car and walked over to her.

She did a doubletake when she noticed him. "What's happening? Any news?"

"Nothing yet." Carver motioned at her car. "Can I get my bags from your trunk?"

"Oh, of course." She pressed a button on her key fob and the trunk popped open.

Carver grabbed his duffel bag and backpack. "Thanks for the ride."

"Thanks for protecting me." Gloria gave him a slip of paper. "This has my number on it. Please let me know if you need anything. I have to go back into town."

Carver took the paper. He took his things into the house and dumped them on the guest room floor. He took a wad of cash from the duffel bag. He dug out a small leather holster and set it to the side.

Leon had given him a Glock 43 to wear as a conceal carry. It was smaller than he liked. It didn't have much capacity. But it was easy to hide, especially with the special holster. It was a small leather pouch that slid inside his pants.

The top of the pouch hung over his belt. When he needed the gun, all he had to do was pull up on the top. That opened the pouch. The pistol hilt would be exposed as with a normal holster. All he had to do was draw it, aim, and fire.

He put the gun into the holster and slid it into his pants right where the right jeans pocket was. He put the cash in his other pocket.

"Guns and gold are the two most important things a person can carry." That was what Rhodes had once told him. Or maybe that had been Leon. Carver couldn't remember anymore. The advice was still good.

Carver went outside. Gloria was gone. Ford was sitting in his unmarked police car, a black Ford with black steel wheels. Like most unmarked cars, it wasn't fooling anybody.

He slid into the passenger seat. Buckled in. "Let's go."

Lucas saw Carver get in. He hurried over and knocked on Carver's window. Ford rolled it down from his side.

"Where are you two going?" Lucas asked.

Ford leaned over so he could see Lucas's face. "I'm taking him into town to get a statement."

"A statement?" Lucas threw up his hands. "This is my jurisdiction, Monty! Don't make me file a formal complaint."

"It's not about this. One of his bags was stolen in town."

"Oh." Lucas frowned. "Why not take his statement here?"

"Because he saw someone take it. Thinks he might know where they are."

"Probably an unhoused individual." Lucas backed away.

"When will the autopsy be done?" Carver asked.

"In a few weeks." Lucas turned and headed back to the stable.

Ford rolled up Carver's window. He put the car in gear and turned it around on the gravel road. Then he gunned it back toward town.

Carver looked around the car. There were fast food wrappers and wadded up paper cups in the back floorboard. It smelled like cigarettes and alcohol. "They let you trash an official car?"

"It's just dirty, not trashed."

"Looks bad." Carver studied Ford for a moment. "You're a heavy drinker."

"I can stop and let you out right now if you want." Ford glared at him. "I don't have to help you."

"But you are. And I wonder why."

"I'm not a model citizen or model cop, okay?" Ford bared his teeth in a mock grin. "But I liked Joe."

Carver decided not to press too hard. Something didn't add up about Ford. Cops like him didn't go out of their way to help anyone. He changed the subject. "Gloria tells me the mayor of this town is rotten. Hell, I saw the mayor send a gang member over to stop her from recording with her phone."

"Mayor Herrada just doesn't like her. That doesn't mean she's rotten. It just means she's human."

Carver laughed without humor. "Her associating with gang members would say otherwise."

"She only knows them because her brother is a former gang member." Ford patted the steering wheel with his left hand. "That said, I would stay out of her way. She has a lot of support in this town."

"So, you'd vote for her again? Not Joe?"

"I would have voted for Joe in a heartbeat. I don't like the annexation plans any more than he does—did."

"You really think the mayor is on the up and up?"

Ford bit his bottom lip. Glanced at Carver. "I wouldn't let Gloria get you involved in anything. If something goes wrong, I can promise you the police in El Fuerte won't be interested in due process."

"Because the mayor controls them."

Ford nodded.

"And they'll kill me?"

He looked shocked. "No! That's not what I meant. I'm just saying you'll end up in jail and the paperwork will get lost."

"But you just told me the mayor isn't rotten." Carver stared at him. "Is she, or isn't she?"

Ford blew out a long breath. "I'm just telling you to behave. Because if you piss off the wrong person, there's nothing on heaven or earth that can help you in this town.

CHAPTER 7

The watcher made another note in his notebook.

Big man got into black cop car. The car left the premises and turned toward town.

He picked up his binoculars. They were high-powered. Made the miles between him and the ranch shrink down to almost nothing. His perch on the mountainside gave him almost a bird's-eye view.

It was noticeably cooler up here. The sun seemed brighter. The roads looked like black ribbons winding through a canopy of green and beige.

He'd only been up here an hour but had two pages of notes. It had been a busy morning at the ranch. A morning of unforeseen and unfortunate circumstances.

There had been other watchers before him. Their logs were unsubstantial. There simply hadn't been much to report. No strange visitors. No unusual behavior or activity. Everything had seemed status quo.

The problems that had been anticipated had never manifested. And then all concerns had been considered moot. Until today.

Today changed everything.

There was no cell signal here. No way to instantly transmit his log to anyone. If he traveled five minutes north or south of the mountain, he'd get a signal again. But it took five minutes to hike to his car and ten minutes to drive back down the mountain.

Once things quieted down at the ranch, he'd make the hike and the drive. Then he'd send the log. Then again, maybe it was important that he let them know now. He frowned. This was a two-man job.

It was better to have someone constantly watch while the other left every so often to send in reports. Of course, before today, that hadn't seemed necessary.

He watched the people from the sheriff's office go inside the stable. There was no other outside activity. He'd give it a few minutes and if nothing happened, he'd leave to make a report. It seemed likely someone would want to know about the big guy. The stranger.

The big guy might be a problem. He might be a big nothing. It wasn't the watcher's job to determine that.

He bit the inside of his lip. It was a nervous habit. One that kicked in whenever he had to make a potentially big decision. He finally decided it was important enough to leave his post and go make a report.

If he had a camera with a high-powered lens, this wouldn't be an issue. He could have the camera record while he was gone. Someone told him that they'd tried a camera once. It hadn't worked well.

The lens would get dusty and dirty. The focus didn't work well over such long distances. Having a human do it worked much better. But it would still be nice to have that option now.

The watcher gave it five more minutes. Then he got up. Dusted off his pants. Started the hike back to his truck. In roughly twenty-five minutes, someone would have his report.

CARVER CHECKED THE TIME.

Ford had driven south for about ten minutes then hooked east for another ten. The car slowed and Ford turned into the parking lot of a shabby strip mall. The parking lot was gray and pitted. The long building was faded green.

There was a massage parlor with dark tinted windows. A Latino butcher shop. A Vietnamese noodle restaurant. Down at the end was a sign that said, *Chronic Pain Management*. Ford parked in front of it.

He got out of the car. Carver slid out and followed Ford to the door. The detective opened it. A bell chimed. A young woman with glasses and puffy blond hair looked up from a receptionist desk.

The lobby was full of chairs. The chairs were full of people. Most were haggard looking middle-aged men and women. A few kids were there too. Some were staring at the screens of phones or tablets. Some were playing with toys from a wooden toy chest.

The receptionist narrowed her eyes. She looked from Ford to Carver. Back to Ford. "He's busy."

"Which room is he in?" Ford asked.

"I said he's busy."

Ford leaned over her desk. "Cut the shit, Janine. Or do I need to file a report?"

Her nose wrinkled in disgust. "Go to hell, Monty."

"You first."

She rolled her eyes. Sighed. "Examination room two."

"Thank you, darling."

She wrinkled her nose again. "Go to hell." She looked at Carver. "Who's the meat wall?"

"A new patient."

"Oh, yeah?" Her face brightened. "Tell Arly that I referred him?"

Monty smiled. Leaned over her desk again. "So, you get the referral bonus?"

She made her eyes bigger. "Yes. You wouldn't get a bonus anyway."

Monty looked around conspiratorially. Leaned a little closer. "Usual arrangement."

She shuddered. "Yes."

"Okay, then you got it." He turned his cheek toward her. "Give me a kiss."

Janine leaned closer. Wrinkled her nose. Kissed his cheek. Wiped off her mouth. "Thanks, babe."

"My pleasure." Ford walked around the desk. Opened the door. Walked into the hall. There were five doorways. Two on the left, two on the right, and one at the end of the hall. They were all closed.

"What's your usual arrangement?" Carver asked.

Ford grinned. Then he seemed to think better of it and wiped it off his face. "Oh, nothing."

"Trading favors for sex?"

"It's not like I could get any otherwise." Ford sighed. "I'm not proud of it, but it's better than nothing, you know?"

Carver didn't reply. The man was crooked but at least he was being helpful. For now.

Ford stopped outside the room marked three. He put a finger to his lips. Put his ear to the door. He listened for a moment, then quickly twisted the knob and opened the door.

A short, chubby man with a crown of hair around a bald spot gasped and looked at the door. A painfully thin man was sitting on an examination table. His eyes were red, and his skin was drawn back from his eyes.

The balding guy was wearing a white lab coat. He looked like a doctor. Maybe he was. Maybe he wasn't. He looked like the kind of guy who was one false prescription away from losing his medical license.

"Damn it, Ford." The doctor put a hand over his heart. "Why do you always burst in on me in the middle of an examination?"

Ford made air quotes. "An examination." He laughed. "Just give the poor man his prescription and let him go."

"I'm trying to make sure he still needs it."

"Please, doc!" The patient clasped his hands in a beggar's pose. "I need it so bad! I really, really need it! I can't survive." Tears trickled down his cheeks. "Not without it."

The doctor patted the patient's shoulder. "Calm down, Oscar. You still need it."

Oscar calmed immediately. Wiped away his tears. Smiled gratefully. "Thanks, Doctor Palmer."

Palmer took out a pad. Scribbled something on it. "Here you go. Make sure you read the brochure about the dangers of opioids, okay?"

"Oh, yeah, I'll read it for sure." Oscar took the paper and hurried out of the room.

Palmer turned to Ford. He looked curiously at Carver. "New patient?"

"Not technically. Not for pain management, anyway."

"Okay." Palmer said it slowly. Like he was trying to figure out a new angle he hadn't heard of before. "Care to explain?"

Ford closed the door. Leaned on it. "You do toxicology screenings, right?"

"I'm required to do them for some patients, yes. To make sure they're not mixing dangerous meds."

"Good." Ford crossed his arms. "I have a post-mortem tox I need run. And I need it done quietly."

Palmer's eyes widened. "An overdose?"

"No." Ford waggled a hand. "Maybe. But not the kind you're thinking. The victim might have been drugged before death."

"A murder?" Palmer looked interested. "Why does it need to be kept quiet?"

"Because it happened on Lucas's territory."

"That son of a bitch again?" Palmer looked to the side and pretended to spit.

"Yeah."

Palmer rubbed his hands together. "It's not free, you know? That's an easy five hundred, minimum."

"Is it, though?" Ford pushed off the door. "Unless I'm forgetting something, I still own you, Palmer."

"Yeah, but it's hardly fair you make me pay for something like this!"

Carver held up a hand. "It's fine. I'll pay."

Ford groaned. "That's not how it works."

"I don't care how it works. I need results." Carver took out a wad of cash. Peeled off five hundred dollars in twenties.

Palmer took it. Counted it. "It might cost more."

Carver stepped closer. Towered over the doctor. "It'll cost five hundred and be done right. Okay?"

Palmer gulped. Nodded. "Yes, sir."

Carver stepped back. Leaned against a counter. "How long will it take?"

"It depends on how busy the lab is. They usually turn around a post-mortem in three to four weeks."

"I need it in a week."

"That would require extra money to bump it to the front of the line."

Carver clenched a fist hard enough to crack his knuckles.

Palmer held up his hands. "But I'll pull some strings and get it done."

"Pull those strings hard." Carver relaxed his hand. "How long does it take?"

"If it goes through all the proper procedures, then it can take weeks." Palmer started listing things on his fingers. "You have confirmatory testing, quality control, a review board of pathologists, and so forth."

"That's not exactly keeping it quiet," Ford said.

"Well, in this case, you just want confirmation that a drug was in the blood, right?"

Ford nodded. "I just need to know if someone pumped the victim full of something first."

"Then that should show up relatively quickly, provided the blood isn't too badly degraded."

"It's fresh enough." Ford lifted his shirt and pulled a small, insulated bag from his waistline. He opened it. Produced three frosty vials of blood.

Palmer took them. Held one up to the light. "I'll drive them over to the lab myself."

"Won't that look suspicious?" Carver asked.

He shook his head. "No, I do it all the time."

"He has a guy on the take." Ford grinned. "Someone who makes sure fentanyl overdoses aren't properly reported."

"That's why the good detective here owns me," Palmer said. "He busted me. Made me his confidential informant."

Carver didn't care. "What's your personal cell number?"

Palmer looked uncertain but rattled off the digits.

Carver put them into his phone. He wrote his number down on a piece of paper. Handed it to Palmer. "Text me the instant you have something."

"Yes, sir." Palmer took the paper. "You have my word."

"For what it's worth," Monty said. He nudged Palmer. "Make sure to tell Janine I referred my friend here."

"You realize then I'll have to pay her the referral bonus." Palmer sighed. "I'm literally paying for you to get laid."

"Better than jail, am I right?" Ford nudged Palmer in the ribs with his elbow.

Palmer winced. "Yes. Please stop that."

"Don't pretend you aren't using your position to get some nookie too, doc." Ford grinned. "That's why I like showing up unexpectedly sometimes."

Carver didn't need to hear anything else. He opened the door. Walked down the hallway. He looked at the faces in the waiting room. Gaunt faces. Desperate faces. People dying for their next fix. The next fix that might kill them.

He went outside to the car. Ford came out a moment later. He sauntered over to the car, a little skip in his step. He was an easy guy to dislike. Crooked as hell. But he was useful for now. So long as he didn't decide to turn on Carver later.

Ford unlocked the car and dropped inside. Carver got in.

"Hot damn, I've got a date!" Ford rubbed his hands together.

Carver leaned back in his seat. He thought about what came next. What if the toxicology report came back positive? Maybe someone slipped Joe a sedative. Made it easy to lay him down and get the horse to stomp him.

He needed more information.

Ford steered the car onto the road and turned west. "You're being awfully quiet."

"You would've voted for Joe, but otherwise, you're a loyal supporter of the mayor."

Ford raised an eyebrow. "Was that a question or a statement?"

Carver just stared at him.

Ford cleared his throat. "I support her, yes."

"You'd do anything she ordered, no questions asked?"

"She wouldn't ask me to do anything, but yeah. Orders are orders."

Carver nodded. "All the local cops toe her line?"

"Yeah, willingly." Ford patted the steering wheel. "She's the boss."

"Her brother was a former gang member, not a current one?"

"That's what she says."

"Are there a lot of gangs in this town?"

Ford shook his head. "There used to be several, but the feds cleared them out a few years ago. It was part of a big initiative by the last governor to clean up gang violence in the LA area." He chuckled. "The new governor released a lot of the gang members. He said they weren't a major threat and that his predecessor was too zealous."

Carver wasn't surprised. Especially not if Enigma had something to do with it. "How many gangs?"

"Three, but in name only. La Familia, the Aztecs, and Abuela's Boys." He stopped at a red light. "They decided to unite to keep fighting between gangs to a minimum because that was what got the governor to involve the feds the last time."

"How did they unite? A peace treaty? A gentlemen's agreement?"

"Crossbreeding."

Carver nodded. "Marriages of convenience."

"Yep. It also helped that they're mostly Latino."

"From the same countries?"

Ford shrugged. "No idea. Mostly Mexican if I had to guess."

"Is the mayor native born?"

He shrugged again. "I don't know. She doesn't have an accent, so she was probably born here."

Carver had more questions, but he didn't trust Ford enough to ask him. He could probably find out more from the internet. Despite being a local cop, Ford didn't seem to know much about the ground situation.

He was probably too busy drinking and gambling to do any actual work.

Traffic was a little heavier on the way back, so it took thirty minutes to get back to Joe's. The sheriff's cars were gone.

Ford parked next to the stable. They went inside. It looked like someone had tried to hose away the blood and had not done a very good job of it. There were black streaks leading to the drain. A faint pink circle where Joe's head had been.

Andrea was sitting in a chair next to the stain. She was staring at it, her face locked up in grief and pain. Her eyes were red. Her skin was blotchy. She wasn't crying. She was probably cried out. Dried up.

She was holding one of the pictures from the desk. The one with the gold frame. Carver couldn't see it, but he knew what it depicted. It showed Joe and Andrea holding frozen margaritas. They were smiling. Looking happier than any humans had a right to look.

And now Andrea was more miserable than any human should be.

Ford cleared his throat. Spoke in hushed tones. "Um, I'm going home to get ready for my date. Let me know when Palmer texts you."

Carver nodded. He walked over to Andrea. Put a hand on her shoulder. Comforting someone wasn't exactly his strong suit. He could fake it in a life-or-death situation. But not now.

Andrea touched his hand. She stared at the picture. "Happiest years of my life, Carver. It's all downhill from here."

"I'm glad you two had that."

She laughed. Looked up at him. "Joe always said you were bad at the emotional stuff."

"Joe was a different person after he met you." Carver smiled. "He went from being a grumpy old man to a happy one. And I'm glad he found happiness. God knows it's rare enough."

Andrea teared up again. "The rarest thing ever. I'm blessed to have met him. To have had all this time with him. And now I'm faced with...nothing. A big emptiness until I die."

"Yeah, pretty much."

She laughed. A genuine one this time. "Carver, did anyone tell you that you'd make a great counselor?"

"Rhodes told me I should do it just so she could laugh her ass off."

"Who's Rhodes?"

"A former commander. A former friend."

"Former?"

"She's dead now."

"Oh." Andrea patted his hand. "I'd like some time alone if you don't mind."

Carver nodded. He left by the side door. Walked past the garage. Went into the house and back to Joe's office. He sat down at the computer and read the subject lines on the emails. He found one titled *Help Please*.

It was from a guy having problems with the mayor. He wanted Joe to come talk to him. Joe had replied. Told him they could meet. That meeting was supposed to have been later today.

Was it a coincidence or a piece of the puzzle? There was no way to know for sure unless he met with the guy.

And that was what he was going to do.

CHAPTER 8

Carver was going back to town.

He found Joe's truck keys hanging in the kitchen next to the door. The door led to a covered walkway. The walkway led to the detached garage. It looked more like a small house than a garage. Too fancy to just keep cars in.

The garage door was locked. A key on Joe's keyring opened it. Most folks who lived this far out in the country wouldn't bother to lock their doors. They'd feel safe. And they'd mostly be okay. But it only took that one time to shatter the illusion of safety.

Joe was the careful type. Special forces training usually did that to a person. Joe used to tell him there was a fine line between being prepared and paranoia. He said it was better to be paranoid than dead.

It was a rule Carver lived by. He'd spent years being prepared and never had a problem. At least until Morganville, Georgia. These days being paranoid kept him alive.

There was a nice black Range Rover on his side of the garage. A new black Dodge Ram pickup in the middle. He walked around the front of the pickup. It had large offroad tires and was raised a few inches higher than normal.

It looked clean. No dirt on the tires. No caked dirt in the wheel wells. It looked like it had hardly been driven.

There were two more vehicles in the garage. One was an old Honda sedan. The other was a classic Dodge Ram pickup. It had medium sized tires and looked like it hadn't been lifted like the new Ram.

There was dried mud on the sides and the wheels were dusty. That was the truck Joe normally drove. He probably purchased the new Ram and decided he didn't like driving it as much as the old pickup.

The old Ram had the same classic front end as the Ramcharger Carver had abandoned in San Francisco. He still felt a pang of regret about it, but he couldn't drive it anymore. The people who wanted him dead could find that thing on a traffic camera in a heartbeat.

The classic Ram's key was on the keyring. The fob for the new Ram was on there too. Carver used it to unlock the new truck. He stepped on the siderail and swung inside. He pushed a button to start the engine.

It rumbled to life. The gas tank was three quarters full. That was good because this thing probably didn't get great mileage with the large tires and modified suspension.

It still had that new car smell inside. The leather was fresh and clean. No wrinkles or marks. The floormats looked pristine. The odometer showed 122 miles. Yeah, Joe had driven this thing off the lot and parked it.

The garage door opener was on the passenger side sun visor. He pressed the button and the middle door opened quickly and silently. Carver pulled out of the garage and closed the door. He drove down the concrete driveway and onto the gravel road.

He used the GPS on his phone for directions to a place called Albert's Salvage. It was on the northwest side of town. On a street called El Fuerte Industrial Boulevard. There was a collision repair shop, a used tire store, and an oil change shop along the way.

There wasn't much in the way of apartments or houses. It wasn't a residential part of town. In that sense, the name of the street was accurate. But there didn't look like much industry happening. Most of the shops looked closed. Most of the parking lots were overgrown with weeds. Any industries had closed up shop a long time ago.

One of the few places still in business was a rundown grocery store called Herbert's with the usual suspects sitting on a bench outside. Three old men. One smoking a cigar. They were laughing and talking. Just idling the day away.

Carver reached the salvage yard. There was a tall metal fence all around the property. It wasn't chain-link. Someone had planted metal poles into the ground and welded steel plates to them.

The steel had been painted black to prevent rust. So far, the paint seemed to be holding its own. In this arid climate, there wasn't enough moisture or salt to make the metal oxidize very fast.

There was a rolling gate at the front. It was made with steel bars instead of plates. Probably because it would be too heavy otherwise. It was secured with a heavy-duty chain and padlock. Carver pulled up to it and got out of the truck.

There was a dirt road on the other side of the gate. The road went to a red brick building. The road continued past the building and went between rows of old cars and piles of metal.

It looked like a typical salvage yard. At least from what Carver had seen. There was a poster with Joe's face on it taped to the gate.

It said *Joe Donnely for a better tomorrow*. Even after seeing the box of posters in Joe's office, it was still jarring seeing Joe's face plastered on something like that.

There was a red button next to the gate. It said *Press for service.* He pressed it. A moment later, an older black man walked out of the brick building. He walked up to the gate. Looked Carver up and down. Looked at his truck.

"How can I help you, sir?"

"Are you Albert?"

"Yes, sir. And you are?"

"Carver. I'm here for Joe."

Albert frowned. "For Joe? I thought we were meeting in person."

"That was the plan, but something came up."

"Oh." He looked a little disappointed. "Well, come on in." He unlocked the gate. Pulled on it. Opened it wide enough for the truck. He pointed toward the red brick building. "You can park there."

Carver drove through the entrance and parked. He slid out of the vehicle.

Albert closed the gate and locked it. "Let's go inside." He walked to the brick building. Tugged open the door and went inside.

Carver entered and closed the door behind him. The room on the other side was small and cluttered. There were shelves with car manuals and car parts. Boxes of miscellaneous parts. An old wooden desk with a worn-out chair. There were two metal chairs on the other side.

Albert sat in the chair behind the desk. Carver sat in one of the metal chairs. It creaked and wobbled. He leaned back and got comfortable.

"Well, I guess I'll tell you what I was going to tell Joe," Albert said. "But I'd like to know why he couldn't be here."

"I'll tell you, but first, let's talk about your problem."

Albert nodded. "The annual bike rally is coming up. I got a letter from the mayor's office telling me I couldn't have it without the proper permits."

"You said it's an annual bike rally?"

"Yes. I've been hosting it for over twenty years now. It was part of Mayor Davis's revitalization plan, back in the day." Albert chuckled. "Probably because he was an avid biker himself. He gave me a perpetual permit. He said it was good until hell froze over."

"So, you should be good."

"Yeah, except Mayor Herrada found out I supported Joe. At least, that's the only thing I can think of."

"Did she specifically mention it?"

Albert shook his head. "No. The letter used that roundabout political talk. The kind where they say something without saying something specific."

"Can I see the letter?"

"Sure." Albert opened a desk drawer and pulled out a wrinkled envelope. He handed it to Carver.

Carver removed the letter. It was wrinkled, like it had been crumpled up then smoothed back out again.

"Sorry about that. It just burned me up when I read it, so I balled it up and threw it across the room."

"Understandable." Carver read the letter. It was short and sweet.

Mr. Albert Jones,

It has come to our attention that you are not supportive of our community and are, in fact, actively working against the values that make our city great. Mayor Herrada takes great pride in the progress we've made and will not allow deplorable elements such as you drag our great city down.

To that effect, we are requiring you to file a new permit for any activities at the salvage yard. Unless and until you decide to support your community, you will not benefit from our generosity.

Sincerely,

Allegra Hernandez

Official Spokesperson for Super Mayor Jessica Herrada

Carver noticed the last name of the letter writer. "Is Allegra Hernandez related to Captain Lucas Hernandez?"

Albert grinned. "That's his sister."

Carver took a picture of the letter. He folded it and put it back in the envelope. "The letter seems pretty direct to me. Unless you support the mayor, they'll directly act against you in any way they can."

"You noticed the signature?" Albert took out the letter and pointed to the last line. "Super Mayor Jessica Herrada. Like she's some superhero."

"I noticed." Carver didn't keep up with politics, but he'd never heard of a super mayor. "It's a self-appointed title?"

Albert laughed. "Yeah. It's on all the political billboards all over the town too."

Carver had seen the billboards. He'd filtered them out like background noise, but now that he thought about them, he remembered seeing *Super Mayor* on a couple of them.

He got back to the matter at hand. "The question is, can they revoke your perpetual permit?"

Albert got up and walked to the bookshelf. He removed a picture frame from between two car manuals. Slid it across the desk to Carver. "That's the original permit. A copy is filed with the city too."

Carver read it aloud. "Albert Jones has the blessing and permission of the city of El Fuerte to hold the Annual El Fuerte Bike Rally at Albert's Salvage. This permit cannot be revoked and shall continue in perpetuity. It can be inherited by subsequent owners of Albert's Salvage yard even if the name is changed. Signed Mayor Marquis Davis." Below was a list of city council members who'd also signed.

Albert slid another picture frame across the desk. It showed a large group of bikers posing in front of Albert's place. He pointed to a big black man with a happy grin on his face. "That's Mayor Davis. He never let anything come between him and his Harley."

Carver pointed to a familiar face standing next to the mayor. "That's you?"

Albert grinned. "I was a young'un. I'd opened this place maybe five years before and was struggling. Mayor Davis and my dad were friends. He saw an opportunity to throw me a bone and did it."

"Where is Mayor Davis now?"

"He served three more terms. Best years this city ever saw." Albert sighed. "Black, white, Hispanic, Asian—it didn't matter in those days. We were all brothers and sisters in this city. When the rest of LA was burning, we held firm." He straightened and his chest puffed out a little. "We were El Fuerte. The Fort. Then Mayor Davis retired. His wife died and he took his Harley and said he'd ride the Earth until the day he died."

Albert wiped a tear from his cheek. "I reckon he's still out there riding somewhere."

Carver didn't say anything for a minute. He knew what he had to say, but it felt important to give Albert a moment.

Albert took a deep breath. Smiled like he wasn't feeling like smiling. "I don't know what Joe can do to help, but I won't abandon my principles no matter how those thugs at City Hall threaten me. Will you tell Joe that?"

"I can't."

Albert blinked. "Why not?"

There was no good way to frame it, so Carver just came out and said it. "Joe is dead."

Albert shot up from his chair. "What? Did they kill him? The mayor's thugs?"

"He was supposedly kicked to death by a horse."

Albert's knees gave out. He dropped into his chair. "Ain't no way. Whoever is selling the idea that Joe Donnely got kicked by a horse is selling snake oil."

"I agree."

The other man stared at Carver for a long minute. "Who are you?"

"I knew Joe in the service. He was my mentor. We served together in the SEALs."

"Joe was your brother in arms."

"Yeah. He was family."

"I was Army back in my teens." Albert touched his left arm. "I was out in five years. Broke my arm in two places in a bar fight."

Carver leaned forward. "You broke your arm in a bar fight?"

"Yeah. I wasn't the one fighting. I was trying to break it up." He shook his head. "Some huge MP came barreling in there and took down the two Army Rangers who started it. I just got caught in the middle."

"You planned to make a career out of it?"

Albert shook his head. "I wanted the GI Bill. Thought I'd be the first in my family to get a college degree. It didn't work out. But when I came back, there was a new community college and trade school in town, thanks to Mayor Davis. I got a certification in welding and started my salvage business."

Carver wrote down his number on a slip of paper. Slid it across the desk. "Text or call me if you need help. I don't know what I can do about the permit. I don't think Joe could have done anything about it either. You might need a lawyer."

"I can't afford a lawyer. I make a living. Nothing more, nothing less. It gets me by. And the bike rally is my biggest business of the year. It draws people from all over the country. People who work on classic cars. Rich people who donate to my business. And those people do a lot of business in town too. Other business owners pay me to point the bikers to their places."

"And you just host them?"

"I'll show you." Albert got up. He winced and held his left arm. Barked a laugh. "Still aches like a son of a gun even after all these years." He went to the door. "Come on."

Carver followed him outside. Albert slid up a garage door on the right side of the building. Inside was a golf cart. Not the battery powered kind. This one had offroad wheels and a push to start engine.

It looked brand new. Sparkling clean aside from a little dirt on the wheels. Carver sat on the passenger side. Albert got in and pushed the start button. The cart hummed to life and purred quietly.

He pulled out of the garage. Drove down the dirt road between rows of cars. Ahead was a wall of stacked school buses. It stretched from one side of the property to the other. Sheets of metal were welded to the bottoms of the buses to keep people from crawling underneath them.

Albert pressed a garage door opener on the sun visor. One of the buses rolled up and Carver realized it was just a bus painted on the side of a rollup door.

"Impressive."

Albert grinned. "It was my nephew's idea. He's an artist. One of those folks who can draw a photorealistic picture of anything with just a pencil or a piece of charcoal."

"I thought that was a real bus."

"Everyone does when they first see it." Albert beamed. He drove them under the bus that made the doorway. On the other side was something unexpected.

The wall of buses continued. In some places there were cargo containers stacked two high. Probably because he'd run out of buses. But that wasn't the impressive part. What caught Carver's eye was the small old west town built right in the middle.

Carver heard the roar of an engine behind them. He looked back. Saw a red pickup racing toward them. It flashed its lights. Honked its horn. It raced past them and skidded to a stop about ten yards ahead of Albert's cart.

"Friends of yours?" Carver said.

Albert shook his head. "No." He hit the brakes and the cart skidded to a halt.

The pickup was jacked up higher than Joe's Ram. It was almost ridiculously high. Four doors opened. Four men got out. Three of them climbed down metal steps on the side rail. The last guy was tall enough that he didn't have to use them. It was Hugo.

The same guy who'd bullied Gloria.

CHAPTER 9

Hugo looked ready to fight.

Albert glanced back. "How in the hell did they get in? I locked the gate."

Carver remained in his seat. He observed the four men. They looked small compared to Hugo. He figured they were around five feet seven inches, give or take. Bulges under their shirts told Carver all he needed to know.

They were packing.

He slid out of the seat. Positioned his hand near his concealed holster.

Hugo grinned. "Well, look who we have here."

"Get off my property!" Albert got out of the cart. "How did you get in?"

"Isn't this a place of business?" Hugo smirked and looked at his companions as if he was asking them the question. "The gate was open. We came in."

"The gate was locked!" Albert made a shooing motion. "Get off my property!"

"Or what?" Hugo grinned. "You'll call the cops?"

"The man asked you to leave his private property." Carver stared them down. "I suggest you do that."

Hugo shook his head. "We'll leave, but you're coming with us. I need to teach you some manners."

They'd come specifically for Carver. Not Albert. He hadn't seen anyone following him. No one could have possibly known he was driving Joe's pickup. And since Joe hadn't driven it much, no one should know whose it was.

Somehow, they did.

The four men were clumped up close together. Almost side-by-side. That was convenient. But Carver didn't want to start a shootout. Someone had sent these people here which meant they couldn't just disappear without someone knowing who did it.

"You deaf, gringo?" Hugo raised his shirt to reveal a holstered gun. It was ridiculously large and coated with chrome. Probably a Desert Eagle. "You're coming with me."

"You followed me here for one of two reasons. The person you work for sees me as a threat, or this is personal, and you want revenge for the incident in the park."

"No one sees you as a threat, gringo." Hugo laughed. "I'm just here to escort you out of town and teach you some manners along the way."

"Escort me out of town?" Carver hadn't heard that one before. "Not going to happen."

"You're not wanted here."

"By the mayor?"

"By me. By anyone." Hugo patted his Desert Eagle. "You don't have much choice."

Carver nodded at the truck. "That's yours?"

"What do you think, pendejo? Of course it's mine."

"Big, jacked up truck. Giant shiny gun. Just how hard are you compensating?"

One of Hugo's companions laughed and quickly repressed it. The others didn't react. They probably didn't speak English.

Hugo bared his teeth and pulled his gun. Carver yanked open the holster pouch. Drew his Glock. It wasn't a great pistol for accuracy, but he was willing to take a chance against such a big target. He squeezed off a shot.

The Glock popped. The Desert Eagle sparked. Hugo shouted in alarm and dropped it. His companions started to reach for their guns.

"Next one with a gun in their hand gets a bullet in the head." Carver held his gun steady. "Now, get in the truck and leave."

"This isn't over, pendejo!" Hugo spat on the ground. "I will bury you!"

"Or, I can bury you and your friends now if you'd like." Carver shrugged. "It's a win-win."

One of the men spoke urgently in Spanish to Hugo. The big man shook with rage. Then he bent over to pick up his gun.

"No." Carver shook his head. "That's mine now."

Hugo's face burned red. He rattled off a stream of curses in Spanish. Carver had heard most of them before. The unfamiliar ones were probably regional.

"Do you kiss your mother with that mouth?" Carver waved the gun toward the truck. "Get going before I think better of it."

Hugo spat in Carver's direction. Then motioned for his men to get into the truck. He got in no problem. The shorter guys struggled to hop up onto the siderails. Carver began to think letting them get back in the truck was a bad idea.

The windows were tinted. They could shoot at him. Hugo could grab one of their guns and shoot through a window. Apparently, Hugo thought better of it. He revved the engine. The wheels churned up dirt and grass.

Then he sped off back for the exit.

Albert whistled. "Damn, you shot that gun like in an old western."

Carver motioned at the small old west town before them. "Seemed appropriate, given the surroundings."

Albert laughed. "You must be a real crack shot to hit something that small."

"It was big and shiny. Easy to hit." Carver holstered his pistol. Tucked the pouch back into his jeans.

"I think you're in for a heap of trouble now."

"I knew that from the moment I met that guy." Carver frowned. "The question is, how did they know I was here?"

"You met that guy before?"

Carver nodded. "He was threatening an older Hispanic woman who was recording the mayor."

Albert whistled again. "Good to know I ain't the only one the mayor is after."

"I can see why this is a popular venue for bikers." Carver walked toward the old west town. "You have vendors who man the stores?"

Albert nodded. "Jesse and his cousins take over the saloon. My helper, Rodrigo and his family use a building for cooking Mexican food. Carlton and his boys do barbeque out of another building. And representatives from Harley and other vendors set up booths. It's a big event. Nothing like Sturgis, South Dakota, of course, but it's big for this area."

"How long does it last?"

"All weekend." Albert dropped back into the cart. "All said, I've heard millions of dollars are spent in and around town. A lot of bikers get hotel rooms or go to the campground. They go to restaurants and stores in town."

"And the mayor is okay losing all that tax money because you decided to support her opponent?"

"Sure sounds like it." Albert looked back down the dirt road. "You think those troublemakers are gonna ambush you when you leave?"

"It wouldn't surprise me." Carver sat down in the cart. "You have a legal right to hold the rally. Seems like it would hold up in any court."

"Not locally." Albert shook his head. "The last election swept out all the old timers from the mayor to the judges, to the city council. Lots of young folks decided it was time for a change, I guess. Kids these days work for tech companies and make more money in a year than I'll make in my lifetime. They're spoiled. Think all the old rules are too harsh."

"Is that the demographic in this town now? Young tech workers?"

Albert shrugged. "I don't know. Just seems that way. All them kids making videos on their phones all the time. Pulling dumb pranks for views. My grandkids are into that stuff."

"You're married?"

"Fifty years next month." He grinned. "Best part of my life even if she wants to kill me half the time. But she doesn't live out here. She stays with her mom so she can take care of her."

"Do you know any lawyers? You might need someone who can take this to court." Carver shrugged. "I don't know what else to tell you. Joe probably would have said the same thing."

"I don't have time. The rally starts this weekend."

"And they just sent you the letter?"

"Of course, they did." Albert huffed. "They knew I wouldn't have time to do anything. My nephew set up some internet pages for it, so that's about the only way I can get the word out if I have to cancel it."

"How many people come to this thing?"

"Over two thousand last time."

Carver whistled. "How would the mayor stop you if you didn't cancel?"

"I don't know, but I have a feeling I'm going to find out."

"You're not canceling?"

He shook his head. "And I'm not going to pretend to support the mayor. It's the principle of the matter."

"I think Joe would approve."

Albert smiled. "Yeah, he would. He and Andrea come every year." His smile faded. "But not this year. He's dead. I can't hardly believe it." He started the cart and turned it around. Drove it back to the brick building in silence.

Joe's new Ram had a long scratch down the side.

"Those thugs keyed your car!" Albert parked next to the truck.

Carver got out and walked around it. "At least they didn't puncture the tires."

Albert inspected the chain and padlock on his gate. "They cut it with bolt cutters."

"The cops won't do anything?"

He shook his head. "They'll take a report and promise to look into it. But it's all lip service, especially for me."

Carver opened the truck door. "You have my number. Call or text if you need something."

"You think you'll come out to the rally?"

"When does it start?"

"Noontime this Friday is when people will start rolling in."

Carver climbed into the seat. He nodded. "I'll try to come."

Albert drummed his fingers on the cart's steering wheel. "Be careful, Carver. I've heard rumors about people disappearing around here. Ain't no telling what those thugs will try next." He got out of the cart and pushed the gate open.

Carver turned the pickup around and drove out. He knew for certain a jacked up red pickup hadn't followed him here. Even a half blind civilian would notice something like that following them.

He didn't see Hugo's truck anywhere nearby. That didn't mean they weren't lurking somewhere. Waiting. Despite their apparent disregard for law and order, he didn't think they'd try a drive-by shooting, but it was better to be ready just in case.

Actually, it was better to be proactive. The next time Hugo tried something it wouldn't be so overt. He'd try to jump Carver. And there was another problem. They had someone watching Joe's place.

That was the only way Hugo could have known where Carver was and what vehicle he was driving. Someone might be watching the road into town, or they might be watching the house from a distance.

It seemed most likely that they were watching the house. That was the only way they'd noticed the new pickup truck leaving the house. That was the only way they could have known that Carver was driving.

He wasn't having much luck with vehicles. His classic Ramcharger had been marked by Enigma and tracked every time it was spotted by a camera. Now Joe's new pickup was known by the local gang.

And that was fine. Just fine.

It went back to something Joe said before a mission that had been compromised before it got off the ground. Joe talked the upper brass into going through with it anyway.

He'd said, "If the enemy knows something you don't, that's their advantage. When you know the enemy knows something, then it's your advantage."

The young officer in charge decided to let Joe's experience outweigh his judgment. What would have been an ambush turned into a slaughter of enemy forces. Joe let the officer take all the credit and glory.

He never cared about that kind of thing. He preferred keeping a low profile. Keeping his head down and doing what needed to be done. He was the guy who helped Carver turn his street smarts into military tactics.

Authority figures were nothing new to Carver. He'd fit right into the military. But his parents had been brutal. They'd whipped him into shape literally. Any mistake was met with a physical response.

Joe was the exact opposite. He was demanding but patient. He explained everything. Made sure everyone under his command understood why they were doing what they were doing. What he expected of them.

Now it was time to put some of Joe's best advice to good use.

Carver drove back to Joe's house. Parked the truck in the garage. Andrea's Range Rover was there. That was good. He needed to talk to her.

He went inside the house and back to the guest room. He removed his high powered monocular from the duffel bag. Then he went into the main room where the den, kitchen, and living room were all one big space.

Andrea was sitting at the kitchen table. A laptop was open in front of her, but she wasn't looking at it. She was staring blankly out of the back window. She blinked. Glanced at Carver.

"Hi."

Carver sat down across from her. "Was Joe acting normally these past few weeks?"

She stared blankly at him for a moment.

"Sorry. I should have segued into that." Carver shrugged. "I tend to get straight to the point."

She smiled. "Just like Joe. He always said he saw a lot of himself in you."

It was Carver's turn to blink. "He told you that?"

Andrea frowned. "He never told you?"

"No. He wasn't exactly an effusive kind of guy."

"I guess I forgot what he was like before." She released a shuddering breath. "He was different with me. He let go of everything he was holding inside." Andrea reached across the table and touched Carver's hand. "He was proud of you. Really proud. Especially when you got called to serve on an interagency special force."

"He knew about that?"

She nodded. "Peter Sullivan always kept him in the loop."

"Makes sense," Carver said. "Joe basically made Commander Sullivan's career."

"He made a lot of people's careers." Andrea pulled her hand back. "He was a teacher and a leader. The kind of man who improved the people around him."

"He was the best." Carver was still processing what she'd said. Joe had been proud of him. He'd known about his appointment to Scion. Or at least known generally about it. Sullivan must have known about it because the request for Carver's reassignment had come to him for approval.

"To answer your earlier question, yes, Joe was acting a little differently than usual. I thought it was because he was gearing up for a political campaign." Andrea bit her lower lip. "He would leave the house and be gone longer than usual. He also bought that old

Honda and started driving it more often. When he did, he usually didn't come home until late."

"He didn't drive the new pickup very much."

She smiled. "He got it because he thought it would be nice having a new truck. But he didn't like it and kept driving his old pickup. He said it was comfortable and broken in."

Carver nodded. "Lowkey and reliable. Like Joe."

Andrea stood. She went to a cabinet with a glass door and opened it. She pulled out a bottle of tequila. She opened another cabinet and took out two small glasses. She brought it to the table then poured two fingers into each glass.

Carver took one. She took the other. She held up hers. "To a good man. To Joe."

"A good man." Carver clinked his glass to hers. They tossed them back. The tequila was a cheap silver. It didn't taste good, and it burned. It was also Joe's favorite brand for some reason. Probably for the same reason he preferred his old Dodge to a new one. Probably for the same reason he didn't own a mansion.

Andrea didn't wince at the taste of the tequila. Carver remembered from his last visit that she could toss back drinks with the best of them.

She poured another round. Carver made the toast this time. "Rest in peace, Joe." His voice cracked a little when he said the name. He felt a deep pang of regret. He wished he'd visited Joe a lot more than he had.

He wished he could sit back and listen to his calm voice. Listen to him talk about the old days. Laugh about the times they almost got killed. Reminisce about the people they'd lost. Talk about what he thought the future would hold.

Carver noticed Andrea had already downed her drink. She was watching him with an understanding look. Like she knew what he was thinking. She knew Joe better than anyone. Whatever she felt was magnified exponentially.

He tossed back the shot. Winced at the burn. His eyes watered a little. He set the glass down. "Something happened today."

Andrea leaned back and waited for him to continue without comment.

He told her about Hugo. About Albert's problems. About his suspicions that someone was watching the house.

"I think Joe was murdered. I don't know how. I don't know who did it." Carver stared at his hand and flexed it. "I'm going to find out and someone is going to pay for what they did."

Andrea reached across the table and gripped his hand tight. "You have my blessing, Carver. And I will help you however I can." Her Latina accent grew stronger. "I will spill the blood of our enemies for justice."

Carver squeezed her hands. "For Joe."

"Yes." She hissed. "For Joe."

CHAPTER 10

Carver went for a walk outside.

He took the bottle of tequila with him. Strolled down the driveway. Stretched his arms and looked casually around. He occasionally tipped the bottle back to his lips and pretended to drink.

The terrain to the south was slightly hilly, but mostly flat. There were hills rolling into mountains to the north. There was a tall hill directly behind the house to the west and small rolling hills to the east.

The gravel road leading from Joe's went about two miles before reaching a four-way intersection. From there, a person could keep going straight until the road ended at the paved highway leading into town.

If they turned left, they'd drive five miles before the road ended at a cattle ranch. If they went right, they'd go about three miles before the gravel road reached the highway that crossed east to west across the north part of town.

That highway went past Albert's place. Staying on it would take you to Pasadena.

There was a vantage point at the four-way intersection. But it wasn't a great vantage point. Anyone sitting on top of the hill there would be easily visible. The tall hill behind the house offered a good view too.

But it was too close. The scrubby bushes and trees were poor concealment without heavy camouflage. That was true of most nearby vantage points. Which meant the safest place to watch from was far away.

It meant the best places to set up an observation post were the mountains to the north. A person with any kind of high-powered magnification could watch from there. Cameras could also be used but they weren't ideal. Not from that distance.

Carver's former team had had access to the best cameras. Ones with high-powered lenses. They could be remotely controlled. But the lenses were big. They couldn't be easily concealed. From that distance, concealment wasn't as important.

Even civilians could get their hands on similar cameras these days. And it didn't really matter. Whether it was a camera or a person, Carver needed to locate them without them knowing.

He pretended to drink from the bottle again. Looked at the mountains to the north. Something dead north would be best. If the watcher was too far east or west, the sun would get in their eyes. Keeping the ranch due south provided the best view.

And Carver had a good idea which mountain was being used.

THE WATCHER WATCHED.

He made notes. *The big guy is standing outside. He's drinking tequila straight from the bottle. He looks drunk and sad.*

He continued watching. Continued taking notes. The big guy's shoulders were slumped. He looked defeated. Like he was going to drink himself into a coma.

The big guy eventually went back into the house. He returned outside a few minutes later. The tequila bottle was almost empty. He had a brown bag with another bottle inside of it. It looked like he was going to drink himself into a stupor.

The watcher wished he could record this. It would be easier to send a video instead of taking notes. He'd grown up before the advent of smartphones. Writing with a pen and paper used to be normal and natural to him.

Then he'd grown used to everything being digital. Writing was tedious now. But it was what the client requested. Everything would be written down. A picture would be taken of the notes. The picture would be texted using an encrypted app.

He would then delete the image from his phone and empty the deleted items. It was a real roundabout way of doing things, but the client got what they wanted.

The big guy cocked back his arm and tossed the empty tequila bottle into the scrub brush at the edge of the yard. He opened the bottle in the brown bag and took a long drink from it. Before long, he was staggering.

He walked out of sight around the house. He appeared at the back of the house, staggering through the back yard, around the side of the house between it and the garage. Then he walked into the front yard.

The big guy bent over and heaved. A stream of vomit spattered on the ground. The watcher didn't know how he was still standing after so much tequila and whatever was in the brown bag. He kept watching and jotted down a summary of the last few minutes.

The sun was starting to get low in the west. His position was almost directly north of the ranch so the sun passed from left to right without ever impeding his view. That was one reason why he'd chosen this location.

The client wanted twenty-four-hour surveillance. The only time he could leave was to make reports. They only wanted reports if the big guy left. They didn't care about the woman.

The watcher was only human. He couldn't stay awake for twenty-four hours straight. So, he'd requested help. He needed someone dependable. Someone who was okay staying up all night to spy on someone.

He also needed better equipment. The binoculars didn't have thermal vision or night vision. They were only good during the day. He'd purchased them himself. He'd asked the client for equipment that could watch during the night.

The big guy went into the garage. The middle door rolled up. The big pickup roared out. It skidded onto the gravel. Weaved back and forth. He was probably going back into town.

The watcher didn't leave just yet. He kept watching until the pickup reached the four-way intersection. It kept going straight. Straight toward the highway. Well, relatively straight anyway. The pickup was weaving all over the road.

The big guy would be lucky to make it into town without crashing. He was drunk as a jaybird.

The watcher watched for a few more minutes. Then he hurried back to his vehicle and started the drive down the mountain to send his report.

CARVER KEPT DRINKING.

He was putting on a show in case someone was watching. He kept watching the north even as he staggered around the yard. He covered a hundred yards one way then reversed course. The glint of sunlight on a lens caught his eye on the second circuit.

Whoever was watching was using a high-powered lens. They were zoomed all the way in. Which meant they had to rotate to keep Carver in sight. Even if they were well concealed, the sun would eventually hit the lens.

Now he knew for certain that there was a watcher. And he knew exactly where they were. He just had to figure out the second part. How they watched him enter town and knew where he was going.

The watcher on the mountain probably texted someone in town. That person waited where the highway entered town and watched. That seemed the most likely scenario. They'd probably followed Carver from there.

No, that wasn't it. Carver would have noticed a tail. It was something else. Something elementary. Probably traffic cameras. He'd noticed a few of them in town as a matter of habit. He must have missed one.

Carver went inside. Looked through the pantry. There wasn't much canned food except for chicken noodle soup. That would work fine. He opened the liquor cabinet. Found a bottle of wine still in a brown paper bag.

He removed the wine. Went to the refrigerator. Found a glass bottle of orange juice inside. There was only a couple of sips left, so he drank it. He put some water and the chicken noodle soup inside and shook it up.

He put the bottle in the bag. The tequila bottle was too full for how much he'd pretended to drink. So he emptied it into a tall glass. Put a little water in the bottom. Went back outside to the front yard.

He polished off the water in the tequila bottle. Tossed it into the bushes. He staggered drunkenly. Pretended to drink from the bottle in the brown bag. He walked around the house. When he was out of sight, he took a mouthful of chicken noodle soup and chewed it.

He stopped chewing and walked back into sight of the watcher. He staggered. Bent over. Heaved and spat the soup onto the ground. It was chunky and slightly yellow. The perfect texture for fake vomit.

Carver walked around the garage and out of sight. He went into the house and retrieved his duffel bag. He used the covered walkway to the garage. Got into the new Dodge. Opened the garage door and gunned the engine.

The Ram screeched down the driveway. Skidded onto the gravel road. Carver almost lost control. He managed to stay out of the ditch at the last moment. At least it probably looked more convincing.

He kept up the act until he passed the four-way intersection. After that, the road went downhill out of sight. The watcher would text someone ahead. The person ahead would be watching a camera. Carver just had to figure out where it was.

The gravel road ended at the highway. He took it south into town. There was a camera at the first traffic light. It was high up on the pole and easily visible. He'd probably seen it earlier and not given it much thought.

Mainly because he thought the new Ram was camouflage enough. He hadn't imagined that someone was watching Joe's place. Had they been watching it for a while, or only after Carver arrived?

That would be one of many questions the watcher would have to answer. Including the most important one. Were they watching the house when Joe was killed?

For now, they'd help him in ways they couldn't imagine.

The sun was going down. His stomach was rumbling. It was time for dinner. He found a diner and parked out front. It was already busy with the dinner crowd. He went inside and found an empty seat at the bar.

An older woman took his order within a minute of him sitting down. She called out his order for a double cheeseburger and side of hashbrowns, then poured him a cup of black coffee. It was fresh.

That wasn't surprising given the number of patrons. Maybe it was a little surprising this many people were drinking coffee at dinner time, but Carver wasn't going to complain. He downed the coffee before his hamburger arrived.

He ate, and drank another two cups of coffee. He looked at the map on his burner phone and located some motels. Then he paid in cash and left.

It was dark outside. He looked around the diner's parking lot. Looked at the neighboring parking lots. Didn't see anyone sitting in a car watching him.

But he did see someone in the park across the street. A young man was sitting on a bench beneath a streetlamp. He was looking at his phone. Occasionally looking up and right at Joe's pickup, then looking back at the phone.

He was Hispanic. Probably fifteen or sixteen. Maybe younger. He hadn't noticed Carver, probably because the diner's parking lot wasn't very well lit. Almost every time he looked up from his phone, he looked at the truck.

The pickup had been spotted on the camera. There were two more traffic cameras between the diner and the first camera. One of them was next to the traffic light at the intersection near the diner.

The camera probably saw him pull into the diner parking lot, but it wasn't angled to watch this way. The kid had been sent to wait and watch. He'd see which way Carver went and let someone know.

Carver pretended not to see the kid. He staggered like he was still drunk. Got into the truck. He backed out, stopping and starting like he didn't have full control of his body.

He pulled into the intersection and drove toward his first pick for a motel. Sure, he could stay at Joe's house, but he had other plans tonight.

The kid hopped on a battery-powered scooter and started following him. The traffic lights slowed Carver enough so the kid could keep up. After a few intersections, Carver reached the outskirts of town.

There were no more traffic lights and mostly open highway. He accelerated and left the scooter behind.

The motel was about a mile down the road. It was a single-story place, shaped like an L with the management office at the base of the L. The Blue Star Motel. It was just like every other cheap motel across the country.

Carver went inside the office. The manager asked for an ID. Carver showed him cash and said he didn't have an ID. The guy shrugged. Took the money and gave him a metal key on a keyring with a plastic tag that had the room number on it.

"Where is this room located?" Carver asked.

"Far end. Is that okay?"

Carver nodded. "It's perfect." He got back in the pickup. Drove it to the end of the motel and parked directly in front of his room.

He looked around. The kid on the scooter had probably texted someone. The last traffic camera had been at the edge of town. He hadn't seen any others in the last mile.

There wasn't much out this way except for gas stations and this motel. It wouldn't be hard for someone to find him.

And that was exactly what he wanted.

He had a little while before that happened, so he went into the motel room. He messed up the sheets. Made it look like someone had been sleeping in the bed. He took his backpack and opened it.

He dropped a dirty worn shirt on the floor. Dropped a small pair of pants on the end of the bed. The clothing was far too small to be his. They were some old garments Leon had accidentally stuffed into his backpack when they were camping.

Carver had planned to throw them away but had never gotten around to it. Now they would come in handy. He took a towel from the bathroom. Dampened it in the sink. Dropped it on the floor outside the bathroom door.

He turned the television on. Left the volume low. The light from the TV was visible through the curtains even when they were closed. It would make it appear someone was inside.

Carver slung on his backpack. He removed his duffel bag from the truck and shouldered the strap. He walked around the back of the motel and all the way to the end. An old burgundy Buick was idling on the shoulder of the road.

He opened the back door. Slid the duffel bag and backpack inside. Opened the front door and dropped into the passenger seat.

A young black man looked him up and down. "You're even bigger than my uncle said."

"I'm Carver."

"Ronald." He held out his hand.

Carver shook it. "Thanks for the lift."

"My pleasure. Anything to help Uncle Albert."

"You have someone coming to pick you up?"

Ronald nodded. "My cousin will be here in a few minutes. I just want to ask you to take care of my car. It ain't much, but it's all I got."

"It's old but pristine. I can tell you take good care of it."

"I bought it myself. My dad said it was the only way to teach me the value of a dollar."

Carver grinned. "Did you learn the value?"

"Oh, I learned it the hard way." Ronald laughed. "You better believe I won't forget it."

An old blue Ford pulled up behind the Buick. "That's my cousin. Good luck with whatever it is you're up to."

"Better you don't know."

Ronald turned off the car. Handed the keys to Carver. "Take care of her." He got out. Walked to the passenger side of the Ford and got in. It rumbled down the street.

The Buick had a bench seat, so Carver slid over to the driver's side. He drove the car back to the highway. Turned into a diner parking lot across the road from the motel.

He turned off the engine. Leaned back and waited.

He would have company soon.

CHAPTER 11

Unwelcome company arrived at the Blue Star Motel.

It wasn't Hugo's big red pickup. This one was white. The tires were oversized and the suspension was lifted slightly, but it looked reasonable by comparison. The exhaust didn't rumble either.

The truck had a crew cab. Four doors. A six-foot bed. Two men got out of the front. Three men got out of the back. Hugo was the driver. The two short guys he'd been with were there too.

The other two men were a little taller, a little bigger than Hugo's compatriots. They all drew handguns the minute they stepped out of the truck.

Hugo pointed at the door to Carver's room. It was one of only two rooms with the lights on. The other one was several doors down, closer to the office. That room didn't have Joe's big pickup parked outside of it.

That made it easy, even for someone like Hugo to know which room was the right room.

Hugo motioned his companions to the door. Two lined up on one side. Two on the other. Hugo lashed out with his foot and kicked the door. He did it all wrong. He hit it with the toe of his boot. The door didn't budge.

One of the new guys motioned Hugo back. He got in front of the door. Leaned back on one foot. Raised the other and slammed the flat of his foot right next to the door handle. The door budged a little.

He'd done it right. The problem was the door jamb was metal. The latch was metal. Metal wouldn't break like a wooden door jamb. If Carver had been in there, he already would have shot through the door the moment he heard the noise.

Hugo and company gave up on the door and smashed the window with a rock. One of them scrambled through the window, got tangled in the curtains, and fell inside. It was like watching the three stooges and their two inept cousins.

The door opened a moment later.

They went inside. Carver watched them with his monocular. They saw the bed, the clothing, the towel. They checked the bathroom. Returned outside. One of them pointed to the restaurant where Carver was sitting in the Buick.

Hugo nodded and they ran to the four-laned highway. Waited for some cars to pass. Ran across the road. They tucked their guns into their pants to conceal them.

Carver leaned his seat back. He was in the corner of the parking lot and not near the front entrance. But it was better to be safe than seen.

The men went into the restaurant. It was a typical diner. Big windows all the way around. There were booths, a bar, a bathroom, and the cooking area behind the bar. Hugo and pals looked at all the people inside.

One checked both bathrooms. Shook his head. Hugo asked a waitress. Showed her his phone. He probably had a picture on it. She shook her head. Asked another waitress. That waitress shook her head too.

No one had seen Carver.

Hugo walked outside. Put his phone to his ear and started talking. He threw up a hand. He looked angry and confused.

Carver couldn't read his lips, but he knew Hugo was telling his boss that he couldn't find the target. And now the window was smashed out of the motel room so Carver would know something happened the minute he returned.

Hugo and company walked back across the road. Hugo pointed at them. Said something. Probably along the lines of, you wait here until he comes back. The men nodded.

Hugo went to the pickup. Climbed in. The other four guys stayed where they were. They started cleaning up the glass. Tried making the window look like it wasn't busted open.

One of them picked up a rock. They threw it at the parking lot lamp. Missed. They picked it up and threw it again. The glass shattered and the lamp went out. The darkness concealed the broken window.

They'd probably go inside and wait for Carver to come back. One of them would keep watch through the window. The moment they saw him, they'd ambush him. Maybe take him prisoner. Maybe shoot him on the spot.

At least, that was what they were planning to do. None of that would happen. They'd spend the rest of the night watching the motel room. Waiting for someone who was never coming back.

Carver turned his monocular toward the management office. The manager wasn't there. He was probably in the back room. Probably watching TV. Probably hadn't heard the thugs breaking the room window.

That was good. It was best if he remained unaware and non-reactive.

Hugo's pickup backed out. Carver started the Buick. He pulled up to the parking lot exit and watched the pickup turn right out of the motel parking lot. He gave it a small head start then turned in the same direction.

Hugo drove straight west for a while. Then he took a road that angled southwest through a residential neighborhood. The homes were small and bunched close together. Chain link fences surrounded most of the yards.

There were a lot of pickup trucks parked in driveways. Many looked banged up and beaten. They were work trucks. A few had the kind of jacked up trucks like Hugo's. Most didn't have second cars.

Hugo turned onto another street. This one had a small strip of businesses. Super Mercado grocery store, Eduardo's bar, and San Miguel Carniceria. He parked in front of the restaurant. Got out of the pickup. Went into the bar.

Carver drove into the parking lot. He stopped the car in front of the bar entrance. Looked through the window. Hugo was inside sitting on a stool. He spoke to the female bartender. She got him a beer. Popped off the metal top. Put the bottle in front of him.

He started drinking. He looked at his phone then looked up at an angle. There was probably a television behind the bar.

Carver backed the Buick into a spot with a clear view of the window. He leaned the seat back a little and watched.

Hugo checked his phone every so often. He downed seven beers over two hours. Then he stared at his phone for a long time before making a phone call. He spoke briefly. Nodded. Ended the call.

He put cash on the counter. Got up and left. He stepped outside. Stretched. He got into the pickup. The engine started. The lights came on. It idled in place for a few minutes before shifting into gear.

The pickup backed up. Turned right onto the street. Carver gave it a few seconds, then followed. There were two cars between him and the pickup. Unless Hugo was perceptive, they provided plenty of camouflage.

The pickup took a couple of more turns through residential neighborhoods then turned into a driveway. The house looked like most of the others in the area. Single story. Small porch with concrete stairs. Chain link fence and cracked concrete driveway.

Carver parked on the street behind another car. He lowered his window and watched.

The lights were off in the house. Only a porch light was on. Hugo knocked on the door. He checked his phone. Lifted it to his ear. Held it there for a few seconds, then angrily stared at the screen.

He pounded on the door. An inside light came on. The door cracked open. Hugo pounded his hand on the side of the door. The door opened all the way. A woman was there. She looked sleepy. Dressed for bed.

She shook her head. Held out her hands in a shrug. Hugo said something else. She shook her head.

He pounded the door open. Grabbed her by the neck and pinned her against the door. He held a fist in her face. She winced. Started crying. Nodded.

They went inside. In addition to being an asshole, it looked like Hugo was a woman beater. Probably a rapist too, judging from the interaction. Carver considered his next move. This was a tricky situation.

He didn't want the woman to see him. Maybe she'd keep her mouth shut. Maybe she wouldn't. Carver reached into his backpack. He pulled out a black hoodie. It wasn't cold outside, but that wasn't the point of wearing it.

He got out of the car. Put on the hoodie. Pulled a cloth facemask on to cover his nose and mouth. It was the same kind of outfit that helped him blend in during his time in Oregon and San Francisco.

It didn't help much in these parts. People didn't wear hoodies in the mild weather this far south. Some wore facemasks, but not nearly as many as those in the cities further north. But it would do the trick just fine.

He went to the front door. It was unlocked. He gently turned the knob. Opened it. Slipped inside and closed it. He heard Hugo talking in Spanish. He was talking in loud, demanding tones.

The woman responded in Spanish. Her voice was pleading. "Please stop, Hugo. I'm still hurting from the last time."

"Shut your mouth, bitch. I give you money to help with your kid. This is how you pay me back whenever and however I want."

"Please no." Her voice was shaking.

"I said shut up!"

Carver was standing in a small foyer. The light was on. He switched it off. He stepped through the open doorway and into a den. The lights were off. He left them off. The voices were coming from the right. He looked into the doorway on the other side of the den.

There was a small, dark hallway. A bedroom was to the right. The bedroom lights were on. Hugo was holding the woman by the back of her neck. He was kissing her. Her face was screwed up in disgust, but she couldn't recoil.

Carver considered his options. Hugo was a big boy. He had a big, meaty head. Presumably, he had a brain inside that head. Hitting someone on the back of the head didn't guarantee knocking someone out.

It wasn't like the movies. Even if a blow to the head knocked them out, it might cause serious damage. Carver didn't want to cause too much damage. He needed Hugo to answer questions.

A blow to the head wasn't the best tactic. He wished he had some of the fancy knockout juice he'd used on occasion while abducting people for the US government. The closest thing he had was fentanyl.

Fentanyl wouldn't knock someone out, but it would certainly make them easier to control. It also might kill them. The problem was, it might not work fast enough, and Hugo was a big boy.

Carver wasn't picky about the method. He just didn't want the woman to scream and run out of the house. She probably wouldn't have space to get out of the room. It would be the scream that mattered.

Hugo was gripping the front of her throat now. Choking her and kissing her. She might not be able to scream if she wanted to.

Carver decided to give Hugo a taste of his own medicine. He walked into the room. The woman was squeezing her eyes shut and grimacing, so she didn't even see him. Carver leaned back on one foot and lashed out with his other.

The flat of his boot hit Hugo hard in the back of the knee. The big man howled in pain. His hand released the woman and reflexively went for his leg. He was also falling, so his other hand reached out to steady him.

But the blow was too hard, and the pain was too much. He started to fall backwards. Carver wrapped an arm around Hugo's neck. He positioned the crook of the elbow right over the Adam's apple, so his forearm and bicep squeezed the sides of the neck.

He used his other arm to lock the grip and apply extra pressure. Hugo was falling backward, flailing, and choking at the same time. The woman fell onto her bed, gasping.

Hugo shouted in alarm. As if his brain only just realized his blood supply was being cut off. He thrashed. Gripped Carver's forearm with his hands. But his carotid arteries were being squeezed shut. His brain wasn't getting blood. And he'd blown all the air out of his lungs when he shouted in pain.

The woman sat up. Her eyes were wide. She tried to shout, but her windpipe had been gripped too hard by Hugo. She couldn't even muster a scream.

Hugo slumped. Carver counted off a few seconds, then released him. He put a finger to his lips. Spoke in Spanish. "Be quiet and I won't hurt you." His accent was rusty, but it got the message across.

Tears pooled in the woman's eyes. She shivered. Nodded. Carver pulled out Hugo's wallet. It was stuffed with big bills, mostly hundreds. He took it all. Tossed it on the bed next to the woman.

"Keep quiet about this. Don't make me have to come back and eliminate a loose end."

She looked at the cash. Looked at him. Nodded fervently. "I won't say anything ever. I promise. I have a little boy."

Carver nodded. He checked Hugo's pulse. It was still there. He wouldn't be down and out for long. Carver opened Hugo's mouth. Put a drop of fentanyl under the man's tongue. Put another drop just because he was a big man.

He capped the fentanyl bottle and made sure it was secure before putting it back in his pocket. That was one liquid you didn't want to get on your skin. Just getting it on you could get you high or kill you.

Carver lifted Hugo under his armpits. He dragged him out of the bedroom. It was like dragging a three-hundred-pound sack of potatoes behind him. Lifting that much weight wouldn't be a problem if it was balanced like gym weights.

A limp human body was anything but balanced. It had arms, legs, and a torso. Things that would flop around and throw you off balance if you tried to pick it up or move it. If he wasn't careful, he might throw out his back.

Dragging the body was the easiest way, even with the arms flopping around. The woman watched in silence. She ran ahead and opened the front door for Carver. Once he was through, she closed the door. Latches and locks clicked into place.

Carver dragged the body to the pickup. He took the keys from Hugo's pocket and opened the back door. It was a good thing the pickup was normal height. It would be impossible to get Hugo's dead weight up into his red pickup.

He got Hugo's torso partway onto the back floorboard. Then he went to the other side and dragged him over the transmission hump until he was mostly in. He closed the door. Walked back around the truck to the other side. Bent Hugo's legs up so he was inside and closed the other door.

Hugo would regain consciousness soon, but the fentanyl would keep him slow and compliant. He was a big man, but two drops should be enough to keep him down for the time being.

Carver climbed into the driver's seat. Cranked the ignition. Backed the pickup out of the driveway. He started driving to a spot he'd picked out earlier. Taking the man out of town was ideal, but he didn't want to get too far away from the Buick since he'd need to leave the pickup with Hugo.

Because after tonight, Hugo wasn't going anywhere.

CHAPTER 12

Carver steered into a gas station.

It was an old gas station. It looked like it had closed down a long time ago and sat unused for decades. It was on the southern highway leading into town. There was a strip of closed businesses on the same stretch of road.

One had been a restaurant. Another a computer parts store. The other building had no signs on it. Just the metal frame where a sign had once been.

Carver drove around the back of the garage. The area was fenced in, but the gate hung open. There were old cars in the back and neat stacks of used tires. He parked behind the tires. Dragged Hugo out of the back of the truck.

He leaned the big man against a rusted Toyota with weeds growing through cracks in the hood. He slapped Hugo gently a few times. The man groaned. His eyelids fluttered.

The fentanyl dose might have been too strong, considering Hugo had seven beers in his bloodstream too. That was okay. Carver had time. He sat down on a stack of metal wheels and waited.

Hugo opened his eyes and groaned about fifteen minutes later. His eyes widened slowly when he saw Carver.

Carver had his Glock out. The fentanyl was still weighing Hugo down, but it was better to be safe than sorry.

Hugo tried to stand. He managed to rise a few inches before falling back down. It looked like he was fighting gravity and losing. He finally gave up and stared sullenly at Carver. "What the hell did you do to me?"

"I have some questions for you."

"I'm not answering, pendejo."

Carver slid a knife from a sheath hidden beneath his shirt. He stepped closer. Knelt next to Hugo. "How are you feeling? A little numb, maybe?" He traced the blade down Hugo's arm.

The other man winced. He tried to move his arm and failed.

"Looks like you're feeling something." Carver saw desperation in Hugo's eyes. The big man was used to being in control. He was the one who usually handed out the beatings.

Not today.

"What happened to Joe Donnely?"

Hugo looked confused. "Who?"

"Joe Donnely."

His eyelids fluttered. "Is that the guy running for mayor?"

"Yes. What happened to him?"

"What do you mean? I don't know anything about the guy." It looked like he was telling the truth.

Carver switched subjects. "Why are you after me?"

"Why do you think?"

"Who sent you after me?"

Hugo's nostrils flared. "Nobody sent me. I want payback."

"Someone sent you to Albert's. Who was it?"

"It was all me."

"You're lying. Someone is watching the ranch. They saw me leave. The traffic cameras picked me up when I reached town. Someone sent you after me."

"No, they didn't."

Carver pressed the point of the knife to Hugo's neck. Hugo winced. He tried to move his hand to protect himself but the fentanyl made his arm too heavy to move.

"Don't make me guess who sent you. Tell me, or I'm going to start poking holes in you."

"I don't know!" Sweat beaded on Hugo's forehead. "I get texts telling me where to go and what to do sometimes. The sender calls himself Anonymous. You can look on my phone!"

Carver turned on the phone. "What's the password?"

"Ten seventy-one."

Carver typed in the numbers. The phone unlocked. He opened the texts. The most recent ones had been sent to a woman named Elisa. Probably the woman Hugo had been assaulting earlier.

The texts were in Spanish. The first one asked if she was awake. The next one said he was coming over. When she didn't reply, he sent another saying she'd better be home when he got there. The next few detailed what he'd do to her if she wasn't home or if she didn't answer the door.

Carver tapped the back arrow. He saw a text from a blocked number. He opened the conversation. There were only a few texts in the conversation.

The first one was about the salvage yard. *Go to Albert's. The man from the park is there. Apprehend him and message me.*

Hugo had replied after his failure. *He was armed. We couldn't get him.*

The next one was about the motel. *Target is staying at Blue Star Motel. Do not fail to apprehend this time. Notify me and await further instructions.*

"Where are the rest of the texts?"

"I was told to delete them every day. So that's what I did."

Carver clicked the back arrow. He looked through the other texts. Most were in Spanish. The most recent were to four men, telling them to meet Hugo somewhere or pick up things for him. None of them explicitly said what they were doing or why.

One of the men had sent a text to Hugo a few minutes ago. Saying they hadn't seen any activity. Asking how long they should wait. It had been nearly three hours since Hugo left. Carver almost texted them back.

He thought about telling them to go home. He decided to let them wait it out. It might be good knowing where to find them.

Carver looked through the texts but didn't find anything incriminating. "It looks like you know better than to discuss illegal activities in text."

"I'm not an idiot, pendejo." Hugo struggled to move an arm and managed to lift it a little further.

"What's the incentive? Money?"

"Yeah. I get paid in cryptocurrency through a decentralized exchange. It's anonymous and untraceable."

Carver was familiar with the payment scheme. Tracing the chain of transactions back to the sender was impossible. At least as far as he knew. "What kind of things does this person tell you to do?"

"All kinds of things. Picking up packages and delivering them. Driving to the airport to pick up people and take them places. Capturing people and beating information out of them."

"Basic thug work."

Hugo scowled. "I'm no thug. I'm a businessman."

"A businessman who bullies little old ladies?"

"That dumb bitch was harassing the mayor. I can't stand political activists. They think they're superior to everyone else. I just wanted to teach her a lesson."

Carver mulled it over. Hugo was a run of the mill thug. A street-level enforcer kind of guy. An errand boy. "Your anonymous boss never told you to go to the Donnely ranch? He never asked you to do anything related to Joe Donnely?"

"No, nothing, just..." Hugo trailed off.

"Just what?"

"They asked me to go talk to some vet that Donnely took his horses to. I had a list of questions to ask."

"What's the name of the place?"

"Equine Vet Services, I think."

"What were the questions?"

Hugo frowned like he was trying to remember. "Something about husbandry. About sperm storage. About treating horses for broken legs. I was posing like someone who was interested in horse breeding. They were supposedly the best vet for that kind of thing."

Carver tried to make sense of that. "And the vet answered you?"

"Yeah. It was strange. Real strange."

"How so?"

Hugo huffed. "Why send someone like me to ask those questions? You could probably look up that information on a website."

"Were any of the questions related to Joe?"

"Nothing in particular. Just that I heard the famous Joe Donnely took his horses there. So, I was interested to know what made that vet so special."

"And did they give you a reason?"

"Yeah, a whole list of them. Just like I said."

"Did they ask you to steal sperm samples or anything like that?"

"No. The vet doesn't keep those things around. They're too valuable. They told me specimens are locked up in a secure place. They wouldn't even tell me the location."

That made sense. "You think your boss wanted to execute a heist?"

"Maybe. He might be some tech millionaire who wants to breed horses for all I know."

Carver considered that notion for a moment. Anything was possible. "And that was the only task related to Joe Donnely?"

"Yeah." Hugo clenched his fists. He lifted an arm more easily. "You must be confident, gringo. You didn't even tie me up."

"I didn't see the need to."

"No?" Hugo grinned. "You plan to fight me fair this time?"

It didn't sound like Hugo knew anything else of importance. Carver tried another line of questioning. "Does the mayor ever ask you to do things for her?"

"No."

His nostrils flared and his left eye twitched. He was lying.

Carver put the knife to Hugo's throat again. "Tell me the truth."

"Nothing big. She asks us to pull up her opponents' signs and trash them. She asked me to pay a visit to a city councilman to get him onboard for one of her projects."

"She pays you for this?"

"She keeps out of our business in exchange for our help."

"And your business is?"

"Wouldn't you like to know?" Hugo yanked his head back and rammed an uppercut into Carver's jaw.

At least, he tried to do that. Carver had seen it coming from a mile away. He leaned back. Watched the uppercut miss. Then he aimed the Glock and put a bullet in Hugo's fat head. The big man's eyes flared, and his mouth dropped open.

He lunged for Carver one second and dropped dead the next. It wasn't exactly how Carver wanted it to go down, but it was more satisfying. He'd wanted it to look like a car accident. The bullet hole was going to make that difficult, but not impossible.

Carver picked up the shell casing. The slug had exited the back of Hugo's head and hit the metal wheel behind it. Carver used the night vision on his monocular to sweep the area. The bullet was still hot, so he switched to thermal and found the glowing object a few feet away.

He picked it up with a gloved hand and pocketed it.

There was a steadily growing pool of blood under Hugo's head. Carver went to the pickup and looked behind the back seats. There were a bunch of old towels there. They were probably used by Hugo and gang to clean up messes like this.

There was also a surprise hidden beneath the towels. A rifle. He pulled it out. It was no ordinary rifle. It was a bullpup. The magazine was behind the trigger instead of in front of it. More specifically, it was a Tavor X95.

He rocked out the magazine. The rounds were NATO 5.56. That meant this was the 16.5" barrel. At least, that was what he vaguely remembered. This wasn't his rifle of choice, but he wasn't going to complain.

He'd always take a nice weapon that wasn't linked to him. His other weapons weren't linked to him or anyone else. They didn't even have serial numbers. This one did. It might be linked to Hugo, or it might be stolen.

It didn't matter. He dug four boxes of ammunition from beneath the towels. He set them and the rifle aside. Then he got back to business with the towels and the big slab of flesh bleeding out on the asphalt.

Carver wrapped a towel around Hugo's head to stanch the bleeding. Then he dragged the body to the pickup and bucked it into the driver's seat. The body slumped in the restraints, leaning on the steering wheel.

Carver pushed the body upright. He yanked hard on the top part of the seatbelt to activate the locking mechanism. It locked in place and held the body against the seat.

There were bags of cat litter inside the old gas station. The bags were old and rotten, and litter had fallen out over time, but since it was just clay, it still worked fine. Carver put a pile of it over the pool of blood. He used an old broom to wipe away the drag and scuff marks.

Then he got into the passenger side of the truck. It was a bench seat, so he sat close to Hugo. He pushed the dead man's feet to the side. He put his foot on the brake and started the engine.

Driving was a little clumsy, but he managed to back up the pickup. Turn it around. Get it on the road. He drove it down the highway to another spot he'd seen on his way into town. The highway went up at a steep angle.

There was a rocky mountain on the north side of the road. On the south side there was a wide shoulder and a metal railing to keep people from driving off a steep cliff and into what looked like a dry riverbed. A gulch.

It was a long way down. The ground below was covered in boulders and rocks that had probably rolled down the mountain slope and across the road into the gulch. He knew it was a gulch because there was a green sign on the side of the road that said *Devil's Gulch. No parking on this side of road.*

The railing there was bent and broken. It looked like a car had smashed through it and gone over the edge before. The railing was rusty. It had been like that for a long time but hadn't been repaired. That was good for what he had planned.

Carver slowed down and angled the pickup toward the gulch. He checked Hugo's phone one last time. He could take it, but it might be tracked by his anonymous benefactor. There was a new text from one of the men watching Carver's motel room.

It simply said, *Nada.* Nothing.

Carver considered responding but decided not to. There might be a tactical advantage to pretending to be Hugo, but judging from the previous texts, Hugo usually just let them do their thing with minimal input.

Probably because he was too busy drinking and assaulting women. If Carver gave them orders to do something strange, they might get suspicious. It was best to let them do their thing and he could plan around it.

Carver put the phone on the dashboard. He pulled the towel off Hugo's big head. Dropped it in the floorboard. He grabbed Hugo's pants leg and dragged the man's big, booted foot onto the accelerator.

The weight pressed the pedal to the floor. The engine roared. Carver moved his foot off the brake.

He slipped out of the passenger door just as the truck's tires squealed and the vehicle rocketed toward the gulley. It angled off course. Smashed into the unbroken railing a few feet behind the broken section.

The truck plowed through the metal. It flew over the ledge and out of sight. Headlights flashed in the darkness as the truck flipped.

Carver ran to the edge and watched. This wasn't the first time he'd done something like this. Even after all this time, he still liked to watch. There was something entertaining about watching something roll down a hill.

It could be a wheel, a boulder, or a pickup truck with a body inside. It really didn't matter. Maybe it was childlike fascination. Maybe it was satisfaction for a job well done. He didn't know or care.

He watched until the truck hit something close to the bottom of the gulch. Metal screeched and buckled. The headlights went out. The truck engine roared, sputtered, and turned off.

There were no flames. No explosions. There usually weren't. Sometimes the metal sparked and caught the gasoline on fire, but not this time. Even if the truck caught fire and burned Hugo to a crisp, the big hole in his skull would tell anyone at a glance that he didn't die from the accident.

Maybe they would think he died in a drive-by shooting. Maybe they'd realize he was killed first, and the accident was staged. It really didn't matter. Carver's Glock was unregistered and didn't have a serial number.

Carver had worn gloves so there were no fingerprints. He had the bullet casing and slug so there was little to no evidence about the gun that killed Hugo. It was tied up about as neatly as could be expected.

Unfortunately, Carver hadn't learned much. Hugo hadn't been entrusted with the kind of information Carver needed. He'd just been an errand boy for whoever was pulling the strings. Maybe his anonymous handler was connected to Enigma.

Things didn't feel quite the same here as they had in San Francisco or Oregon. Enigma had vast resources. They'd previously sent kill squads, not low-level street thugs. That didn't mean this unknown person wasn't connected, but he wasn't jumping to any conclusions just yet.

Most importantly, did Hugo's unknown boss have anything to do with Joe's death? It was possible his death had nothing to do with the mayoral race. It might have something to do with his horses. Maybe horse sperm was valuable.

Carver didn't know enough about it to say one way or the other. But he knew who would. It was the same place Angel had mentioned earlier. Equine Veterinary Services. Maybe someone there would remember Hugo's visit.

He was a big guy. His tattoos and jewelry practically screamed gangster. Someone like him should stand out in memory. The only catch was Carver had just killed him. If he spoke with someone at the vet's office and mentioned Hugo, that could implicate Carver.

Because Hugo's death would most likely make the news. If someone at the vet's office saw or heard the news, which was likely in this town, then they'd remember Carver.

It probably didn't matter that Hugo asked the questions. It was more important to know exactly what the questions were and to find that out without triggering memories of Hugo's visit.

Maybe Andrea would know the answers. Texting her was out of the question. The ranch was being watched and for all he knew, her phone was bugged. He needed to take her a burner phone. That could wait until the morning.

He walked back into town to get the Buick. Whenever he saw a car coming, he concealed himself. He didn't want anyone to remember a lone man walking down the highway in the middle of the night.

It took him an hour to get to the car. He drove it back to the abandoned gas station and picked up the X95 rifle. He was far enough out of town that he decided to test fire the rifle. It was always good to make sure an unfamiliar gun actually worked.

The gun sight had night vision. That made it easy to aim and fire at night. He backed up fifty yards. Popped off a couple of rounds into a stack of tires. The shots went clean through right on target.

He backed up another fifty yards. Aimed. Fired. Hit the target right where he was aiming. The scope was calibrated and accurate. Hugo must have been a real gun enthusiast. Or else he'd stolen the gun from someone that was.

Carver put the rifle in the Buick's trunk. The duffel bag with his other rifles were there too. Next up, the Blue Star Motel. He had to park the Buick somewhere safe for Ronald to retrieve it, and then go get Joe's pickup.

Getting the pickup was easier said than done if Hugo's men were still watching the motel room. If they were gone, then he'd get in the pickup and go. If they weren't, then the night was about to get a lot more violent.

And Hugo might have four more friends joining him in the afterlife.

CHAPTER 13

Carver drove west away from El Fuerte.

It didn't take long to reach the bustling outskirts of Los Angeles. He found an electronics store and went inside. Purchased a pair of new burner phones. They were low-end smart phones, not flip phones.

Basic phones were fine unless you had to text someone. Then they became a liability. He didn't want Andrea using her personal phone. It might be infested with spyware. It might be perfectly clean. He didn't know for sure, so it would be best if she had her own burner.

Carver borrowed scissors from the clerk to cut open the sealed plastic packages. He activated the phones and turned them off to save battery life. He already had a burner phone for himself, but it never hurt to have another one on hand just in case.

Carver had learned the hard way about losing his phone in San Francisco. The encrypted messaging app he used to contact Leon and Paola couldn't simply be replaced. The numbers it guarded couldn't be recovered.

He'd sent Paola's contact information to Leon as a backup in case he lost his phone. He also created a new encrypted email account as a backup means of communication. Leon and Paola had done the same.

Paola had been curious about his reasoning for it. She'd sent a long email detailing her life since they'd gone their separate ways. Carver had thought it unwise for her to send that much information, but he'd read it three times before deleting it.

It was the last question Paola asked him that still stuck in his memory. *Why do you care, Carver?*

It was a damned good question. They'd been together for months. She'd wanted more. He hadn't. She'd decided to move on with her life. She'd let go of Carver. Apparently, he hadn't quite let go of her even though he knew it was for the best.

Carver pushed aside those thoughts. They were unproductive. He dropped into the Buick and headed back to El Fuerte. He drove past the gulch where Hugo's corpse was resting inside the pickup truck.

He didn't even slow down. He kept driving. From one side of town to the other. Back to the restaurant across the road from the Blue Star Motel.

He used the monocular to scout the area. The streetlight and other exterior lights were off since Hugo's men had broken them. The management office lights were still on. It was getting late, but some offices stayed open until midnight.

There was no sign the manager had come outside or been alerted to the broken window and defunct lights at the far end of the motel.

Night vision didn't pick up any bogeys in the area. Infrared didn't show any heat signatures inside the room. It was possible the men had packed up and left. It had been a long while since Hugo had left.

Their last text to Hugo had said, *Nada.* They hadn't seen anything. They'd probably texted him the same thing again at least once since Carver had sent their boss's corpse hurtling into the gulch.

Maybe they'd seen nada for long enough and decided to leave.

The monocular picked up movement at the corner of the motel. There was a pinpoint of heat there. He switched to night vision. Saw smoke. Someone was smoking around the corner. Someone was waiting.

Hugo and his four men had arrived in the pickup. The pickup was at the bottom of a gulch, so they'd have to walk home or catch a ride. It looked like at least one of them was waiting outside. Why weren't the others waiting inside?

Carver swung the monocular around and found out why. Four men were sitting in a gray SUV. There was nothing basic about the vehicle. It was a Dodge Durango SRT Hellcat. Basically, an SUV version of a Charger.

The driver of the vehicle was a new addition to the crew. He must have brought food, because the three passengers were eating from paper bags. The driver was staring at the motel. He gestured at the building and started talking.

The guy in the front passenger seat said something in response. They were probably wondering why Carver hadn't returned. It was almost midnight. They were also probably talking about Hugo.

It was likely that they knew their boss had gone to the bar. They probably knew he might visit that woman too. Maybe it was nothing unusual for them to do all the hard work while Hugo got his rocks off.

Carver was tired. He just wanted to retrieve Joe's pickup and go back to the ranch. But that wasn't going to happen. At least, not easily. And not without bloodshed.

Killing was messy. It didn't matter if you were in a foreign country or your homeland. A trail of corpses was hard to conceal. People interacted with other people. They went out into the world and did things.

The disappearance of a single person would cause a ripple effect. The people closest to them would notice their absence. They would ask questions. They would look for answers. A person would have to be an absolute isolationist to go missing without anyone noticing.

Killing required a delicate balancing act.

Deleting Hugo's men would mean four less people who could kill Carver in the future. But it would make a mess. The trick was to make the mess look like someone else's mess.

Hugo's sort lived violent lives and often died violent deaths. That made Carver's situation a little easier. He just had to finesse the course of events to his liking.

Carver studied the Durango. It was sitting in a dark parking lot diagonally across the street from the motel. They could see their guy hiding at the end of the building. They probably planned to join him once they finished eating.

Carver weighed the pros and cons. He considered three plans. Kill them here. Kill them somewhere else. Leave them alone and find another motel to sleep in, then get the pickup in the morning.

Killing them somewhere else was best. But he'd have to take a route away from the traffic cameras. The last thing he wanted was for Joe's truck to be spotted in a high-speed chase with him behind the wheel.

Carver had mapped out a camera-free route on his walk back to the Buick. He hadn't done it for fun. It was absolutely necessary to find ways into town that avoided traffic cameras and any buildings that might have cameras outside.

It had resulted in cutting through residential areas. People might have cameras on their homes, but those were usually watching the front porch and not the road. Plus, whoever was watching the traffic cameras probably didn't have access to private ones.

Carver mapped out the plan in his head. If Rhodes were alive, she'd tell him it was terrible. She'd sketch out a superior blueprint in a few seconds. Something that didn't require a lot of luck. It was a good thing he was relying on skill and experience, not blind luck.

The rifles minimized the luck aspect. He also had the Tavor X95. He'd inspected it. He'd fired it. He knew it worked. He knew the scope was accurate out to a hundred yards at least.

And that was good enough for him.

The targets thought they were doing a good job watching the motel. They were wrong. They had a great view of the west side of the building and the motel room, but that was it. Unless they had a fifth man standing on the east side, they'd left a giant hole for Carver to walk right through.

Carver drove the Buick to the back of the restaurant. He parked it. Got out and slung the X95 over his shoulder with its strap. It was nice and light compared to his other rifles. Firing it at the tires had felt good. Real good.

Hopefully a live fire situation would go just as smoothly.

He circled around the back of the restaurant. Walked west down the back street for a block. He walked north to the sidewalk. Looked down the street with his monocular. The men were still in the car.

There was no sixth man watching the eastern side of the motel. The streets were empty. It was late. Just past one in the morning now. It was time to kill.

Carver looked up and down the east-west road. He looked north and south. No cars. No sign of police. Just two large billboards with the mayor's smiling face plastered on them. At the bottom it said, *Super Mayor Jessica Herrada welcomes you to El Fuerte!*

He hustled across the road. Kept going north along the sidewalk. Cut right down the service road behind the small strip mall there. The bottom of the L-shaped motel was two blocks down.

He covered the distance. There were four windows on the back of the office. The two on the left were cracked open a few inches to let in the night air. They were probably the windows to the managers bedroom. The other two were for the motel lobby.

Carver looked through the windows on the right. Saw the empty front office. He walked a few feet to the open window on the left. Sounds from the television drifted out. There was gunfire. The rumble of running horses. Probably an old western show.

He edged to the open window. Looked inside. He saw a couch. He saw the office manager sitting on the couch. Images from the television were casting different shades of light on the man's face. His eyes were open, but he wasn't watching the television.

His eyes were staring blankly at an upward angle. There was a gaping wound in his left temple. He'd been shot point blank on the right side. And he'd been dead for a while. He must have gone outside for a final check before going to bed.

Hugo's men had seen him coming. Maybe the manager tried to shoo them away. Maybe he'd threatened to call the cops. Or maybe Hugo's men just grabbed him, brought him back to his room and killed him because it was easier that way.

There were no cameras in or around the motel. That was one of the first things Carver usually checked for. If there had been cameras, he would have had to make sure to delete or steal the footage before doing what he planned next.

Going around the corner would risk revealing him to the men in the car. He pushed the bedroom window all the way up. Put one leg through. Ducked inside and pulled his other leg through. The rifle stock banged against the window frame.

He adjusted the strap. Pulled it tighter so the stock wasn't poking up too high. He wore the rifle angled across his back with the barrel pointing diagonally at the ground. The safety was on, and the chamber was clear, but just in case it wasn't, a misfire wouldn't risk taking off anything vital like his head.

Carver double-checked the bedroom for cameras. Didn't see any. There was a hole in the drywall from the bullet that had ended the manager's life. The show on the television was in black and white.

He recognized the main actor, James Garner. He recognized the show too. It was *Maverick*. He'd seen the reruns a lot as a kid. *Bonanza* had been another one. One of his foster dads used to make all the kids in his house watch western movies.

"Those were the good old days," he'd say. "Back when you could do what you wanted and shoot anyone who got in your way."

Apparently, Hugo's men thought this was the wild west. Carver figured it was only fair to join in on the fun.

Carver looked around the room. There was a couch and a television. A small kitchen with refrigerator, stove, and oven. A doorway presumably led to a bedroom. He went inside and found a bed and bathroom.

A chest of drawers was on one wall. A nightstand was next to the bed. Carver opened the drawer on the nightstand. Inside was a cigar box. He opened the lid and found an old-school Smith and Wesson revolver.

The words *357 Magnum* and *Combat Magnum* were inscribed in the barrel. The wooden grip was worn from use, but the gun smelled of oil and looked clean. There was a paper box of ammo and some loose bullets inside the cigar box.

Carver added the dead man's gun to his collection. He opened the cylinder. Checked the chambers. They were empty. He loaded all six. Snapped the cylinder back into place. Rolled it to make sure the action was nice and smooth.

He tucked the box of ammo and loose bullets into a pocket. Stuffed the revolver into his belt loop. It wasn't ideal, but it would do for now.

Carver ducked through the door leading into the office, keeping low in case one of the men had a line of sight into the front windows. He peeked out of the front window with the monocular. The four men were still in the Durango.

There was another car parked two rooms down from the office, but it didn't block the office door. There would be a moment when Carver was visible. Thankfully, Hugo's men had done Carver a favor and turned off the outside lights.

The office light was still on, but if he was quick, he could make it into the darkness before they saw him.

He stood. Cracked open the front door. He slipped through the opening. Crouched outside and shut the door. He dropped to his stomach and looked at the Durango through the monocular. The men were talking. None were looking in his direction.

Carver crouch-walked to the corner. The darkness concealed him, but it was still nice having the nearby parked car between him and the watchers. He continued down the walkway toward the pickup.

He'd turned off the dome light in the pickup earlier. He usually turned off dome lights so they wouldn't activate when the door opened. It was a good habit to have if you were worried about people shooting at you.

He reached the pickup. The odor of cigarette smoke reached him. The man waiting around the corner was only a few feet away. Carver went prone and checked with the monocular. The man wasn't visible, but the smoke from his cigarette was.

Sloppy. Real sloppy. Not that he expected better from street thugs.

Carver crouch-walked to the driver's door. It detected the key fob nearby and the door unlocked. It was just a faint click. The lights didn't blink and the alarm system didn't beep like some did.

He already knew they wouldn't. It had been something he'd checked earlier. Flashing lights and a loud beep were inconvenient when trying to sneak into a car unnoticed.

There was a scraping sound. Like boots on concrete. Carver looked through the truck window and saw a shadow moving down the sidewalk. The man must have heard the locks click. He was coming to investigate.

That saved Carver a few steps. He edged along the truck to the front left. Crouched. Drew the 357 magnum. The man's boots scuffed the concrete as he walked. He probably figured he hadn't heard anything important.

Carver poked around the corner and proved him wrong. There was just enough light to see the man's outline. Carver aimed the revolver. Fired. The muzzle flash highlighted a surprised look on the man's face the instant before his brains flew out of the back of his head.

The loud boom echoed. Carver's ears rang. He hurried to the pickup. Climbed in. Cranked the engine. It roared to life. He slammed the truck into reverse. The big treads chuffed against the asphalt.

Carver tried a reverse one-eighty, but the tires were too grippy. He put the truck in drive and hit the accelerator while lowering the driver's side window. The Durango's lights flashed on. Its engine rumbled.

The game was on.

CHAPTER 14

Carver fired a couple of blind shots with the revolver.

He wasn't trying to hit the men in the Durango. He wasn't trying to scare them off. He was just trying to slow them down a little. The truck was a Dodge Ram TRX. It was no slouch, but it couldn't outrun the Durango Hellcat. Especially not with its larger offroad tires.

The truck roared down the street. He cut hard left. Crossed a couple of blocks. The Durango drifted around the corner. It had street tires and was far nimbler than the Ram.

Carver followed the memorized route. He rolled south and veered into a residential neighborhood. It was a straight shot to the edge of town from here. He gunned the engine. The truck surged forward.

The Durango slid around the corner a moment later. It was a few blocks back. It was fast, but the Ram was already up to speed. It should be able to hold the lead for a little while.

Carver sped past a stop sign. The residential road angled into the highway and ended. He hooked a slight left and went west. He pushed the accelerator all the way down. Within seconds the speedometer needle surged north of a hundred miles per hour.

He looked both ways as he crossed an intersection. He saw a car in the distance. Just a civilian. Not a cop, thankfully. Hopefully there weren't any lurking nearby or his reckless plan would fall apart.

The Durango reached the highway. It was a little further back than it had been. Maybe the driver had slowed down for some reason. Maybe he'd had second thoughts about chasing Carver and then decided to keep chasing him anyway.

That was good. Really good. It gave Carver a few extra seconds of leeway. With this plan, every second counted. The highway angled southwest. Another highway branched due west. Carver took the branch.

He hurtled down the road at a hundred and thirty. Streaked past the abandoned gas station. Roared up the steep climb ahead. The Durango was trying to close the gap. It had to be doing a hundred and fifty.

What was its top speed? One-eighty? Two hundred? He didn't know for sure. At these speeds, the slightest mistake could be lethal. A pothole or even a small bump could send a vehicle flying.

Carver crested the rise and drove out of sight of the Durango. He hit the brakes. Veered onto the right shoulder and into the grass. It took the truck several precious seconds to come to a complete halt.

He jumped out of the truck. Unslung the X95. Ran across the road. Went prone.

The Durango topped the rise seconds later. It was going so fast all four tires left the ground for an instant. Carver aimed through the scope. The SUV was coming right at him. An easy target. He fired.

The front tire on the Durango exploded. The driver lost control. There was no telling how fast he was going. Probably over a hundred and fifty. The driver had been pushing the engine to its limits, that was obvious from the high-pitched whine.

The vehicle careened to its left. The tire caught the road and peeled off. The rim sparked against asphalt. The SUV hurtled right toward Carver.

He jumped to his feet. Ran a few steps to his left and dove out of the way. Rolled onto the asphalt. The Durango hit the shoulder of the road right where he'd been. It skidded into the grass. Flipped sideways. Went through the broken section of metal railing and plummeted into the gulch. Bits and pieces of the car flew into the air, trailing behind like a comet smashing down to earth.

Carver pushed to his feet. He ran to the edge. Viewed the gulch through the monocular. The Durango had flown off the ledge. It had plummeted well past Hugo's pickup and smashed into a boulder.

There was nothing left but twisted metal and a trail of broken plastic. It looked like it had been through a car compactor. Twice.

There was no easy way into the gulch. Not unless he went back a few miles and took the southwest highway. He didn't need to go down there to know everyone in the SUV was dead. All the flipping, twisting, and grinding had been like a giant blender. Churning their bodies into crimson pudding.

Four more dead. Six total, including Hugo. That was enough work for tonight.

Carver picked up his shell casing. The slug had probably bounced off the rim. It could be anywhere. It didn't really matter anyway. He pocketed the casing. Examined the area with his monocular.

There were skid marks from the Durango. Gouges in the asphalt from the metal rim. Faint skid marks from Hugo's pickup. No marks from Joe's pickup. There were no traces that anyone had been prone on the shoulder of the road. The scene looked nice and mysterious.

Just how he liked it.

He cleared the chamber on the X95. Rocked out the magazine. Pushed the unused round inside. He put the rifle on the back floorboard and left the magazine out of it. Safety first.

With that done, Carver drove back to town using the same camera-free route he'd used earlier. He drove slowly. Checked for any other cars on the road. There were only a few driving around at this hour.

He saw a lone police car parked outside the bar Hugo had visited earlier. It piqued his curiosity, so he stopped at the curb and looked through the window. A uniformed patrol officer was sitting at the bar inside. He was talking to a woman. He was also drinking from a martini glass.

There was a decent crowd inside. Apparently, the place was open all night. Apparently, the cop was partying along with everyone else inside. That was good. It was one less cop patrolling the streets.

The town was small, so that might be the only patrol officer on duty at this hour. Whatever the case, it worked out. Detective Ford or one of his people would have a mystery to solve tomorrow.

Then again, the gulch might be in unincorporated LA County. Maybe it would be another mystery for Captain Lucas Hernandez.

Carver accelerated slowly so the engine didn't roar. That was the problem with performance vehicles. The exhaust notes were anything but subtle. He parked behind the restaurant where he'd left the Buick.

The motel should have been a hive of police activity by now. The boom from the magnum revolver should have alerted whoever was staying in the room near the office. But it was just as dead as it had been before he'd blown a hole in a man's head.

It made him wonder if the occupant was dead. After all, those men had killed the motel manager. Maybe the other person had come outside to investigate and also been shot. The restaurant had been closed and there weren't any houses nearby.

It presented an opportunity to further muddle any investigations. Carver looped around the restaurant and hustled across the road to the dark motel parking lot. He found the man he'd shot lying on his back outside his hotel room.

He found the shell casing nearby and left it for the police to find. Then he hurried to the room with the car parked outside. The door was unlocked. Carver eased the door open and looked inside.

There was a large man face down on the bed. A pillow with the stuffing blown out of it was next to his head. Carver used the flashlight on his phone. The man had been shot in the back of the head. The pillow had been placed between his head and the gun to make the shot quieter.

Hugo's thugs were absolute morons. Correction—*had* been morons. Just leaving a trail of bodies between them and their target. There was no shell casing nearby, so at least it looked like they tried to clean up after themselves.

Carver went back to the motel office. He went to the dead manager. He put the revolver in the dead man's hand. Aimed it at the wall. Fired a shot. It boomed insanely loud inside close quarters.

He took the gun. Dropped it on the office floor. It was a revolver, so the shell casing was still in the cylinder. It wasn't the best job he'd ever done staging a scene, but by the time the police tied it to the dead men in the gulch, the chain of events would be almost incomprehensible.

There was an old school landline phone next to the couch. It looked like something from the eighties with pushbuttons on the front. He lifted the phone off the hook. Wrapped the manager's hand around the receiver. Let it fall from the dead man's hand.

It would make it look like he'd tried to call the police before he died. At least, that was the plan.

Carver hurried down the dark walkway. He crossed the road. Looped back around the restaurant where the Buick and Ram were parked. Parking the Buick right across the road from a major crime scene would be a bad idea.

He transferred his stuff from the Buick to the pickup, then drove the Buick down a few blocks to a strip of shops. He parked it near the sidewalk then hoofed it back to the restaurant, texting Ronald along the way to let him know where he could find his car. He didn't get a reply, probably because he was asleep.

Carver drove down the street behind the restaurant and went to the edge of town. He took a moment to examine the area. There were no cameras. The closest one was at the traffic light two blocks from the Blue Star Motel.

The highway left town and linked up with a road that went north and circled the outskirts of town. Carver took the route slowly, checking for traffic cameras on the corners and security cameras on the buildings.

He spotted a traffic cam ahead and took a right into a residential area. The street took him north and then back west. He continued the circuitous route and connected with the northern highway well outside of town and away from any cameras.

That was one more route he could take to avoid being seen. But getting further into town without being spotted on a camera was going to be difficult if not impossible.

He aimed the car north and thought about the problem. It triggered a faint memory. He'd been back in the States on leave. Rhodes had invited him to join her and her family for the Thanksgiving holiday.

She'd told him to use a different map program because the default maps app would take him to the wrong location. She'd recommended something. And he remembered that it had a lot of route details not present in the default app.

It warned drivers about speed traps and locations of police. It had more details when there were wrecks. And it even marked all the spots where there were speed cameras and traffic cameras.

Carver vaguely recalled a word in the name. He typed it into the search bar of the apps store. The third result was the correct one. It was called Way-Go. He installed it. Opened it once it was ready. It zoomed in on his location.

He scrolled down to El Fuerte. The place was full of little icons. He couldn't look at them while he was driving, so he put down the phone and kept his attention on the road.

He was tempted to turn off the headlights when he neared the ranch, but if the watcher was still active, they'd probably already seen them from miles away.

It was likely there wasn't just one watcher. A team of three or four was ideal. They could watch a target in shifts. A minimum of two was necessary for around-the-clock watching. The only way to find out for sure was to pay them a visit.

Carver was too tired to plot out an angle of approach. He knew their general location on the mountain. It gave them a view for miles around. Finding a blind approach would be difficult. But confronting them now might not be the right move.

He knew they were watching. He now knew they contacted someone and that some-one had arranged for Hugo to follow him. With Hugo dead, he could use the watcher to his advantage.

Hugo had received his orders from Anonymous. Maybe the watcher did too. If that was the case, then the watcher probably knew as little as Hugo. It made sense to let the watcher keep breathing for now.

The reasoning was simple. Hugo was dead. The next time Anonymous sent someone after Carver, they'd have to send the next person up the food chain. Maybe that person would know more. Or, they might just be another dumb thug like Hugo.

For now, Carver would bide his time and see what kind of reaction the violent deaths of six gang members would trigger.

He pressed the remote control on the truck visor and the garage door opened almost silently. He backed the truck inside. Closed the door. Retrieved his guns and the X95. He probably should have ditched it somewhere, but it was a solid rifle, and it was probably linked to a gang member. That could be useful.

It might also be a stolen rifle. Hugo hadn't exactly been a law-abiding citizen. The only way to know for sure was to trace the serial number but doing that could also raise alerts if the number was being monitored because of theft.

Joe's house wasn't a secure location. It was being watched. It was known to unknown parties who might have possibly killed Joe. Until the blood results came back, Carver wouldn't know for sure.

There was no reason to believe Andrea was in danger. Unless she was withholding information, she hadn't become entangled in politics or anything else that might have put Joe's life in jeopardy.

Carver, however, was someone they were interested in. Maybe it had just been a personal beef. Maybe Hugo knew Carver had gone to the ranch. Maybe it was his watcher on the mountain.

Maybe the events of tonight would put an end to all of that. Only time would tell. In the meantime, Carver would sleep with one eye open.

There was an alarm zone for the garage. He armed the system. It started beeping a countdown from thirty until it was armed. He left the garage. Closed and locked it. He went to the house.

The door was locked. He unlocked it with the keys Andrea had given him. The alarm inside was armed. It started to beep in warning. He walked across the kitchen to the control pad and disarmed it. He closed the door and locked it. Rearmed the alarm in *At Home* mode.

It was a simple system. There were motion sensors, but they weren't active in *At Home* mode. There was a control pad in the kitchen and another one in the master bedroom. The mode could be switched to *Away* from there to activate the motions sensors.

There were motion sensors in the main open area. They monitored the kitchen, den, and dining area. They were angled so if anyone entered via a window or door, they would be detected.

The windows and doors had their own sensors that would trigger an alarm as well, but an experienced person could easily bypass them. Carver knew how to do it. He also knew how to defeat most home systems.

Of course, when he'd done it in the past, he'd also had access to specialized equipment that made it easier. Doing it with normal tools was far more difficult unless he already knew where the main alarm panel was.

The alarm system was good enough for a home. But he wasn't going to bet his life on it. So, he got a pillow from the guest bedroom. He found a nice, dark nook in the dining area. It was between the wall and a large cabinet that held the good dinnerware.

He put the Glock next to his pillow. Then he went through his relaxation routine and fell asleep quickly. Ready to wake up at a moment's notice.

In case someone decided to pay him a visit.

CHAPTER 15

The watcher had an unexpected guest waiting for him.

A young man with buzzed hair was sitting in his chair, eye pressed to a scope on a stand. The man held up a finger in a *wait there* gesture. He backed his face away from the scope and turned to the watcher.

"Who are you?" the watcher asked.

"You can call me Two."

"Like the number two?"

"Yes." Two rose from the watcher's chair. "I was asked to assist you. We will be watching in shifts. I've brought tents and supplies so we can sleep here."

The watcher nodded. He'd requested help before. Anonymous had finally granted that request. The timing was no coincidence. "It's because of Carver, right?"

Two nodded. "We don't have any intel on him. He's a void."

"That's surprising." The watcher frowned. "No one living in a civilized nation can exist without a record of some kind."

"We know he was in the service with Donnely. We know they're friends. But there are no records of him." Two put his eye back to the scope. "I was provided this MWIR scope." He pronounced MWIR like a word rather than spelling out the acronym. "It's better than binoculars. It's capable of thermal vision for up to seven miles."

"Were we given other operational guidelines?"

Two nodded. "Keep watch twenty-four hours. Make regular reports."

"We need range extenders. There's no cell service up here."

"I was told that's in the works."

"By whom?"

Two put his eye to the scope again. "Anonymous. Until that problem is solved, the person not on watch will go down the mountain and make reports at four-hour intervals."

The watcher saw a folded chair leaning against a tree. He opened it. The cloth mesh was camouflaged. "Am I taking over now?"

Two stood. Stretched. "Yeah. I'm going to set up the tents and get some shuteye. Let me know if anything major happens."

The watcher tried the camouflage seat. It was more comfortable than what he'd been using, so he switched chairs, folded the old one, and set it on the ground. He put his eye to the scope. It was still dark, so the thermal imaging was on.

There was no activity at the ranch, but he saw a coyote loping across the plain and a mountain lion prowling near the base of the mountain. The scope was definitely a major upgrade.

"What's the endgame?" the watcher asked.

Two continued unpacking a tent while he talked. "I don't know. Watch, report, and wait for instructions."

The horizon turned pink. The watcher checked the time. Sunrise in twenty minutes. "Did you observe the ranch last night?"

"I did."

The watcher looked at Two. "Any activity?"

"The new Dodge Ram returned at zero two thirty-three. There was a large male behind the wheel, presumably Carver. The vehicle backed into the garage and the door closed. The covered walkway between the garage and house prevented me from seeing the individual walk into the house, but a light came on a moment later, so I know he did."

The watcher frowned. "He was out all night. Did you read my last report?"

Two nodded. "I read all the reports. He went into town last night at twenty thirty-three."

"And didn't return until after zero two thirty? Was he out drinking?"

"Unknown." Two began unfolding the tent. "That's not our job to know."

The watcher looked through the scope. A light was on in the house. The day was about to begin.

CARVER WAS UP AT SUNRISE.

He'd slept four solid hours and felt good. He vaguely remembered a dream about Paola. They were on a beach, talking about something, but the fragments faded away before he could grasp them.

He went to the guest bathroom to shower. There was a note from Andrea on the bed. It had probably been there last night, but he hadn't come into the room until now. It said that she'd be in town most of today.

It didn't say why. Didn't say where. It wasn't important.

He showered. Put on fresh clothes. It was his last pair of decent cargo pants. The others had holes and tears in them. The shirt and pants from last night had Hugo's blood sprinkled on them. He'd have to dispose of them and refresh his wardrobe.

He paused outside Andrea's bedroom door. He considered knocking to make sure she was okay. She wasn't okay. No one would be after suffering a loss like she had.

Carver took Andrea's note and crumpled it up. He dropped it in the trash in the kitchen. He found a notepad and wrote a note for her.

I got you a burner phone and installed an encryption app. My number is already in it. Don't send any important information using your personal phone. Communicate with me using the burner.

He wrapped the note around the phone and put it in front of her bedroom door. He got his duffel bag and backpack and left, rearming the alarm system on the way out.

He put his stuff in the rear floorboard of Joe's pickup. He'd put his bloody clothing into a plastic grocery bag to keep them separate from everything else. He checked the interior of the Dodge carefully and didn't see any blood on the dark leather.

It was probably clean, but he wanted to be sure, so he pulled his tactical flashlight out of the duffel bag and turned out all the lights in the garage. He put it in UV mode and shined it on the leather. It was clean as a whistle. The floorboards were clean too.

He checked the back seat. Also clean. His duffel bag had splotches on it. So did his backpack. No telling what had made those, but definitely not Hugo's blood. He shined the black light around the cabin. It was clean.

The truck had hardly been driven, so that was no surprise.

Carver got out of the truck and went to the old pickup. He shined the light on it. There were smudges and blotches on the outside. The inside looked clean. The old vinyl seats didn't stain easily.

The pickup bed had small stains here and there. There were a lot of streaks. It had probably been cleaned with strong chemicals at some point. It had probably been used for hauling feed and manure, and all the other things required on a horse ranch.

A gooseneck hitch was in the middle of the bed. There was a wide metal brace around it, probably to strengthen the bed. The truck was an older Dodge. Judging from the odor, it was a diesel. Probably a one-ton pickup because the horse trailer at the other end of the garage looked big.

Carver checked the sedan next to the pickup. The outside was clean. The interior had a large spot on the back headrest. Someone with a lot of hair care products might have been sitting there.

He went to the horse trailer. It looked like it could carry four horses. There were stains all over the wood flooring. Probably from horse pee and fecal matter.

There was another garage door in the wall behind the trailer. Carver had noticed it before but hadn't given it much thought. It occurred to him that there was no back exit out of the garage. He gauged the distance from the front wall to the back wall. This was just a section of the entire garage.

He pressed the button next to the door. It rolled up. The room beyond was dark. Carver felt the wall and found a switch. He turned it on. It shined on a new section of garage just a little narrower than on the other side.

There was a mechanical lift in this section. A big metal tool chest. A long metal workbench. Shelving with an assortment of car parts. It was the vehicle on the lift that caught Carver's attention.

It had the Dodge logo on the front, and it resembled a truck, but Carver hadn't seen one like this before. He saw a repair manual on the workbench. It was open to a diagram of an engine. He closed it and read the title. It was for a nineteen fifties Dodge Power Wagon.

The truck on the lift looked like it had been fully restored. There was an empty oil pan and funnel beneath the truck. A new oil filter on a rolling workbench next to it. Joe had been planning to change the oil and had never gotten around to it.

Now he never would.

The red paint was new and shiny. The steel wheels were painted white. The tires had an old-school offroad tread. It was nice. Really nice. Before Joe moved and built the ranch, he'd had a normal house close to San Diego.

There had been a classic Dodge Charger in that garage. They'd stood around it. Drank beers. Talked about what work Joe had to do on it next to get it running. Nothing had changed since buying the ranch. He'd just upgraded his garage space.

Carver left the workshop and closed the door behind him. The main garage was still dark. There was nothing on the floor between him and the far wall, so he started walking. He turned on the tactical flashlight.

It was still in UV mode. His finger was on the toggle switch to change it back to normal light when he saw something. He walked toward the glowing splotch on the tailgate of the new Ram.

There was a hard tonneau cover over the bed. He pressed a button and it retracted, rolling up at the other end of the bed. Carver stood on the rear bumper and looked inside.

The bed was streaked with stains. Big stains and small ones. Some of those stains didn't glow. They were pitch black. Most fluids left a stain that glowed under UV light. There was one that absorbed the light instead.

Blood.

There were spots of it all over the pickup bed. Other parts of the bed glowed slightly as if someone had poured bleach to clean it up. Carver switched to regular light. The pickup bed looked clean aside from a few spots of blood here and there.

The metal had been covered in a rubberized treatment to prevent cargo from scratching the metal. There was a gooseneck hitch in the middle, and a low-profile toolchest at the front.

He switched back to UV. It definitely looked like there had been blood all over the pickup bed and someone had used bleach to try to clean it. That was a mistake. Hemoglobin reacted with bleach to leave a faint glow.

They should have used an oxidizer to remove all traces. Joe would have known that. Maybe he hadn't cared. Maybe this was horse blood. Maybe he'd shot a coyote or mountain lion and tossed it in the back.

That made sense. It seemed strange that Joe would have bought a new pickup only to toss a dead animal in the back and then never drive it again. He'd put a gooseneck hitch in the back which seemed to indicate that he'd planned to use it to haul the trailer.

Carver opened the passenger side door. He opened the glove compartment and found the registration. The truck had been purchased nearly three months ago. But the odometer had barely over a hundred miles on it before Carver had added to the total last night.

He put the registration back in the compartment. It was just enough to pique his interest. Why hadn't Joe driven his new truck very much? The old Dodge one ton was okay for work, but it wasn't nearly as comfortable as a new vehicle.

Carver was sure Joe had his reasons. Maybe it had to do with the stains in the bed. Maybe it didn't. He planned to keep using it for the time being.

He climbed inside. Opened the garage door and left. He went toward town but turned east before he hit the first traffic cameras. The road went straight along the outer edge of town. It turned southeast. There was an empty stretch before he reached the next town.

The maps app located a suitable clothing store not too far away. He drove there and went inside for some light shopping. He picked up four sets of clothing. Black cargo pants, black t-shirts, black boots.

He added another black hoodie to the total along with socks and underwear. It was a lot of clothing, but he wasn't exactly traveling light these days. Not with a duffel bag full of weapons and gear and a backpack.

Plus, it looked like he might be here for a while. Maybe a few days, maybe a few weeks. Whatever it took to make sure that he got to the bottom of Joe's death. That was the only way to be sure Andrea wasn't in danger.

If it was an accident, then she was going to be safe. If it was a political assassination, then the odds were they didn't care about her, and they'd leave her alone. But there was an outside chance it had nothing to do with politics.

There might be another scenario that led to Joe's death. Maybe it was murder, maybe it wasn't. Carver planned to stay until he knew without a doubt that a horse really kicked his friend to death. He wanted to ensure Andrea would be okay. It was the least he could do.

He climbed back in the truck and sat in the parking lot thinking about his next moves. It all depended on how overt or covert he wanted to be. He wanted to talk to the mayor. Ask her face-to-face if she had anything to do with Joe's death.

Seeing her reaction might tell him what he needed to know. It also might tell him nothing and would tell her that he was actively investigating the situation. That could trigger a reaction from her that made everything harder.

It seemed best to remain as covert as possible. To investigate in secret. To remain as invisible as possible. That was provided he didn't get tied to the over half a dozen dead men in the gulch and at the motel.

The blood test results would steer his investigation. It was probably too soon to expect anything, but he texted Doctor Palmer for an update. Then he leaned back and wondered what he would do if the results came back clean.

Carver had seen Joe's face. The marks left no doubt that a horseshoe had struck him in the head at least twice. The force of the blows had nearly caved in his skull.

A notification appeared on his phone. He opened it. There was a message in the secure app. For an instant, he hoped it might be Paola. He didn't know why that was his first thought. The message was almost certainly from Andrea.

He opened the app. Andrea had sent a text. *Can you meet me downtown in the square?* Carver stared at it for a moment before replying. *Sure. ETA ten minutes.*

He backed up. Wheeled the Ram around and got on the road. There was no way to avoid cameras on the way to downtown El Fuerte, so he took the shortest route. It took him fifteen minutes thanks to traffic.

The square was where he'd encountered Gloria and Hugo the day before. There was a statue with the founder of El Fuerte, a park, and some sidewalks. Town hall, a building that looked like a Spanish fortress was at the north side of the square.

It was surrounded by roads on all sides and parking lots on the east and west sides. The place had been bustling the day before and it was still bustling due to the Salvation Day Festival.

Carver didn't know what Salvation Day was. It had something to do with local history. Maybe it was religious. Maybe it was something completely different. He didn't know or care.

What he did care about was parking a big truck. There was no room around the square, so he drove down side streets until he found something a block away. He got out and walked toward the square.

A newspaper box displayed the local paper, *The El Fuerte Gazette*. It featured a picture of Joe outside his ranch. The headline read, *Local Rancher Killed in Accident*. Carver put fifty cents in the slot and took a paper.

The article by Breanna Taylor was short, simple, and to the point. *Local Rancher Joe Donnely was killed in a tragic accident Friday morning when a horse he was training kicked him twice in the face. He was found dead by his helpers who reported it to the police. Mr. Donnely is survived by his wife, Andrea.*

No mention of an investigation or autopsy. No real details at all. It was the top news story, but the writer hadn't even tried to stretch the story out to a full half page. It was barely a paragraph.

The office for the Gazette was a few paces away from Carver. It was small, like most local newspapers. He considered asking the reporter when and how she'd heard the news. Had Detective Ford told her, or someone else?

It probably wasn't important, but it was worth asking. It could wait until later. Carver wanted to find out why Andrea wanted to meet in the square. He hoped she wasn't going to do something rash.

As he neared the square, he heard the whine of microphone feedback. A man spoke to a large crowd gathered near a stage where a live band had performed the day before. The drone of the crowd was too loud for him to make out what the speaker was saying.

Carver crossed the road and into the square. He checked his phone. Andrea hadn't messaged again. She hadn't told him where in the square to meet. A familiar voice boomed over the speakers.

"Can I have your attention, please?"

He looked at the stage. Andrea was holding the microphone. She locked eyes with him and nodded as if acknowledging he was there. Then she spoke.

"Hello everyone. My name is Andrea Donnely. Today, I'm announcing my intention to run for mayor of El Fuerte."

The crowd roared.

— • —

CHAPTER 16

Monty got the call at six in the morning.

A patron of Ray's Diner had noticed something strange when entering the diner for breakfast. He'd seen someone lying on the sidewalk across the road at the Blue Star Motel. He figured it was another drug addict enjoying his high.

But the figure didn't move at all. So, he'd called 911 just in case. A paramedic arrived thirty minute later—their department was understaffed and inundated, so thirty minutes was a great response time for them.

The paramedic found a Hispanic man with a bullet wound in the head. She had notified the police. The switchboard had sent patrol officers to secure the scene and notified Monty.

His ringing cell phone had jarred him out of a drunken sleep. He'd taken Janine out drinking last night. She'd just wanted to skip straight to the sex and go home, but he'd wanted the full experience.

She'd loosened up after a while and enjoyed herself. Then he'd brought her to his place and given her the best two or three minutes of her life. Maybe. Probably. He'd been pretty drunk and numb. It had been good for him, at least.

Then he'd rolled off her and fallen asleep. When the phone woke him, she was gone. She'd probably left the instant she could. It didn't make him feel good about himself, but hey, sex was sex.

Monty was at the motel now. He was looking at three dead men. Phil Smith, the owner of the Blue Star, a guest who'd signed the ledger as John Smith, but whose ID had the name Bruce Joyner on it. And lastly, an unknown Hispanic man with no ID.

All three men had died of gunshot wounds to the head. From what Monty could tell, the Hispanic man had killed Bruce Joyner. Phil had killed the Hispanic man. Someone else had shot Phil.

There was also a bullet hole in the wall of Phil's apartment. It looked like he'd gone back to call emergency services. Someone had entered the room. He'd shot and missed. They'd shot and nailed him square center in the forehead.

No other guests had signed in, but the key to room thirty wasn't on the pegboard in the office. The window had been broken, presumably by a rock lying on the floor inside. The key to the room was also inside.

There were some clothes inside. A shirt and a pair of pants. Sized for someone around five feet, six inches. There was a towel on the floor outside the bathroom. The shirt and pants looked about the size of the Hispanic man, name unknown. He was five feet, five inches and thin.

Monty formed an image in his head. The Hispanic man, call him Juan Doe for the report, was the guest in room thirty. He wasn't alone. Maybe he'd brought a woman with him.

There was an argument. Maybe the other guest had gotten into an altercation with him. They shouted at each other about something. Juan went into his room. There were footprints on the door.

It looked like Joyner had tried to kick the door open. The metal frame was too strong, so he picked up a rock and threw it against the glass. Juan emerged from his room with a gun.

Joyner ran back to his room. He couldn't close the door in time. Juan forced him face down on the bed. Put a pillow on his head. Pushed the muzzle of the gun against the pillow. Fired.

That would have slightly muffled the shot, but not enough. The owner, Phil, heard the shot and got his gun. He came outside to investigate. He saw Juan walking back to his room. He ran after him. Saw the gun in the other man's hand.

When Juan turned to face him, Phil panicked and shot him in the head. He ran back to the office to call 911. The phone was off the hook. It looked like it had been in his hand. Then the other unknown person entered the office, presumably with Juan's gun.

Phil had probably put the gun down. He tried to pick it up and fire. He panicked and shot the wall. The unknown person shot him. Phil's head wounds matched Bruce Joyner's. The crime scene investigators would confirm that.

This was anything but a nice, neat package, but he felt like he'd nailed the course of events. Finding the unknown shooter would confirm that. Hopefully the CSI people would find a stray hair or fingerprint that would lead to that person.

The vehicle Juan had driven was gone. There were some skid marks that looked like someone had backed up and gotten out in a hurry, but they were just black streaks. No tread patterns that could lead to identifying the make and model of the tires.

It was probably a truck. Most of the Hispanic men in these parts drove them. Judging from the width of the marks, he felt certain they'd been caused by large tires on a heavy vehicle. Maybe a half-ton or one-ton pickup.

His phone rang. "This is Ford."

"You still at the motel?" It was dispatch.

"Yeah. Just waiting on CSI."

"They want you at the one sixty next to Devil's Gulch."

"That's not our jurisdiction."

She sighed. "I'm just telling you what Chief Lynch told me."

"Ten-four." He ended the call. Shook his head and wondered why they wanted him across town and outside of their jurisdiction. And where in the hell was CSI? They should have been here by now.

He dropped into his car. Started it. Headed across town toward whatever mystery awaited him there. This had better be good.

CARVER GRIMACED.

This wasn't good. Not good at all. Andrea was running for mayor in place of Joe. She didn't look like a newly grieving widow. She was in jeans and a t-shirt. Cowboy boots and a ballcap. She was wearing makeup. Not too much. Just enough to look natural.

Her eyes were a little red around the edges, but they looked fierce and determined. Not sad.

She must have been up all night. Absolutely wracked with grief. Crushed with loss. She'd turned that into anger. Determination. Defiance. If someone had killed Joe to keep him from running for mayor, then she was going to show them that they'd failed.

Andrea was going to pick up where Joe left off and defeat Jessica Herrada. And if Joe had been murdered, she was painting a huge bullseye on her back.

"Joe had a vision for El Fuerte. A vision where land isn't forcibly annexed. Where new taxes aren't levied on the backs of hard-working citizens. Where the mayor and city council are held accountable for paying exorbitant amounts of city money to their cronies." Andrea pointed at the town hall. "Mayor Herrada, give us back our city!"

The crowd cheered. There had been maybe a hundred people before. Now the crowd had doubled. Whatever events had been scheduled for today were on indefinite hold until Andrea finished talking.

A big black Chevy Suburban with dark tinted windows screeched to a halt at the curb. Four men in black suits piled out. They big guys. All business. A couple looked like former military.

One of them opened the back door. Jessica Herrada stepped out.

She was wearing a tight-fitting black dress and heels. Her hair was thick, black, and straight. She stood and glared at Andrea. Motioned to her security detail. They cleared a path through the crowd with her in the middle.

"Mayor Herrada, are you here to defend your indefensible actions? Are you here to resign immediately so the citizens of El Fuerte can start to recover from the financial wounds you've inflicted on the city? You have turned a five-million-dollar surplus into a ten-million-dollar deficit!"

One of the security detail held his hand out to Andrea. She shook her head. Tried to speak. The man yanked the microphone from her hand. Feedback squealed. He handed it to Mayor Herrada.

She smirked. "I see you've wasted no time turning the tragic death of your husband into a political campaign." Herrada rolled her eyes. "I hope everyone can see what this woman is doing. I'm so sorry for your loss, Mrs. Donnely, but it's just disgusting that you would try to use this to fuel your own political ambitions."

Andrea replied, but Carver couldn't hear her without the microphone.

Herrada feigned a sad look. "Joe Donnely was a good man. A worthy candidate for mayor. But he wasn't eligible to run, and neither are you. Your home is outside the city limits."

Andrea smiled and said something else.

Herrada blinked. Shook her head. "Now that's just sad." She turned to the crowd. "Mrs. Donnely, I want you to know that we all join in mourning for the loss of a local icon. Joe Donnely knew how to pick breeding horses. He knew how to pick winners. I want to believe that you're just sad and angry at his loss. But you've hijacked this festival and put a black stain on the celebrations."

"Let her speak!" Someone in the crowd shouted. "Let her speak!"

"No!" Someone else shouted back. "I want music, not this!"

More and more in the crowd started chanting. "Let her speak. Let her speak."

Herrada raised a hand. "I'm afraid she's broken the law by using city resources to announce her political ambitions. She's not allowed to simply disrupt official city procedures in this manner."

The chant grew louder. "Let her speak!"

A school bus pulled to the curb. People started piling out it. They hurried into the square, some of them holding up signs.

Vote Jessica!

Citizens for Super Mayor Jessica

The new arrivals started a counter chant. "Super mayor! Super mayor!"

Herrada grinned and winked at one of the men in her security detail. A Caucasian with buzzed hair and a muscular frame. He nodded back at her.

She raised a hand, and the crowd went silent. "This farce has gone on long enough. Let's get back to the music!"

The people from the bus cheered and started chanting again. The musicians were ushered to the stage. They took the microphone and started playing.

Andrea tried to leave the stage, but Herrada's security detail detained her. They took her off the stage and toward town hall.

Carver sighed. He didn't think they'd do anything to Andrea, but he wasn't sure he wanted to take the chance.

He started walking around the crowd toward Andrea. A police officer emerged from the other side. He talked to Andrea. Turned her around and put handcuffs on her. Then he marched her away.

Mayor Herrada's eyes met Carver's. Her gaze narrowed. She said something to the same man she'd winked at earlier. Motioned to her security detail in a *stay here* gesture. She approached him by herself.

When they were a few feet away, Herrada smiled and extended her hand. "You must be Mr. Carver."

He looked at her hand. Didn't take it. "You mind telling me why they arrested Andrea?"

"Mr. Carver, I'm afraid she's broken the law. It's just a misdemeanor. She'll be out by morning." She lowered her hand and feigned a sad look. "I'm very sorry about Joe."

"How do you know my name?"

"Joe told me about you." She smiled fondly. "You might find this hard to believe, but he and I had a good rapport. We talked a great deal about the future of this city."

"I do find that hard to believe."

"I understand, but you also know next to nothing about anything here. After all, you only just arrived yesterday."

"And yet you know my name and what I look like."

Herrada looked him up and down. "You're hard to miss, Mr. Carver."

"Just Carver."

"Back when Joe and I were discussing annexation plans, he told me a little about you and his time with the Navy SEALS."

"Why would I ever be a subject he discussed with you?"

She smiled softly. "We were talking about his time with the SEALS. I was asking him to consider becoming our police chief since he has such a depth of experience. He said he had a better candidate for the job, and named you."

That didn't sound believable at all. It sounded like she made it up on the spot. Joe knew Carver didn't have any interest in law enforcement. It was a hard, thankless job even in the best of circumstances.

It was too similar to military life for his tastes. He'd told Joe that once he was out, all he wanted was a beach, minimal work, and relaxation.

Carver didn't call out the lie. Herrada had taken a look at him and thought she'd stroke his ego. The next thing she'd do was offer him the job. He simply nodded. "Yeah, I can imagine Joe saying that."

"Our chief is retiring soon. It would be amazing to have someone of your caliber taking his place." Herrada stepped closer. She put a hand on his arm. Squeezed gently. Looked up at him with her big brown eyes. "We need someone with your skills leading our law enforcement. The compensation and benefits package is excellent."

She was a beautiful woman. She exuded confidence and charisma. It was no wonder she'd been elected. It was no wonder that she still had a following despite abusing her power. She'd make for the perfect psyops operator.

Then again, there wasn't much of a difference between politicians and psyops operators. That was why she was doing just fine despite her borderline criminal antics.

Carver returned a smile. "That's a hard offer to turn down. Maybe we can discuss it over dinner."

Her smile turned warmer. She rubbed his arm. "I'd like that a lot. Maybe you can tell me some fun stories about your time with Joe over a glass of wine."

"Sounds great." Carver knew he couldn't do anything about Andrea's situation.

Andrea had used herself as bait. She'd wanted Carver here to see what the mayor's reaction would be. Within a few minutes, he knew all he needed to know about the mayor. She was smart and manipulative. She knew how to talk to people. How to turn a losing situation into a winning one.

She could do anything she wanted in this town, and no one would stop her.

The mayor hadn't even been at the festival. Someone must have told her what Andrea was doing. She'd arranged for a busload of her supporters to come here to counterprotest in a short amount of time.

Then she'd come here, nipped things in the bud, and sent Andrea to jail for the night. It was masterful work. Carver could appreciate that. He could also turn things around on the mayor. Use her tactics against her.

And find out if she had anything to do with Joe's death.

CHAPTER 17

Monty couldn't believe what he was seeing.

The twisted, mangled remains of two cars at the bottom of Devil's Gulch. There was no hairpin curve here. The road was straight. There were reflective markers all along the side of the road.

In fact, no one had died here in his lifetime. At least, not that he knew of. In one night, five people had gone over the side.

Two patrol cars were parked on the opposite side of the road from the drop-off. There was no ambulance. It had already been and left. They hadn't been able to access the gulch. There had been no signs of life to rescue anyway.

Police chief Bart Lynch stood precariously close to the edge, a pair of binoculars up to his eyes. He lowered them and glanced at Monty. He looked older than sixty-five. His skin was wrinkled and covered in age spots. But he was still spry for his age.

He turned to Monty. "I need you to go down there."

"How?"

"I've got Perez bringing quads on a trailer. He'll meet you down the hill." Lynch offered the binoculars to Monty. Pointed downslope. "There's a way into the gulch but it's only accessible by foot or smaller motorized vehicles."

Monty took the binoculars and looked where Lynch was pointing. The bottom of the gulch was littered with boulders and scrubby trees. The sides were steep and rocky. They were less so near the bottom of the slope.

"Why are we here? Isn't this LASD territory?"

Lynch pointed toward the vehicles. "Do you recognize either of those vehicles?"

"It's hard to tell what kind of vehicles they were. Pickups?"

"The tags belong to a white Ford F-150 and a Dodge Durango Hellcat. The Durango was reported stolen from Los Angeles a month ago. The pickup belongs to Hugo Alvarez."

Monty recognized the name. "He's in a local gang, right?"

"Abuela's Boys," Lynch said. "Both vehicles came out of El Fuerte and ended up at the bottom of the gulch. I spoke to the mayor. It's a local problem and she wants it taken care of by our people."

"And Lucas just agreed to that?" Monty examined the skid marks on the road. He took pictures of the guard rail and figured out that the pickup had rammed through one area while the Durango had gone through the already broken section.

"What do you think?"

Monty nodded. Of course he'd agreed. Whenever it came to issues of jurisdiction, he'd do whatever the mayor wanted. Even though she technically had no authority over him whatsoever.

"Lucas tells me you were giving him some guff about the Donnely situation." Lynch took his binoculars back and looked at the cars. "He says you were commiserating with that newcomer, Carver."

"Carver and Joe were friends. They served together in the Navy." Monty shrugged. "He was coming to visit his friend only to find out he'd been killed that same morning. I was just trying to smooth things out."

Lynch lowered the binoculars. He studied Monty for a moment. "That better be all it is. I'm retiring this year and I expect you to toe the line until I'm gone. The last thing I need is you raising Cain like you did in the Fuentes case."

"That little girl's death wasn't an accident." Monty felt the heat rising in his face. It had been a long time since he'd thought about it. He clenched his fists. "It wasn't an open and shut case."

"That's what I'm talking about." Lynch cleared his throat. Spat over the side of the cliff. "Sometimes you get awfully righteous for a man who drinks on the job, gambles his paychecks away, and turns prostitutes into his confidential informants just so he can get laid."

Monty choked back a retort. "It's over and done. Long in the past. This isn't the same thing. Joe got his face kicked in by a horse and his friend is upset about it. He'll probably stick around to comfort the wife for a few days and move on."

Lynch chuckled darkly. "Comfort how?"

Monty stared at the wrecks below. He thought about what Gloria had told him. Carver had confronted Hugo in the town square. Now Hugo was probably in the white pickup. Probably mangled to hell.

Did Carver have something to do with this? Or were the gangs fighting again?

"Perez is here." Lynch pointed down the road. A patrol truck had pulled to the shoulder at the bottom of the hill. It was pulling a metal trailer with two black and white quad cycles on it.

"Why me?" Monty asked. "Landry isn't back from vacation yet?"

"He's on extended personal leave, not vacation. Besides, it's about time you earned your pay." Lynch nodded at the gulch. "Get your ass down there and tell me what you find."

Monty walked across the road to his patrol car. He saw a black SUV speeding out of town toward them. He got into his car. Made a U-turn. The SUV came to an abrupt stop in the middle of the road and nearly hit him.

The driver stared at him coldly. Monty backed out of the way and the SUV drove past and to the chief's car. He finished his turn and started downhill. He looked in his rearview mirror and saw the driver open the back door of the SUV.

The chief walked around and climbed inside. The driver closed the door. The mayor had leased four identical SUVs for the city. Some people had raised a stink about them because they found out the lease prices were nearly a hundred and fifty grand per vehicle.

It was also no coincidence that the dealership was owned by the husband of a city council member. Those people were making serious bank through their elected positions. Monty was sure the chief wasn't hurting either.

Most of the police force had gotten hefty raises. At least those that signed the loyalty pledges to the mayor. Those that refused had been let go. Monty had signed on, of course, but he'd burned all his bridges during the Fuentes case.

His raise had been stripped. He hadn't been fired, but he'd been relegated to the backlines. They knew about his gambling and drinking. They knew he was no model citizen or cop. So, they probably decided it was best to let a known quantity fill up a slot rather than risk bringing in someone new.

Thinking of the Fuentes case made his face turn hot. He shook it off and kept driving downhill. He parked across the road from the patrol truck. Perez had already unloaded the quads. He frowned at Monty.

Perez voiced what was plain on his face. "Why are you here? Where's Landry?"

"The golden boy is on extended personal leave, so you're stuck with me."

The new quads were painted black and white. They even had sirens and lights built on. The mayor bought her boys all the fun toys to keep them happy. Perez pushed the start buttons on both quads. They thrummed to life.

"You sober enough to drive one?" Perez smirked.

Monty didn't reply. He took the quad on the left. Pressed the accelerator with his thumb. Tested the brakes. It had been a while since he'd been on one of these things. He slipped the gear into reverse.

Backed it up a short distance to clear the trailer. He drove off the shoulder and into the scrub grass. There was a five-foot drop that looked precarious even for the quad.

Perez got on one. Put on a helmet. He gunned the quad. Spun it in a circle. He straightened up and sped off the road and straight at the drop. The quad flew over the edge. Landed easily down below on its suspension.

Monty couldn't bring himself to do the same. He eased diagonally down the slope. The quad almost flipped, but he leaned hard left to keep it upright and managed to reach the bottom without dying.

Perez shook his head. He said something, but the helmet muffled his words. He spun his quad ninety degrees and headed into the gulch, dodging around rocks and boulders. Monty followed him at a slower pace.

The gulch floor was treacherous. Lots of big rocks. Lots of scrub brush. Lots of tight spaces. Perez navigated a path that took them fifteen minutes to reach the wrecks. He turned off his quad. Pulled off his helmet.

Perez went to the mangled remains of the pickup and glanced inside. He looked away. Shivered. "That's gotta be Hugo. He's too big to be anyone else." He started walking toward the Durango.

Monty looked inside the pickup. There wasn't much left of the passenger compartment. It was crushed on all sides. It looked like it had landed upside down and somehow rolled onto the side before landing back on its wheels.

He walked to the other side. Hugo's head was turned toward the window. It was bloody and cut from the jagged remains of the dashboard. But it was easy to see the hole in his forehead. The crash hadn't killed him. A bullet had.

He looked up. The boulder the pickup had smashed into blocked the line of sight from the top of the cliff. Only the rear of the pickup was visible to anyone above.

He pulled on his nitrile gloves. The pickup door was hanging on broken hinges. Hugo was leaning sideways into the seatbelt. His lower body was pinned to the seat by the dashboard and the engine.

Monty examined the back of Hugo's head. There was a gaping wound there. Definitely a bullet wound. Had the Durango been pursuing him, or had it been the other way around? None of the glass had survived the impact so there was no way to know if the bullet had entered through the windshield.

He walked to the Durango. It was in even worse condition than the pickup. It looked like a twisted hunk of metal and plastic. Parts trailed all over the gulch floor. A severed arm was on the ground. Bits of flesh. Even a foot.

Perez was looking inside, his lips peeled back in disgust. "There isn't much left of anyone inside. They're all jumbled up in the front of the cab. Probably not wearing seatbelts."

Monty thought back to the guard rail. He looked up at the top of the cliff. He couldn't see the guardrail from here, but he knew where it was. The Durango had traveled a lot further than the pickup.

He looked inside the cab. There were four bodies inside. They were piled in the front of the cab like broken dolls. Blood and viscera were everywhere. One of the men had struck the boulder headfirst. The skull was crushed, and the body was folded up on itself.

They'd need dental records to identify that one. The others had enough features left to possibly identify visually. He took pictures. The forensics team would take samples and do the rest of the crime scene work.

He didn't recognize any of the men. He was pretty sure they were all men. There were guns among the bodies. Three handguns and a couple of rifles. They were covered in blood and bent metal, so it was hard to know the makes and models.

Perez reached into what had been the back of the Durango and pulled out a bent rifle. He chuckled. "Not even the guns survived this wreck."

"Why are you touching that without gloves?"

Perez tossed it back into the wreck. "So, Detective. What do you think happened?" He said it sardonically. Like Monty's title was a joke.

Monty showed him the pictures of the road and guard rail. "High speed chase. Looks like Hugo was chasing them. They shot at him. Hit him in the head. He went off the road without pressing the brakes. They must have lost control and gone over the edge right after that."

"Why in the hell would they be running from a single man?"

"I don't know." Monty showed him the skid marks from the Durango. "Judging from the way the marks angle and the scrapes in the asphalt, I think the front tire blew out. Caused them to go over the edge at close to a hundred and forty miles per hour. Maybe more."

"No wonder there's nothing left." Perez took the phone and scrolled through the pictures. He flipped too far and got a picture of Janine naked on Monty's bed. He smirked. "She doesn't look too bad for a hooker."

"She's not a hooker." Monty snatched his phone back. "The big question about all this is why would Hugo be chasing a car with four armed men? He's the kind of guy who lets his minions do the work for him."

"You know a lot about this guy."

"Because I've tied a lot of investigations back to him and his boys." Monty tucked his phone away. "Not that anything comes of it. The mayor's brother used to run with Abuela's Boys, so they're untouchable."

"Good boy." Perez patted Monty on the cheek hard enough to make it sting. "That's what we like to hear from you."

"You already knew about Hugo."

"Of course I do. They leave us alone and we return the favor. Mayor's orders."

"Exactly." Monty forced a grin. "So, what are our orders with this mess?"

"ID the men in the Durango. Figure out how they're connected to Hugo. We need to know if there's a new gang in town." Perez leaned on the mangled car frame. "Maybe if you do a good job with this, you'll be back in the chief's good graces."

"What makes you think that? I've been on the outs for two years now."

"Call it a hunch," Perez said. "Even with Landry on personal leave, I'm surprised they called you."

Monty was just as surprised. The motel crime scene looked like a domestic argument that had spiraled completely out of control and left three men dead. On any other day, it would've been big news.

But a personal acquaintance of the mayor's had died in a high-speed shootout. Five men were dead. This was going to explode into something big.

And all hell was about to break loose.

CHAPTER 18

Carver had a date with the mayor.

She'd invited him to dinner that night at her home. Then a member of her security team had hustled over. Taken her aside and whispered in her ear. Her eyes had flared. She'd excused herself and been hustled off to the waiting SUV.

The car had screeched out of the parking lot and sped away. It was no mystery where they'd gone. Someone had discovered the cars in Devil's Gulch. The mayor's day was about to get a lot more interesting.

Carver left the town square. He walked across the road to the police department. It was a three-story building designed to match the Spanish fortress look of the town hall. It looked good. The tall black iron fences and gates around the motor pool enhanced the curb appeal.

He walked in the front door. The inside was a departure from the fortress look. It was contemporary with light gray and black hues on the walls and trim. The front desk curved gently outward from one wall to the other.

There was a secure door with a keypad on the left side of the desk. A thick plexiglass window prevented anyone from vaulting over the desk to get inside. A hallway behind the secure door presumably led to offices and the holding cell.

The outline of a large silver police badge was centered behind the desk. It said *El Fuerte Police Department* inside the outline.

A clerk in police uniform looked up from her computer screen and at Carver. "How can I help you?"

"I'm here to see Andrea Donnely."

She raised an eyebrow. "Are you a family member?"

"No. The mayor sent me."

She blinked. "I'll need to see some ID."

"Oh, really?" He leaned his elbows on the counter. "You want to see my ID?"

The clerk gulped. "I'm sorry, I don't recognize you."

"Do you know everyone on her security detail?"

She shook her head. Bit her lip nervously. She looked him up and down and seemed to come to a decision. "Okay. I'll have someone escort you."

"Are you serious?" Carver gave her a dark glare. He took out his phone. "I guess I'll have to call her to get this sorted."

"No, wait!" She hit a button and the magnetic door lock clicked open. "Just come in. I assume you know where you're going."

"Yes, I do." Carver looked at her name badge. "Officer Nichols."

Her face flushed. "I'm sorry. I didn't know you were with the mayor's security team."

He sighed. "I won't mention it to anyone, okay? We're both just doing our jobs, right?"

She managed a smile. "Yeah. Thanks."

"You're welcome." He strolled through the door. Walked down the hallway. He entered an open area that looked like a workroom. There was a copier, tables, and stacks of files. There were two offices on the left with the names Detective Monty Ford and Detective Brent Landry.

There were two more offices on the other side, but they were jammed with filing cabinets and boxes. There was a large room with a whiteboard and rows of chairs inside. Probably the briefing room for daily assignments.

A staircase led to the second floor. There were no signs anywhere to direct him to the holding cell, but he doubted it would be on the second floor. He followed the hallway around a corner and found a desk next to a metal door.

There was a computer tablet on the desk. He tapped it and the screen turned on, revealing a sign-in sheet. There were three names on the sheet. Carver didn't recognize any of them.

The computer monitor was tied into the cameras in the holding rooms and the hallway. He saw Andrea sitting in the first cell. The other cell cameras were off, presumably because they had no occupants.

He disabled the hallway camera and Andrea's cell camera with a few clicks of the mouse button. He didn't want there to be a recording of him talking to her.

He pressed the green button next to the door. The magnet hummed and the door clicked open. He pulled it open. There was a wide hallway on the other side.

There were six doors on each side. Windows next to each of the doors. There was no door handle inside. No button to release the lock either. Carver took the chair from the desk. It wasn't heavy enough to prop the door open, so he put it between the door and the jamb.

He looked into the first window. The glass was an inch thick with thick metal mesh reinforcing it. There was an intercom speaker next to the window. He saw Andrea lying on the bed inside, staring blankly at the concrete ceiling.

Carver pressed the intercom button. "Andrea, can you hear me?"

She flinched. Sat up and stared. "They let you in here?"

"Kind of." He motioned her over. "What were you thinking?"

She walked to the glass. Stared at him for a few seconds before answering. "It wasn't a stunt, Carver. I'm really running for mayor. I signed a lease on an apartment this morning and will be moving in so I can meet the thirty-day minimum for residency."

"I wish you would have told me."

"Why would I tell you, Carver?" She shook her head. "You're Joe's friend. You and I barely know each other."

"Yes, but I'm—"

"What? Protecting me? Looking after me?" She laughed. "I'm picking up where Joe left off. I'm doing what needs to be done to fix the damage this mayor has done to the town. I may not have been a SEAL, but I was an attorney. I know my way around the law."

"I'm not sure the law applies in this town."

"It doesn't matter!" Her eyes filled with ferocity. "I'm doing this."

Carver held up his hands in surrender. "I won't do anything to stop you. I will give you some advice. If Joe was murdered, then you're painting a bullseye on your back for whoever did it."

"If someone kills me then it proves that Joe was murdered." She put a hand on the glass. "If that happens, you need to kill whoever did it, Carver. Kill them and put them in the ground for Joe." She glanced up at the camera in her room as if suddenly realizing it was there.

"It's disabled," Carver said.

She blinked. Shook her head. "You're just like Joe. Hyperaware of your surroundings. I just don't know how anyone could have sneaked up on him and killed him."

"I don't either. But I'm looking into things. I might be doing some things you don't like. It's important you don't interfere."

Andrea narrowed her eyes. "What kind of things?"

"I'm having dinner with the mayor."

Her mouth dropped open. "Are you kidding me?"

"No." He put his hand where hers was. Pressed it to the glass. "Just trust me, okay?"

She nodded. "I'm sorry I didn't tell you my plans. Joe respected you, so I should too."

"You're right." Carver shrugged. "We hardly know each other. Just know that I'm going to find out what really happened. And if anyone gets in my way, they won't be there for long."

Fresh tears trickled down her cheeks. "Thank you, Carver."

He backed away from the window. "It's best if you don't mention this visit."

"I won't."

Carver left. He put the desk chair back where it had been and enabled the camera in the hallway and Andrea's cell. He wasn't ready to leave the building just yet.

He detoured upstairs and remained on the landing so he could peek around the wall. There was a wide-open room taking up most of the floor. Cubicles. The clicking of keyboards, ringing of phones, and the hum of multiple conversations.

At the back of the room was a large, windowed office. The blinds were closed so he couldn't see inside. There was a name stenciled on the door. *Chief Bartholemew "Bart" Lynch*. Carver wondered why people did that. Why put your full name and your nickname in quotes? Why not just put the name you go by?

It was one thing if he went by Bartholemew "The Hammer" Lynch. But Bart was a common shortening of Bartholemew. And in any case, it didn't matter.

What mattered was the other room taking up even more real estate than the chief's office. The Operations room. It was windowed too. It didn't have blinds, so he could see everything inside of it.

There were four desks. Four chairs. Four people. There were several giant screens on the wall. Four columns by three rows. One column for each person in the room. Each screen was at least eighty-five inches. Each screen was divided into four images.

It was clear from the cars driving under the cameras that they were the ones attached to the traffic lights. Other cameras were on side roads. It looked like the entire area around the town square was monitored.

A red square appeared around a car as it drove through an intersection. The woman at the desk in front of that column of monitors, clicked the image and pulled it up on the large monitor on her desk.

She must have clicked to track the vehicle because the image changed every few seconds to a different camera with the car centered on the screen. The car entered a parking garage across the road from the town square.

Cameras inside the structure followed its progress. It parked. The camera zoomed in and focused on the occupant. A middle-aged Asian woman stepped out of the car. She picked up a briefcase and turned for the garage exit.

Carver saw a familiar vehicle on the monitor of the neighboring desk. A red square was around the vehicle. That vehicle was Joe's truck.

He used his phone to snap several pictures. There was a server rack in the corner. Probably private storage for the footage they kept. These people were watching everything that happened in town.

There were eight cubicles in the office. He saw the tops of heads in six of them. Two weren't occupied. He couldn't tell if there was any equipment in them or if the people just happened to be out.

From what he could tell, they were clerks, not police officers or detectives. This seemed to be an administrative level. Carver was about to leave when a door opened in the back wall of the operations room.

A man in a dark suit emerged. The door swung shut behind him. He walked to the woman who'd been watching the approaching car and spoke with her. The man was Latino. He was tall, with dark hair, bronzed skin, and a neatly trimmed beard.

He typed on the woman's keyboard. Said something to her. Went to the back wall and tapped on it. Carver zoomed in with his phone. The image was a little grainy, but he could barely make out a keypad recessed in the wall.

The keypad didn't light up. It was almost camouflaged against the wall. The man tapped in four digits. He didn't even try to cover up the keypad while he did it. He pushed the wall. The door opened, and he went inside. That was interesting.

A red square marked another car on another monitor. Carver recognized the compact SUV at once. It was Gloria's red Toyota. Given what he knew about the woman's history with the mayor, it was no surprise that she was being watched.

A woman rose from a cubicle. She pulled off a headset and started walking toward the stairs. Carver quickly made his way down. He took a left. Walked back through the secure door, past the reception desk and through the lobby.

The receptionist glanced at him, and quickly looked back down when he looked at her. He exited the building and stepped outside.

Carver checked his messages. Still nothing from Doctor Palmer. The results might not be back today. That was okay. He had other leads to chase.

The first one was the veterinarian. A phone call would probably suffice, but that was no way to conduct an investigation. There was a reason cops went to homes, knocked on doors, and questioned people face to face.

It was the same reason you didn't phone in an interrogation. The investigator needed to see body language. See if the person's skin flushed or paled. See if their eyes twitched or their nostrils flared. They needed to hear the person's voice.

The veterinarian probably had nothing to do with any of this. She might also be at the center of everything. The sperm of Joe's prized stallions might be a reason for his death. Maybe someone wanted to buy some, and he refused.

Maybe someone wanted to take sperm directly from the source. Maybe they'd met with Joe to discuss it. Joe declined the offer, and someone killed him for it.

Carver's gut feeling told him the chances were slim, but it was a thread that needed to be accounted for and he wasn't going to ignore it. People had killed for less.

He got in the pickup and put the address in the maps app on his phone. He drove in the opposite direction. Cut through a residential area with no cameras. After meandering through the backstreets for a while without spotting a tail, he started following the blue line on the map, altering course to avoid cameras until he was out of town.

It was a twenty-minute drive to Equine Veterinary Services. It sat on a large plot of land. The building was shaped like a barn. There was a normal front door and several rollup doors. Probably so people could back horse trailers inside.

Carver went in the normal door. A man at the front desk greeted him when he entered. "Welcome to Equine Veterinary Services. How can I help you?"

"I'm here to speak to Beth Gatti. I'm with Joe Donnelly."

He blinked a few times. "Are Ron and Angel no longer helping him?"

"I'm not a helper. I'm a personal friend of Joe's."

His eyes brightened in understanding. "Ah, okay. Did you have an appointment?"

Carver shook his head. "It's an important personal matter that can't wait. Can you see if she's available?"

He pressed his lips together. Like he was making a decision. He nodded. "Okay. I'll ask her." He left through the door behind the desk.

Carver sat down and waited. He'd barge through the door if he had to, but it was best to see if this worked first.

The receptionist returned a few minutes later. "She'll see you. Just go through the door, take a right, and walk all the way until you enter the stable."

"Thanks." Carver followed his instructions. There were only a few offices in the hallway behind reception. He took a right at the junction and went through double doors and into the stable.

The stable looked similar to Joe's. Except there were some stalls with large medical equipment inside. There were large padded platforms with wheels that looked big enough for horses to lie on.

There was a wide-open area in the middle of the stable. A woman in green scrubs was leading a gray horse in circles. She was walking backwards. Paying careful attention to the horse's legs. She stopped. Ran a hand along the horse's front left leg and nodded.

Another woman in blue scrubs took the reins and led the horse over to another stall. The woman in green pursed her lips and looked at Carver. She walked up to him. Held out her hand. "I'm Beth."

He shook her hand firmly. "I'm Carver. A friend of Joe's."

She released his hand. "I'm a little busy today, Mr. Carver."

"Just Carver."

She nodded. "How can I help you, Carver?"

He didn't preface the next sentence at all. Just laid it out plain and bare to see her reaction. "Joe is dead."

Beth's mouth hung open for a few ticks before she gasped and put a hand over her lips. "What?"

"Sunshine kicked him twice in the head. Killed him."

She gasped again. Shook her head emphatically. "That's impossible! Joe would never—" She blinked. Her face paled. She wobbled on her feet. "I need to sit down."

Carver caught her by the arm. He guided her over to a chair against the wall. She sat down and stared blankly, mouth agape. He let her take all the time she needed. Unless she was an amazing actress, she was genuinely in shock.

Beth swallowed hard. Took a deep breath. "This isn't possible. No one with Joe's experience would ever get kicked once, much less twice, and even much, much less in the head!"

"So I've heard. But the imprints on his head looked exactly like a horseshoe."

"My God." She shuddered. "The imprints match the size and shape of Sunshine's shoes? His are custom fitted."

"From what I could see, yes. But I'm no expert."

Beth licked her lips. "Why did you come here in person to tell me this?"

"I have some questions."

"You're not a detective? Just a friend of Joe's?"

"We were in the Navy SEALs together. I'm ensuring his death was an accident."

She blinked. "You think I had something to do with it?"

He shook his head. "No. I just want to know if there's a reason someone might kill him. Someone said horse semen might be valuable."

Beth seemed to regain some strength as a familiar subject came up. "Yes, it's extremely valuable. Perhaps more valuable than liquid gold. It's cryo-preserved in high-security straws and kept in a secure facility."

"Did Joe have any horse semen that valuable?"

"Yes, certainly. He produced several amazing racehorses. He sold some of them and retained breeding rights so he could keep their frozen sperm for future generations."

"Did he have any issues with this? Any people who might potentially kill him over something like this?"

She shook her head. "The sperm is kept in secure facilities. While I do offer husbandry services, I don't keep any product on the premises. Joe sent his products to Cryo Systems."

"Maybe someone wanted to buy sperm and he refused to sell it."

Beth shook her head again. "He used my husbandry services as an intermediary, and I know for a fact that he didn't turn down reasonable offers. No one was upset or angry at him for negotiating as far as I know."

This sounded like a dead end, but Carver still thought it was worth the trip. "So, Joe would bring in a horse and ask you to milk it for semen. Then you'd send it off to storage for him?"

She nodded. "He was always here in person to monitor the process. It's required by our insurance and by regulators that a representative be here."

"Did you ever have to operate on his horses?"

"No, but he brought in his best horses for regular checkups and molds."

"Molds?"

"Yes, we take extremely detailed scans of the horse's skeleton, muscles and skin to form a virtual mold. So, if the horse breaks a leg we can reconstruct everything exactly, if possible."

"Don't they usually shoot horses that break their legs?"

She laughed. "Goodness no. Not in this day and age. It's not the wild west here anymore."

"Are these molds valuable?"

"Only to the horse owner and us." Beth spread her hands in a shrug. "I'm sorry. Inasmuch as the cause of Joe's death seems impossible, I just can't think of any reason someone would want to kill him. Maybe it was an accident."

"Joe was a little shorter than me," Carver said. "Can you demonstrate how a horse might be able to kick me in the face?"

She frowned. Looked up at him. Glanced at a horse in a nearby stall. "Sunshine is normal height for a stallion. His legs can rear as high as your face, but—no. She shook her head. "You'd have to bend over directly behind him."

"The first kick would send me flying backwards, right?"

"Most people, yes." She walked around Carver, examining him like he was a horse. "It's possible that Joe was pressed against a wall."

"He was in the middle of the stable. Not even close to a wall."

She tapped a finger on her chin. "If Joe somehow ended up behind the horse and bent over just right, it's possible. Maybe the first kick wasn't as hard as the second."

Carver grunted. "Even a love tap from a steel horseshoe would knock me on my ass."

"Sunshine is still a bit wild. He could have started bucking and twisted around so Joe was in a vulnerable position. But even so, a single kick would knock a person back."

"So, a second kick would hit nothing but air."

"Yes." She nodded. "Nothing but air."

"Thanks for your time." Carver headed out.

"Wait." Beth caught up to him. "How is Andrea?"

"Not well. Did she come here with him often?"

"They usually came together. He always had his arm around her shoulder or hip. They were, I don't know, inseparable. It was honestly quite beautiful to see a couple so in love."

Carver didn't have a response to that. "Thanks again for your help." He thought of something else. "Did Joe ever bring a wounded horse here in his pickup truck? Or maybe a dead one?"

Beth flinched, like the question was totally unexpected. "He only brought horses here the right way—in a trailer."

"Understood." Carver left the stable and exited the building. He climbed in the Ram and sat there for a few minutes. There was a notification on his phone. It was a text from Doctor Palmer. The blood results were in.

His blood was clean. No sign of drugs except traces of caffeine. Probably from coffee.

Carver stared at the message. Now he really was out of ideas. Maybe Joe's death was just an accident. Maybe he hadn't been murdered by one of the mayor's people.

Maybe it was time to mourn his friend and move on.

CHAPTER 19

Monty watched the CSI team.

They were wearing their bubble suits, as everyone jokingly called them. The coveralls covered them from head to ankle. Nitrile gloves protected the hands. Most of them wore regular shoes and put covers over them.

Some wore regular surgical facemasks and safety glasses. One had a protective plastic faceplate to protect against splashing bodily fluids. None of them wanted to be potentially exposed to infected blood.

"God what a damned mess." Perez circled the wrecks like a vulture. "You think they got cash in one of those cars? I should've checked."

"You think CSI will pocket anything they find?"

He nodded. "I know I would. You still got to give the chief his cut, but money is money."

"Yeah." Monty doubted there was a hoard of cash in either vehicle. Maybe a few hundred dollars in wallets, but that was about it.

There wasn't anything else he could do at the scene, and he had a lot of paperwork to fill out for the motel. He climbed back on his quad and headed back to the shallow end of the gulch. It had once been a river that had long since dried up and disappeared.

Droughts were common in this arid region. But when there was rainfall, the water would rush down the mountains through the gulch. One time the rainfall had been so heavy that the gulch became a viable river again for a short time.

The water level rose and took out a bridge. Boulders rolled down the mountain and blocked the highway for days until the county sent heavy equipment to break up the rocks and push them into the gulch.

Monty drove past the place he'd used to enter the gulch. He found an easier incline and got the quad up it without tipping over. His hands were shaking. Not because of excitement or nerves, but because he hadn't taken his customary morning tequila shots.

He hadn't taken the shots because he'd been too busy to go to the store to replenish his stock. Between Joe's death, the motel murders, and now the gulch, it was looking like another full day of work with no breaks.

Life was raw dogging him hard this week.

He parked the quad next to the trailer. Got in his car and drove up the hill to the chief. The chief was leaning against his car. Arms folded over his chest. A sour look on his pockmarked face. The mayor's SUV had left fifteen minutes ago, and he'd been up here alone ever since.

Chief Lynch turned his head toward Monty. "Of all the damned weeks for this to happen, it had to be now."

He didn't have to say exactly what he meant for Monty to understand. Lynch was stuck with his worst detective. His beloved golden boy was probably basking in the sun on a beach somewhere.

"I've got a working theory."

Lynch raised an eyebrow. "Let's hear it."

"It was a high-speed chase. Hugo was pursuing them."

"I'm going to stop you right there," Lynch said. "In what universe are four armed men in a Durango running from a single guy in a pickup?"

"Right now, it's the only thing that makes sense." Monty wished he'd kept the theory to himself. "Hugo was shot in the head. Probably by one of the guys in the Durango. The front left tire of the Durango blew out. The driver lost control. Everyone went over the cliff."

"That's got to be the dumbest theory I ever heard."

Monty really wished he had some tequila. He plucked another theory out of thin air. "The other possibility is that Hugo and the men in the Durango were pursuing someone else. At least two people in another car. One of them shot Hugo and hit him in the head. He went off the cliff. They shot at the Durango and blew out the front tire and sent it over the edge too."

Lynch nodded. "Sounds a lot more plausible to me. Any evidence of this mystery car?"

Monty shook his head. "I only see two sets of skid marks. It's possible the mystery car was fast enough to get up here a few seconds ahead of Hugo. Shooting accurately while in a moving vehicle is difficult. It's possible they had time to get up here and line up good shots."

"Agreed. Maybe an ambush?"

Monty shook his head. "If it was an ambush, the vehicles probably wouldn't have been traveling at such high speeds."

"Well, well, well." Lynch pulled a pack of cigarettes from his shirt pocket. "That's a better theory than I would have expected from a drunk." He slipped a cigarette in his mouth. Tucked the pack back in his shirt pocket. "The mayor says this case is a top priority."

"What about the Blue Star Motel?"

"It's on the backburner." Lynch lit the cigarette and took a long draw. "What happened there, anyway?"

"Looks like two people were staying in room thirty, the unit at the far end of the motel. They got into an altercation with the guest in room thirteen." He couldn't remember the names, so he pulled out his notepad. "Bruce Joyner in room thirteen tried to kick down the door to room thirty. He failed and used a rock to smash the window. The unknown Hispanic male in room thirty—I'm calling him Juan Doe—came out with a gun. Chased Joyner back to his room. Put him face down on the bed. Put a pillow between the gun and Joyner's head and shot him."

Lynch's eyebrows arched. "Jesus H. Christ."

"Yeah." Monty kept reading. "Phil Smith, the owner, came out with his three fifty-seven magnum revolver and put a bullet between Juan's eyes. Juan's unknown companion chased him back to the management office. Shots were exchanged and Phil took one in the head."

"Hard to believe they're such good aims." Lynch pulled a flask from inside his car and took a draw. "Headshots all around. Especially with a three fifty-seven. Long barrel or short?"

"Long. Probably eight inches."

"Must've been a close-range shot."

"Probably just a couple of feet if I had to guess."

Lynch nodded. Took another draw from his flask. His face flushed. "I don't know if CSI will have time to visit the scene. Might just have to clean it up and run with your version."

"I'd like to ID Juan."

"Did he have anything on him?"

"A wallet with cash. No ID, no car keys."

"I'm starting to wonder if we've got a new gang trying to force their way into town."

Monty shrugged. "I don't know. There's not much else I can do until CSI files a report."

"There's plenty you can do." Lynch blew a cloud of smoke. He got in Monty's face. "Get a couple of our boys and canvass the area. Maybe someone saw something last night."

"Yes, sir." Monty turned on his heel and got in his car. He knew of a couple of places to look. He'd start there before involving anyone else. He drove back into town. Stopped outside Eduardo's. It was a popular bar for the locals on this side of town.

It was already open for business. The lunch crowd was inside. Most were sitting in booths and at tables. He went to the bar.

A skinny old Hispanic man spoke in Spanish.

Monty sighed. "You speak English?"

"Si."

"That's still Spanish." Monty tapped the counter. "Two shots of silver tequila."

The bartender understood that. He poured two shots. Drank one. "Gracias."

"That wasn't for you!" Monty downed his shot. It burned a line straight down to his stomach. The effects were almost immediate. His hands stopped shaking and calm returned. He turned his focus to the bartender. "Was Hugo here last night?"

The man nodded. "Si."

"What time?"

The bartender waggled his hand. "Not sure."

Monty put cash on the counter. "Two more shots, please."

The bartender grinned. Poured the shots. He held one in a toast. Monty clinked his glass against the other and they downed the shots.

The bartender spoke with a heavy accent. "Around ten. He stayed for about two hours. He was texting someone before he left."

"Any idea who?"

The bartender shrugged.

Monty slapped more cash on the counter. "Two more shots?"

The bartender took the cash. Poured a single shot and put it in front of Monty. "Sabrina Diaz. She doesn't like him, but he pays her bills."

Monty downed the shot and showed the man his empty wallet. "I'm out of cash, but I have two more questions."

The bartender nodded. "I'll put on your tab."

"Please do." Monty looked around to see if anyone else was taking an interest in the conversation. No one was even looking at him. "Was Hugo here with anyone else?"

"No."

"Do you know where Sabrina lives?"

The bartender took out a metal filing box. He took out a manila folder and a pen. Handed it to Monty. "Put your name on the folder tab. Put your name and address on the paper inside."

"Jesus, you were serious about putting it on my tab." Monty pulled his badge from another pocket. "You understand that you have to answer my questions, right?"

"Put your name on the tab." He pushed the pen toward Monty.

"Mother effing—" Monty put his name on the tab. The paper inside was gridded like accounting sheets. He put his name and address on it, then pushed it across the counter.

The man put in the date and dollar amounts.

"A hundred dollars?" Monty gritted his teeth. "Look, the mayor put this investigation as the highest priority."

The bartender flinched like he'd been struck. His grin vanished. He wadded up the paper. Tossed it and the folder in the trash. He poured another shot and pushed it across to Monty. "I'm sorry. You should have led with that."

"Next time I will." Monty tossed back the shot. "Sabrina's address, please."

The bartender pulled a folder from his metal box. He pulled out a sheet. Copied the address to a napkin and pushed to Monty. "I've heard she'll do anything for money."

"Now I'm getting free shots and advice?" Monty stared him down. "Something bad happened. The mayor is pissed and on the warpath. I have to find out who did the bad thing before this spirals out of control."

"I understand."

"Good. How about you give me back the money for the shots?"

"Señor, I'm scared of the mayor, but not that scared. There's an ATM down the road if you need money."

Monty took the napkin. "It was worth a try." He looked around. "Did anyone else talk to Hugo last night?"

The bartender shook his head. "No. He watched TV and looked at his phone a lot."

"Did you see his texts?"

"Not really. I saw something about a blue star, I think. Maybe it's a new drug? Who knows with people like him?"

Monty stiffened. "As in the Blue Star Motel?"

The other man furrowed his brow. Put a hand on his chin. "I don't know. All I saw was blue star. Nothing about a motel."

"That's very helpful. Thanks." Monty hurried out. The Blue Star might be connected to the dead men in the gulch. But how?

He checked Sabrina's address. It wasn't too far. He wondered if the bartender was right. Would she do anything for money? It sounded like Hugo gave her money and she probably gave him other things.

Monty was feeling good. Nothing like a few shots of tequila to brighten his day. He drove through the neighborhood. The houses were old and shabby. The yards were full of old rusting cars and kids' toys.

It was a poor area filled with Hispanics and a handful of Asians. Probably ninety percent of local crime happened here. Chief Lynch had shown everyone a crime map of the city a few months back. There were dots on the map indicating reported crimes. This area was filled with them.

He called the station. Dialed the extension for traffic control. Rudy Daniels answered the phone. "Hey this is Monty. I need camera records pulled for midnight all the way to four AM. I have descriptions of the vehicles in question."

"I've already been going over them. Chief Lynch wanted the recordings reviewed. We had the Durango on the east side of town at eleven thirty-three PM. Nothing else after that. The white pickup wasn't recorded either."

"You checked with the usual private camera owners?"

"Yep. They submitted footage too. Caracas Bank had footage of the Durango on the east side at roughly the same time as the other footage."

"No signs of them chasing another car?"

"Nope. They were driving normally."

"Thanks." Monty ended the call. There were cameras all over town. It was hard to avoid them unless you wanted to. He knew where most of them were and avoided them whenever possible. He didn't like the traffic department having records of him.

It was possible Hugo avoided them as well. Which meant there'd be no footage of what happened last night. It would be another dead end.

He thought about Sabrina again. Wondered if she was good looking. Wondered if she'd really do anything for money. He decided to find out. There was a small neighborhood convenience store down at the corner.

Just a few miles down was the old, abandoned gas station and mechanic shop. Past that was the mountain and Devil's Gulch. He stopped at the store. There was an ATM in the back. He put in his card and punched in two hundred. Changed his mind and put in three hundred. He might go to the track later.

The money came out. He put it in his wallet. He was walking out when he saw a security camera. It was inside but pointed at the window. He followed its line of sight. It was looking at the road.

He went to the cashier. "Do you save the camera footage?"

The girl nodded. "Yeah."

"I need to see it." He flashed his badge.

She didn't seem to care. "Okay." The store was empty, so she led him to the back room. There was a monitor hooked up to an old computer. A keyboard and mousepad on the table. She sat down and moved the mouse.

The screen flicked on. There were four images on the computer. One from a camera in the back corner of the store looking out toward the front. A camera looking out from the front corner. A camera behind the cashier. And most importantly, a camera looking out at the parking lot and the street.

"I'd like to see footage from that one." He pointed to the parking lot camera.

She minimized the camera screens. Opened a folder on the desktop and browsed to one named *Parking Lot Cam*. She opened the folder and scrolled down a long list of files, stopping when she reached yesterday's date and a timestamp of eleven PM.

"Just double click the files to play them." She stood.

"Do the cameras trigger on motion or are they always recording?"

"They're always on but only record motion." She raised an eyebrow. "Anything else?"

"No, thanks." He sat down. Played the clips one by one. The ones around eleven PM were longer. Cars passed by on the road every few seconds. None of them were the white pickup or Durango.

Monty kept looking. It was at 1:33 in the morning that he saw the white pickup. There was one person inside. All he could see was the outline. No face. No identifying features. But the figure was big enough to be Hugo.

The truck drove past at a normal pace. The next two videos were other cars. One was an old Buick. The other was an old truck. The video file at 2:12 AM was a different story. A large black pickup sped past. Right behind it was the Durango.

"Bingo!" Monty pumped a fist. He restarted the clip. Slowed it down when the black pickup shot past. It was going fast, making the truck a blur. But it looked like a Dodge Ram. A nice one. The front end was sporty. It was probably a TRX.

There was a single figure inside. The silhouette was as big as Hugo. Had he switched to another truck? That didn't add up.

Monty continued playback at half speed. The Durango sped into view seconds later. Four figures inside. One of them was leaning out of the window, a rifle in hand.

"That doesn't make sense." Monty thought it over. Had Hugo switched to the white pickup later? There was no way he would have had time. The Durango was just seconds behind and traveling faster than the Ram.

Monty played the last clip of the night. The black Dodge Ram passed by going back into town. There was just enough light from a streetlamp to see the driver. Not enough for a positive ID, but enough for him to see that it wasn't Hugo.

He saw the arm. It was thick and muscular. He remembered where he'd seen the truck before. And he knew exactly who it was.

Carver.

CHAPTER 20

Carver wasn't going anywhere.

Maybe Joe had been killed in a freak accident. Maybe someone had held him down and made the horse stomp in his face. Neither seemed likely. He couldn't even visualize it.

Joe was hyper vigilant. It would be hard to take him by surprise. It was obvious he'd been alerted by something. He'd even patrolled the perimeter with his rifle before returning to the stable.

Maybe the horse had gone crazier than usual and that made it easy for someone to get the drop on Joe. It didn't seem likely, but it was a possibility. It occurred to Carver that he didn't know much about the horse in question.

Andrea had told him a little about Sunshine. Just that he was almost broken. Almost trained. That didn't mean anything to Carver. Did it mean the horse might buck and kick or was it past that?

There was one way to find out. There was no camera footage from the day of Joe's death but there was plenty of footage from before then. Maybe he could see how Sunshine behaved from the stable camera.

He was already driving back to the ranch. Since the blood results came back clean, he hadn't known what else to do. Reviewing the camera footage was something, at least. There was also the matter of the watcher.

It just didn't make sense to have someone watching the ranch. Especially now that Joe was dead. Why bother? It only reinforced Carver's suspicions that there was more to Joe's death than an accident.

He backed the truck into the garage. Went inside to Joe's office. Turned on the laptop. He looked through the apps. Looked through the documents folders. There was one labeled *Sunshine*.

Carver opened it and was presented with a list of video files. He started with the first one from several months ago. Joe's old pickup was parked in front of the stable. The trailer was hitched up to it.

Joe was in frame. He was leading a sleek black horse into trailer. He went inside and came out a moment later. He closed the rear gate. "Mayhem is good to go."

"Are you excited, babe?" It was Andrea's voice.

Joe grinned. "Like a kid in a toy store." He waved her over. "Let's go."

The camera moved toward him. It reversed to show Andrea and Joe. He had his arm around her. He was looking at her. Grinning like an idiot. He kissed her cheek. She kissed him. The video ended.

Carver dropped into the chair and shook his head. He'd seen glimpses of that Joe the last time he'd visited. It had been a night and day difference from the Joe he'd known pre-Andrea. And it was nice. Real nice.

That was happiness. Real happiness. Probably the rarest thing on Earth.

He cleared his throat. Went to the next file. Andrea was recording Joe as they rode horses across a grassy plain. A horse stood atop a hill in the distance, the rising sun casting him in silhouette.

It looked magnificent. Like something you'd see in a movie. Except the horse didn't rear up on its hind legs and whinny.

Joe whistled. "Damn, he's spectacular. Look at the way the light glints off that dirty coat of his."

"He's a sight all right." The camera shifted to another man on horseback. "I think we'll have an easier time catching him with the tranquilizer gun."

Joe shook his head. "Where's the challenge in that?"

The man laughed. "Have it your way."

Joe was on the black horse he'd put on his trailer. "Mayhem loves a challenge."

"Yeah? Well, Nugget will give her one."

Joe groaned. "I hate that name."

The man snorted. "Well, he's your horse now. You name him what you want."

The camera panned back to the horse on the hill. "Sunshine," Andrea said.

Joe looked at her and grinned. "I love it."

They reached the base of the hill. Sunshine stood at the top, staring down at them like a king to his subjects.

"Bill, can you circle around back?" Joe said. "We can drive him back toward the reliable fenced area. Give him a little less room to run."

"You got it." Bill clicked his tongue, and his horse began trotting around the base of the hill.

Joe strapped a bodycam around the top of his cowboy hat. He looked at his phone. It displayed the video feed. "This is going to be fun."

"I can't wait to see my cowboy in action."

Joe chuckled. "Never thought I'd go from a SEAL to a cowboy, but here we are."

"From an ocean dweller to a land lubber." She laughed. "Go get 'em hot stuff."

The video ended. The next video picked up moments later. This one was from Joe's bodycam. He was chasing Sunshine, a lasso in his right hand. He spun it around. Tossed it. Barely missed the stallion's neck.

Sunshine looked like he was just trotting. Every time Joe made a throw with the rope, he accelerated out of reach. He turned sharp left. Bill was there, trying to keep him from changing direction.

Sunshine trotted right past him. He wasn't intimidated by a person on a horse. He wasn't letting them herd him.

Carver skipped through sections of the video. It went on for an hour before Joe finally got a rope around Sunshine's neck. The stallion stopped running. He turned and watched Joe. Joe wrapped the rope around his saddle horn.

He was laughing. "Man, I haven't had that much fun in, I don't know—years."

Bill was sagging in his saddle. "Fun? I'm all tuckered out."

Andrea came into frame, delight plain on her face. "That was amazing."

"You haven't even gotten him in the trailer yet," Bill said. "Believe me, it's not over yet."

The video ended. The next one was recorded from Andrea's phone.

Joe got off his horse.

"Careful, baby," Andrea said.

Joe walked up to Sunshine. The horse whickered. Tossed his head. Joe held his hands in front of him. He touched Sunshine's neck. The horse tried to nip him. Joe blocked the attempt with a hand.

He patted down Sunshine's neck. Down to his back. The horse nipped again. Tossed his head. He turned in place, like he was trying to knock Joe out of the way.

"He's got a lot of energy left," Joe said. "I've never seen a horse this fast with this much endurance." He patted Sunshine's haunch. The horse whickered in annoyance and tried to turn, but the rope kept him from rotating too far.

"Careful babe," Andrea said.

Joe gripped the mane. The horse was tall. He somehow vaulted himself up onto Sunshine's back. The stallion reacted instantly. Bucking and twisting. The only thing preventing him from spinning in circles was the rope.

"Baby, you're crazy!" Andrea shouted.

Joe held tight to the mane. His legs gripped the horse's sides. Bill watched with a stunned look. Like he couldn't believe what this madman was doing.

Carver grinned. Joe was a patient man. But when he felt it was time to act, he did it without hesitation. The man was cautious but fearless when the time was right. That was what made him a good squad leader.

But Sunshine was a little too much for even Joe to handle. He slid off and rolled out of the way. Dusted himself off and walked away.

He grinned at Andrea. "Not too bad for an old man."

"Baby, you're not old. Forty-nine is young."

Bill gave her a doubtful look. "I'm only thirty-five and there's no way in hell I'm jumping on a wild stallion."

Sunshine calmed down. His sides were heaving. He stared at Joe with his dark eyes, like he was plotting revenge.

"Well, I think he's finally tired." Joe climbed back on Mayhem. "Let's try to lead him."

He guided his horse forward. The rope pulled taut on Sunshine. At first, the stallion glared defiantly at him. Tried to pull back. But he was too tired. He gave in started following.

"Damn." Bill whistled. "You sure you haven't been wrangling horses all your life?"

"Just for a few years now." Joe shrugged. "I never in a million years thought it'd be something I'd want to do."

"Well, you're a natural. And Nugget—erm—Sunshine is an impressive horse. Wish I had the money to indulge in breeding, but it takes a lot of money."

"So, I've discovered." Joe glanced back at Sunshine. "He's not much of a kicker, is he?"

"You noticed that too?" Bill nodded. "He's a bucker and a twister. Back when me and my boys were trying to break him in the corral, we got behind him a few times when he twisted. I thought for sure someone was going to get kicked, but he never did."

They kept talking about horses on the way back to the trailer. Carver skipped through to the end. He watched more videos. Most of them were of Joe trying to break Sunshine. Most of them were recorded with a camera on a tripod.

Andrea was almost always there cheering him on. Laughing at his mistakes. Nursing his bruises when Sunshine got the better of him. It was fascinating seeing Joe act like this.

He'd been more reserved when Carver saw him, even with Andrea around. It was clear he completely let down his guard with her around. They were so natural around each other.

The more Carver watched, the angrier he became. His friend was dead. He and Andrea had been robbed of something probably more precious than anything else in the world.

And there was something else. Something Bill had told Joe in an earlier video. Something that was proven true in every video Carver watched. Sunshine wasn't a kicker. He bucked, twisted, tossed his head, and would just about flip himself sideways trying to dislodge Joe.

There were multiple instances where Joe got knocked down. Where Sunshine's hindquarters were right next to him. The horse could have stomped him. He could have kicked him. But once Joe was knocked on the ground, Sunshine did what most males would do.

He turned to face his fallen foe. Looked down at him with contempt. His lips would pull back from his big horse teeth and he'd toss his head like he was gloating. Carver didn't know if that was unusual with horses.

Joe looked at Sunshine as a challenge. Sunshine looked at Joe in the same way. They were both trying to break each other. Two dominant males trying to come out on top. It was clear Joe respected Sunshine.

Carver didn't know if horses could respect humans. Maybe they could. Maybe that was what happened when you broke a horse. Either way, it was clear that Sunshine could have seriously injured Joe by stomping him on multiple occasions.

Sunshine never did. He'd just calmly turn to look at his fallen challenger and do that horse smile. Sometimes, he'd even bend over and snort in Joe's face. Joe would laugh and nod. He was keeping score too.

"Sunshine one hundred. Joe zero." Then Joe would get up and do it all over again.

It was like watching two men fighting. After one won, the victor would help him up. They'd shake hands. Then they'd go rest and come back and fight it out again the next day.

There was no way in hell Sunshine killed Joe. Absolutely no way. He had no proof. No idea how it had happened. But he knew a couple of things.

Sunshine was a rare breed. He was a sprinter but with excellent endurance. The two traits didn't often go together, at least from what Joe said in some of the videos.

Carver skimmed through months' worth of videos. Joe was able to actually ride Sunshine around a little before the horse decided enough was enough and bucked him off. Once Joe was off, Sunshine acted like his best friend.

He'd let Joe brush him down. Let him do all the normal horse maintenance stuff. Maybe because he thought Joe was his servant. That probably wasn't far from the truth considering how much work Joe put in to making Sunshine part of the family.

There weren't as many recent videos. Joe probably figured he didn't need to record every single session. In the last three, Joe was able to ride Sunshine all around the ranch without getting bucked off.

Sunshine was still annoyed, as evidenced by his ear flicking and head bobbing. He'd still buck unexpectedly, as if reminding Joe who owned whom. And at the end of the last video, Joe was talking to Andrea.

He was grinning like a kid at Christmas. "I rode him for a mile today. I think it's time to take him out for a longer ride."

"I'm so proud of you," Andrea said. "You always find a way to do what you want to do."

"I couldn't do any of it without you." They kissed. Hugged. Joe looked at the camera. He grinned and reached over. The video ended.

Carver heard a door open and shut. He closed the laptop. Eased to the office door, the Glock ready.

Keys clinked on a countertop. A woman sighed. A chair leg scraped against the floor. Carver went into the kitchen and saw Andrea sitting at the table. She was staring blankly at the wall, tears in her eyes.

"I thought they were keeping you overnight," Carver said.

"They cut me loose early. They didn't say why."

Carver sat across from her. He took her hands. Squeezed them. "How are you?"

She blinked. Looked at him as if suddenly realizing he was there. "I feel like a giant knot of pain, Carver. Like I don't know what to do with myself. I'm lost without Joe."

"I watched his training videos. I saw the one where you all caught Sunshine. Bill said he wasn't a kicker. The other videos proved that."

Andrea's eyelids fluttered. She pulled her hands away from Carver and rubbed her eyes. "I'd forgotten about that. I watched Joe train Sunshine. That horse never tried to hurt him. It was like watching two men wrestle every day for dominance. Like they were competitors, not enemies."

"I got the same feeling," Carver said. "Someone killed Joe. My gut tells me I'm right. Nothing I can do will ever make things right. But I can damned well make sure whoever did it suffers."

She wiped tears from her face. "I want whoever did this to suffer, Carver. I want them to feel this pain they caused me."

"I don't think it's possible for them to feel the loss you're feeling." Carver stood. "What you two had was about as real as it gets. I'll do my best to make sure they get a taste of that. I promise."

He walked to the fridge. Looked inside. There were two six-packs of beer inside. Joe had probably bought it just because Carver was coming to visit. He took one. Twisted off the cap and took a draw.

"Andrea, did Joe ever mention anything about people trying to steal horse sperm?"

She shook her head. Smiled. "Joe said most breeders use a secure cryonic facility. Everything is locked down and accounted for, just like money in a bank."

"Joe always hated banks."

Andrea chuckled. "Yeah. He didn't trust anything easily. So, he interviewed several places before making a decision."

"How much sperm does he have stored?"

"I have a list. Most of it is from Mayhem. He also was looking into oocyte cryopreservation."

Carver blinked. "Can you say that again in English?"

"Oocytes are the eggs from mares. Beth told him it was the next big thing a couple of years ago."

"Because high quality sperm is nothing without high quality eggs."

"Exactly." She took out her phone and scrolled down it. "Joe sent me a document about it, but it's been so long that I don't know if I can find it."

"I assume the same facilities that store the sperm can store the eggs?"

"Yes." She stopped looking at her phone. "We talked about it a lot. We talked about anything and everything. I loved seeing him so excited."

"You weren't bored with all the horse talk?"

"Not in a million years, Carver." She sighed. "I love horses. I grew up as a poor farmer's daughter in Mexico. My dad was a hard worker. He did anything he could for his family. But he wasn't a kind man. He was quick to anger, and I can't count the number of times he slapped me or my sisters."

The story sounded familiar to Carver. Not because she'd told him but because people in other countries had similar upbringings. He kept quiet and listened.

"One day he brought home a pony. It was a sick little thing. He said we could use it on the farm." Andrea bit her lower lip and went silent for a moment. "I fell in love with him. I named him Amigo and did everything I could to make him healthy. I gave him vegetables and corn every day."

She blew out a breath. "My dad got so angry when he found out I was giving Amigo our grain. He slapped me so hard I saw stars. He forbid me from touching the horse again. I was devastated because I felt like he was my horse. But every time I tried to get near him, my dad would grab me and slap me. He told me I stole from the family because I gave the horse the grain we could have sold."

Carver sipped his beer and kept listening.

Andrea's face brightened. "Then a lifetime later, I met Joe. I was court-martialing a former SEAL. He was called as a witness. We became acquaintances, and then later, friends. He retired and I left to pursue private law."

"Joe never told me that," Carver said. "He didn't tell me much about how you met."

She laughed. "That's Joe."

Carver nodded. "That's Joe."

Her smile faded. "Then one day, he asked me to come see him. To see what he was building." Her lip quivered. "It was a small stable with two horses."

"Another thing I didn't know about," Carver said.

Andrea nodded silently. "He took me to see his horses on our first date. I started crying and he asked what was wrong. I told him that story about Amigo. He squeezed my hands and told me that even if I didn't want to date him, that I could always come visit his horses and ride them any time. He said I could feed them all the grain I wanted."

Fresh tears formed on her face. "I just knew right then that this was a good man. A kind man." She pressed a hand against her chest. "I felt it in my heart and knew he was the one." She looked miserably at Carver. "I know it sounds silly."

"It's not." Carver sipped his beer. "Your dad worked hard. He was focused on survival by any means. He was strong in some ways, and weak in others. That doesn't make him bad. Doesn't make him good."

"You have a very blunt way of stating things, Carver."

He nodded. "Joe was the same. Where do you think I got it from?"

She laughed. "I should have known."

"Before I met Joe, I didn't say what was on my mind. I figured people wouldn't like what I said. Joe told me that was their problem, not mine."

There was a pounding on the front door. The doorbell rang several times. Carver picked up his Glock and hurried over to a window. He put his back to the wall and looked outside.

"Carver!" It was Monty. "I need to talk to you now."

Carver holstered the gun. He opened the door. Monty didn't waste any time. He took out his phone. Showed Carver a still image. An image of Joe's truck.

An image from last night.

— • —

CHAPTER 21

Carver was caught.

It was him. Monty had him dead to rights. But that didn't mean Carver had to admit anything. "What am I looking at?"

"Don't play dumb." Monty tried to push past him and inside, but Carver was a wall. "Can I come inside?"

"I don't know. Can you?"

"May I?"

"Why?"

"Because I want to talk about last night!"

Carver considered it. Maybe Monty was on his side. Maybe he wasn't. Maybe he wasn't on anyone's side. He seemed like the loner type. No, not a loner. An outcast. Maybe he could be recruited.

Carver stepped to the side. Monty nodded. Walked past. He smelled like tequila and cigarettes.

He nodded at Andrea. "Hello, Mrs. Donnely."

She nodded back. "Detective."

"How much have you had to drink?" Carver asked.

Monty ignored the question. "What happened last night?"

"I went out for drinks. Got back late."

"Yeah? Where did you go?"

"About an hour west of town to a Texan Grille steakhouse. Talked to a bartender named Lisa." Carver had been there two days ago on his way to El Fuerte.

Monty could call and find out it wasn't true. Unless Carver managed to reach Lisa first and ask her to confirm his story. Then he had a fifty-fifty chance she'd play along.

The detective nodded. "Take a look at this and try again." He played a video. Joe's Ram sped past, with the Durango in hot pursuit. It returned via the same route moments later.

Carver had obviously overlooked a camera. This one was looking out through a window at a parking lot. He could only see part of the sign, but it was enough to tell him it was the small convenience store a mile or two from the abandoned mechanic shop.

Monty set his phone on the kitchen counter. Stared at Carver. "Start talking."

"About what?"

Monty played another clip. This one of Hugo's white pickup driving past. "This got me to thinking. What happened to Hugo? How did he end up at the bottom of Devil's Gulch?"

Andrea gasped. "What?"

Monty kept talking. "I drove along the same route. I stopped at the old gas station." He scrolled to another photo. "And I found this."

There was a black stain on the old concrete. It was speckled with little chunks. Hugo's blood and brain matter. Probably some bone fragments too.

"Looks like coyote puke," Carver said.

Monty clenched his fists. "I'd like to see the black Dodge Ram I saw parked in the garage yesterday."

"You have a search warrant?" Carver said.

"You're going to make this difficult, aren't you?"

"I'm not making anything difficult, Detective." Carver put extra emphasis on Monty's title. "I'm cooperating, but that doesn't mean you can perform a search without a warrant."

Monty turned to Andrea. "May I have your permission to see the truck?"

She shook her head. "Not unless you explain why. I don't know what these videos are about."

Monty played the video back to Joe's truck and paused it. "Is that your husband's truck?"

She looked at it. "It's a black Dodge Ram. That could be anyone's truck."

"It's a high-performance model. A TRX. Those are not that common."

"The salesperson told Joe it was the most popular model." Andrea shrugged. "I've seen dozens of them around town."

"Maybe you ought to just come out and tell us what you're trying to accuse us of," Carver said.

"I'm not accusing both of you." Monty looked like a man who'd shown a winning hand only to have it trumped by the last player at the poker table. "Just you!"

"Of what?"

"Of killing a shit load of people last night." He waggled a hand. "Or at least knowing how they died."

"Yeah? Are you going to arrest me?"

Monty stared at him for a moment then shook his head. "No. I already fed the chief a story that makes sense. I think he'll run with it unless I show him this."

"Now, why would you do that?" Carver said. He knew the answer. It went back to his earlier thoughts. Monty was an outcast. He'd seen it in the way Captain Hernandez treated him and talked about him.

Monty didn't reply. He looked down.

Carver asked another question. "Are you on the take, Monty?"

The detective flinched out of his silence. "I was. Well, technically I was never taking cash under the table. But the mayor makes sure that her loyalists are well paid."

"Legal bribery." Carver nodded. "So, what happened to you, Monty?"

"I—I got righteous." He dropped into a chair. Rubbed his cheeks with both hands. "It was just once. And that was enough."

"Righteous?" Carver went to the fridge. "Want a beer?"

Monty shook his head. "You have tequila?"

"Yes." Andrea went to the liquor cabinet. She opened the door and paused. "Silver, reposado, or añejo?"

"Silver, please. Herradura if you have it."

"I do." She got it. Pulled out shot glasses. Salt from the cupboard. A lime from the fruit basket on the counter. She sliced the lime. Set it on the counter. "You want a shot, Carver?"

He shook his head. "Beer is fine."

She poured shots for herself and Monty.

Monty raised his glass. "To Joe."

"To Joe," Andrea said in a shaky voice.

Carver held out his beer bottle. "To Joe."

Monty tossed back the shot. Winced. Drew in a deep breath. "Perfect."

"Start talking," Carver said.

Monty poured another shot. Downed it. Then he started talking. "There was a missing girl case. A Mexican girl from south LA. Ten years old. The Amber alert said she was last seen outside El Fuerte being forced into a black windowless van with a tall roof."

He took another shot. "I found the van on the southeast side. At least it matched the description. I called it in. The chief told me to back off and wait for SWAT. So, I backed off. SWAT never came. Two days later, we found the girl dead inside an abandoned warehouse just half a mile from where I'd seen the van."

Andrea gasped. "Oh, God."

Monty rubbed his eyes. "You could tell she'd been abused. Bruises on her arms and wrists. Ligature marks on her ankles. Bruises on the throat. Bruises on her privates." He cleared his throat. A tear trickled down his cheek. "She was in a dirty gown. Nothing else. I knew what happened to her. I just knew."

"What happened?" Andrea said. "You found who did it?"

Monty shook his head. "I tried. The chief told me to lay off. He told me to take a vacation, that I was too emotionally involved. He said the golden boy would investigate."

"Who's that?" Carver said.

"Brent Landry. He does what he's told. Chief Lynch loves him like a son."

Carver nodded. "Let me guess. You kept investigating. Pissed him off."

"Exactly. I found a van that matched the description of the one that took the girl. A black Merecedes Sprinter van. I saw some suspicious looking men driving it. I followed them. There was a chase. I got in a wreck." He clenched his fists. "The chief found out what I did. I gave him hell. He gave me a suspension and a pay cut. He told me to go back to being a useless drunk and gambler. That I had a more secure future that way."

"Ouch." Andrea winced. "Were you drinking and gambling back then?"

Monty nodded. "I was good at ignoring things. At doing what I was told. But that little girl—that girl's name was Angela Fuentes." He poured another shot. Held up his glass. "To that poor little girl, Angela Fuentes. I hope you found your peace." He downed the shot without waiting for anyone else.

Andrea drank a shot solemnly. "To Angela."

Monty wiped away tears. "Once upon a time, I was married and had a little girl. I was a good detective in the LAPD. I was mostly honest. You know how things are."

"Not really," Carver said.

"My wife was carjacked. The thief took off with my little girl in the back." He gripped the tequila bottle. Took a long draw. "She was only six." His voice cracked. "The carjacker was an addict. We later found out that he sold her to someone for heroin."

"My God!" Andrea got a fresh bottle of tequila and poured herself another shot. "What happened?"

"The man who bought her sexually abused her. Another drug addict reported it. We found my daughter, but not before she was abused multiple times."

"I'm so sorry, Monty." Andrea reached over and touched his arm.

"My wife was furious with me. She said I didn't do enough to find our daughter. My chief had pulled me from the case because it was a conflict of interest. I still did what I could, but without the resources of the department, what could I do?" Monty sighed. "I blamed myself too."

Andrea patted his arm. "But it wasn't your fault."

He nodded. "I know. But I was so sick to my stomach about it that I started drinking. It got so bad my wife took my daughter and left me. I lost my job. I ended up down here because this was the only city that would hire me." He laughed sarcastically. "I'm not even good at being a crooked cop."

"You did the right thing. Drugs and street crime are one thing. But sexually abusing children is absolutely evil." Andrea pounded her shot glass on the counter. "I would kill anyone who did that."

"Oh, I did." Monty grinned almost maniacally. "Bail reform and crime reform let that pedophile back on the streets. He was just some homeless guy, so he was able to melt back into the massive homeless population. But I tracked him. I followed him." He nodded to himself. "I sent him off good and proper."

Carver studied Monty carefully. He was being genuine. He was admitting to first-degree murder, too. But he wasn't ready to spill the beans about Hugo and pals just yet. "Let's just leave last night as a mystery, then. No need for anyone to know details. And I'd prefer that you delete that camera footage."

"Already did it," Monty said. "I deleted it from the store's computers. Copied it to my cloud storage first, of course."

Carver folded his arms. "You plan on deleting it from there, too?"

"Maybe."

Carver raised an eyebrow. He said nothing.

Monty gulped. "I just want someone to help me with the case. You were a former Navy SEAL with Joe, right? Can you help me? I just want to do one thing right in my life."

Carver gave it some thought. This town was definitely rotten. The mayor seemed to be at the core of it. But looks could be deceiving. It was best to get some definitive information before making any decisions.

He looked Monty over. "Will you be my inside man?"

Monty straightened a little. "Absolutely. What do you want me to do?"

"Delete those files for starters."

He set his phone flat on the table. Opened a cloud storage app. Deleted the files. "They're gone."

Carver nodded. "Okay. Now, tell me what you told the chief about last night."

"It was just a working theory, but he seemed to buy it." Monty told them his scenario about the motel and the wrecked vehicles in the gulch.

It was a good theory, given the limited information. Carver hadn't tried to stage anything. He'd just tried to make the scenes as confusing as possible. Monty had somehow turned the chaos into logic.

"The mayor paid the chief a personal visit while I was at the gulch. Probably because Hugo was one of her loyalists." Monty held his hands out in a shrug. "I just want to know what really happened."

"I'll give you my theory," Carver said. "Just remember that anything I tell you is purely hypothetical and shouldn't, under any circumstances, be shared with anyone else."

Andrea looked interested. "Did you have something to do with their deaths?"

"Of course not." Carver put a hand to his chest. "I'm strictly non-violent. Just like Joe."

She laughed and quickly repressed it. "Oh, I'm sure you are."

"Here's what I think happened," Carver said. "I think this Hugo fellow was angry at someone for humiliating him in public. He was intimidating a little old lady and some guy put him in his place. Let's call this guy Bert."

"Bert?" Monty groaned. "Fine. Tell me about Bert."

"Bert was going to see Albert at his salvage yard when Hugo and his boys showed up and tried to jump him. But Bert was armed and shot the gun out of Hugo's hand." Carver tsked. "Poor Hugo got humiliated again and left."

Carver continued. "Bert knew Hugo wasn't done. So, he went into town and got a room at a motel, knowing Hugo would pay a visit." Carver told the rest of the story of Bert. About blowing out Hugo's brains, sending his truck over the cliff, and then baiting his buddies at the motel to follow him.

"Wow, this Bert is one deadly man," Andrea said. "I think Joe would have loved to meet this guy."

"Joe probably taught Bert a thing or two about how to pull something like this off."

Monty looked shocked. "I think I'm glad I'm on Bert's side."

Carver put a hand on Monty's shoulder and squeezed. "You made the right decision."

The detective gulped. "Yeah, I'm sure of it. What do you want me to do next?"

"I have a small checklist. Let's start with the hard items first." Carver went to Joe's office and retrieved the laptop. He showed Monty the gap in the footage from the security cameras. Showed him how the wi-fi had been off right at the time of Joe's death. "I called the company and spoke with a rep. They told me there was no scheduled update to the modem, but the one here updated all on its own."

Monty nodded. "That's suspicious."

"Yeah. And I need someone to track down exactly what happened. Can you do that?"

"I have a contact in the LAPD cybercrimes division who's good with that kind of thing and loves a mystery." He nodded. "He might help me trace it."

"Excellent. Let's start with that. Find out how it could have happened." Carver rapped his fingers on the counter. He turned to Andrea. "I need to know why Joe never drove his new pickup after he got it."

She looked confused. "Well, he said he preferred the old one."

"That's it?"

She nodded. "He just said the old one was more comfortable. I never questioned the decision."

"Well, I think I know why he stopped driving it. At least in general." Carver stood. "Let's take a walk into the garage."

Andrea looked unsure. "Why? What did you find?"

"I'll show you." Carver got his tactical flashlight.

Monty took the bottle of tequila by the neck. He swigged a little more. Nodded. "Let's go."

They went to the garage. Andrea reached for the light switch. He shook his head and turned on the flashlight. He retracted the tonneau cover.

Monty stared at the empty bed. "Is it invisible?"

"Sort of." Carver switched to UV mode. The glowing streaks and black stains appeared.

Andrea gasped. "Why is it glowing like that?"

Monty looked more closely at a black stain. "Spots of blood."

Carver said nothing.

"Animal blood, probably." Monty looked at Carver. "Right?"

Carver shrugged. "Can you take a sample and find out?"

"Yeah." He looked at the glowing parts. "Looks like bleach was used. That's not a good way to clean it up." He walked toward the door. "Let me get my kit."

"Blood? Bleach?" Andrea looked shocked. "Joe had something dead back here?"

Carver nodded. "He didn't say anything to you? Didn't act strange?"

She shook her head. "The man was a trained killer, though."

"True." Carver switched back to normal light. "When did he stop driving the truck?"

"Maybe a week after he bought it." Andrea looked stunned. "He was using it to drive around town and plant election posters. He wanted a new truck because he thought the old one might turn off some voters who thought he wasn't successful. He said it was all about psyops."

Carver grinned. "Yeah."

Monty returned from outside. "Can you switch back to UV?"

Carver obliged. Shined it on the bed. Monty scraped a few samples and put them in a vial. "Guess I'll take them to Palmer for analysis."

"You do that. And dig into the wi-fi issue." Carver walked to the wall and turned on the lights. "Also, the ranch is being watched."

Andrea gasped. "Watched?"

He nodded. "I noticed it yesterday. I assume someone is still watching."

"From where?" Monty said.

"The mountain to the north." Carver flicked off his flashlight. "The watcher saw the Ram leaving for town. The traffic cams picked it up once it got to town. That was how Hugo knew Bert was at Albert's Salvage."

Monty groaned. "How long are you going to keep using Bert? I'm helping you. There's no need to keep pretending."

Carver checked the time. "I've got to get cleaned up."

It was almost time for his date with the mayor.

CHAPTER 22

The date with the mayor would be big.

Carver would gauge her body language. Ask some probing questions. See what kind of reactions he got. The mayor was smart and manipulative. She was either a natural or she'd been trained.

He wasn't sure which, but he was going to find out.

Andrea looked confused. "Why are you getting cleaned up?"

Carver kept walking toward the garage door. "I've got a date." He left the garage. Headed to the house.

"A date?" Monty caught up with him. "With whom?"

"The mayor."

Andrea's mouth dropped open. "You're really going through with this?"

"No." He went inside the house. Picked up his beer where he'd left it and took a swig. "She talked to me after they led you off in handcuffs. She was interested in talking. I want to find out why."

"So, it's not a date. You're just meeting to talk."

"I'm having dinner at her house."

She stared at him in horror. "You're going into the lion's den?"

"Lioness's den," Carver said. "I'm going to interrogate her."

Monty took another draw of tequila. "You're insane. She keeps a minimum of four men on her personal security detail twenty-four seven. You'll be having dinner with them too whether you want to or not."

"That's a lot of security for a small-town mayor." Carver sipped his beer. "She's either showboating or she's up to no good. I'm going to find out why."

Monty's expression changed from concern to realization. "You're not going to go Bert on them, are you? Am I going to be investigating the mayor's corpse tomorrow?"

"No." Carver shook his head. "That would be stupid."

Monty breathed a sigh of relief. "Thank God."

"If Bert needs to kill her, he'll make it look like a gang hit."

"I don't know if you're being serious." Monty stared blankly at Carver. "And can you stop with the Bert bullshit?"

Andrea put a hand on Carver's arm. "Tell Bert to do what he needs to do. Bert has my blessing."

He nodded. "Bert will."

Monty threw his hands in the air. "Okay. I'll go see Palmer about the blood and get on this internet business."

"Text me when you have something," Carver said.

Monty opened the front door. "You'll be the first to know." He left.

Carver showered. He put on a fresh pair of black cargo pants and a t-shirt. He probably should have purchased something a little nicer for his date, but hopefully the mayor would understand.

When he was driving the Ram out of the garage, he wondered if the watcher was still watching. And if he was, why? Did he think Carver was a new threat? Or was Andrea part of the equation?

Depending on how his date with the mayor went, he might need to pay the watcher a visit tonight.

He plugged the address into the GPS and started driving. The house was on the east side of town right next to a lake and nature preserve, a large green space on the map. The green was deceptive because the land was just as arid as everything else. There was grass, some beige stone and gravel, and lots of scrub brush and trees.

The route took him along the edge of the preserve before reaching a gated community. The gate was made of black iron bars with sharp tips. There was a tall wall made of concrete and native stone that wrapped around the community.

According to the satellite view in the map app, the wall ran the entire perimeter. It probably cost more than half the homes on the south side of El Fuerte. There was a concrete path running alongside the wall.

Two stone guard houses guarded the gate. A man stepped out of each of them. One ran a mirror along the bottom of Carver's truck while his dog sniffed it. The other motioned Carver out of the vehicle.

Both guards wore suits, and both looked like they'd done time in the service. They were all business. Completely professional.

Carver stepped out of the Ram. He lifted his arms and let the man frisk him. "Pretty fancy digs for a small-town mayor."

The guard said nothing. He finished frisking Carver. The other guy finished his inspection. He went back inside his guard house. The other guard stared hard at Carver for a moment before speaking.

"Don't try anything stupid. If you do, you won't be walking out of there, I promise."

Carver didn't reply. He got back in the pickup and waited for the gate to open. The guard made him wait a few extra seconds before opening it.

The lawn on the other side was lush and green. There were tall trees that weren't native to this area. Oaks, hickory, maples, all planted in beds with rich, black soil and bark. The road went straight, branching into subdivisions.

Most of the houses in the first subdivisions were three stories with three or four-car garages. Some were built in the stucco style that was common in these parts. Others were traditional brick or stone. One looked Victorian with spires and tall iron gates.

The deeper in Carver drove, the bigger the houses were. The larger the plots of land. There was a proper mansion on a hill to the south. It was large, white, and probably had twenty bedrooms.

The larger houses all had their own gates and guard houses. Most of the walls looked decorative. Like the owners decided it wasn't worth fortifying the land since the outer wall already did that for them.

The mayor's house was on the next road to the right. It was white stucco with beige and black stones for the foundation. The roof was made of barrel clay tiles, similar to the ones common in Mediterranean climates.

A tall iron fence guarded the perimeter. It was tall with sharp barbs at the top. The metal looked thick and durable. It was most certainly not a cheap decorative fence, but a heavy-duty barrier.

Unlike the lush green lawns of the neighboring homes, the mayor's one adopted the beige and brown tones of the natural landscape but with large saguaro cactus plants interspersed with smaller spherical cacti.

There were dozens of agave plants and other succulents. There were palm trees, lots of bushes with pointy leaves, and a lot of native rocks and gravel. It looked like similar landscaping surrounded the house.

From a tactical perspective, it was a nightmare landscape. Trying to low crawl the front yard would be like dragging yourself through needles. There were too many cactus plants to avoid and the spiky succulents around the windows were enough to deter even hardened veterans.

It was a fortified hacienda.

Carver stopped at the guard house. A guy who looked identical to the ones out front got out and frisked him. He patted a handgun in its holster while looking Carver dead in the eyes. He didn't say a word, but the gesture was enough to send the message.

Carver didn't say anything either. He got back in the truck and waited for the gate to open. The guard made him wait. No doubt they wanted to assert dominance early and often. But they were laying it on a little thick with the intimidation routine.

Trying to assault the mayor out here would be more trouble than it was worth. She was far more vulnerable when she was driving around with her entourage. Not that Carver was planning to kill her. At least, not unless he found out she was complicit in Joe's death.

The gate finally opened. He drove around the semicircular driveway. A man in a butler's uniform was waiting there. Carver stopped the truck. Got out.

"Mr. Carver, please follow me." The man turned and walked toward the huge front door. It looked twelve feet tall and was made of steel.

The butler opened the door. Carver walked inside, touching the door frame on the way in to confirm that it was sturdy material. There was no way in hell the mayor of a town like this could afford this place.

Housing was already astronomically expensive in California. He'd learned that first-hand in San Francisco. Even in a state with lower cost of living, this place would cost a couple million to build, minimum.

The foyer was huge with a domed ceiling and marble tiles. Two curving staircases went to a walkway that crossed the space like a bridge. It went left and right, presumably into different wings of the house.

A pair of guards stood inside the foyer. They wore handguns at their hips and had rifles leaning against the walls. They stared at Carver as he passed by.

The butler led him through a large open den and into a large kitchen with shiny stainless-steel appliances. There was no need for an open concept floor plan because every room was big enough to be a normal house in its own right.

That was why Carver was confused when the butler led him down a hallway and through a doorway into what looked like a separate living space. It was a suite buried inside a mansion, complete with a kitchen, bedroom, and den.

The mayor was in the kitchen. Gone was all the jewelry and fancy clothing. She was in jeans and a t-shirt. And she was cooking something that smelled delicious.

She looked up from the stove and smiled. "You came!"

"You didn't think I would?"

"I wasn't sure." She added a pinch of seasoning to the meat in the pan. "I hope you like beef."

"I do."

"Have a seat." She motioned to the barstools in front of the granite countertop. "Want wine or a beer?"

Carver sat. "What are you having?"

She pointed to a glass of red wine. "It pairs well with the steak."

"Then I'll have that."

She picked up an empty wine glass and filled it halfway. Set it in front of him. She held up her glass. "To new acquaintances."

Carver clinked her glass. "To new acquaintances." He sipped the wine. It was good. Hopefully it wasn't poisoned. "I'm a little confused by your accommodations, Mayor."

"Please call me Jessica, okay?"

"Okay."

She smiled. "This isn't my house. But I do rent this suite."

"You rent a suite in a mansion." Carver looked around the room. "That's strange."

"It's affordable."

"If someone could afford to build this house, why would they need to rent out a suite?"

"This was an in-law suite built by the original owner. Their company went bankrupt, and the bank foreclosed on the house." She turned off the stove and took plates from a cabinet. "The bank hasn't been able to sell the place. It was on the market for so long that they decided to put it up for rent. The rent for the mansion is unaffordable, but I talked them into renting the suite."

"You talked them into it or strongarmed them into it?"

"It's a national bank, Carver." She piled food on a plate. "I don't have any control over their decisions."

The food smelled good. Really good. It was chopped steak, diced onions, and cilantro on corn tortillas. "Tacos?"

"Yep." She brought the plates around the counter and set them on a small wooden table. She placed hers at the head of the table and gave Carver the seat next to hers. It seemed symbolic. Like she was making sure he understood his place.

Carver joined her at the table. "It smells amazing. Do you enjoy cooking?"

"I prefer cooking to eating out." She patted her stomach. "It's better for the body."

Carver folded the tortilla around the ingredients. He took a bite. The steak was cooked medium. The onions and cilantro complemented it perfectly. He nodded in approval. "It's delicious."

She grinned. "Thanks." Jessica bit into hers. She wiped her mouth with a napkin and sipped her wine.

Carver ate in silence. He decided to let her do the talking. She finished off her first taco before she spoke.

"Where are you from, Carver?"

"All over the place." He picked up his second taco. "Military family."

She ate her last taco in silence. Waited for Carver to finish his. Then she took the plates into the kitchen and put them in the sink. "Want to wash your hands?"

Carver walked around the counter and washed his hands. Eating tacos was a messy business. He went back to the table.

"Let's talk in the den." Jessica picked up her wine and walked to the brown leather couch. She sat down at the closest end, crossing one leg so she could face sideways.

Carver sat down next to her. He angled toward her but didn't mimic her sitting style. "On to business?"

She nodded. "On to business."

Carver already knew what she was going to say next. It was obvious from the way she paused to consider her words.

"I would like Andrea to withdraw from the race."

"Afraid she'll win?"

Jessica nodded. "I am afraid of that. But not for the reasons you think."

"I'm listening."

Jessica put a hand on Carver's leg. "You've noticed my security detail."

"Who can miss it? You have a small army."

"I know, right? How much money do you think that costs?"

"At California wages? Probably thirty bucks an hour minimum."

"Probably, yes."

"You don't even know what you're paying your own people?"

She sighed. "Carver, these men aren't so much guarding me as they're keeping an eye on me."

Guarding and keeping an eye on someone could be interpreted as having the same meaning. But her tone of voice told Carver it wasn't the same meaning. If anything, it was the opposite meaning.

"Are you saying you're a prisoner?"

"No. Not exactly." She gulped down the rest of her wine. Got up and poured herself another glass. "I'm free to go where I want. I can do what I want. But they're always with me. Always watching. Always ensuring that I'm doing my job the way I'm supposed to."

"And how are you supposed to do your job?"

"However they tell me to do it."

Carver frowned. "Told by whom?"

"I can't say anything else, okay?" She looked around the room.

Carver had already noted that there were no visible cameras. But that didn't mean anything. "You think someone is listening?"

"A friend brought me a bug detector. I scan this place frequently. But I'm scared I missed something." She rubbed her hands together nervously. Leaned closer and spoke in a low voice. "Carver, you need to convince Andrea to drop out. It's not because I want to win. It's because I'm afraid for her safety if she runs against me."

"That's an interesting angle. But I'm going to need to know more. A hell of a lot more."

She pulled herself closer to him. Leaned forward and spoke softly. "I won the mayoral election fair and square. For the first time in El Fuerte history, the entire city council and the mayor were females."

"Congratulations," Carver said dryly.

"Our city was getting overrun with asylum seekers. There were many families. Many legitimate asylees. But there were also criminal elements. They began to take over the town. We asked for federal assistance and were ignored by Border Patrol and the White House." Jessica shook her head. "It was getting so bad that the citizens tried to recall me."

"Gloria told me about that."

Jessica bristled at the name. Her eyes darkened. But she kept on with her story. "A man came to visit me one day. He told me that his boss would help bring law and order back to the town. But that we would owe him favors."

"Typical," Carver said. "Was he a local?"

She shook her head. "No. He was from a cartel. He didn't say which one. I refused his offer. It turned out it was an offer I couldn't refuse. Because then his people started making life miserable for me."

"They didn't threaten to kill you?"

She shook her head. "They thought I'd be a valuable asset."

"And now they own you," Carver said.

Jessica looked down. "Yes. And if Andrea runs against me, they might kill her."

CHAPTER 23

Carver hadn't expected this.

The mayor was at the mercy of a cartel. Supposedly. He wasn't quite sure he believed her yet. He did, however, believe that Andrea was in danger whether Jessica was telling the truth or not.

"Did they kill Joe?"

She looked confused. "His horse kicked him to death."

Carver shook his head. "I've got expert analysis that says the horse didn't. I've watched hours of videos. The horse in question isn't even a kicker. He's a bucker."

"I spoke with Captain Hernandez. He says the marks on the face are identical to the horse's horseshoes. The size and imprints match perfectly."

"It's interesting that a captain in the sheriff's department would share that with the mayor of a city with no jurisdiction over the scene."

She nodded. "I understand how it looks, but I've cultivated a good relationship with LASD out of necessity. Cartel crime transcends borders."

"Cartel crime that you can't stop. That you won't stop."

"The cartel that's threatening me has competitors. I'm supposed to arrest them."

Carver noticed she was talking at conversational levels again but was still sitting close. She looked scared, but it might be an act. "Explain to me what stopping a bike rally at Albert's Salvage has to do with cartels."

"Nothing, but my handler told me they don't want a lot of attention on the town." Jessica put her hands on Carver's. "At least, that's what they told me."

"It seems like it'd be a great opportunity to sell drugs."

"It's really not," she said. "The people attending the rally aren't the same as biker gangs you see on TV. They aren't all violent thugs who traffic drugs. These are people from all walks of life. Some are rich, some are middle class. Some are even with law enforcement."

Carver didn't know enough about biker demographics to question her response. It was possible the cartel was making her do it. It was possible she simply didn't like Albert and was being vindictive because he supported Joe.

"I can tell you have doubts," Jessica said. "I warned Joe about it too."

Carver studied her face. He couldn't tell if she was telling the truth or not. "What did he have to say about it?"

"He said he'd think about it. I even told him I'd try to exclude his property from annexation since that was the primary reason he was running." She shrugged. "The annexation was already on hold until December, so he wasn't eligible to run as a non-citizen."

"Andrea seems to have solved that problem by renting an apartment."

Jessica smiled. "She seems to think it's a clever move, but it's a method politicians use all the time to run in jurisdictions they'd otherwise be ineligible for."

"Seems pretty clever for someone who's not a politician."

"I can give her that much." Jessica's hands lingered on Carver's. "She'll need thirty days to establish residency, and she'll need fifteen thousand signatures on a petition to get her on the ballot."

"Really?" Carver frowned. "That sounds excessive."

"Don't blame me. Blame Mayor Davis. People loved him back in the day, but he was as crooked as they come." She smiled fondly. "He pushed that rule through the city council to keep others from running against him. He also had them attach annual increases to the mayor's salary, so he got paid like a king."

Carver wasn't surprised. Politicians didn't produce anything. They didn't run a company that needed profits in order to pay wages. They had police power to tax people at whatever rates they wanted.

They could vote higher wages for themselves at the risk of getting themselves voted out of office. But they could also make it harder for anyone to run against them by abusing that power.

What Carver needed to know was whether Jessica was the same kind of politician, or someone with good intentions who was at the mercy of a cartel.

There was another important question that needed asking. "When did you warn Joe?"

Her brow furrowed and she looked to the side like she was trying to remember. "It was just over a month ago, I think. Why?"

"Just curious." He switched subjects. "Where are you from?"

She blinked and went silent, like her mind was switching gears. "My parents moved here from Mexico. I was born in San Diego."

"You still have a hint of an accent."

"My parents spoke mostly Spanish at home." Jessica smiled fondly. "And I grew up in a Spanish-speaking part of town."

"Mostly Mexicans?"

She nodded. "My mom cleaned houses and my father did whatever construction work he could get."

"You come from a big family?"

Her face grew sad. "My mother wanted more children, but she was diagnosed with ovarian cancer. She didn't have health insurance, of course, but there were local doctors who tried to help her. They did what they could, but she died two years later."

"And your father?"

"He died in a construction accident."

Carver patted her hand sympathetically. "I'm sorry to hear that."

"Thank you, Carver." She looked down. Her long black hair cascaded to cover her face. "I took whatever work I could find. Mostly waitressing. I went to community college for a couple of years and finished my business degree at UCLA."

She looked up. Her eyes were red. Tears trickled down her cheeks. "I don't know what to do now, Carver. I worked so hard to get where I am, and now I'm trapped in a nightmare."

Carver tried to be skeptical, but it was hard looking into those eyes and not seeing the sincerity. He'd nearly lost his life to a crying woman once. He and Joe had been undercover, gathering intel for a retrieval mission.

They'd grown thick beards and worn local clothing, so they'd fit in with the general population of Kabul, Afghanistan. A politician's family had been kidnapped by the Taliban and they were assigned to get them out.

Their cover had been blown and they didn't know it. They'd come across a woman crying in an alley. Her face was bloody and bruised. She held out her hands and begged for help in the Dari language.

Carver wasn't anywhere close to fluent in the language, but he understood that much. He'd been moved by her tears and distress. He'd jogged toward her to help her. Joe had snatched him back at the last instant.

Just before Carver's foot hit a tripwire hidden in the dust. The woman jumped up. Brandished an AK-47 and fell an instant later when Joe shot her in the head. Four men jumped from behind cover and opened fire.

They'd barely gotten out alive.

That lesson had stuck with him. A constant reminder to always be vigilant. To never trust a person you don't know.

That hadn't stopped him from helping Paola even though she could have just as easily been faking her distress. Was Jessica really in trouble? Or were these alligator tears?

His gut told him to proceed cautiously. And that's what he would do. But he would play along in the meantime.

Carver wiped Jessica's tears away with his thumb. He caressed her cheek. "I'm sorry."

She gripped his wrists desperately tight. "Can you help me? Can you get me out of this mess?"

"What do you want me to do?"

"I don't know." Her chin quivered. "I sent secret messages to people at the FBI and even the governor's office. The FBI never replied."

"What did the governor's office have to say?"

"I received a message that said, *Do as you're told.*" She shivered violently. "I was so scared I felt sick. I thought, this is it. They're going to kill me."

"Apparently, you're too valuable."

"I don't even understand why." Jessica's shoulders hunched. She leaned against' Carver's shoulder.

He put an arm around her. Kept a sympathetic look on his face. "I'll help you, but I don't know how."

"I don't know either. It just feels good to be able to tell someone everything."

"Aren't your wardens suspicious about my visit?"

"I told them that you're friends with Joe and Andrea and that I need to talk to you to convince Andrea not to run."

"What did they say?"

"They don't talk to me much. I assume they asked someone further up the cartel chain and they approved it."

Carver had seen similar situations before. Noah, the former kingpin of San Francisco held multiple people hostage through fear and intimidation. He'd made them work for him. He and his henchmen were dead now.

Killing the Brazilian cartel thugs in Morganville, Georgia had fixed a problem there. Killing people had solved a lot of problems all over the world when Carver had been in the dark ops organization known as Scion.

But southern California was a different animal. The border was practically wide open. Gang members could come across anytime they wanted without fear of Border Patrol.

Carver could kill them by the dozen and there would be endless wave after wave of replacements coming from the south. They would send kill squads or specialists instead of their low-level thugs, and someone would eventually kill him.

Whatever he did, he'd have to stay off the radar. He'd have to act covertly. And if he screwed up, maybe Monty could cover for him.

"I'll help you, Jessica." He smoothed her hair back from her face. "I don't know how, but I will."

"And you'll give Andrea my warning?"

"Yes. I don't want her in danger."

A smile broke through her tears. "Thank you, Carver." She leaned forward on her knee and kissed him. "Thank you."

He pulled her closer. Kissed her harder. She smiled. Stood and took his hand. Led him down the hallway and into a small bedroom.

Jessica pulled up on his shirt, but she wasn't tall enough to pull it over his shoulders. Carver finished the job for her. Then he lifted her dress. It was tight but elastic and came off easily. She was wearing matching lingerie. A sure sign she meant for this to happen.

Maybe she was the enemy. Maybe she was manipulating him. Willing to do anything to get him on her side.

Carver was willing to take that chance.

MONTY WAS PAINFULLY SOBER.

His body had worked through all the alcohol, and he hadn't had anything to drink for hours. Having a clear mind made it easier to pore over the data from the forensics department. The CSI team had submitted information as they processed it.

Their assessment of events followed Monty's closely. Except they thought there was a third vehicle involved. One that Hugo and the men in the Durango were chasing. Someone in the fleeing vehicle had fired and struck Hugo.

His truck had flown off the road. Shortly after that, a bullet struck the front tire of the Durango. Sent it hurtling into the gulch behind Hugo's car.

They'd reached that conclusion because one of the men in the Durango had been a known associate of Hugo's. They couldn't identify the others. There were no matches in dental records or other databases.

Tattoos on two of the men tied them to a gang out of LA but failed to provide a positive ID on either. It looked like there was no way Carver could be implicated.

The motel crime scene had all but been forgotten. A team hadn't been sent there because they hadn't had the resources. So, the bodies had been bagged and tagged and sent to the morgue. Only the painted outlines and bloodstains remained.

"Monty."

He flinched. Looked up from the papers. Saw one of the CSI team standing a few feet from his desk. "Lia?"

"I need to review the Blue Star case. I need you to come with me to examine the scene."

Monty stood. Tried to straighten his wrinkled shirt. "It's nearly eleven at night. Can't it wait until the morning?"

"The chief told me to work it all night if I have to. The others are still doing lab work for the Devil's Gulch case."

"Okay." He realized his shirt was a hopeless case. Probably because he'd slept in it the night before and hadn't bothered changing. Lia was an older Hispanic woman. Probably in her forties.

She wore the trademark glasses of a lab geek, but he'd never seen her in a lab coat. Not even when she was in the lab. She favored jeans, t-shirts and boots, and her hair was usually in a tight ponytail.

"Don't look at me like that," she snapped. "Get your act together and let's go."

Monty blinked. "Look at you like what?"

"You were looking me over. Practically salivating." She stepped closer and snapped her fingers in his face. "Look me in the eyes or don't look at me at all."

"You can't control what I look at."

"Want to bet?"

Monty huffed and pushed to his feet. He could understand why she didn't want some ugly drunken has-been with blotchy skin looking at her. If she looked like him, he wouldn't want her looking at him either.

Then again, he'd paid money for sex with women that were uglier than him. These days, he wasn't even sure how he'd ever landed a wife back in the day.

Lia sighed. "I'm sorry, okay? It's been a hectic day, and I can't put up with anyone's shit anymore."

"I understand perfectly." Monty wiped the potato chip crumbs off his shirt. "Your car or mine?"

"We'll take a van." She walked to the elevator and pressed the button.

They took it down to the first floor. Monty followed her outside to one of the high-roofed lab vans and waited for her to unlock the doors. He climbed into the passenger side. The interior stank of pot.

There were burn marks from cigarettes on the upholstery and ashes in a coffee cup in the center cupholder. He opened the glove compartment and found a bag of weed and a bottle of Hennesey inside.

Lia nodded at the bag. "Make me a bowl, please."

Monty found the glass pipe in the glove compartment. The weed in the bag had already been crushed and seeded, so he stuffed some in the pipe and handed it to her.

Lia put the pipe in her mouth and steered the van out of the fenced-in carpool.

Monty laughed. "You look like a sailor or something."

She smiled. "Light me."

"Bite you?"

She took the pipe out and repeated herself. "Light me."

Monty dug the lighter out of the glove compartment and held the flame to the pipe while she puffed until it lit. She rolled down the window and blew smoke outside.

Lia sighed and rolled her neck. "God, I hate working late. I don't even understand why the chief even cares about this motel crap."

"Maybe because there are three bodies."

She laughed. "Oh, yeah. Guess you're right." She took another long draw. Held it in her lungs for a few seconds. Blew it out the window. She glanced at Monty. "Want a hit?"

He shook his head. Held up the Hennesy. "I'll just drink."

"Better get a replacement if you drink it all, or Cory is going to be pissed."

Monty didn't feel like pissing off anyone else, so he stuffed the bottle back in the glove compartment.

"Good boy." Lia grinned. Took another hit. "Did you file a report on the motel yet?"

"Yeah. Should I summarize?"

"Yes." Lia leaned back her chair. Kept one hand on the wheel and another on the pipe.

Monty told her his theory then summed it up in a single line. "A domestic disturbance that went horribly wrong."

"Sounds like a gang member was involved," Lia said. "That's the element that made it go wrong."

Monty studied her figure. Her breasts weren't large, but they stood out against her slim figure. Her arms were tanned and slightly muscular.

"I told you not to look at me like that." She didn't even glance at him.

"I'm not looking at you in any kind of way," Monty said.

"You're looking at my tits." She set the pipe in the coffee cup. Smoke drifted up from it, tickling Monty's nose. Lia put her other hand on the wheel. "I don't feel like getting written up for kicking your ass, but I will if you don't stop."

Monty forced his eyes forward. "I'll wear a blindfold if you'll just shut up."

She laughed. "I'd love to see that."

They arrived at the Blue Star Motel. She parked in front of the office. Monty got out and stared at the human outline on the sidewalk. At the dark stain on the concrete.

"Walk me through it," Lia said.

Monty pointed to the room in the middle. The one where the man had been shot on the bed. He couldn't remember the man's name. It didn't matter anymore. "It started here. This guy got angry at the other tenant. Probably loud noise or something. He went down to the other guy's room and pounded on the door."

They walked to the end door. She examined the footprints on the door. The smashed window and the rock on the floor inside. Monty took her through it step-by-step, mimicking the motel manager when he came out and shot the Hispanic guy.

He took her into the manager's back room, showed her the hole in the wall. The blood on the couch. "The last person took off after killing the manager."

"Did they steal anything?"

Monty shook his head. "Doesn't look like it."

She walked around the scene. Used tweezers to collect something from the couch. Used a scalpel to scrape dried blood from the cushions. She did the same for the sidewalk and the motel rooms.

A black car pulled into the parking lot. The windows were tinted too dark to see through even in broad daylight. A short Hispanic man got out of the passenger side. His left arm was covered in tattooed skulls and flames.

With him was a Caucasian man. Buzzed hair. Stony face. Military through and through. He looked familiar. Monty had seen him before. He just hadn't been paying much attention. Then it came to him. This was one of her top security men.

He wasn't just a guard. He was like an advisor or something too. Monty vaguely remembered the guy talking to Chief Lynch. He'd seen him around the office at times. Entering the operations room and looking at the cameras.

Monty had never seen him with this tattooed guy. It looked like they were working together. Like they were partners or something.

And they looked like bad news.

CHAPTER 24

Carver rinsed off in the mayor's shower.

She got up and joined him before he could get out. "I really enjoyed that."

"Me too." He kept playing his part. The knight in shining armor who'd do anything for the damsel in distress. "How are you feeling?"

"Much better." She hugged him and let hot water course down her body. "I know you'll think of a way to get me out of this."

"What makes you think I can do that?" He'd considered asking her about the person or persons watching Joe's ranch. Just to see her reaction. But it felt more advantageous to seem unaware of them.

"Because you were a SEAL like Joe." She looked up at him. Rested her chin on his chest. "I know you have your ways."

"You may not like everything I do," Carver said. "I might do things that confuse you. You'll need to pretend to be angry with me to protect yourself."

Her forehead wrinkled. "I don't understand."

"I'll be doing things to elicit a reaction from people. It'll help me gather information." She nodded. "Okay. I trust you."

He smoothed back her wet hair. Leaned down and kissed her. "Good."

Jessica sighed in contentment and kissed his chest. "I could stay here all night."

"Me too. But I've got to go. I need to talk to Andrea."

"Please do. She's in way over her head."

Carver turned off the water and dried off. He put his clothes back on. "Walk me outside?"

She nodded and hooked her arm in his. They walked back through the den and through the kitchen.

A ringtone started playing. A phone on the kitchen counter lit up. *Video Call Incoming*. There was a man's picture on the screen. Probably the contact picture. The man had buzzed hair and a stern look to his face.

Carver nodded at it. "Your boyfriend?"

She sighed. "No. One second." She picked up the phone and clicked to answer.

"We're here," a cold voice said.

"Let me call you back, okay?"

There was no answer but the phone played another sound and Jessica put the phone down. She'd been holding the phone toward her so Carver couldn't see who was on the other end of the video call.

Presumably it was the man in the picture. He looked like most of her other security detail. Former military types. Or at least men who like to pretend they were in the military.

"Sorry about that." She smiled. "I don't even know why they were calling me."

"Where were they?"

"They're here waiting outside." She shrugged. "Always keeping an eye on me." She led him out of the front door.

A guard outside the suite door stepped out of the way and shadowed them through the mansion and out of the front door. Carver kissed Jessica long and hard.

She bit his lower lip. Winked. "Drive safe."

"I'll keep it under a hundred." Carver got in the Ram and drove off. The gates opened on his approach and the guards waved him through. He drove to the main gate and the guard there did the same thing.

He looked for the man who'd called but didn't see anyone matching the picture. Carver had a feeling that the man was somewhere else. Somewhere Jessica had told him to go. He hoped it wasn't to the ranch.

He'd noticed something else. When he'd kissed Jessica, the guard who'd followed them out got a look in his eyes. Like he was holding back anger. Like he wanted to say something but couldn't.

His entire body had gone rigid. Like it was taking him everything not to aim his rifle at Carver and open fire. He was jealous. Angry.

Carver recognized the man. He'd been one of the security detail who'd arrived in the town square with Jessica. She'd looked at him several times. Something had passed between them. Maybe this guard was someone special.

Maybe she was sleeping with him. Maybe she just pretended to be interested in him so she could manipulate him. She was an attractive woman. She'd use it to her advantage to get at least one of her supposed captors on her side.

It was just something to keep an eye on. Something to be wary of. Controlling someone with emotion was a double-edged sword. It could lead to unintended consequences. One of those being that guy shooting at Carver even if she told him not to.

Once Carver was out of the gated subdivision, he turned toward town. He stopped at a gas station to fill up. While the gas was pumping, he removed a device from his duffel bag and turned it on.

He walked around the truck, checking the wheel wells and under the truck. The scanner didn't find any signals. No signs that the truck had been tagged or bugged. They'd had ample opportunity to do so.

They might have known he would check. They knew he was a former SEAL. They'd assume he'd be careful. Methodical. And if the watcher was employed by them, they had surveillance on him anyway.

Carver paid for the gas with cash. He got back in the truck and opened the map app that tracked camera locations. He added the camera from the convenience store. There was a residential street he could take to avoid that camera.

Not that it mattered now.

He noticed an unread text from Monty. *Looks like you're in the clear but there's a pair of dangerous looking guys at the motel talking to one of our CSI people.* The text was twenty minutes old.

Carver thought it over. There was no reason to go to the motel. No reason to risk being seen near there and possibly linking him to the bodies. But he was curious about the man Monty described.

He replied to the text. *Can you get a picture of them?*

Monty's reply came seconds later. *I'll try.*

Make sure your flash is off. Carver had seen people die for dumber mistakes.

I was just making sure it's off, Monty sent back.

Carver started driving. He cut through town since it didn't matter if the truck was seen on traffic cams. He imagined it was on a monitor in the operations room with a big red square around it.

That made it very inconvenient for getting around unnoticed in this part of town. If he still had access to the same high-tech equipment he'd used in Scion, it would be a cinch to put a tap on the feed.

One of the techs would duplicate the feed on their monitors. They'd be able to loop it, alter images, or replay old footage so the people in the operations room would essentially be blind.

Carver had retained some of the surveillance equipment he'd used in San Francisco, but he'd returned the most valuable item—a leech. When placed next to cell phones, computers, or other digital devices, it could break into them and download their contents.

Judging from what he'd seen during his time in the police station, there was a lot of useful information on the computers in the operations room. But the most valuable information was sitting behind the hidden door in the back.

If they were willing to brazenly spy on the people through the various cameras located around town, what were they doing in secret behind that door?

Thanks to the pictures Carver had taken, he could zoom in and see the locations of all the cameras. But that wasn't going to help him sneak into the center of town. Not unless he procured an unknown car and drove it there.

He wasn't willing to use Ronald's car again. Or any car that could be tied to someone in the city. He'd have to get one outside the city limits.

But solving the car problem was just a tiny piece of the puzzle. He had to get inside the police department without being seen. That would be a major obstacle since they had cameras surrounding the place.

His cell phone vibrated. Monty had sent two images. Carver pulled to the side of the road and stopped. He opened the image.

The first subject was Hispanic. A middle-aged male, probably late thirties. He looked like the standard bad guy. A mean look on his face. Ample tattoos. A couple of scars. Black clothes. He was talking to a woman with long black hair.

The tattoos on the man's arm drew his attention. A vine of flames with small skulls hanging from the shoots. Some of the shoots were bare, leaving room for the addition of more skulls.

Carver counted forty-three skulls from the man's wrist to the top of his forearm. There was room for one more skull before starting on the bicep. The skulls near the wrist had thin black slashes in them.

Each skull was a kill. Each slash was an additional kill so the tattoo didn't run out of real estate too soon. Carver counted the skulls and slashes. Over a hundred and thirty kills for this man.

There was no telling if that was an impressive number or not. Most of the time, these cartel killers weren't going up against skilled adversaries. They were killing regular people, catching them by surprise with a bullet to the head or a knife to the guts.

Maybe the guy was a first-class assassin. Maybe he was a regular old contract killer. Maybe he was just a thug with a gun. There was no way to tell without actually sizing the guy up in person.

The man's homicidal acumen wasn't the most important thing to know. What Carver needed to know was why the guy was in town, who he worked for, and most importantly, why he was at the motel.

The answer to the latter question seemed obvious. He was connected to Hugo and his men. He was probably sent by the cartel leader to find out why in the hell six of his men were dead. If Monty did his part, the man would think a rival gang was involved.

The second image was of a Caucasian man. Buzzed hair. Emotionless face. It was the same guy who'd called Jessica. Carver was glad to know he wasn't at the ranch.

Carver sent another text. *Did they just send the two men? Or are there more?* He resumed driving to the ranch. Monty didn't reply for a while. Carver hoped he hadn't ended up as another slash on the Hispanic man's tattoo.

He'd almost reached the ranch when Monty replied. *Four men total. The car windows were so darkly tinted I couldn't see.*

Carver pulled over to the shoulder of the road and stopped to type a response. *Who's the woman in the first image?*

Lia, one of our CSI team. She's fully invested in the company Kool-Aid.

The tattoo guy and buzz cut guy were asking her what happened. Probably because they knew the man Carver had shot in the head at the motel.

Carver sent another text. *Does Lia believe your version of events?*

I think so. But if she finds out the dead Hispanic guy here is tied to Hugo, then it might all fall apart.

Carver thought of another reasonable scenario. *Lead them to think a rival gang is involved.*

Monty replied again. *I will if they ask me anything. They're just ignoring me.*

Maybe it was mistake not to go by and see these men in person. Maybe going there was an even bigger mistake. Carver didn't plan on trying to lead another carful of killers off a cliff. At least not tonight.

It got him to thinking about what Jessica told him. She'd told Joe about the cartel connection. She'd told him it was dangerous, and he needed to drop out. She'd told him that just over a month ago.

Joe wouldn't have taken her warning at face value. He would have needed to confirm what she told him was true. And if he did find out it was true, he wasn't the kind of man to let that kind of rot infect his city.

He was a man of action. He wasn't the kind who bitched and moaned about something then sat idly by and hoped someone else would take care of it. Today's society was full of empty talkers. Of people with no skin in the game.

They were people of words, nothing more.

Carver had no problem imagining what Joe had done next. He'd gone looking for trouble. And he'd probably found it. That trouble had gotten him killed. Somehow, they'd framed it as a being kicked to death.

How they'd done it was a mystery. But Carver's gut told him it was a frame. It told him that they couldn't outright kill him because people would believe the mayor had something to do with it and they didn't want to lose their golden goose.

In the end, it didn't really matter how Joe had been killed. He was dead and Carver was going to kill anyone even remotely connected to his friend's murder unless they killed him first.

Hugo didn't have anything to do with it. Carver felt sure of that. Joe would have seen that idiot and his boys coming from a mile away. If he had to guess who did it, it would be one of the men at the motel. One of the men in the images Monty had sent him.

Carver got back on the road and went to the ranch. He backed the pickup into the garage. He got out and put a hand on the steel wall. It was thick and insulated. That might be important.

If the watcher was spying day and night, he'd need thermal imaging from that distance. It was too far for night vision. It would likely be using MWIR, midwave infrared. It meant the insulation would block his heat signature, but if he poked his head out of the door, it would glow like a beacon.

Sneaking up on the watcher would require a more elaborate plan. He'd have to approach from a completely different direction. And in this case, it would be better to do it during daylight. That might seem counterintuitive, but it would be unexpected.

And doing the unexpected was the only way to keep breathing.

THE WATCHER MADE ANOTHER NOTE.

Dodge Ram arrived at 12:41. Driver appears to be Carver. It backed into the garage. Subject appears to be in garage.

The watcher had taken the night shift. Two had left for reasons left unexplained. The watcher knew better than to question him. It was best to keep doing his job and ignore everything else.

He yawned so hard his jaw cracked. He poured himself another cup of coffee from the thermos. He took a sip, and the steaming hot liquid burned his tongue.

"Damn it!" He took a piece of ice from the cooler and put it on the burned spot. It didn't make it feel much better.

He leaned back and kept watching. The new chair was much more comfortable. The MWIR scope was amazing. Another yawn sneaked up on him. He carefully sipped the coffee and slapped his cheek to keep himself awake.

He jerked awake. Checked the time. It looked like he'd been out for almost an hour. The watcher sipped his coffee. It was cold now. He tossed it all back. Hoped it was enough to keep him awake for the rest of the night.

There was the crunch of gravel and the rumble of an engine. Something was coming up the mountain. Ambient sound carried long distances in the still of the night.

The sounds gradually grew louder. He wasn't expecting anyone. Had Carver come this way while he was asleep? Or was it Two? He frantically considered what to do. The engine grew louder until it was on the gravel road near camp.

The watcher put on a pair of night vision goggles, picked up the handgun, and positioned himself behind a tree, just like Two had shown him.

The engine shut off. He couldn't see it through the camouflage netting and trees. He stayed still and waited. Wondered if he'd see Carver's hulking form walk into view.

A man walked into camp. It was Two. Then another man appeared. A man the watcher didn't recognize.

Had the stranger taken Two hostage? Was Two bringing a third person to help them? The watcher hadn't been prepared for this situation. He decided to remain hidden. To wait and see what happened.

The two men walked alongside each other. There were no weapons drawn. No indications anyone was under physical duress. They appeared to be simply walking and talking.

The watcher remained where he was.

The men reached Two's tent. Two stopped. He looked in the watcher's direction and nodded grimly. "You're still hiding. Good."

The watcher didn't reply. He wasn't going to do anything until he heard the safe phrase.

Two went silent for a moment as if drawing out the tension. Then he finally spoke the code phrase. "Baked beans and rice."

The watcher breathed a sigh of relief. He set the gun down and emerged from behind the tree. "Who is that with you?"

"That's not important."

"Is he here to help us keep watch?"

Two shook his head. "No."

The watcher didn't ask anything else. It had been dumb to pose even a single question. These were not the sort of people you wanted to know about. It was best to keep his head down and do his job.

So, he sat back in the chair and put his eye to the scope. There was no sign of Carver. He'd probably gone inside long ago right before the watcher nodded off. The kitchen light had been on all night. It was still the only illumination in the house.

The watcher was just glad it hadn't been Carver who'd shown up. Even though there was no way he could know he was being watched, the watcher had a feeling that the man knew more than he was letting on.

There was something about the way the man walked. The way he looked at his surroundings all the time even when he was pretending not to. The man was dangerous. And there was no telling what he'd do if he found out he was being watched.

He kind of reminded the watcher of Two. Except Two was nowhere near Carver's size.

Two and the stranger continued talking in Spanish. It could have been any language, but it sounded like Spanish to the watcher. He tried to pick out a few words here and there, but they were simply talking too fast.

The Dodge Ram abruptly sped out of the garage. It turned toward town and kept going straight. The watcher noted it. He turned to Two. "I'm sorry to interrupt, but Carver just left the ranch. He was only there for an hour."

Two stopped talking to the stranger. He shooed the watcher out of the chair. Put his eye to the scope and watched. "What in the hell is he up to?"

He turned to the stranger and spoke in Spanish again. There was a small amount of light at the campsite. It was shielded by black fabric to ensure it couldn't be seen from the ranch.

The stranger was standing near it. He looked Hispanic. He was wearing a black T-shirt and black pants. His right arm was covered with a tattoo. It looked like flames with skulls on them. He looked like the kind of guy you didn't want to run into in a dark alley, or anywhere, really.

The stranger replied to Two. He finally said a word the watcher understood. "Vamos!"

The stranger rushed back to the truck. Two got out of the chair. "Let me know if he comes back."

The watcher had more questions, but he held his tongue and nodded. "Okay."

Two jogged to the truck. It spun around on the gravel and took off down the mountain. Something big was happening tonight. That was the only reason someone like that stranger would be up here, right?

They must have planned to do something else but since Carver left, they'd changed their plans. The watcher didn't know what they had planned, but whatever it was it couldn't be good.

Maybe Carver was going to die tonight.

CHAPTER 25

Carver imagined what Joe would have done after the mayor warned him.

He'd come home. Write down a checklist of to-do items. Then he'd arm himself and start investigating. He was good at undercover ops. He'd taught Carver everything he knew.

That was why Carver could make an educated guess about what Joe had done. Since the mayor's security guards were supposedly with the cartel, that would be the logical place to start. Watch them when they were off duty and see where they went.

If they were really with a cartel, they'd probably be staying in a house with the others. That was the way a lot of these organizations worked. They liked to keep the muscle in one location. They didn't want them getting their own homes, finding wives, and starting families.

That was counterproductive. It made them vulnerable. Only those higher up the ladder earned those kinds of perks. Only they had access to something resembling a real life. Everyone else was considered disposable.

The cartel in question might be a kinder, gentler cartel. But it was doubtful.

It was also doubtful that the mayor's wardens left the gated community where she lived. It was just as likely that the cartel owned that mansion and housed their men there. Surely, Joe would have discovered that.

One month, Carver thought. That was a lot of time to discover things. Joe had probably realized the same thing about the mayor's guards that Carver had. He'd probably confirmed that they did, indeed, stay at the mansion.

It made sense that the cartel would want them close to Jessica at all times. They needed to be able to respond to anything at a moment's notice.

Okay, so what was the next thread to follow?

He thought about Lia, the woman with Monty. She was talking directly to a hired killer. Someone who was probably higher up the ladder within the cartel. Where had that guy come from?

The cartel owned the town. That meant they had a hub of operations inside the city limits, or somewhere close by. The killer might not work at the hub, but he'd almost certainly go there at some point.

It seemed likely that Joe had found the location. He'd watched it. Studied it. Had he actually done anything about it?

Carver looked at the pickup. Another fact clicked neatly into place. Joe had purchased the pickup shortly before his meeting with Jessica. He'd stopped driving it shortly thereafter. After whatever happened to make the stains in the pickup bed.

He thought of something else. Something he should have thought of already, but he'd overlooked it time and time again. He climbed into the pickup. Pushed the start button. The electronics came on.

The touchscreen turned on. It was huge. Probably twelve inches at least. And it had several options he hadn't even looked at since he'd been using his phone for everything.

A home screen appeared with multiple options. *Radio, Media, Phone Apps, Vehicle, Phone, Settings, Help, Navigation.*

Carver tapped *Navigation*. More options appeared. He tapped *Favorites*. Nothing was in the list. He tapped *Recent*. A short list appeared. Three items. One was his home address. The next was to a restaurant in Los Angeles.

The third one didn't have a name associated with it. Just an address. And it was on the northwest side of El Fuerte. It was the last place this pickup had been until Carver started driving it.

Maybe that was the place where he needed to go.

He checked the GPS app on his phone. There were no traffic cameras within a mile radius of the place. It was right where two main highways intersected. It was on a route that came from the border and went into LA.

Carver noticed the date for the restaurant in LA. It was from two days before. He wondered if it had anything to do with the last address. Maybe Joe had gone to LA on business and looked for a place to eat. The GPS didn't track everywhere he'd been. Only that he'd looked for directions to those places.

He tapped the restaurant. Directions appeared. It was thirty-seven miles there and back. Seventy-four miles round trip. Another eleven miles from the ranch to the second address. Twenty-two miles round trip.

Add in two trips from the ranch to El Fuerte and that could easily add up to the one hundred and twenty-two miles that were on the odometer before Carver started driving it.

Carver pulled up the unknown address on his phone. He put it in satellite view and zoomed in. There was no business name. The overhead view showed a rectangular building. A large parking lot.

And right next to it was a place Carver had already visited. Albert's Salvage. Puzzle pieces clicked neatly into place. Things that seemed unconnected suddenly connected.

Jessica was acting for the cartel when she forbid Albert from holding the bike rally. Not because Albert was supporting Joe. But because the salvage yard was right next to the cartel's hub of operations.

There had to be something in that unnamed building that the cartel didn't want anyone finding. If Albert's place was overflowing with bikers, one of them was bound to see something they weren't supposed to.

That was now Carver's working theory. The next step was proving the theory true. Because if nothing was there, then all the cartel stuff went out the window and he'd be back to thinking it was Jessica who didn't want the bike rally. And she was punishing Albert for supporting Joe.

Carver didn't want to wait another day to check it out. It was dark and he was equipped for the job. The watcher would see him, of course. They'd wonder what he was up to so late and tell someone.

And that was exactly what he wanted to happen.

TWO GUNNED THE ENGINE.

The truck wound its way down the mountain. He had to be careful. A single mistake and the truck would slip over the edge and tumble down the steep slope into the trees.

His passenger seemed unconcerned. He wasn't even wearing a seatbelt. It was pure machismo, that much was certain. Two thought it was stupid. The man might have over a hundred kills, but that didn't mean he couldn't die in a car accident.

"What's your name?" Two asked in Spanish.

"You can call me Domingo." He gripped the handle above the door. His muscles tensed from holding on, betraying the calm look on his face. "That is all you need to know."

"I need operational information," Two said. "Why is this guy important?"

"I know what you know." Domingo looked out the side window at the darkness. "Watch him and find out where he goes."

"Is he supposed to lead us to something?"

"I don't know."

They reached the bottom of the mountain. Two took the eastern highway. It hooked due south after a mile and would deliver them to the outskirts of the eastern side of town. They were probably twenty minutes behind.

"Do we have spotters in town?" Two asked.

"Just the cameras." Domingo released the door handle. He turned his cold, black eyes on Two. "You should stop asking questions if you know what's good for you."

"I'm just trying to understand the objectives." Two kept his eyes on the road. "Am I supposed to covertly follow him or chase him down?"

"Do what I say, gringo, and nothing more." Domingo pulled a knife and rotated the blade as if it was supposed to glint menacingly in the moonlight. "I won't ask you again."

Two looked at the knife. He could take it and cut the other man's throat before he knew what happened. These untrained thugs thought they were tough. They were nothing, especially compared to a man of his skills.

Rather than slit the other man's throat, Two shrugged and went silent.

They finally reached town. Domingo kept staring at his phone. His lips were turned down in a permanent scowl, so it was hard to determine if he was angry or just patiently waiting on new information.

Two didn't ask. He slowed down for a traffic light and stopped. He tapped his fingers on the steering wheel and waited. The light turned green. He slowly accelerated. Domingo didn't tell him where to go, so he went straight.

He followed the speed limit. It was late and there was almost no traffic in this part of town. The road entered a square roundabout at the town square ahead. He turned right and drove next to the park.

Tall, black lamps lit the square bright as day. The trashcans were overflowing with garbage. Trash littered the area around them. A broken guitar was lying on the band stage. A large festival sign with the mayor's face hung front and center at the sidewalk entrance to the square.

Two pulled to the side of the road and awaited further instructions. Domingo kept staring at the texts on his phone.

He let the silence linger for a few seconds before finally asking a question. "He wasn't spotted on cameras?"

"No." Domingo looked sullen and angry.

"Okay. Well, we know where the cameras are. We know where he'd have to go to avoid them."

Domingo narrowed his eyes. "How do you know?"

Two showed him the map app. "Users mark the locations of traffic cameras and cops." He zoomed out. "The only way to avoid cameras when you come into town from the north is to take this residential road east or west. It hooks up with the highway on the west side and connects to neighborhoods on the east side."

"How does this help us?"

"It means we know the target went one of these ways. Since we entered town from the east side and drove across town without seeing him, I think it's safe to say he went west."

Domingo tilted his head slightly. "You think you're a detective or something?"

"No. I'm just making an educated guess." Two leaned back in his seat and waited for the man to make a decision.

Domingo studied the map. His eyes flared slightly. "Go here." He jabbed his finger on a location. The app put a pin on the map.

Two studied the route and pulled back onto the road. He took the first right out of the roundabout and headed for Route 45 to the north.

"You don't need to put it in the GPS?" Domingo asked.

"No." Two took a left. The address was a mile ahead on the right.

Domingo slapped the dashboard. "Don't go to the address. We need to be covert."

Two took a left into a side street. He drove behind the businesses, turned off his headlights, and used the streetlights for illumination. He stopped at the next intersection. The target building was about a block north, just across the road from the former police station.

Domingo got out. Two got out and followed him. They were at the edge of town. Most of the streetlights were out. The storefronts looked old and dilapidated. They'd been abandoned long ago.

A few still looked operational. But even they looked old and tired. Like they were barely hanging onto life. Maybe it was because they were all closed at this late hour. Or maybe they looked just as dead during normal business hours.

Domingo paused at the end of the street. He knelt next to a building. Looked across the road. A long chain link fence ran along the road on the other side. There was no sidewalk, and the area was overgrown with weeds and tall grass.

There was no light emanating from the other side of the fence. No signs of life. The nearest light was about a hundred yards to his right on the left side of the road. It lit the signage for the neighboring property. Two could make out the words from here.

Albert's Salvage.

Domingo typed something on his phone. Probably a warning. Two pretended not to notice. He pretended not to know anything. That was what he'd been told to do. *Act like you don't know anything.*

So, he played stupid.

He took out his compact monocular. Pressed himself to the side of the building. Edged the monocular around the corner so he could look without being seen. He switched to thermal. It wasn't very powerful, but it was good enough for this distance.

Domingo pulled a handgun. He remained crouched, looking up and down the street. It looked like someone was going to die tonight.

Carver reached the outskirts of town. He took the residential road to the west to avoid the cameras. He reached Albert's a little while later. He'd texted ahead. Albert was still awake. He apparently wasn't sleeping well since the bike rally was starting tomorrow and he wasn't sure what would happen.

The gate to the salvage yard rolled open. Carver went inside.

Albert closed the gate and went to the window. "Park around the back of that shed. Just in case."

Carver drove around the back of the shed. There was a small, enclosed carport there. It was a good place to hide the truck, though he wasn't anticipating any company since Hugo was dead and he'd avoided all the cameras coming into town.

Still, it was better to be prepared. Joe always told him to expect the problems he didn't think would be a problem and everything would go wrong according to plan. Basically, expect the unexpected.

This was no different. Hugo was dead, but the watcher was still there. Someone else could be sent. Someone who might be smart enough to figure out where he'd gone.

He walked around the shed. Albert was there, a curious look in his eyes. "I welded a new bar onto this side of the gate," he said. "They gonna need a heavy cutter to get inside this time."

"It'll be someone different this time," Carver said. "I heard Hugo and his pals had a car wreck."

"They did?" Albert frowned. "They're dead?"

"From what I heard." Carver shrugged. "Probably drinking and driving. You know how it is."

Albert winked and grinned. "Oh, I know how it is." He clapped his hands. "I've never been this happy to hear about another man's passing." He sobered quickly. "Why did you come tonight? You hear that something might happen?"

"Did Joe come here at all in the days before he died?"

"Only one time. He just wanted to plant a sign out front. Asked for my support. I told him I was happy to do anything to get that criminal, Mayor Herrada, out of office."

Carver looked west. It was too dark to see the fence on the west side. "How far is it to the fence?"

Albert didn't even have to think about it. "A hundred and twenty yards. This place is the size of three football fields lined up side-by-side."

"Big place."

Albert nodded. "My great grandfather bought the land for cheap back in the day. It was all sand and scrub brush and everyone figured it was worthless. He wanted to start a horse ranch because people were still using them for primary transportation back then."

"Early nineteen hundreds?" Carver asked.

"Yep. But he did other work to get his dream off the ground. Can you believe he went from repairing wagon wheels to automobiles?"

"That's quite a life."

Albert smiled. "Yep. I wish I'd been alive back then. It was still the wild west out here."

"I take it you're a big fan."

"Oh, I love westerns." He pretended to fast-draw revolvers. "Pow!"

"What do you know about the building to the west of your property?"

Albert blinked as if switching gears. "Oh, that place? It used to be a warehouse. Then it turned into a skating rink. When that failed, an auto parts place tried to make a go of it. Then it was going to be the site of a Wal-Mart, but those plans fell through. Someone said it was bought by a company from out east. I don't know if that's true or not."

"You ever see activity over there?"

Albert shook his head. "I got a big wall around this place, so I don't see what the neighbors are doing, and they don't see what I'm doing."

"No cameras?"

"Just out front. I never saw a reason to put them anywhere else."

He looked west. "Why?"

"I'm just tracking down leads. I think Joe went to that building a few weeks ago. I want to know why."

"How do you know he went there?"

"His GPS." Carver took out his phone and showed Albert the date. "Did he come here on that day?"

Albert shook his head. "No, he came by probably a month before then. It was right around the time he kicked off his campaign."

"Mind if I wander over and have a look?"

"There's a big stack of cars there. You'd have to climb them to see over the fence."

"Not a problem." Carver started walking.

"Hang on. I'll give you a lift in the cart."

Carver shook his head. "It's too loud. Probably better if you don't come. Keep an eye on the gate and let me know if anyone shows up."

"You expecting someone?" Albert asked.

"No, but after Hugo's surprise visit, I don't want to take any chances."

Because the next guy might be even more dangerous.

CHAPTER 26

Carver looked at the tall stack of crushed cars.

He looked between the cracks and could see the steel plate fence on the other side. Albert didn't play around when it came to border security.

He stepped up on the crushed roof of the bottom car and hauled himself up to the next one until he reached the top, some five cars later. The metal creaked and groaned threateningly, but the stack didn't wobble in the slightest.

Carver went prone and looked over the fence at the neighbor's yard. The building was large, brown, and nondescript. There was no signage out front. The parking lot was cracked and overgrown with weeds.

He used his monocular in night vision to zoom in. There were windows but they were boarded up. There was no light leaking around the edges. He used infrared. No heat signatures. No signs of life.

That didn't mean anything. The boards might have tape around the edges. The walls were concrete blocks and brick. They were thick enough to conceal heat signatures inside.

There was a camera facing the front of the building. It was big and clunky, like something that might have been installed decades ago. He couldn't tell if it was working.

He spotted a smaller hump on the building near the southeast corner. A newer camera. One that could have been installed in the past five years. The night vision picked up a slight twinkle around the edges. That twinkle meant the camera had infrared and it was on.

It took a matter of moments to find two more cameras along the east side of the building. One halfway down and the other above the loading bay doors. Carver worked his way down the wall of cars, keeping low in case an unseen camera was looking his way.

He stopped when he was even with the back of the old warehouse. There was a tall chain link fence along the back, topped by coils of razor wire. There was a chain link fence running parallel to Albert's sheet metal fence, also topped with razor wire.

There was a space of about ten feet between Albert's fence and the chain link fence. A small section of no-man's land that would be hard to cross without the right tools.

It was hard to tell without proper light, but the razor wire coils looked springy. They weren't sagging or broken as if they'd experienced years of neglect. Carver risked a look with his tactical flashlight. He aimed it straight down and shielded the light with a hand.

He got a glimpse of shiny new metal. The fence and the wire were relatively new. He flicked the flashlight off quickly and tucked it in a leg pocket. He shot Albert a text. Telling him he was going to keep watch for a few hours to see if there was any movement.

Carver took a position with a clear view of the entrance. He remained prone even though the bent and broken car roof was uncomfortable. A bit of seat cushion was poking out of the window. It smelled old and moldy, but he ripped off a chunk and put it under his stomach.

It wasn't exactly comfortable, but it was more bearable. He put his eye to the monocular and kept it aimed at the street. It only took fifteen minutes to notice something, and it wasn't on the property. It was across the street.

A man's head poked around the corner for just an instant. It was lower to the ground than it should have been, indicating the man was crouching or kneeling. A moment later, a monocular poked around the corner, looking up and down the street.

There were two possibilities. One—someone else was casing the building, or two—someone was looking for him.

Carver kept watching while he thought it through. The second option was most likely. The watcher told someone that Carver was on the move. They expected him to show up on camera when he reached town. But he didn't because he'd avoided the cameras.

They deduced that Carver knew about the cameras and had taken a route away from them. They knew he could have gone east or west. There was nothing important to the east, but there was certainly something important to the west.

Their next deduction was that Carver must have somehow known about this place. Maybe because they knew Joe had known about it, or maybe it had been pure instinct. It didn't matter. Carver was here. They were here.

He just had to make sure they didn't see him. Right now, they were looking for confirmation. He wanted them to keep guessing.

The man at the corner carefully used his monocular to look up and down the street. If he looked up at all, he might spot Carver. There was a twisted piece of the roof that partially shielded him from view. But it wasn't enough to keep him hidden.

If the guy focused on the wall of crushed cars, there was a good bet he'd spot Carver with night vision. If he switched to thermal, then Carver would stand out like a beacon. That was assuming the monocular had those capabilities.

Turning back to Joe's wisdom, it seemed best to assume that it did. That Carver was seconds away from being exposed. He slowly backed over the side of the cars. Put his foot on the next car roof down.

He stood there so he could look through the space between the cars. The view of the road wasn't as good from there. He couldn't see the monocular anymore. That was fine because it meant the other man couldn't see Carver either.

Carver shifted to the right. He kept going until he put the warehouse between him and the man with the monocular. Then he climbed back to the top and looked through his monocular. He was no longer in the line of sight of the man with the monocular.

He couldn't see the front gate of the warehouse either. It seemed doubtful that anyone entered the property that way. The building was supposed to look abandoned. Which meant any traffic would come from somewhere else.

It was also possible that there was plenty of traffic to the place, but it went unnoticed due to its location. Without extended reconnaissance, it was hard to know.

Carver worked his way down the car roofs and settled down with a view to the back of the warehouse. Albert's property was larger, but the wall of cars ended about fifty yards past the back fence of the warehouse.

He went all the way to the end to look at the property behind the warehouse. There wasn't anything there. Just a vacant lot. But there was something on the lot that caught his eye. Tire tracks carved through the scrub brush.

The tracks went to the back of the fence. There wasn't an obvious gate there, but Carver spotted a pair of support poles right next to each other. There were no hinges, but there were three latches.

The latches held the chain link to the support pole. Springing the latches would release the fence. Cantilevered gate rollers allowed the gate to slide open. The rollers were small and almost unnoticeable. They'd done a good job making the gate look like just another stretch of fence.

The well-worn dirt road leading to the secret gate, however, was a dead giveaway. The only reason it wasn't highly noticeable was because it was shielded by Albert's car stack and fence on one side and a hill on the other.

The only way to see the road was from the road to the north. The empty lot to the north of the warehouse was overgrown and the entrance to the dirt road was partially concealed by weeds. Most people wouldn't give it a second glance.

The dirt road had deep ruts in it despite the rocky soil. Those tracks weren't caused by light cars. They were caused by heavier trucks. Trucks hauling cargo.

The cargo was almost certainly drugs. The drugs were probably concealed in ordinary-looking cargo which added to the weight. The width of the tire tracks indicated trucks with double tires on the back.

He didn't think the tracks were from semi-trucks, but he couldn't discount them either. There was plenty of room to maneuver a semi-truck in the loading zone, but driving a big rig down the dirt road would be risky.

Carver swept the monocular back and forth, studying the area. The rocky hills concealed the road on the west. Albert's fence and car stacks concealed it from the east. It offered the perfect clandestine route for trucks to approach the warehouse unseen.

It might also be the perfect way for Carver to infiltrate.

The warehouse was about twenty feet from the gate. The east-facing loading docks were another fifty feet forward. A truck would drive through the gate and angle east to line the trailer up with a loading dock, then back up to it.

The eastern side was also the only place with doors. There was a ground-level rollup door about ten feet from the northeastern corner of the building. Next to it was an ordinary entry door. The only other doors were on the raised loading docks.

The northern side of the building had no ladders, no doors, nothing. Just boarded windows that were too far off the ground to be useful even if he could remove the plywood covering them. The gutters, however, looked like cast iron pipes. Provided they were still firmly attached to the building, they might offer a way to reach the roof.

The first challenge would be reaching the vacant lot. He could try to reach it from Albert's place, but he'd have to overcome significant hurdles first. The first would be getting over Albert's fence. Then he'd have to get over the fence guarding the abandoned lot.

A couple of ladders would do the trick. He could leapfrog them. Put both ladders against Albert's fence. Climb one to the top, pull the other one up and lower it on the other side of the fence. Step over the fence to the second ladder, pull up the first one, set it down, and then repeat the process to cross the chain link fence.

But ladders wouldn't be easy to conceal. Even if he laid them both down, there weren't enough weeds to hide them. If a truck arrived, the driver would see them and alert the warehouse.

The best approach would be via the dirt road. He'd have to drive all the way around the salvage yard and find a place to hide the truck. Then he could approach on foot. Since the gate didn't seem to have locks, he could simply unlatch it and slide it open wide enough to squeeze through.

He wondered if Joe was dead because he'd done the same thing Carver was now contemplating. Maybe. Maybe not. That wasn't going to stop Carver from trying. But first he had to fine-tune his plan.

Then he'd see if there was anything inside this building worth killing for.

TWO WATCHED THE BUILDING.

There was no activity. No sign that the target was here. Not unless he'd hidden the truck and walked. That was what Two would have done. Parked the truck half a mile away and walked. If the target had done that, he would have reached the building just a minute before they did.

Domingo remained crouched, the monocular glued to his eye. He swept it back and forth. Left to right, but never up and down. The man didn't seem to think in three dimensions. The target might be on a roof. He might even be on top of that wall of wrecked cars in the salvage yard.

Two almost suggested it but didn't feel like dealing with a cranky contract killer. That wasn't part of the plan. There were enough complications as it was without drawing more attention to himself.

Domingo growled and backed away from the corner. He tapped on his phone. Probably sent another text. "You were wrong. I don't see anyone."

"There are plenty of places to hide around here." Two leaned against the brick building. "Where else would he have gone at this hour?"

Domingo stared silently at his phone.

"Let's drive around the building. Take a look at the perimeter." Two pointed to the wall of cars in the salvage yard. "What if he's up there?"

The other man narrowed his eyes. "How would he get in there? Look at that fence. Look at that gate."

"Maybe the owner let him in."

Domingo laughed without humor. "At this hour? As you said, gringo, there are few places he could go."

"Okay. So, what now?"

Domingo lunged at Two. He put his hand around the taller man's neck. His knife was suddenly in his hand, the point a scant inch from Two's jugular. "I told you to stop asking questions."

Two stared at Domingo's dead, black eyes. "I'm trying to help. That's hard to do without information sharing."

"And you don't need to know anything." Domingo pressed the point hard against Two's neck. "You need to keep quiet and follow my orders."

"Okay, fine!" Two trembled as if he was frightened. "What are your orders?"

Domingo grinned, showing the gold crowns on his front teeth. "Good gringo. See? You're learning." He sheathed the knife and released Two. "For now, we wait. We watch. And you keep your mouth shut."

Two kept his mouth shut and nodded. He was itching to kill this idiot, but he held back. It was better to conceal his abilities. To act helpless and frightened. Then when it came time to kill, it would be a complete surprise to the other person.

He and Domingo were, of course, on the same side. Working for the same people. At least on the surface. The cartel was a family. Families sometimes had disagreements about who should be in charge.

Domingo was loyal to one family member. Two was loyal to another. In general, they both wanted the same thing. But if push came to shove, Two would remain loyal to his family member and eliminate anyone who got in the way.

Until then, he would act like a nobody. Like a regular guard for hire. Hiding in the camouflage of mediocrity had always worked out well for him. It was no different now, despite how irritated he was with Domingo.

The hum of an engine drew Two's attention to the south. A silver sedan appeared under a streetlight to the south. Its headlights were off. Domingo glanced at it, then went back to watching the building.

Two caught a glimpse of shadows in the vehicle. He wasn't supposed to know about them, but he did. He knew all about the operation. All the players. As a lowly guard, they didn't pay him much heed.

He was the proverbial fly on the wall. Always listening. Always watching out for the boss. Making sure everything was going according to plan. Making sure these people were doing their jobs right.

The car pulled to the curb. Four men got out. One of them spoke in lightly accented English. "What is the problem?"

The accent wasn't Spanish. The men had tanned skin, but their features weren't Latino. That was because they weren't from South America.

Domingo nodded at Two. "The watcher thinks Carver might be around here. He might know about the warehouse."

"How is that possible?" The same man who'd spoken stared down the street at the warehouse.

"I don't know." Domingo nodded his head at Two. "He's the one who suggested it. I'm beginning to think this is a waste of time."

"Explain."

Domingo turned to Two. "Yes. Explain."

Two pulled out his phone and opened the map app. He highlighted the route from the ranch to the building. "Carver arrived back at the ranch. He was only there for an hour or so before he abruptly drove back toward town. The cameras didn't pick him up entering town, so I suspected he'd taken a route through a residential neighborhood toward this building." Two turned the phone around so they could see the route and the marked camera locations. "He could have gone east or west along these northern routes, but I don't know why he would have gone east."

The man studied the map. Nodded. "Your reasoning was sound. I will take precautions."

Domingo folded his arms over his chest. "I think he's wrong. I've been watching and haven't seen Carver anywhere around here."

The man narrowed his eyes at Domingo. "You may go. We will take care of this."

Domingo shrugged. He walked back toward the truck and gestured for Two to come with him. He stopped at the driver's side door and held out his hand. Two gave him the keys, then went to the passenger side.

Two watched the men climb back into the silver car.

Domingo grunted and spoke in Spanish. "Why are we dealing with Arabs? I don't trust them." He looked at Two and laughed. "You didn't even know they were Arabs, did you?"

Two shook his head. "I thought they were Latino."

Domingo burst into laughter. "Stupid gringos."

Two, of course, knew they were Arabic. He knew their names and which country they were from. He knew why the cartel had partnered with them. They were strategic reasons someone like Domingo wouldn't understand.

But he played along anyway. "Why are we dealing with Arabs?"

Domingo sneered and made a show of looking Two up and down. "For the same reason we deal with people like you. Because the boss thinks it's good for business."

Two nodded. "Whatever the boss says is right."

"Yeah, and don't forget it." Domingo flashed his knife and grinned. "When someone forgets that I'm the one who puts them in the ground."

Two let Domingo have his illusions. The truth was, the man was nothing compared to his older brothers. They'd been top-tier killers. Not because they could shoot a gun or wield a knife. But because they were pros at making murders look like accidents.

Unfortunately, they were dead. They'd died at the hands of one of their targets. Someone who'd somehow avoided the death they'd had planned for him and killed them instead.

And now that someone was here in town.

— • —

CHAPTER 27

Carver saw movement.

The regular door swung inward. Four men filed outside. The last one out closed the door behind him. They were carrying rifles at the low and ready. They had handguns holstered at their hips. Survival knives sheathed on their thighs.

They were wearing black fatigues and black ballcaps turned backward. These were no ordinary warehouse security guards, that was for certain. These guys looked ready to kill an intruder on sight.

Carver remained tucked away at the end of the wall of cars. He was up against the thick sheet metal fence separating Albert's place from the neighboring property.

A gap in the metal allowed him to peer through with his monocular. He watched the men stand outside the door for a moment.

They were talking. One of them made a circling movement with his finger. *Take a look around the building*, he seemed to be saying. Normal operating procedure.

One of the men pointed toward the salvage yard. He pointed up at the wall of cars. The man who'd made the circling motion nodded and unclipped a radio from his belt. He spoke into it. Nodded again.

When he held the radio, he released the grip on his rifle and let it hang from the strap. At first glance it looked like an M4. But the grip design caught Carver's attention. It was one he'd seen before.

The grips on most American rifles were smooth or covered in small bumps to increase grip. This one had ridges on the front and back. The barrel shroud and stock designs also looked familiar, but he couldn't place the make and model.

There were so many variations of the M4 that no one could possibly remember them all. Carver knew the most popular models by sight. But the rifles these guys were carrying weren't popular. At least, not in these parts.

He zoomed in on the holstered handguns. The grips looked different. They weren't Glocks. They had a design similar to the rifle grips. It was hard to make out much detail in night vision. The manufacturer's name was probably engraved in the metal, making it impossible to see without light.

It was the faces of the men that helped make the link. These men weren't Hispanic. They were Arabic. The weapons were made in the United Arab Emirates. Manufactured by Caracal. If he recalled correctly, the rifles used 5.56 ammo and used gas pistons to reload the chamber.

Did that mean these men were from the UAE? Were they Emiratis or from another Middle-Eastern country?

Carver watched the men split into two groups of two. They walked opposite ways around the building. They moved cautiously, one sweeping the side and rear, the other keeping eyes front.

He started the timer on his watch.

These men were well trained. Probably current or former military. They were Arabic and carrying UAE manufactured weapons. And they were somehow tied to local Hispanic cartels. They had to be if they were operating in their territory.

What possible reason could there be for that?

The UAE was a major hub for weaponry. They manufactured and sold everything from small arms to weaponized drones. But if they were selling weapons here, then why weren't the gang members packing Caracal handguns?

The immediate answer was obvious. Caracal weapons would stand out to local law enforcement. Glocks, Colts, H&K, and other major weapons brands were common in the wild. But if there was a sudden rash of Caracal weapons being found, then that would stick out.

Carver didn't think the warehouse was a hub for illegal weapons dealing. It could be drugs. Could be just about anything. And it seemed there was now an Arabic connection. Or maybe there was no connection at all.

These might be freelancers. Mercenaries. Men without allegiance to anyone. It just so happened that they preferred a specific brand of weapons. They might have even been in the UAE military at some point and kept their service weapons.

Joe loved to say, "Just because it looks like a duck doesn't mean it's a duck." That was his way of saying, don't make assumptions just because something looks, swims, and quacks like a duck.

Motion drew Carver's attention to the warehouse roof. A fifth man was standing at the edge, scanning the wall of crushed cars with a monocular. He turned to look further back into the salvage yard.

The brand name FLIR was easily visible on the side of the monocular, so it almost certainly had multiple advanced modes like thermal vision and more.

Albert's plate metal fence was thick. Metal blocked infrared rays. Even if the man was using thermal, he wouldn't spot Carver's heat signature through the metal.

The man walked to the back corner of the warehouse and looked at the concealed road and surroundings. His movements were precise and deliberate. He was taking his time. Being thorough.

Carver started the second timer on his watch.

After the man on the roof finished surveying the hidden road, he walked further down the edge of the building and began scanning the other part of the boundary.

The man who'd been watching from across the road had obviously warned the people in the building. He'd somehow surmised that Carver was in the area. Once they made a few circuits without seeing him, would they remain as vigilant?

Guarding a place like this was probably ninety-nine percent boredom and tedium. Routine probably consisted of sitting around, watching monitors for activity. Playing cards. Watching television. Maybe reading romance novels.

Tonight was an exciting deviation from the norm for the guards. But now that they suspected Carver might know about the building, would that change their routine? Or would they keep their ears perked just a bit more than usual?

The four men on the ground finished their patrol and met back in front of the door fifteen minutes later. They spoke for a few minutes. One of them said something and the others laughed. Another one replied to the first and they laughed again.

They might be military trained and deadly, but they were still as normal as any other soldier. Which meant they might make the same mistakes as most soldiers.

The man on the roof returned to the side of the building. He leaned over the edge and said something. Carver couldn't make out the words, but it sounded Arabic. One of the men on the ground replied to him.

The man on the roof nodded and went back to scanning with the monocular. The four men on the ground split back into pairs and resumed their patrol. Carver started his timer again.

The ground patrol had taken eleven minutes to complete a circuit. The rooftop sentry had taken a little over ten minutes.

Infiltrating tonight seemed like a bad idea. Most people would agree. Most people would call it a night and wait until the guards were settled back in. Most people wouldn't see the opportunity for what it was.

A place like this didn't want to draw attention to itself. They wouldn't have a large contingent of guards. The more people you had, the more mouths you had to feed. The more resources you had to consume.

It would necessitate someone actively replenishing food and other resources. They would consume more water and power and the utility bills might draw someone's attention. This kind of covert installation would be manned by a maximum of ten people.

But judging from their reaction to a possible intrusion, it seemed far more likely that these five men represented the entire contingent. At most, there was one more person inside the building watching the camera feeds.

Joe would tell Carver he was being impetuous. That he should gather several days' worth of intel before even thinking about going inside. He'd probably put on a ghillie suit and sit in one place for three days without moving.

Rhodes would probably order the techs to plant surveillance gear and settle in for the long haul before deciding to do anything. It wasn't uncommon for the team to gather two or three months' worth of data before acting.

If Leon was here, he'd already be convinced that these people were up to no good. He'd want to circle in behind the patrolling guards and eliminate them in pairs. Then he'd snipe the man off the building.

Once everyone was dead, then he'd be ready to investigate and find out what was going on inside the building.

Carver didn't have the luxury of sitting around for days. He didn't have high-tech gear to rely on. He could probably kill the guards but doing that would trigger a chain reaction. He didn't know what that reaction would be, but it would be bad.

It would almost certainly put Andrea in danger. And if Jessica had been telling the truth about her situation, it could get her killed.

The gangs would know without a doubt that Carver was involved. There would be no way to disguise it as a rival gang hit. It would drive him underground. It was important to play this as close to the chest as possible.

And that meant taking advantage of this momentary opportunity. Which meant he'd have to improvise a better way of penetrating the warehouse perimeter. That also involved getting over Albert's tall sheet metal fence which would be a challenge in and of itself.

He texted Albert. *Is there another way out of the salvage yard? I need access to the neighboring property.*

Albert replied quickly. *You about to do something stupid?*

Maybe.

There was a moment's lag before Albert replied again. *There's an emergency exit back just before the wall of buses. If you go inside that bus at the far back corner on the western side, you can go out the back door. But it swings shut behind you and you can't get back in without a key.*

Carver looked down the fence toward the buses, some fifty yards distant. He shot a short reply of thanks to Albert then hustled along the fence toward the wall of buses. About halfway down, he checked the warehouse roof.

The rooftop sentry wasn't visible. The timer had reached six minutes, so if he kept to the same pace, it would be four more minutes before he returned to the eastern side of the building. Hopefully he was consistent, or this was going to be a lot harder than it needed to be.

Carver reached the wall of buses. Albert had fortified the buses with braces and metal beams buried in the ground every few feet. Otherwise, it would be an unstable tower. A disaster waiting to happen.

The doors to the buses on the lower levels were blocked by plates of metal welded over the openings. Carver went to the bus closest to the fence. There were no visible hinges. No handle. Nothing to indicate it opened.

He put his fingers under the metal plate and tugged. Hinges creaked, and the plate rotated open. There were dual direction spring hinges hidden on the back side of the plate. He slipped inside the bus and eased the door shut so the spring hinges didn't slam it closed.

The inside of the bus was pitch black. Carver raised the monocular and looked around. The windows were blacked out but there was just enough ambient light to see that there were no seats inside the bus. It was wide open all the way to the back door.

He made his way to the back. A heavy metal latch secured the door from the inside. He pushed the lever. The door swung open on spring hinges just like the ones used on the front door.

The timer hit ten minutes. Carver cracked open the door and aimed the monocular at the building. The rooftop sentry was back. He was looking down and talking, presumably with the guards on the ground.

It looked like they'd been there for a few seconds. It might have taken them less time to make the circuit. They might have been slightly less vigilant on the second pass. The rooftop sentry kept talking.

Carver wondered if they were debating doing another patrol. It was highly likely. After all, this probably wasn't part of their daily routine. They normally stayed indoors and out of sight. They didn't want to be outside doing guard duty.

If they were diligent, they'd keep patrolling for a while. If they were lazy, they'd go back inside.

The rooftop guy straightened. Stretched and yawned. He put his hands on his hips and sighed. He didn't have that same attentive look as the guys on the ground. The guy in charge had probably told him to keep patrolling and he didn't like it one bit.

He finally put the monocular to his eye and started sweeping it in Carver's direction. He rotated back and forth, carefully examining the area along the concealed road from the fence to the hill and back again.

He lowered the monocular. Walked west along the roof. Started scanning the area on the other side of the hill. Once he finished there, he moved to the western side of the building.

Carver had already started the timer. He had six minutes to cover forty yards. He took an empty rifle magazine from his backpack and put it between the bus door and the latch to keep it from closing all the way.

He hustled to the chain link fence. Pulled his eight-inch bolt cutter from the backpack. Made short work of the links at the post and slid through the opening. He was in the abandoned lot now just a few feet from the dirt road.

He snipped one of the wires connecting the fence to the post and used it to secure the bottom of the clipped fence together so it wouldn't hang open. If someone came this way, they'd have to look closely to see the opening.

Then he hustled toward the chain link gate. He kept an eye on the timer and an eye on the roof. There was no cover out here. The chain link fence blocked him on the left and it was a long run to the small hills on the right.

It might be dark, but Carver's heat signature would stick out like a sore thumb. If the rooftop sentry returned, this stretch of road would turn into a shooting range and Carver would be the target. Unless the guy was a real slouch, it wouldn't be too hard hitting a moving target out here.

The timer kept ticking down. Carver reached the gate with two minutes to spare. He'd already studied the latches with the monocular, so he knew how to operate them.

The release levers were accessible from either side of the gate. Probably so delivery drivers could open the gate themselves. But they were designed to be opened with a tool. Probably pliers or something similar.

Carver had brought several tools, but not pliers.

The bolt cutters were the closest thing he had. Since the levers were thick and there was no danger of the cutter actually cutting through them, he clamped the cutting end on the top lever and twisted.

The top latch released. He repeated the process for the other two. It took thirty seconds to open them. It would have taken fifteen seconds with a pair of channel locks. He was down to one minute and thirty seconds on the timer.

He pulled on the gate. The rollers were well oiled. It slid open easily just enough so he could squeeze through. Then he closed it behind him.

One minute left.

He heard talking. The guards were getting close. He used the bolt cutters to close the latches. It felt like it took forever. He hurried from the gate to the north side of the building. The door was right around the corner.

Thirty seconds remaining.

Someone cleared his throat. Carver looked up. The rooftop sentry was directly overhead. If he so much as glanced down, he'd see Carver.

And it would all be over.

Chapter 28

Carver didn't panic.

He pressed his back to the wall. Looked at the dark silhouette on the roof. He raised his monocular for a clear look. The man on the roof had a foot on the lip of the roof. He was staring blankly at Albert's property without the monocular.

Then he put the monocular to his eye and started sweeping left to right. Carver slid around the corner to the door. He tested the knob. It wasn't locked. He eased the door open and slipped through.

It was pitch black inside. Carver put the monocular to his eye and activated night vision. He was in a large, open space with very little ambient light. The windows were boarded up, but there were rows of skylights on the roof, allowing in just enough moon-light for night vision to work.

Carver switched to thermal imaging. No heat signatures glowed. He switched back to night vision. The place looked big and empty. He walked along the wall. Found the raised loading dock platforms.

He felt his way around them and eventually reached the other wall. The cargo bay stretched from one side of the warehouse to the other. He followed that wall to the back of the bay. It was about a hundred feet, maybe more.

There was a stretched SUV limo parked in the back. Next to it was a sedan. There were two large rollup doors that probably led to the interior of the warehouse.

The rollup doors didn't budge when he pulled up on them. There were buttons on the wall. They presumably opened and closed the doors. Everyone was still outside patrolling and unlikely to hear anything, so he tested the buttons. Nothing happened. It seemed there was no power to the controls.

Carver moved along the back wall and reached an area that looked like it had once had a rollup door. That door had been removed and the opening had been bricked up. There was another section just like it a few feet down, but a regular door had been installed in the middle.

He twisted the handle. The door opened. Light spilled out from the other side, blinding the night vision. Carver lowered the monocular and blinked spots out of his eye. He pocketed the monocular and drew his Glock. Just in case.

There was a hallway in front of him. He stepped inside and closed the door behind him. It was a long, carpeted hallway. The carpet was clean. The walls were painted a modern shade of gray. The place smelled like new construction.

The hallway was long and lined with multiple doors. The first doors on the left and right were open. The last door on the left was open. There were closed French doors at the end of the hallway.

There were dull sounds from the open doorway near the end of the hallway. It sounded like a television.

He peeked into the first door on the left. There was a full kitchen on the other side. Stainless steel appliances. Granite countertops. The whole nine yards. The floor was slate. Someone had gone all out to make it as nice as possible.

He cleared the room and moved to the one across the hall. It was a game room complete with pool tables, card tables, and a bar with well-stocked shelves. There was even a video game console in front of a large TV.

The next few doors were closed but unlocked. He eased them open one at a time. Looked inside. They were bedrooms, each one with top-notch furnishings. Each with big bathrooms and tiled showers.

There were signs of occupancy in five of the rooms. Clothing on the bed or floor. Personal items here and there. The sixth room was clean. The bed was made. There were no clothes in the closet. No messes in the bathroom.

That bolstered Carver's theory that there were only five men here. It made him wonder why they'd gone to such expense to build a residence inside this warehouse when it seemingly only housed five people.

Maybe there were more rooms on the other side of the French doors. Maybe those weren't as well furnished. Maybe they had rows of bunkbeds for ordinary henchmen while the Arabs got the best rooms.

It seemed doubtful. If this was where they housed cartel members, it was woefully understaffed. This place should be crawling with thugs. Carver saw no evidence there was anyone here except for the five men he'd already seen.

He continued investigating. The last door on the left led to a large room with a leather couch, end tables, and a big screen television mounted to the wall. A half-empty beer sat on a coaster on one of the end tables. Condensation dripped down the sides. Someone had been drinking it just moments earlier.

The murmur of the TV was what Carver had heard when he first entered the hallway. A show was on. Carver didn't recognize it or the actors. Then again, he didn't watch a lot of television.

The French doors at the end of the hallway were locked. There was a keycard reader to the left. He could probably kick the doors open if he wanted to, but that wasn't on the menu now.

There was something of note in the TV room. A metal door in the far wall. It was the only one he'd seen so far. The other doors were the standard kind you'd find in residences. What secrets was this one guarding?

He walked across the room and examined the metal door. It opened inward toward him, but there were no visible latches. He'd brought his slim jim, but it wouldn't open this door. This door had a magnetic lock.

Carver tugged on the handle. The door didn't budge. He examined what he could see of the jamb. It looked like the entire surface area was a magnet. There didn't seem to be a way to release it.

Normally, there would be a card reader next to the door or a button that would release the magnetic lock. Nothing like that was present here. Maybe it was opened with a smartphone or tablet.

The next anomaly was the light fixture on the wall above the door. It resembled an old-school police light. The ones they referred to as bubble-gum machines.

A loud laugh echoed down the hallway. A door slammed shut. Carver peered around the doorway and saw the men coming back inside, talking loudly in Arabic. Three of them went into the kitchen.

The third guy went into the game room across the hall. The fourth guy was making a beeline in Carver's direction. Maybe he was the one who'd been watching television. He was also the guy who'd been on the roof.

Carver looked around the room. There were two slatted doors on the other side of the room. He opened them and wasn't surprised to find a large closet on the other side.

There was a shelf filled with books and board games on the right. There were plastic boxes stacked on the left. In between them and the shelf was just enough room for Carver to squeeze into.

He closed the doors and wedged himself inside. He looked through the slats at the room beyond.

The roof sentry entered the TV room. He said something in an annoyed tone and dropped onto the couch. He took a long drink from the beer bottle and used the television control to rewind the show, presumably back to where it had been before he'd gone outside.

Carver couldn't see much of the TV from his position. He could see the back of the man's head on the couch and the door. The show was in English with Arabic subtitles. It was some kind of reality show about people who were getting married.

After thirty minutes, Carver wasn't sure which was worse torture. Listening to the TV show or being wedged into a closet without being able to sit down. Against his better judgement, he was seriously considering stepping out and killing everyone just so he could leave.

Carver leaned his weight against the plastic boxes. They creaked slightly, but the TV drowned out the sound. It alleviated some weight from his feet. He was a little annoyed that his feet were bothering him at all.

He'd been in plenty of situations where comfort wasn't an option. Remaining motionless for hours in a ghillie suit during snowstorms and heat waves. Crawling through thick black mud in a marsh because the helicopter missed the drop zone by miles. Hanging upside down from the bottom of a truck to infiltrate a base.

He was getting soft. There were no two ways about it. Unless he adopted a daily regimen to counter the effects of civilian life, he was going to be less and less able to do the things he'd been trained to do.

Then again, that was the point of civilian life. He wasn't supposed to have to deal with these things anymore. He could be sitting on a beach with Paola, sipping drinks and watching their kids play in the ocean.

He almost shuddered. But something else caught his attention first. The lights in the room were flickering. No, not the lights. A light. The one over the locked door.

The man on the couch groaned. He paused the TV. Got up and pulled out a radio. He spoke into it. Carver didn't understand most of it, but the first word the man said was a name. A moment later, another man entered the room.

Carver recognized him as the guy who'd been leading the guards on the ground. Now he had a name to go with the face. Yusef.

Yusef didn't say anything to the other guy. He walked over to the metal door. Carver didn't have a great view from this angle, so he took a risk and cracked open the closet door. With the TV paused, the room was almost silent.

The closet door made a faint *snick* when it opened. The two men didn't seem to hear it from across the room. They were standing in profile to him, so he was careful not to open the door too much in case they saw movement in their peripheral vision.

Yusef touched a keycard to the side of the door jamb. The flashing light turned off. There was a faint buzz and a click. He tugged the handle, and the door swung toward him. The two men went inside. The door swung shut behind them.

Carver remained in place for a count of thirty. Then he eased out and jogged across the room. He looked down the hallway. A man was standing at the door to the bar room. He was talking to someone inside.

It didn't look like anyone else was coming this way. He went to the metal door. Pulled on the handle. It didn't budge. He studied the door frame. A slim card reader was built into the side of it.

It was set flush to the surface and was the same color as the door frame. It was hard to see even when looking directly at it. Why they'd chosen to camouflage it was a mystery since the door was so noticeable.

Since there was no way through the door and the other men were in the hallway, it looked like he might have to spend the night in the closet. That certainly wasn't ideal, but there wasn't much else he could do without going on a killing spree.

The metal door was embedded in a cinderblock wall. The wall was painted gray. It had probably been painted to bring it into aesthetic alignment with the rest of the residential space. Carver had seen the same cinderblock wall in the other rooms on this side.

It was an original wall, not part of this new residential construction, meaning it ran from the floor all the way to the ceiling and spanned most of the length of the warehouse.

Carver imagined the layout of the warehouse. It was a large rectangle with the cargo bay taking up a section of the eastern side. The cinderblock wall intersected the cargo bay wall in the middle and divided the western side of the warehouse into two large sections.

The residential area was in the northern section, and the southern part was a mystery. What could they possibly be hiding over there? Drugs? Illegal weapons? It could be anything.

The metal door was a new addition. Maybe there had been other doorways leading to the south side of the warehouse, but they'd been bricked up and painted over.

All of that was interesting, but it didn't help him get out of here and he didn't feel like going back into the closet. He was going to have to find another way out.

Yusef seemed to be the only person with the keycard. He was a single point of failure. If something happened to him and the keycard, did anyone else have access? Was there a backup on the premises? Maybe in one of the bedrooms?

There was another set of slatted doors in the TV room. Probably another closet. Maybe this one would have more room.

Carver opened the doors and found the HVAC system and a tankless water heater. The ceiling inside was different. It wasn't drywall. It was a panel ceiling. Designed for easy access to the service space.

There was a metal shelf with HVAC filters, water filters, janitorial supplies, and other odds and ends. There was a rollaway toolchest, automotive supplies, and a small stepladder.

Carver tugged open the top drawer on the toolchest. It was fully stocked with socket wrench sets. The sockets were neatly arranged in a nylon tray with the sizes imprinted below them. One row was entirely devoted to 10mm sockets for some reason.

He closed that drawer. Checked the next one. Found a large rubber mallet, a claw hammer, and a handsaw. He closed that drawer too. It was good to know he had options if he wanted to build something.

The third drawer had something useful. A pair of pliers. They'd come in handy for opening the gate latches, provided he made it out of here in one piece. He tucked them into his backpack and closed the drawer.

There was an open space to the left of the HVAC system. Bits and pieces of ceiling panel were sprinkled on the floor there. Carver picked up the stepladder and unfolded it. It only had four steps, but that was more than enough for him to reach the ceiling.

He pushed up the panel and looked into the space above. There was enough light for him to see pipes, wires, and ductwork. He shined his tactical flashlight into the darkness. It was a giant void.

The light glinted off the glass skylights in the warehouse ceiling far above. The top of the residential area was framed with steel beams and metal studs. Flexible ductwork ran along the top of the beams.

Metal electrical conduit ran in neat rows along the center and branched off to the various rooms. Water was piped in through white polyethylene pipes that branched into smaller red and blue pipes.

Sheets of plywood had been affixed to the walls where the windows were. Carver could probably use the hammer from the toolbox to smash his way out, but the sound would be enough to wake the dead. It wasn't a viable option.

A massive cargo hoist ran lengthwise along the ceiling. A large hook hung from a platform at the far end of the main beam. Metal wheels sat on metal rails along the wall, allowing the beam to move back and forth. The hook platform could likewise roll back and forth along the beam.

It looked old and rusty. Like it hadn't been used in ages. The hook dangled about twenty feet above the residential area. That was too far to reach. But there was a ladder on the far wall. It was enclosed with a safety cage to keep climbers from falling.

The cage and ladder had been cut a few feet above the residential space. There was a climb of about forty feet to the catwalk above the hoist track. From there, the skylight was almost within reach. If only he had a ladder.

Carver looked down at the stepladder. It might be enough. But getting it up into the ceiling after him would be tricky. He turned off his flashlight and holstered it. Dropped into the utility closet.

There was a spool of twine on the metal shelf. He cut himself a length with his knife. Tied it to the top of the stepladder. Then he tied the other end to a framing beam above the ceiling. There was a loud metallic click.

Carver quickly got off the ladder and pulled the closet door closed just as the metal door opened. He left the door open just a crack so he could look through it.

Yusef came through the door with his companion just behind him. Loud booming laughter echoed behind them. A man walked out behind them. He was Caucasian. Just under six feet tall. Fairly muscular, but not overly so.

His hair was cropped short. He was dressed in gray urban camouflage and carrying a compound bow. A quiver of arrows was slung across his back.

But that wasn't the most noticeable thing about him. The thing that stood out the most was what covered his face, his outfit, and his hands.

Thick, crimson blood.

CHAPTER 29

Carver really wanted to know what was behind that door.

The man covered in blood was laughing and talking loudly. Not in Arabic. Not in English. It wasn't Spanish, either. It was Slavic. Maybe Russian. Maybe Ukrainian. It was hard to hear him because the air rushing through the HVAC system drowned it out.

Someone else laughed in response to whatever the man said. Another man emerged. His face and clothing were also streaked with blood. Two more men emerged from behind the metal door.

The door slammed shut behind them.

One of the bloody men spoke in accented English. "Yusef it was amazing. Well worth price." The accent sounded Russian, but it could be from another Slavic language too.

Yusef bowed slightly. "I am glad to hear this. Please follow Hassan. He will take you to decontamination. Your ride will be waiting to take you back to your hotel."

Hassan, the guy from the roof, bowed slightly at them. "Would you like something to drink or eat?"

One of the men grinned and spoke loudly. "Vodka?"

The other men raised their fists and shouted. "Vodka!"

Yusef left the room and went right. Hassan led the men to the left to the locked double doors. Presumably to decontamination, whatever that meant. Was that just a fancy way of saying showers? Or was there something more to it?

Carver couldn't see into the hallway from this location. He'd have to step outside the utility closet and move to his left. It wasn't worth the risk. He had other tasks that needed completing.

He closed the closet door. Climbed the short stepladder. Pulled himself up onto a support beam above the ceiling. Used the twine to pull the ladder up after him. He folded the ladder. Slid the ceiling panel back into place.

Then he turned on his tactical flashlight. The metal support beam offered a relatively easy way to traverse the area. He walked slowly. Moving too fast would cause the metal to ring like a bell.

He crossed over the area where the double doors were. He heard water rushing through the pipes. Heard the splash of water on tiles. Heard men laughing and talking.

They were definitely talking in Ukrainian. Carver wasn't fluent in the language, but he'd learned enough of it to get by during his time in the country. To the untrained ear, the language sounded like Russian. In practice, the two languages were very different.

It didn't much matter. Carver could carry on a very limited conversation in either language. When he was young and naive, he'd committed to becoming fluent in the languages of any countries he was stationed in. He'd purchased books. Listened to audio. Watched videos.

He'd learned that it was nothing like the movies. Learning to speak one language like a native was extremely difficult. Learning to speak multiple languages like a native was something that only happened in the movies.

Due to the nature of his work, he couldn't just go out and talk with the locals. That was what it took to achieve real fluency in any language. Instead, he'd gained functional knowledge. The only languages he could carry on a real conversation in were Spanish and Portuguese.

Even then, he wasn't going to fool native speakers.

One of the men said something about money. Another said he was hungry. The others laughed. It sounded like they were in a large tile room with multiple showers.

Carver knew it was best to keep moving, but he was curious to see what else he could understand.

Another man said something about Los Angeles. About getting food and something about a night club.

One of the other men said, "Club Paradiso?" in heavily accented English.

The previous man said, "Tak! Tak!" That was Ukrainian for yes.

It was already one in the morning. These guys probably wouldn't get to LA until long after the clubs were closed.

Carver listened a moment longer, then kept walking. The showers turned off. The men went silent, presumably as they toweled off.

Hassan spoke in English. "Gentlemen, you will find your clean clothing in the next room along with your souvenir packages, several bottles of vodka, and a selection of recreational pharmaceuticals."

The Ukrainians started shouting about vodka again. Carver used the noise to walk a little faster. He reached the ladder. The lower portion had been cut off when the residences below were built. The bottom rung was about head height for him. The metal safety cage started just a few feet above that.

He gripped the rung and pulled on it to ensure the wall brackets were still sturdy. The ladder was rock steady. He pulled himself up, hand over hand. Then he pulled the stepladder up behind him.

It was narrow enough to fit between ladder and cage. He considered pulling it after him with the twine, but it would probably bounce around and make a racket. Instead, he held it above his head and climbed the ladder one-handed.

It was a longer climb than it had seemed from across the room. He reached the catwalk at the top and set the stepladder down. Then he unfolded the stepladder beneath the skylight and climbed it.

By standing on the top step, he was able to reach the glass. It was standard for an old skylight—a thick pane of glass set in a metal frame. If he'd brought a hammer from the toolchest, he could easily break it.

But that would make a lot of noise and broken glass would rain down on the ceiling below. Several of the glass panes had broken over the years. They'd been replaced with plywood instead of glass.

The pane next to this one had been given the plywood treatment very recently. The wood looked new. There was even a faint odor from the silicone adhesive used to seal it to the metal pane.

The adhesive was waterproof, but it was soft and flexible. Not as good as other construction adhesives. Carver put his hands near the lower edge of the plywood. He braced his feet on the stepladder and pushed upward, straining his shoulder muscles.

The plywood peeled away from the adhesive. The skylight angled upward so he couldn't quite reach the top half. He considered jumping while pushing, but the stepladder was small. One wrong step and he'd fall over the edge of the catwalk and give the people below a surprise.

He wished he'd brought along a crowbar from the toolchest. It would make this task several magnitudes easier.

Carver wedged his fingers beneath the loose side of the plywood. He muscled himself up like he was doing a pullup. Put his head against the plywood. Pushed the plywood with his head.

The silicone finally lost its grip. He swung an elbow over the skylight frame. There was a metal vent stack a short distance away. He grabbed it. Pulled his torso onto the roof. His legs were still dangling over the void.

Carver dragged himself forward with the vent stack. The plywood wobbled on his legs. It tilted sideways, threatening to fall through the skylight. He pincered it with his feet an instant before it fell.

He breathed a sigh of relief. The plywood was half an inch thick and measured four by three feet. It was a substantial hunk of wood that would have bounced off the catwalk and smashed into the ceiling of the apartments below.

He kept the plywood wedged between his feet and used the vent stack pipe to pull himself all the way onto the roof. He gently released the plywood and took a moment to collect himself. Then he stood and stretched to work out the kinks.

The roof was flat. The skylights were not. They angled up from the surface in a triangular formation. They were the kind of old-school skylights that had gone out of fashion decades ago. Maybe as far back as the sixties.

The glass was secured by metal frames. Most of the glass panes were still intact. Some were cracked and worn, but the glass was thick and hardy. It would take solid blows to break one. Trying to pry apart the metal pane would be no easier.

This pane had been broken recently. Even the outside layer of plywood still looked relatively new. It didn't show the effects of weathering from months of exposure to the sun like the other wooden panels.

The second anomaly was the metal pane. It was warped and uneven. Like it had been pried open and then hammered back into shape.

Carver looked around to ensure that he was alone on the roof. Then he shielded his tactical flashlight with a hand and closely inspected the pane. The old paint looked burned and scorched. Someone had used a torch on it.

Once the metal softened, something flat had been used to pry it up. The entire frame showed signs of high heat and bending. With the frame out of the way, the glass would have nothing holding it in.

A heavy-duty glass suction cup with a handle could have then been used to pull the glass out quietly. The glass had probably been laid back in place afterward, but it wouldn't have been weathertight.

All it took was a cursory glance at the metal to see it had been tampered with. It looked like someone had taken a hammer or mallet to the frame to bend it back into place. They'd probably broken the glass while doing it.

They'd glued the plywood over the hole and called it a day. The edges were smooth and straight. They'd probably purchased it precut from a lumber supply store, or had it cut there.

It only reinforced what Carver had already suspected. Joe had been here. He'd been inside this building. This was his handiwork.

Carver thought about the blood on the Ukrainians. About the blood stains in Joe's pickup. What in the hell was going on inside this building? Why were Arabs guarding it? Why were Ukrainians visiting it? What did the local Hispanic gangs have to do with everything?

Who was the watcher working for? Who had been watching the building from across the street?

He imagined a likely scenario. Joe had somehow discovered this place. He'd observed it for a while. Probably a week minimum knowing how he always did his due diligence. Knowing that he never went on a mission without proper preparation.

Carver had broken into this place on barely more than a whim. He had only known about the place for a couple of hours before barging inside. And his escape had been facilitated by Joe. Even in death, Joe's careful planning had saved Carver's hide.

How far inside had Joe gone? Had he found a way into the secure sector? Despite all his planning, he couldn't have known what was inside. He would have gone in the same way Carver had gone out.

That meant he'd have seen the old hoist and the top of the apartments below. He'd have probably brought rope and lowered himself inside.

Carver examined the metal vent pipe. There were ligature marks in the rusted cast iron. Signs that a rope had rubbed the surface of the pipe. There were also marks on the lip of the roof. Something sharp had pressed into the old asphalt roofing.

A grappling hook probably. Joe had sneaked in through the gate, tossed the hook up here. Climbed the side of the building. Tied a rope to the vent pipe. Lowered himself onto the catwalk below.

Knowing Joe, he'd brought a backpack with redundant supplies. Another climbing rope, for example. He'd probably walked along the hoist beam, examining every inch of the concrete walls.

Once he'd investigated the area, he'd climbed down the ladder. Investigated the exterior of the apartments. Found the utilities closet as the best way to infiltrate. Gone inside and seen some of the same things Carver had seen.

But had he gone past the metal door? Had he found another way inside?

He wouldn't have known about the door until he went into the apartments. Carver pictured Joe examining the door and deciding he couldn't breach it without making a lot of noise. Being a careful and deliberate person, Joe would have left, planning to return with the right tools for the job.

Joe had never had that chance.

Something had happened. Something to leave the blood stains in his pickup truck. Something that caused him to get killed. He had been murdered. The only remaining question was how.

Carver's fists clenched. The occupants of this building almost certainly had something to do with Joe's death. He had no proof. Just a gut feeling. And that was good enough for him.

A diesel engine rumbled. Carver saw headlights coming from the north. Coming from the concealed back road. He laid the plywood over the metal pane, just the way it had been. There was no silicone glueing it down, but it was heavy enough to remain in place under its own weight.

He had another problem now. Unlike Joe, he didn't have a rope. The building was about two stories high. Even dangling over the side from his fingertips, the distance was too far to drop. The cast iron gutter pipes he'd noticed earlier might be sturdy enough for him to use.

He went to the eastern side of the roof above the cargo bay. The lip of the roof was only a foot high. He'd have to go prone to hide behind it. But it was dark up there and unless Hassan ventured back out to the roof, no one was likely to see him.

A cargo truck stopped outside of the gate. It wasn't a semi-truck. It was a twenty-five-foot moving truck. The kind people could rent to transport all the crap they'd accumulated over the years.

The driver got out and unlatched the gate. He pushed it to the side. Got back in the truck. Drove it onto the asphalt. He backed up to the nearest loading dock, just a few feet from the door Carver had used to get inside.

The loading docks were raised to match the height of a semi-trailer. The cargo truck was the same height, so its back end fit firmly against the dock pads. Carver went prone next to the skylight.

Lights snapped on in the loading bay. They weren't the massive old ceiling lights that hung from the rafters. These were LED lights installed on the walls all around the bay.

They bathed the place in cold, white light. Carver could see the stretched SUV limo, the black sedan, and the rollup doors leading into the mystery area. He wondered if they were about to open those doors.

The truck driver entered through the ground-level rollup door. He walked up the ramp to the concrete platform. Yusef and Hassan emerged from the apartments and met him.

The driver was Caucasian. He was a young guy with a pot belly, a worn blue cap, and scruff on his chin. He rolled up the truck's cargo door. He pulled a hand truck from inside. Stepped inside the truck. Came back out with a stack of bottled water packs.

There were forty bottles of water in each pack, according to the writing on the side of the package. The driver set the stack aside. He went back into the truck and came out with another stack.

He put it next to the first. Then he waved with his hand, as if telling someone to come over. But he wasn't waving at Yusef or Hassan. He was waving in the direction of the truck.

Someone was inside it.

CHAPTER 30

An Asian man emerged from the truck.

He was wearing a backpack and designer clothing. He was middle-aged. Two young boys and a short woman came out with him, sticking close to his side. Another young man emerged. He seemed to be alone.

Then a flood of people poured out of the truck. Hassan motioned them to keep moving so there was room for everyone. After a couple of minutes, the truck was probably empty but the loading bay was crowded with about fifty people.

There were families, young, single men, a smattering of single women, and even some kids that didn't seem to be with adults.

There were Asians, Hispanics, and other races mixed in the group. People not just from south of the border, but from all over the world. It was no surprise to Carver. The border was long and porous. It was easy to just walk into the United States unchallenged in some areas.

Coyotes, i.e. human smugglers, were responsible for some of the traffic. But most of it was just people packing up what they could carry and walking thousands of miles across South America to reach the southern border.

It seemed Yusef and his boys were helping people once they got across the border. They probably picked them up before Border Patrol got them and brought them here. Or maybe it was something more insidious.

The truck driver cut open a package of bottled water and started handing them out to the migrants. He went into the truck and wheeled out a stack of boxes with various brand names stamped on the side.

He cut open a box and started handing out potato chips and other snacks. The migrants snatched them up like they hadn't eaten in hours. They'd probably been cooped up in the dark back of the cargo truck the entire drive.

One mother put her toddler on the floor and started changing his diapers. One young woman was holding her stomach and looking distressed. Yusef pointed to a row of portable toilets against the far wall. Migrants began rushing toward them, eager to relieve themselves.

This was quite an operation.

A group of Asians remained next to Yusef. He spoke with them. One of them showed him a booklet. No, not a booklet. A red passport. Carver used his monocular to see it more clearly. It was a Chinese passport.

Yusef took the passport and inspected. He nodded. Smiled. Carver tried to read his lips, but he couldn't make out a single word. He put his ear to the glass, but the drone of background noise drowned out everything else.

The woman with the passport pulled a phone from her purse. She was well dressed and clean. It was obvious she hadn't hoofed it across South America to get to the border. She'd been driven there along with the others in her group.

The woman unfolded the phone into a large screen. She pressed her thumb to the screen to unlock it. She opened an app. Carver zoomed in with the monocular for a closer look. A big number was at the top of the screen.

Beneath the big number was a colored graph, green and red. That was a cryptocurrency app. The number was the amount of funds available. The specific cryptocurrency was Tether. Carver had used that particular currency many times.

Unlike other cryptocurrencies, Tether was pegged to the U.S. dollar. Its price varied only hundredths of a cent. In other words, you wouldn't lose your shirt if you put all your money into it because the price didn't fluctuate.

The number on the woman's screen was over ten million dollars. She tapped options on the screen. Entered an encrypted crypto wallet ID. Transferred half a million dollars.

Yusef checked his phone. Grinned and nodded. Hassan went into the apartments and returned a moment later with a briefcase. He opened it and turned it so the Chinese woman could see the contents.

It was filled with cash. On top of the cash were several blue passports. U.S. passports. One for each of her companions. Another bundle had Texas drivers' licenses.

The woman unfolded a piece of paper that was bundled with the passports. She opened it. Carver focused on it and took a picture. The sheet listed several addresses located across multiple states.

Carver had an educated guess about what was happening. About what went on in this place. Foreign nationals were taking advantage of the open border. They were coming in with other migrants and asylum seekers.

Yusef and his boys were providing them with cash in US dollars, fake IDs and apparently even houses. The foreigners were paying in crypto to hide the transactions. They were hiding these people among ordinary migrants.

He had a bad feeling about what became of the other migrants. The blood on the Ukrainians seemed to be proof enough that Yusef was also trafficking humans. Maybe providing them to people willing to pay top dollar.

Carver had seen it in other countries. He'd seen humans hunted like wild game. He'd seen them sexually abused. Seen their organs harvested and sold to the highest bidders. There was no limit to the horrors that might await those migrants.

Yusef took out a bullhorn and cleared his throat. By now, most of his guests had finished using the bathrooms. He spoke in Spanish. "Please gather around."

The migrants wandered over, forming a semicircle in front of him.

Yusef spoke again. "Welcome to America!"

The migrants broke into cheers, clapping, waving their fists. Only the Chinese contingent remained unmoved. Probably because they didn't speak Spanish.

"As promised, we have your passports, your driver's licenses, and your citizenship papers ready."

More cheers erupted.

"These are all authentic and legal. They are not forged, meaning you have all the rights of American citizens."

The group cheered louder. People hugged. Danced in place. Laughed and cried.

"Now it is your turn to adhere to the agreement you made." Yusef gave them a deadly serious look. "You will be assigned a place to live. Some of these places will be houses where you may live with multiple families. Some will be apartments. You will be expected to pay a small amount of rent."

The crowd was more sober now. Nodding in response to his demands.

"We, of course, will be monitoring our investment. We will make sure you are living in the assigned homes. And most importantly that you are doing your civic duties when it comes time to vote."

There were a few scattered cheers. Most of them looked eager to comply. Carver couldn't blame them. Instant citizenship and a place to live sounded like a sweet deal.

Yusef nodded. "Good. Form a line and come get your papers."

Two of his men unfolded a table and set several boxes on them. The migrants approached either singly or in family groups. The men gave them passports, driver's licenses, everything a citizen needed.

Carver zoomed in with his monocular. He couldn't make out the text, but the driver's licenses were all for the same state—Utah. That seemed like a strange destination since the state wasn't exactly friendly to illegal immigrants.

Then again, these people wouldn't be illegal—not technically. If these documents truly were legitimate, then it meant someone in the federal government was processing the citizenships. But how were they getting driver's licenses?

Those were given by the states, not the feds. All it took was a few people at the right government agency to make it happen. Once the information was entered into the database, everything else was automatic.

Carver wondered why the Chinese contingent had been treated differently. Maybe because of the language barrier. Maybe because they were paying for their documents. They might have made separate arrangements.

It wasn't long before everyone had their documents.

Yusef held up his hands to silence them. He put the bullhorn back to his lips. "Please board the truck. It will be departing in exactly five minutes." He turned off the bullhorn with a squeal of feedback and handed it to Hassan. Then he turned and spoke to the Chinese again.

The migrants went back into the truck. The Chinese went in last. The woman who'd spoken to Yusef wrinkled her nose in distaste before she boarded. It probably reeked of body odor and urine. There was no way someone hadn't relieved themselves inside during the journey.

The truck driver closed the cargo door and latched it. He took a stack of twenty-dollar bills from Yusef. Carver estimated it was about a thousand bucks. The driver closed the cargo bay door. Walked down the ramp. Went outside and got back into the truck.

The diesel engine rumbled to life. Carver got up and went to the lip of the roof to watch. The truck drove to the gate. The driver got out, opened it. He drove through. Got out and closed the gate. Drove away.

Carver went back to the skylights. Yusef and Hassan were talking. Nodding. Looking pleased with themselves. The Ukrainians emerged from the apartments, escorted by two of Yusef's men.

Yusef's men escorted the Ukrainians to the stretched SUV limo in the back of the bay and opened the doors for them to get in. Once they'd boarded, the SUV drove through the loading area and down the ramp to the rollup door next to the door Carver had used to enter.

Another man opened the rollup door. The SUV exited the building. The driver opened and closed the gate on his way out.

The cargo bay lights flicked off. The apartment door opened and Yusef and his boys went back inside.

It seemed Carver had been wrong. Partially wrong. The migrants weren't being traf-ficked so people like these Ukrainians could do horrible things to them. They were being used for some other nefarious purpose.

This place was a processing center. They were giving migrants legal citizenship papers and other vital documents, then giving them cheap housing to live in. He didn't know why Utah was their destination but felt certain there was a good reason for it.

Was this what Joe had discovered? Was this what had cost him his life?

Carver glanced at the time. It was going to be daylight soon. He needed to get the hell out of here before then. First, he walked to the other side of the roof. The side over the restricted area. There were no skylights.

It looked like they'd been removed and replaced by steel plates. The plates were welded together. The seams looked relatively new. Like this had been done just a few months prior. Then again, the dry air and lack of rainfall meant it took surface rust longer to set in.

There was definitely no way in from above. He looked over the side of the building. The windows weren't boarded in on this side. They were bricked up. He'd need a sledge-hammer or a welding machine to get inside the restricted area.

Carver went back to the other side of the roof. He crept up to the northeast corner. Found the gutter. It was the original cast iron pipe. A bit rusty but solidly anchored to the brick. Carver tested his weight on it. It held just fine.

He swung a foot over the edge. Gripped the pipe with both hands. Pressed his feet to the wall and used friction to get into position. The rough, rusty metal and thick metal anchor bands made it unsuitable for sliding down. Not unless he wanted to shred his hands.

Even the gloves he'd brought weren't up to the task. They were just to keep his fingerprints off anything incriminating.

Carver worked his way down the gutter. He saw the flare of lights. Heard an engine. It was still ten feet to the ground, but he dropped the rest of the way to the asphalt. He dropped to his stomach and pressed himself into the darkness at the side of the building.

This was apparently a busy place this time of night. Moments later, another cargo truck pulled up to the gate. A different driver got out. An older guy with long, gray hair. He opened the gate and drove through. He didn't get out to close it behind him.

The truck drove past the corner of the building and presumably backed up to the cargo dock. The engine shut off.

Carver rose to a crouch. He scuttled along the building. Got right up to the corner. He heard a door open and close. He looked around the corner.

No one else was in the truck. This one was a little shorter than the last. Maybe ten feet long. He heard shouting from inside the cargo bay. It was Yusef.

"You are not scheduled for tonight and you're at the wrong place! Why are you here?"

Someone replied with a northern American accent. Presumably the truck driver. "I couldn't hold them any longer. I was running low on supplies."

"This is most irregular. This is against protocol. We don't take these deliveries."

"I didn't have a choice. I really didn't. No one was answering at the other place."

"And what if there is more cargo delivered to the waystation in the meantime?"

"I put one of my guys there to watch."

Yusef spoke in Arabic. Another man replied. Probably Hassan. A door opened and shut. The driver shouted in concern.

"Hey, what are you doing?"

"You will remain perfectly still while we inspect your truck. We had better not find anything suspicious."

"You won't find anything! I told you I had to come because I was out of supplies, and I need more money."

Someone was going to come outside any moment now. Carver decided not to stick around. He ran through the open gate. It was still dark out, so he ran down the middle of the dirt road to avoid stumbling over the rocky terrain.

A moment later, one of Yusef's men stepped outside. He had a mirror attached to a pole. The kind used to examine the underbody of a vehicle. He had some other gadgets with him as well. One of them looked like a bug detector.

These men weren't playing around. It sounded like they were ready to kill the driver if he was up to something. While smuggling foreign spies into the US was normally a bad thing, the people in power didn't seem too concerned with such things these days.

It was unlikely local law enforcement or the federal government would raid the place even if they knew about it.

Carver kept going until he reached the concealed door back to Albert's property. It wasn't all that concealed since he'd propped it slightly open, making it easier to spot. He went back into the bus. Closed and latched the door behind him.

Then he hiked back to Albert's shop. He was tired. Driving back to the ranch would take too long. He decided to sleep in the truck.

Albert came outside before Carver climbed into the back of the truck. "Where have you been? I thought for sure something happened to you."

"I'm fine. Everything is fine. I'm just going to catch some shuteye in the truck."

"No need for that. I got an extra bed."

Carver nodded. "If you don't mind."

"I don't mind at all." Albert motioned him to follow.

Carver got his backpack and duffel bag and went past the shop to the small house behind it. The inside was surprisingly clean and roomy. Albert led him through the den, down a short hallway, and to a bedroom.

"It's got its own bathroom," Albert said. "If you get hungry, there's food in the fridge. Make yourself at home."

"Thank you." Carver shook his hand. "I'll explain things more in the morning, okay?"

"I can't wait." Albert smiled and went to a bedroom at the end of the hallway. He closed the door behind him.

Carver went into the bedroom. He showered off and climbed into bed. It was just a twin sized bed, but it was better than the cramped confines of the truck. He was exhausted, but he couldn't stop thinking about the building next door.

Joe had been there. He couldn't imagine anyone else infiltrating a place with a grappling hook and torch. Those were signature hallmarks of Joe's careful planning and execution.

His fists clenched. He should have kept Joe up to date with his burner numbers. Then he could have called Carver for help. They could have done this together. Because one thing was certain. If Carver had been here to help, things wouldn't have gone wrong.

Joe would still be alive.

CHAPTER 31

Monty had been on the phone all morning.

He'd been getting the runaround. Everyone referred him to someone else. No one had answers. KalTel operated like every other giant company. The phone system was automated. When you asked for tech support, it told you to reboot your modem and go through several more steps, each time asking, "Did that solve your problem?"

Monty kept shouting, "Give me a human!" until the robot voice finally relented and told him he was being transferred to a live representative.

Then another long wait would ensue during which he'd be treated to horrible on-hold music that sounded like it had been created by a person with a 1980s Casio keyboard.

When a human finally answered, they were almost always a computer-illiterate employee who was reading from a script. They always asked the same questions. "Did you reboot your modem? Did you restart your PC?"

Once Monty got past that layer of nonsense, he'd ask them the same question he'd asked all the others before him. "I think my modem was hacked. Can you help me?"

There didn't seem to be an answer in the script because the support representative would go silent for a moment before telling him they had no idea what to do. They would then escalate the ticket to level two support.

Another long hold would ensue, complete with the god-awful on-hold music. Monty felt his sanity ticking away. Once he even caught himself clapping along to the music and promptly wished he had a bottle of tequila handy.

Monty had repeated this task eleven times from seven in the morning to now almost noontime. Only about thirty minutes of that had been talk time. The rest of the time, he'd been on hold.

Now he was back on the line for the twelfth time. He'd already been escalated to level two. The level two tech people knew a thing or two. But they still didn't know much. Most of the level two people would check Andrea Donnely's modem, tell him it was fine, and then end the call.

This woman sounded no different than the others. Monty decided it was time to play another card.

"Look, I'm a detective with the local police. I know for certain that someone hacked that modem and caused it to update perfectly in synch with a time that a man was murdered. I need to find out how it was done."

He hadn't been telling that to everyone because he assumed that whoever did it wouldn't want to be caught and would just lie. Plus he didn't want rumors to spread at the call center and give the perp advanced warning.

The tech worker gasped. "You're serious? This isn't a prank call?" She sounded uncertain.

"Look, I'll come see you personally, badge in hand if that works. I'm just sick of getting the runaround."

"Wow." She blew out a breath. "I have no idea how to do something like that, but there's a very specific protocol for staging modem updates. It has to go through a vetting process and multiple approvals before the file can be staged for updates."

"So, you can't just update one specific modem?"

"The files are tagged as updates for specific modem brands and models. So, if Model XYZ needs updating, the file is tagged for only that model. I only know this because the chief technology officer included it in a daily bulletin a couple of weeks ago. Apparently, someone mistakenly sent out an update for Goodwin N40 modems that wasn't compatible and bricked them."

Monty nodded. "Okay, well, this brand of modem isn't Goodwin."

"Thankfully, hardly anyone has Goodwin modems. The N40 model is so old it barely even works with our system anymore. They're basically cheap, generic Chinese modems you can get for thirty bucks. Maybe fifty people across the entire state have the N40 model. Well, they had them, anyway. Now they're garbage, thanks to the bad firmware update."

The timing caught Monty's attention. "You said this happened two weeks ago?"

"Yeah. Hang on." She went silent for a moment. "Ten days ago." She went silent again. "That's strange."

Monty's ears perked. "What's strange?"

"Another Goodwin N40 update went out three days ago. Unscheduled. Which makes no sense, because like I said, they would have all been bricked."

"Who sent the update?"

"I mean, it doesn't matter since you said the modem in question isn't even a Goodwin."

Monty sighed. "Yeah. But the timing is precise."

There was a long silence punctuated by a gasp. "Holy shit."

"What?"

"The make and model of the modem is usually automatically detected. But the log shows that someone went in and changed the model ID for the modem in question. That made the database think the modem was a Goodwin N40. Then it was changed back a day later."

"Someone there had to do it, right?"

She blew out a breath. "Yeah. It wasn't a hack. It was an inside job."

"Okay, this is extremely important. Can you find out who did it?"

"I can't. My supervisor can."

"Okay. This is very sensitive information. Don't tell anyone, not even your supervisor. I'm going to come in person. What's the address for his location?"

"We're in a call center just north of Pasadena." She gave him an address. "This is exciting. Should I sneak you in the back door? Because security won't let you in the front without approval."

"That would be perfect."

"Okay. I'll need to sneak you onto the campus too. I take my lunch break in forty minutes. We can meet somewhere outside, and I'll sneak you in."

"You're doing an awful lot to help me. I don't want to get you into trouble," Monty said. "Maybe I should just go in the normal way. Get a visitor pass and all that."

"All I can say is they don't even let food deliveries inside. We have to meet them at the front gate. Even if you came here to visit someone, they would make you do it outside. Unless you have a warrant, of course."

Monty didn't have a chance at getting a warrant. "Why such high security?"

"I mean, part of this building is a massive datacenter and cloud storage. I think the state of California hosts storage and servers here. It's a high-sensitivity installation."

"Yeah, that makes sense." Monty gave it some thought. "But if I pop out of nowhere, won't security hustle me out in record time?"

"Yeah, you're right." She sighed. "Okay, I'll get Brad to go to lunch with me. He's always flirting with me anyway. It'd be easier to talk to him outside. Then he can go back and find out who did this."

"Perfect." Monty paused. "What was your name again?"

"Oh, it's Alice. Let me give you my personal cell so we can text."

"Alice, where are we meeting?"

She gave him the address of a restaurant about a mile east of the call center.

Monty jotted it down. "Okay. I'll see you there in thirty." He ended the call. He had several texts from the chief.

I still don't have your report about the motel or Devil's Gulch. I want it on my desk ASAP.

On his desk was a misnomer since everything was electronic these days. Monty hadn't written a single word of that report. He'd been too busy with other things. For one thing, he'd gone to question Sabrina, Hugo's girlfriend.

Well, technically not a girlfriend. He'd paid her bills and used her for sex. More like a sugar baby, if anything. The bartender had been right about her. She'd do just about anything for money.

Monty had tested that theory and she'd taken him to bed for a couple hundred bucks. She'd also spilled the beans about Carver's visit and how he took down Hugo. She'd only told him that once Monty said he was helping Carver.

Sabrina had mixed emotions about Hugo's death. He'd been a steady source of support and now he was gone. Monty had offered to give her some help in exchange for regular visits. She'd agreed.

The chief might be mad at him. His life might suck. But today was a good day. He'd found a lead on the modem and had enjoyed the company of a woman last night. Things were looking up.

He'd even shaved and showered and not touched a drop of alcohol yet this morning. Maybe today was the day he became a new man. Maybe today he could finally put the past behind him.

Monty opened the drawer on his desk and stared at the tequila bottle in the brown bag. He'd picked it up on the way to work. He normally filled his coffee cup with it. But not today. He grabbed it and headed for his car.

CARVER STABBED A SAUSAGE.

Albert had cooked a big breakfast. Eggs, sausages, and biscuits. He was drinking a cup of coffee and watching Carver polish off his second helping. "It won't be long before the bikers start rolling in."

Carver finished chewing a biscuit and washed it down with coffee. He hadn't told Albert anything yet. Hadn't told him about the operation happening next door. But it was only fair that the man knew the truth.

"I know why the mayor doesn't want you having the rally."

"It's because I don't support her, right?"

"She told me last night that the town is controlled by a cartel. That she has to do what they say." Carver set his fork on the plate. "They told her to shut down your bike rally."

"Okay, but why?"

"Because of what's going on in that building next door." Carver finished off his coffee. He got up. Picked up the coffee decanter. Poured himself another cup. He sat back down. "The information I'm about to give you might put you in even more danger."

Albert leaned forward eagerly. "I am all ears, Carver."

Carver told him what he'd seen. He told him that Joe had been there too. That something had happened that night to leave the bloodstains in the back of the pickup.

Albert whistled. "What's the point of giving those illegals papers and sending them to Utah?"

"Maybe to tip elections in a different direction."

"That makes a lot of sense," Albert said. "They look at past election results and see how many thousands of people they need to change the landscape."

"Maybe. But they'd have to process a staggering number of people. Seems like someone in the federal government would notice and report it." Carver stabbed another sausage. "A lot of that group last night was made up of kids who won't be of voting age for another decade."

"What if that's not the only operation?" Albert said. "What if this is just one of many?"

"That would make more sense." Carver bit the sausage. "The border is pretty porous in these parts."

"Over four million illegals have entered the country over the last three years," Albert said. "If they processed even a fraction of them, that's enough to tip elections in most major cities."

Carver nodded. This had Enigma written all over it. The shadowy organization had its fingers in pies all over the country. It owned several large cities along the west coast. Now it had plans to get its people into power in other cities.

The cost had to be staggering, but it wasn't that hard when Uncle Sam was actively helping you. Not to mention Enigma seemed to be funded by some heavy hitters in the investment community.

The companies that controlled trillions of dollars in retirement funds were using those funds to purchase homes in hot markets. They were outbidding ordinary people. Causing a housing shortage, ostensibly so they could rent the properties.

But what if they'd been purchasing the homes for this migrant scheme all along?

His phone buzzed. He saw a text from Monty. *Got a lead on the modem. Headed to Pasadena.*

Carver stared at the text. *I'm coming with you.*

Too late. I'm meeting with a source in ten minutes.

Carver stood abruptly.

Where?

Monty sent an address.

"I've got to go." Carver finished off his coffee and went to the room to grab his things.

"Wait, what about the bike rally?"

Carver had been giving it some thought. There was no good answer to the situation. "Do you want to hold your ground or avoid confrontation altogether?"

"I want to hold my ground. But I don't want anyone to get hurt."

"I don't know what I can do to help. But now that we know why they don't want you having the rally, I think it's safe to say that they'll do anything to keep it from happening."

Albert spread his hands helplessly. "So, what do I do?"

"You know many of these bikers?"

He nodded. "I know lots of them. I get hundreds of visits every year. They'll swing by on one of their cross-country trips and even take me out to dinner. Some of them are like family."

"Okay, then use that to your advantage. Ask them for help. But I wouldn't tell them what's happening next door. That could cause other major problems."

Albert nodded slowly. "Yeah. I'll do that. And just hope nobody gets shot."

MONTY ARRIVED.

The restaurant was in a small strip mall. It was one of those fancy places with avocado toast and soy lattes. He certainly wouldn't be eating anything there. He parked so he could watch the entrance.

He texted Alice. *I'm here.*

She replied. *Five minutes away.*

Don't text and drive, he sent back.

It's voice to text.

That was a joke.

She didn't reply.

He sat back and waited. A dark blue compact car pulled into the parking lot six minutes later. A young woman with blond hair got out of the driver's side. She was tall and thin and wore thick glasses.

A short, older man got out of the passenger side. He was balding and had a thick, round belly. Obviously middle management.

The woman typed on her phone. A message appeared on Monty's phone an instant later. *We're here.*

Okay. See you inside. Monty waited until they went inside. He gave them a moment to get settled in and then got out of his car and went inside.

They were seated at a table for four. Brad was sitting in the chair next to Alice. He was leaning toward her. She was leaning back in her chair, obviously putting as much space between them as possible.

Monty sat down unannounced. Brad flinched like he'd been struck. He blinked. Frowned. Stared at Monty. "Excuse me. We're sitting here."

Alice apparently hadn't told him anything. Good.

Monty took out his badge and set it on the table in front of Brad. He smiled. "You're not in any trouble, but I'm hoping you can help me with an investigation."

Brad looked flummoxed. He looked from Alice to Monty. "Why do I feel like I've been set up?"

"I didn't set you up," Alice said. "This is important."

Brad sighed loudly. "God, you Zennials are so easy to manipulate."

Monty didn't get the reference, so he ignored it. "Brad, just give me a moment to explain everything and I think you'll be willing to help."

Brad folded his arms over his chest. "Doubtful, but we'll see."

Monty told him about Joe. About the suspicious timing of the modem outage which took out the Wi-Fi and disabled the cameras. Alice then explained what had happened with the modem and how the false update had gone out.

Brad looked a little pale after hearing everything.

She put a hand on Brad's arm. "Brad, this was done on purpose. That man might have been murdered and you can help us find out who did it."

Brad wiped his brow. He shook his head. "No, that doesn't sound possible."

Alice looked confused. "You know it's possible. All you have to do is look into the logs and find out who did it. You have access. I don't."

He worked his jaw back and forth. "I can't." He stood. "I'm sorry, detective, but you'll need a warrant."

And with that, he left.

CHAPTER 32

Monty watched Brad leave.

Alice's avocado toast arrived. She bit into it and looked unconcerned. "I don't know where he's going. I drove him here."

Brad stood outside and stared into the parking lot. He seemed to have realized the same thing. He took out his phone and typed on it. Probably ordering a rideshare.

"Damn it." Monty stood. "I can't just let him go. He'll just have someone pick him up. He'll go back to the office and tell someone about this and whoever did it will find out and cover their tracks."

Alice groaned. "It's just crazy how corrupted the system is. All the old people complain about us, but they never talk about changing the system or making it better."

Monty was confused. "What are you talking about?"

"The archaic business culture and how people like Brad always try to protect their corporate overlords."

"Well, circling the wagons is just human nature. Brad is middle management. He sees an outsider like me, and it makes him defensive."

Alice sighed. "Fine. I'll go talk to him. I really want to help solve this mystery, but I'm not going to seduce Brad just to make it happen."

"I wasn't even suggesting you do that," Monty said.

She stood and walked outside. Brad looked up from his phone and smiled at her. It wasn't a warm, pleasant smile. It looked more nervous and embarrassed than anything. They spoke for a few minutes.

Brad nodded several times. Alice grinned and came back inside. "He said he'd look into it."

"Great. And you didn't even have to seduce him."

She shivered. "Thank God."

Brad came back inside. Sat down. He looked less nervous. More confident. Like he'd found a little backbone once he'd decided to help. Typical middle management. "I'll look into it once I get back to the office. But you're buying my lunch."

"Fair enough." Monty got a server's attention and they ordered. Alice was apparently satisfied with just the avocado toast.

The food arrived and they ate. Brad ate in silence and kept checking his phone. He was starting to look nervous again.

Monty tried to reassure him. "Look, you just send me a name and I'll take it from there, okay?"

Brad nodded. "Yeah, I know."

"Brad, you're very brave for doing this." Alice touched his hand. "I'm proud of you."

Brad blushed slightly. Smiled. "I know how you can make it up to me."

"Careful, Brad." Alice sipped her green soy latte. "No sexual harassment."

Brad's blush turned a deeper shade of red. "Is asking someone on a date sexual harassment?"

She narrowed her eyes as if thinking it over. "It's inappropriate since you're my direct boss. I mean, what if I was your boss and I used my power to make you go on a date with me?"

Brad grinned. "That would be hot."

Alice huffed. "Men are disgusting."

Monty kept his mouth shut.

Brad checked his phone. He abruptly stood. "Okay, let's go."

Alice looked at his plate. "But you didn't even finish your sandwich."

"I'm not that hungry." He headed for the door.

Monty and Alice hurried after him.

Brad stood outside next to Alice's car. He looked at Monty. "I'll text you in a little while."

"Thanks," Monty said. "You're doing the right thing."

"I'm just doing what I can." Brad looked around conspiratorially. "Look, there's something I didn't mention."

Monty perked up. "What's that?"

Brad bit his lower lip. Looked at the people walking by. "I-I don't want to say it in the open." He motioned them to follow and walked around the corner of the building.

Alice looked intrigued. "Brad, what is it?" She hurried after him.

Monty thought the drama was ridiculous, but he followed them.

Brad stood around the corner. Alice was there too. Most noticeably standing there were two men in dark suits. Both had shaved heads. One had a thick black mustache. The other had a goatee. Both looked Middle Eastern. Arabic.

Both were holding handguns pointed at Alice.

A black Mercedes Sprinter van was parked behind them. The back doors were open.

"Brad?" Alice was frozen with shock. "What's happening?"

"I'm sorry, okay. I'm so sorry." He was shaking. "I did it, okay? It was me. I didn't know about anyone getting killed."

One of the Arabic men spoke with a light accent. "You will remain quiet, Mr. Garner." Brad clamped his mouth shut. His face blanched.

The other Arab spoke in another language. The first nodded. "Everyone into the van."

"Except me, right?" Brad said.

"You too, Mr. Garner."

Brad shivered uncontrollably. "I'm not going to say anything. That's why I called you. I'll keep quiet!" He sounded more desperate with every sentence.

"There is nothing to fear, Mr. Garner. We would just like to have a word with everyone away from here."

"That's a load of BS," Monty said. He started backing away.

The first man removed a black cylindrical object from inside his suit pocket. He screwed it to the end of the gun. It was a suppressor. A professional silencer. "Don't make me shoot you, Mr. Ford."

"You know my name?"

The man nodded. "Of course, I do. I can shoot you now, or you can get into the van."

"And then you'll shoot me later?"

"I will not shoot you."

"But someone else will." Monty considered making a run for it, but it was ten feet to the corner. A bullet would put him down before he could get even three feet.

The van's cargo space had benches on the sides. A metal cage separated the cab from the cargo. It looked like it was designed to carry prisoners, much like a police paddy wagon.

Brad climbed in first. Alice looked ready to faint. The other Arab man helped her inside. Monty hesitated, then walked to the van. The second Arab man frisked him. Took his service piece and his phone.

"Your phones, please." The first man held out his hand to the others.

Brad and Alice handed them over. The second man lifted a panel in the floor and removed three straps with chains dangling from them. He buckled a strap tightly around Monty's wrists then latched one end of the chain to a metal loop in the floor.

He did the same for the others. Then he pulled three more straps out and strapped their legs to the benches.

"Isn't this overkill?" Monty said. "We're in a cage already." He kept hoping someone would walk by, but the parking lot was in front of the building, not on the side.

Neither man answered. They closed the back doors and climbed into the front. The engine started, and the van rolled forward.

Monty had no doubt this would be the last car ride of his life.

CARVER SWUNG INTO THE PARKING LOT.

A black van pulled out at the same time, nearly hitting him on the way out. Carver didn't bother honking. That wouldn't improve the other person's driving skills.

He saw Monty's car. It was parked with a clear view of the entrance to the restaurant. The man might be a drunk but at least he had some good habits.

Carver backed into a parking space. He used the monocular to look inside the restaurant. From this position, he had a clear view of everything inside.

There was a hostess station in the front. A narrow space with rows of tables in the middle. Only a few tables were in use. The place looked dead. Monty wasn't inside. He would have recognized his balding head even from the back.

Carver got out and went inside. He spoke to the hostess inside. "I'm supposed to meet a friend here." He described Monty.

The girl nodded. "Yeah, I saw him. Old guy. Looks like a heavy drinker?"

"That would be him."

"I remember him because he and some other old guy were sitting with a real young blonde at that table." She pointed to a table near the back. "They seemed to get into an argument. The other guy went outside. The girl went out and talked to him and then they all left together."

"Did you see which car they left in?"

The girl frowned. "Well, the girl and the other guy arrived in that blue car." She pointed to a car parked right outside, clearly visible in the big window. "I don't know what car the heavy drinker arrived in."

"Did you see them leave with anyone else?"

The girl shook her head. "I think I saw them walking down the sidewalk toward the end of the building." She gasped. "Do you think they're doing something sexual behind the building?"

Carver didn't answer. He rushed outside. Jogged to the corner. There was nothing on the side of the building except a dumpster.

The van.

An image of the tall, black van flashed into his head. It was a Mercedes. Windowless. Perfect for abducting people.

He ran back to the pickup. Hopped in and gunned it out of the parking lot. He turned in the same direction the van had gone. It had a good head start on him, but with all the traffic lights, it might not have gotten far.

He weaved through traffic. Made it through an intersection before the light turned red. Kept his eyes focused on the road ahead. A tall black van like that would be taller than cars. It would stand out. But there were a lot of trucks on the road.

If the van was in front of him, he didn't see it.

Maybe it had taken a turn. Carver had glanced both ways at the intersections, but he hadn't seen the van. It could be anywhere by now.

Then he saw it. Two intersections ahead, right behind a semi-truck. Heavy traffic had slowed it down. That same traffic blocked Carver from reaching it. That was fine. Just fine. He knew where it was now.

The light changed at the van's intersection. The semi-truck rumbled into motion, but it was slower than most traffic and the van was stuck behind it. The traffic light turned green at Carver's intersection.

There were two cars between him and the intersection. Both accelerated as if they had all the time in the world to reach thirty miles per hour. Carver couldn't weave around them. The other lanes were just as jammed as this one.

The pickup truck sat high. It gave him a vantage point. But the size was also a con. It kept him from slipping between cars like he could with something smaller. Even though it sat high, it wasn't a monster truck.

There was no shoulder to drive on. Just a sidewalk with poles, benches and all kinds of obstacles. There was no median. Just a double yellow line and more traffic. All he could do was keep his eye on the van and go with the flow.

He maintained the distance for another mile. Then the car in front of him stopped at a yellow light. The van got ahead by an extra intersection. It was still in sight, just barely. The car to his right turned.

Carver gunned it into the empty space before the car behind it reacted. Now he was the first car in line at the light. The other driver honked his horn. The light turned green. Carver sped forward.

He just as quickly had to stop. The next light had turned green but the cars ahead hadn't started to move yet. It was like watching a train pick up speed, if the train used elastic bands to link the cars. The lead cars accelerated. The cars behind them moved seconds later.

The chain reaction was slower than molasses. Some people were looking at their phones. Cars behind them honked to get the drivers to look forward. The van had better luck at its intersection.

It got moving. It wasn't in the left turn lane, but it turned left, right across traffic. Carver wanted to do the same thing, but he couldn't. He was blocked on the left. It would probably be faster to get out and walk.

That wasn't a bad idea. He was in the right lane, so he veered right. Pulled into a bank parking lot. Got out and hoofed it down the sidewalk. He wasn't the fastest guy in the world, but he made good time.

He crossed three intersections in a matter of minutes. The light was already red. So was the crosswalk sign. It didn't matter. The cars were stopped. He ran across six lanes of traffic. Saw the van two intersections down.

Carver picked up the pace. A man on a moped was idling on the east side of the intersection. Waiting for the light to change. Carver made a split-second decision. He grabbed the guy by the back of his shirt.

Yanked him sideways off the seat. The man was completely unprepared. He sprawled on the ground. Carver hopped on the moped. Gunned it down the sidewalk. People dodged out of the way.

He saw the van moving. The light ahead was green. A woman screamed as the moped narrowly missed her. A car screeched to a halt at the next road inches from hitting Carver. The wheels bounced over broken concrete.

Carver was just a block away from the van. It turned right. For an instant, he had a clear view of the passenger. He was an Arab. More specifically, an Emirati, presuming the guy was from the UAE. Even more specifically, it was one of the guys from the warehouse.

The van accelerated out of sight. Carver reached the corner. He turned hard. The skinny wheels skidded. He almost lost control. The rear wheel bounced off a light pole and the moped stopped.

There was nothing but open road ahead. The van was already two blocks ahead. Carver gunned the moped. But it didn't have speed or acceleration. The van was out of sight in seconds. He could chase it all he wanted, but at thirty-five mph max speed, he wasn't catching anything.

He turned the moped around. Drove it back the way he'd come. The man he'd taken it from was standing at the corner. Talking on his cell phone and waving his hands around. Carver got off the moped. Put down the kickstand.

The man looked at him wide-eyed. "I called the police!"

Carver wasn't concerned. "I saw a news story the other day. Nearly a hundred and fifty carjackings happened in this city last month. You know how many arrests?"

The man stared blankly at Carver then shook his head.

"Twenty. And all the perps were released without bail, thanks to bail reform."

"I-I'll take your picture." The man raised the phone toward Carver.

Carver yanked it from him. Looked at the pictures. The man hadn't taken one yet. He held onto the phone and finished his pitch. "You got your moped back in one piece. Do you want your phone back in one piece too?"

The man looked horrified. "Don't break it! I still haven't paid it off yet."

Carver powered the phone off. It'd take a minute or two to start it up again. "Put on your helmet, get on your moped, and go about your day, okay?"

The man reached out with a shaking hand for his phone. "Please don't break it."

"Do what I said, and you'll get it back in one piece."

The man quickly put on his helmet and got on his moped. Then he held out his hand.

Carver unzipped the man's backpack. Dropped the phone inside. Zipped it up. "Okay. Go."

The man started the moped. He turned around and drove away as fast as the wheels would roll. Carver didn't know why he'd bothered bringing it back. The delay had cost him a good ten minutes.

It wasn't like he could have gotten back to the truck in time to follow the van anyway. But that didn't matter. He was pretty sure he knew where they were going. Back to the warehouse.

And God only knew what was going to happen to them there.

CHAPTER 33

Carver didn't go straight back to town.

He couldn't simply storm the warehouse. There were too many armed men inside. Plus, he didn't think they'd outright kill Monty and the others. Or maybe they would. Maybe they wouldn't take them to the warehouse. Maybe they'd take them somewhere else completely.

Just because the Emiratis were based out of the warehouse didn't mean they'd take someone there to dispose of them. But it was still a good bet.

He considered asking Albert to watch the place. To see if the van showed up there. He didn't want to put Albert in danger, but there wasn't much choice. The fact that these people had kidnapped Monty meant he'd been too close to the truth.

The modem outage was connected to Joe's death. Since the Emiratis had kidnapped Monty, that had to mean they were also connected to his death. Carver needed Monty alive. He needed to know exactly what he'd discovered.

Carver texted Albert. Told him what had happened. What he needed. Albert replied and said he'd get one of his nephews to watch from a concealed spot. That they'd never know he was watching.

Speaking of watching, it was time to pay a visit to the man on the mountain. To find out exactly what he knew and why he was watching the ranch. But the only way to do that would be to get there without being seen.

Carver pulled to the side of the road and studied the map. There weren't many roads going where he wanted to go. In fact, there was just a single road going north from the ranch. The mountain was inside a nature preserve.

A single highway went from one side of the preserve to the other. There were a few gravel roads used by rangers to patrol the area. Carver knew because he'd seen them. But they didn't show on the map.

He navigated to the forest ranger website and found a map of the trails and roads used to reach them. One of the ranger roads branched off the highway Carver was on and went north. It wound through a valley between the mountains and ended at a small river.

That river was at the base of the mountain where the watcher was. There was a ranger road on the other side of the mountain. It circled up to the top to a ranger observation post. The watcher wasn't there. He was downslope on the south side.

Carver found the gravel road. There were several large, red signs warning visitors about washouts, boulders, rockslides, and dangerous wildlife. As if to underscore the point, there was a pile of small boulders blocking the left side of the road ahead.

He steered around them. Followed the road down a steep slope and then up the other side. It curved between steep, rocky slopes covered in wildflowers, scrub brush, and short trees. The road was heavily rutted and sprinkled with obstacles.

Carver was glad Joe's pickup had the offroad tires and higher suspension. Anything lower would have bottomed out by now.

It took the better part of an hour to reach the trailhead. There was a gravel parking area and a green box to pay the visitor fee. Carver pulled the truck into the meager shade of a thin pine tree. A nearby sign told him it was a sequoia.

He got out. Strapped on his shoulder holster. Tucked the Glock into one side and the suppressor into the other. He strapped the X95 across his back. Just in case there was more than one watcher up there.

The park service had thoughtfully provided a bridge crossing the river. This was a place for casual walkers, not hardcore hikers. There was also a raised wooden platform for the first hundred yards of the journey. After that, it turned into a rutted dirt path that was nearly overgrown.

Apparently, this wasn't a popular hiking place. Maybe casual hikers from the greater LA area didn't want to take the risks highlighted by the signs at the road entrance. There were probably plenty of other hiking spots closer to LA anyway.

That was probably one reason why Joe chose that spot for his ranch. It was close to nature. Next to a small town. Beautiful country, but not a hotspot for tourists and hikers. It gave him a nice balance.

Then someone had turned that against him.

Carver checked the trail map he'd downloaded. This path was marked green. It went up the mountain a little then circled back down to the parking lot after a mile or two. It met with two other trails.

The blue trail circled around the middle of the mountain for a six-mile hike. The orange path ascended at a steeper angle, winding north and up to the peak where hikers could climb into the observation post.

He followed the green path to the junction and then followed the orange trail. When it turned north, he left the trail and kept going straight up the mountain. It was a steep climb. Treacherous in spots due to loose soils and rocks.

The trees provided a decent amount of cover, but nothing to write home about. As with most places, the arid landscape didn't have a lot of leafy vegetation. It was thicker in spots and almost nonexistent in others.

After a steady climb, he stopped to check his position. There was no cell signal up here. Not even a single bar. That was something worth noting. Unless the watcher had a satellite phone, he'd have to drive down the mountain to find a signal.

That meant there had to be at least two people doing the watching. Probably in shifts. Probably taking turns travelling down the mountain until they got a signal and could send reports.

It meant when Carver had left the ranch, the reports of his departure hadn't been instantaneous. There had probably been a delay of several minutes.

Good to know.

Using his training, he estimated his location relative to the watcher's position. He was more or less at the same altitude and due west of their location.

The vegetation grew thicker to the east. That would benefit him as much as it benefitted the watcher. Even so, he didn't want to approach in a straight easterly line.

Carver climbed higher until he was sure he was at least a hundred feet higher than the watcher's location. That was assuming the watcher hadn't moved, which didn't seem likely. There weren't many other prime locations.

He turned east. Cut through the thicker vegetation until he reached the gravel road that wound back and forth up the mountain to the observation tower at the peak. He kept to the trees on the side of the road.

A small pickup was parked there. Camouflage netting tied to the nearby trees hung over it. More netting concealed it from the side. Anyone driving past would spot the netting easily during the day.

They were probably relying on a scarcity of traffic to make sure no one noticed. They might have even done something to close the road or arranged something with the local forest ranger.

There was more netting in the trees on the other side of the road. The trees and brush were thicker there, concealing it slightly better. It worked in Carver's favor too because it kept whoever was over there from seeing him cross the road.

He wasn't ready to do that just yet. He tested the door on the pickup. It was unlocked. He eased it open. Checked the glove compartment. Found the registration. It belonged to Tamara Goodson of Los Angeles.

That told him one of two things. The pickup was stolen, or Tamara or one of her relatives was the watcher. Carver put the registration back. Closed the glove compartment and the door. Then he set out to find out the answer.

He continued east to ensure there were no other vehicles hidden on the side of the road. Then he went back to the pickup. He kept low and crossed the road. He reached the camo netting and low-crawled beneath it.

There were tents on the other side. Same color as the netting. Low profile and small. Just for sleeping. He crawled around the closest one. The good thing about the sequoias was that they didn't drop leaves on the ground.

The rocky soil was no pleasure to crawl on, but there was no rustling of leaves. No cracking of branches. He was able to crawl between the two tents nice and quiet. From that position he saw the watcher's spot.

They were sitting in a foldout chair. A large monocular was on a tripod in front of them. Camouflage netting covered them from the front. The monocular stuck through a hole in the netting.

It was a nice setup. At least for an amateur. Leaving the lens unshaded meant anyone looking in its direction might see sunlight reflecting off it. You wanted it back inside the netting as much as possible.

The monocular was anything but amateur. It was a nice piece of equipment. Top of the line civilian or military. Technically, it wasn't even a monocular. It was a long-range MWIR single-lens camera with binocular eyepieces.

Did that make it binoculars because of the dual eyepieces, or a monocular because it only had a single telescopic lens? Maybe it was neither of those because it was a camera.

It had a laser rangefinder, thermal imaging, and a range of several miles. It came with all that for a reasonable price tag of about thirty or forty thousand. Carver knew because when he'd been shopping for monocular, he'd looked into pricier options as well.

He could have afforded something like these, but he'd settled for something a little more portable. Something a little less noticeable. This thing looked like a telescope on steroids.

The watcher's head was visible above the top of the chair. He pressed his eyes to the binocular eyepieces for several seconds, then leaned back and sipped from a stainless-steel travel mug.

Carver watched silently for several minutes. There were no signs of another presence. The tents were open, and no one was inside either of them. It seemed Carver had the watcher all to himself.

If he had more time to conduct covert operations, he'd surveil the area overnight. Find out who used the other tent. Learn their patterns. Discover the nature of their operation, all without disturbing anything.

But he didn't have time to mess around. He was just one person with limited resources up against an organization that clearly had virtually unlimited resources. Maybe it was Enigma, maybe it was cartel funded.

Unfortunately for the watcher, this was going to be quick and dirty. Exceedingly unpleasant, depending upon the level of cooperation. Well, exceedingly unpleasant no matter what if this person had anything to do with Joe's death.

The man in the chair obviously wasn't Tamara. He also had earbuds in his ears. He was listening to music or maybe even an audiobook. It was definitely amateur hour up here.

He rose to his knees. Stood. Drew the Glock. Attached the suppressor. There was another foldout chair behind the watcher. Carver picked it up. When the watcher put his eyes back to the binoculars, he walked around the watcher's chair.

Carver set the chair down facing the watcher. He sat down and set the gun casually across his knee, so the barrel was facing the watcher.

The man pulled back from the binoculars. His eyes flared wide with almost comical surprise. He tried to scramble back, but only succeeded in almost tipping over his chair.

Carver pointed to his own ear. The man was frozen for several seconds before realizing what was being asked of him. He was Caucasian. Probably in his late thirties or early forties. His hair was shaggy but not overly long.

He looked like he should be wearing a tweed jacket and teaching college. Not spying on people.

The man pulled the earbuds out of his ears. Set them on the small plastic table next to him. He was visibly shaking. His eyes were still as wide as they'd been a moment ago.

"Hi," Carver said. "You're not Tamara Goodson, are you?"

He shook his head slowly.

"You have an ID?"

He shook his head again. "I was told not to bring anything that could identify me."

"Where is your partner?"

The man glanced back toward the tents. "I don't know."

Carver narrowed his eyes. "I'm going to ask some questions. I'd appreciate honest answers. Otherwise, I'm going to torture you until you do what I ask. Is that clear?"

The man's teeth chattered. He nodded.

"Respond verbally."

"Yes," the man said.

"Okay. What's your name?"

"Greg Porter."

"Where did the pickup come from?"

"It was given to me."

"Who hired you to spy on the ranch?"

Greg shook his head. "I don't know." His eyes twitched rapidly. Obviously lying. Obviously scared of whoever hired him.

"You just lied." Carver sighed. He stood and drew his survival knife. "Every time you lie, I'm going to cut off a finger."

"No, wait, please!" He held up his hands then quickly pulled them back as if he might lose a finger. "I work for the mayor's political campaign. They wanted me to gather dirt on Joe Donnely so it could be used against him in the election."

"They specifically told you to climb this mountain and watch the place? Or did you do this on your own?"

"They wanted me here," he said. "The location was already set up. They gave me high-powered binoculars and recently upgraded them to this camera."

Carver nodded. "Okay. And now for the most important question. What did you see on the day Joe Donnely died?"

"I wasn't here yet. I had a meeting with a campaign staffer."

"Was it a scheduled meeting?"

He shook his head. "They texted me the evening before and asked for an in-person meeting."

That seemed awfully convenient. Carver approached him. Held out his hand. "Give me the notepad."

Greg gave it to him with a shaking hand.

Carver looked at the notes from today. Andrea had sat outside with her coffee this morning. She'd sat for two hours before going back inside. His hand tightened around the notepad. He turned back a few pages to the day Joe died.

The first entry was late morning. It described Monty's arrival. Captain Menendez's arrival. Everything else except what had happened to Joe.

Carver dropped the notepad in Greg's lap. "Were you here when he died?"

Greg leaned back as far as he could. Shook his head. "I promise I wasn't. I got here about the time the police arrived at his house."

"Who is the other watcher?"

"Some military looking guy. He just goes by the name Two. I never even met him until yesterday. He came up here with a Latino man."

"Describe them both."

Greg gave a physical description of them both and the pickup truck they'd arrived in. "When you left for town late last night, they took off after you."

"Did they say anything about what happened to Joe?"

Greg shook his head. "They didn't tell me anything."

"Do you live in El Fuerte?"

"Yes."

"You voted for the mayor?"

"Yes."

"You consider yourself a big supporter?"

Greg nodded. "She's the best mayor we've ever had."

"Unlock your phone and give it to me."

Greg picked up the phone from the table and unlocked it.

Carver read through the texts. There were several conversations with friends. A few texts from a woman named Roberta, the campaign staffer Greg had met with on the day of Joe's death.

The texts to friends were mostly political. Mostly talking about stopping Joe from winning at any cost. Calling him a rich man who was trying to buy his way into the mayor's office. The usual political crap people spewed during elections.

But nothing about killing him.

"How long have you been watching the ranch?"

"A little over a month."

"How many visitors came to the ranch in that time?"

Greg frowned. "No one ever came out there except Donnely, his wife, and the two helpers."

"Did the helpers ever do anything suspicious?"

"No. Similar routine every day."

This was a dead end.

Carver moved his chair next to Greg's. Motioned the other man up. "Take my chair."

Greg did it without hesitation.

Carver took Greg's former seat. He looked through the binoculars. The image of the ranch even from this distance was crystal clear. He could read the numbers on the side of the mailbox. He removed the camera from the tripod and packed it in the hard case nearby.

Greg watched him in tense silence. He looked like a man waiting for execution. Carver had a good mind to do it. This guy was barely a pawn in a game he didn't even know existed. A useful idiot.

Not worth the trouble of killing.

"I'm going to let you go, but you can't stay here," Carver said. "You are going to pack up this campsite and then you're going to get in that pickup and return it to the rightful owner."

"What?" Greg looked confused. "I don't know who that is."

"Your benefactors left the registration in the glove compartment. The address is on it." Carver entered Greg's number into his burner. He'd taken a picture of the registration as well. "I have Tamara's phone number. I'm going to call her in three hours to see if her truck has been returned. If it hasn't, then I'll come for you Greg."

Greg gulped. "I'll do it. I promise."

"And let me tell you something." Carver tapped the suppressor against Greg's forehead. "I had dinner with the mayor last night. She told me in no uncertain terms that she's being controlled by a cartel. That everything she does is by their command. Does that sound like someone you want to be supporting, Greg?"

Greg's mouth dropped open in horror. "What? A cartel?"

Carver nodded. "Now, start packing up the camp. Put everything in the pickup and give it all to Tamara as payment for borrowing her truck, okay?"

Greg nodded fervently. "I'll do it. I promise."

Carver had considered taking the pickup, but there was no direct road back to the pickup. It would take less time to hike back down than to drive the pickup the long way.

"I'll be tracking your phone." Carver handed Greg's phone back to him. Then he picked up the case with the camera and started walking back to Joe's truck. He needed to get back into signal range for his cell phone.

And find out if the van had gone to the warehouse.

—— • ——

CHAPTER 34

Monty rocked back and forth.

The straps kept him firmly adhered to the bench even though the van was rocking along on a bumpy road. They'd put noise canceling earmuffs on him and the others and covered their heads with black bags.

He'd felt a few turns here and there. Heard faint traffic sounds through the earmuffs and a little road noise. But he had absolutely no idea where they were or where they were going.

Monty had tried to talk and had been pistol whipped. Since then, he'd kept his mouth shut. But where they were going was probably not going to be good for his health either.

The van slowed. The bumpy surface turned smooth. The van stopped. It turned and backed up. It stopped a few seconds later. Someone began loosening the straps. His lap and legs were freed first.

The straps around his wrists came off a moment later. The freedom was short lived as a nylon strap held his wrists together. He was jerked upright. Pulled along and helped out of the van.

Someone kept a firm grip on his elbow. He shuffled along with them then had to adopt longer strides as they picked up the pace. He stopped several times. Heard the faint rattle of metal, like a door rolling up.

Then he was pulled along again. After what seemed like a short eternity, he was pushed into a sitting position on something hard. The bag was yanked off. The earmuffs were removed. He was sitting on a folding metal chair.

He was inside a room with cinderblock walls and a concrete floor and ceiling. Alice and Brad were sitting on chairs of their own next to him. There was a metal door on one side of the room, and another one on the opposite wall. There were no handles on either of them.

There were no windows. The room was rectangular. About ten feet wide and twenty feet long. A stainless-steel toilet and sink were in the corner. There was no wall or curtain for privacy.

It looked like a holding cell at a police station, but it wasn't the holding cell at the El Fuerte police station. This room stank of fear and urine. The scent was old, although judging from the wet spot on Brad's pants, he'd added to the aroma.

The room looked old. The concrete was pitted and scarred. It looked as if it had been recently painted, but the paint hadn't been able to overcome the mildew stains.

There were two round LED lights bathing the room in harsh white light. There was a small television mounted on the wall. A web cam was attached to the top of it.

The TV was off, but the light on the camera was on. They were probably being watched.

"Hello?" Monty said. "Where are we? What are you doing to us?"

There was no answer.

Alice stood and ran to one of the metal doors. She pounded on it. "Let us go!"

Brad stared blankly at the wall. He looked terrified and completely oblivious to the large pee stain on his trousers.

"Did someone pay you to hack that modem?" Monty asked.

Brad didn't react.

Monty elbowed him hard.

Brad shouted in alarm. He stumbled out of the chair and fell down. "I didn't know anyone would get hurt. They gave me the update and told me how to do it."

"You didn't already know how to do it?"

"Yeah, I'm a level three tech. I know how to push updates."

"Who told you? Who paid you?"

"I was contacted anonymously. They paid me in crypto."

Monty shook his head. "And you just agreed to do it for money?"

"It was a thousand dollars." Brad stood up and looked at the wet spot on his pants. He looked at Monty. "Are we going to die?"

"Probably." People who kidnapped you and brought you to an undisclosed location usually didn't have your best interests at heart.

The only shred of hope was that they'd put bags over their heads to keep them from seeing where they were going. It was possible they just wanted to scare them so badly that they'd keep quiet and drop the investigation.

The door Alice was banging on opened. One of the men who'd captured them grabbed her by her throat and wordlessly shoved her backwards to a chair and pushed her roughly into it. He then motioned for Monty to stand.

Monty stood.

Alice gasped for air. "Where are we?"

The man slapped her. "Remain seated and quiet. Test my patience and you will be rewarded with pain and death."

Her face went white as a ghost. She leaned back and stared in horror at him.

The man motioned Monty to follow him. He went to the door. There was a magnetic hum and it popped open. Monty followed him into a room with a metal table and chairs on either side. There was a two-way mirror on the wall and another metal door with no handle.

It looked exactly like an interrogation room.

"Sit." The man pointed to the chair on the left side.

Monty sat. He couldn't decide if this was promising or not. It probably wasn't. They wanted to find out what he knew. At this point, he knew too much to keep breathing. But they wanted to be certain before putting a bullet in his head.

The man went to the door next to the two-way mirror. It clicked open. He left. Monty rested his elbows on the table. He stared at the empty chair across from him and wondered who would fill it.

The wait stretched on. There was no clock on the wall. No way to tell the passage of time. It might have been thirty minutes. Might have been an hour. Might have been several hours. Monty didn't know.

He crossed his arms on the table and laid his head on his arms. A klaxon blared. He jerked upright and shouted in alarm. The klaxon whined down to silence. He looked up and spotted a horn in the top corner of the room.

Monty knew what would happen, but he tried to rest his head again. The klaxon blared again. He sighed and sat upright. Apparently, they wanted him off balance for questioning. It looked like he might be here for a while.

The door buzzed open. A man stepped inside. He wasn't Arabic. He was an older guy. A guy Monty knew quite well.

It was Chief Lynch.

CARVER GOT A SIGNAL.

He texted Albert for an update. It didn't take long.

Randall didn't see any vehicles. He's been watching all this time.

Carver asked him if he was absolutely certain. Albert said he was. Which meant the van hadn't gone to the warehouse. So, where had it gone? Maybe they'd taken Monty and the others somewhere else to execute them.

That seemed the most likely answer. Which meant Carver would have to beat answers out of the men in the warehouse. Yusef and Hassan were the ringleaders there. Maybe they didn't know who ordered the modem hack, but they could point him in the general direction.

He reached the bottom of the mountain and crossed the bridge. He was almost back to the pickup truck. He'd have to backtrack down the gravel road to the highway, but he wasn't sure where to go next.

A full-frontal assault on the warehouse would just get him killed. He needed to wait until dark and infiltrate. If the same number of people were still there, his mission plan was simple.

Kill everyone except Yusef and Hassan.

Interrogate them.

He wasn't sure how effective the plan would be. It was likely those two would resist answering questions. It was likely they knew he'd kill them whether they answered or not. But he didn't have time to sit around and hope they said something incriminating.

Even if they were openly talking about Joe, they'd probably say it in Arabic. Unless he planted a bug and recorded everything for an interpreter, he wouldn't understand a thing.

Besides, he wasn't here to solve a crime. He didn't need to build a case for prosecutors or convince anyone that he was right. The only person that needed convincing was him. He just wanted to ensure that he wasn't just killing the branches of an organization that killed Joe.

He wanted to be certain he got them stem, trunk, and root. He didn't want to kill a few thugs only to find out that their deaths scared away the person or people who ordered Joe's execution. He also wanted to find out how they'd staged the scene to look like a horse had done it.

There had been no drugs in Joe's system. Nothing but caffeine. A man who could still infiltrate a two-story building with a grappling hook wasn't the kind of guy who was going to get kicked in the face twice by a horse.

He wasn't going to be the kind of guy you could easily sneak up on. But someone must have done it. Maybe someone with special training. Whoever it was, he couldn't afford to underestimate them.

So, who ordered the hit? The cartel? The Emiratis? Someone else?

There was one thing Carver felt reasonably certain of. Joe had been focused on the horse when it happened. The horse might have been bucking or twisting around. Even a guy like Joe would have been distracted enough for someone to get the drop on him.

Carver hopped in the pickup and gunned it out of the gravel parking lot. He sped down the road, leaving a long trail of dust floating behind him. He wanted to infiltrate the warehouse and execute the men there until someone told him what happened.

Yusef and Hassan seemed to be in charge of a major human trafficking operation. Sure, it wasn't the kind of human trafficking Carver had expected, but it was still highly illegal. A good reason to order someone's death.

They were working with the cartel. The cartel was using the mayor. The mayor's office had used Greg to spy for them. Any of them had motive to order Joe's death.

El Fuerte was covered in a web of connections. At first, the mayor seemed to be the spider at the center. But if she was being used by the cartel, the spider was someone else. The spider was lurking in the shadows.

Carver turned toward town. He took the road northeast to avoid the cameras. Kept driving all the way out to the ranch. He went inside. Andrea wasn't in the kitchen. He went to the bedrooms.

The master bedroom door was open. She wasn't inside.

"Andrea?" He called her name a few times. No answer.

She could have left since the last entry recorded by Greg. He went to the garage. Her Range Rover was still there, and she wasn't in the building.

Metal clattered from somewhere in the garage. Carver walked behind the cars and saw the rollup door to the back area was open. He went inside and saw Andrea standing next to the lift. She was pounding her hand on the control panel.

"Andrea."

She gasped and turned around. "Carver?"

"Yeah."

"What happened last night?"

"There's a lot to catch up on." He looked up at the old Dodge on the lift. "What are you doing?"

Tears filled her eyes. "Joe promised me a ride in that thing. He promised. And then he put it on this hoist and left it there."

"Technically it's a lift."

"Carver, spare me the technicalities."

Carver pointed to a mobile apparatus with a hook and a spool of chain. "That's a hoist." She glared at him. The tears had stopped. "You're trying to distract me."

"Did it work?"

Andrea nodded. Then the tears started flowing again.

"What's the story with the truck?" he asked.

She wiped her eyes. "Joe started working on that thing ages ago. He'd finish with the horses, then he'd come work on this. He got me to help him and it kind of became our collective hobby."

"Sounds nice," Carver said. "Did you get it running?"

"Yes! Joe drove it around a little, then he said it was good to go, but he wanted to change the oil and filter before we took it on a longer drive."

Carver walked under the truck and pointed up at the new filter. "Looks like he already did that. We can lower it and see if it runs."

"That would be great, except I can't get the hoist—the lift—working."

Carver checked the control panel. There was an up button and a down button. He pressed the down button. Nothing happened. Not even a hint of something happening. He looked around the area. Saw an electrical subpanel.

He opened the panel door. The breakers were neatly labeled. The one for the lift was turned off. "Back away from the lift."

Andrea backed away a few steps. "What's wrong?"

"I don't know. The breaker is off. Maybe something broke. I don't want to turn it on and crush you."

She laughed. "Just my luck at this point."

The lift was hydraulic, so the only way that would happen was if turning it on somehow released the air holding up the cylinders. This wasn't exactly Carver's area of expertise, so he would rather not accidentally drop a truck on Andrea.

He clicked the power on. There was a faint click and hum from the lift. He walked over to the lift controls. There were several colored plastic panels at the top. An orange one was glowing. White lettering on it said, *Lock Engaged*.

There were only two buttons on the panel. Up and down. He didn't see anything about a lock. He walked around the lift. He realized the lift wasn't hydraulic. There were metal cables inside the two posts.

The cables rotated and lifted the supports. There was a lever on the side of each post. He pulled a lever and pulled it down. He went to the other side and repeated the process. He went back to the control panel.

The orange light was off. Andrea had already cleared everything from beneath the truck, so he pressed the down button. The lift hummed. The cables spun. The lift lowered the truck to the floor.

"Yes!" Andrea ran to the old Dodge and opened the driver's door. She sat down and drew a deep breath. "It smells so old. I love it."

The interior looked as flawless as the exterior. Carver walked around the outside. "It looks great."

There was a chest in the bed of the truck. It wasn't a toolchest. Not the kind that fit neatly in the bed of a pickup. It was an equipment chest. The kind that was used in the military. It looked old and banged up. It was probably the one Joe had used in the service.

Carver tugged on the heavy metal latches. They weren't locked. They popped out and opened. He lifted the lid. It swung up on spring hinges and stayed open. Inside the chest were several things that immediately caught his eye.

There were two sets of black fatigues. The same kind used for infiltration. There was a full-faced gas mask, several sheathed knives, two Sig P226 handguns with suppressors, and an M4A1 carbine.

These looked like Joe's original service weapons. Items that should have been turned in or you'd get a bill from Uncle Sam for missing inventory. It didn't matter if you were a grunt or elite special forces, the military would get their money for missing bootlaces if you didn't return them.

There was also something else in the chest. A tiny bodycam and a pair of night vision goggles with their own built-in camera. The goggles were broken. It looked like they'd been run over by a car.

The bodycam was intact. And right next to it was the memory stick it fed into. Carver grabbed it. He pulled everything else out of the chest. There was a length of black rope. A compact grappling hook. A line shooter, or what some might call a grappling hook gun.

The grappling hook folded into a cylindrical shape. It was made of lightweight aluminum. This version was medium sized. Ideal for supporting body weight. Tightening a knob on the top would lock it closed. Loosening it would allow it to spring into a four-pronged grappling hook.

The line shooter could be used to launch the hook, but it used CO_2 cannisters. It was too loud to use in most silent infiltration situations. Joe wouldn't have needed to use it for the warehouse. He could have just lobbed the hook to the top.

The tips of two hooks were covered in roof tar. This was definitely the hook Joe had used to climb to the roof. This was the rope that had been looped around the vent pipe. And the dark stains on one set of fatigues marked it as the clothing he'd worn.

Those were bloodstains.

But the real find was the memory stick from the body cam. The camera had still been clipped to the bloody fatigues. It might have recorded everything.

Carver took the memory stick to the driver's side door. Andrea was resting her head on the steering wheel. Tears trickled to the tip of her nose and pooled on the floorboard. She looked up at Carver.

"I found something. Maybe it's nothing. Maybe it's everything."

She blinked. "What is that?"

"The memory stick from Joe's bodycam."

"What's that doing in the truck?"

"Looks like Joe put his things in the chest, put the chest in the pickup bed, and then lifted it and turned off the power so no one would lower it." Carver started walking toward the exit. He ducked under the rollup door and hurried to the other end of the garage.

Andrea hurried to catch up. "What do you think is on it?"

"Answers."

CHAPTER 35

Carver plugged the memory stick into Joe's laptop.

There were multiple files from a night several weeks ago. The body cam would record continuously unless it was turned off. It looked like it had been manually turned off and on several times.

The camera was small. Virtually unnoticeable when attached correctly. This wasn't the same kind used by the police. Theirs was a large boxy shape with storage and battery built into it. This wasn't the same as the helmet cameras used by soldiers in the field, either.

This was a smaller undercover camera. The battery and storage were connected by a thin cable that was hidden under clothing. The camera was a small wafer that could be placed over a button on a shirt.

It had been top of the line years ago, but wasn't much better than what could be purchased on the civilian market these days.

Carver played the oldest video. Mayor Jessica Herrada appeared. It was dark and she was standing on the side of the road, highlighted by the headlights of a truck. The camera shook slightly. There were sounds of feet on gravel.

It seemed Joe was walking toward her. He stopped so he faced the truck sideways. That would prevent the glare from blinding the camera.

"I'm glad you came." Jessica put on her thousand-watt smile. "It's good to see you under less formal circumstances."

"Wish I could say the same." Joe's rich baritone triggered a flood of memories for Carver. He'd forgotten what his friend sounded like.

Andrea gasped and shivered. "It feels like it's been an eternity since I've heard him, Carver." She wiped her eyes and held a hand toward the laptop screen. "Joe." The pain in her voice made Carver glad he'd never felt anything so strongly.

Carver rewound the video since she'd talked over some of the dialogue.

Jessica nodded at Joe's comment. "I understand how negatively you must view me right now."

"What I understand is that the city is trying to annex my property. That my property taxes will increase significantly. That city building codes and ordinances will apply retroactively to my property and cost me significant sums of money to bring up to city code." His hands went out in front of the camera as if he was shrugging. "The city inspector paid me a visit and seemed very smug about how much money I would have to pay after annexation. He even offered to let me pay another fee to avoid such things."

"That fee allows us to grandfather you into the older building codes and property tax millage rates." Jessica's smile didn't waver. "It sounds like a lot up front, but it saves you in the long term."

"That fee is called extortion," Joe said. "I specifically chose my location to avoid being inside the city. To avoid city ordinances and taxes. But the most egregious of the city ordinances is that I would no longer be allowed to have a horse ranch because the rules don't allow for livestock or farm animals."

"I'm sure we could reach an arrangement." Jessica reached toward him, but the camera backed up a step as if Joe avoided her touch.

Andrea grinned. "Don't let that bitch touch you, Joe."

"Let's get down to brass tacks," Joe said. "You called this meeting because I announced my run for mayor. You, the city council, and the police force are all crooked as a barrel of snakes. I won't negotiate with you. Instead, I'll do my best to replace you."

Jessica sighed and gave him an understanding look. "And therein lies the rub, Joe. The polls show you leading. I'll give you that. But in this town, the polls don't matter. In this town, the votes don't matter, either."

"Are you telling me you'll manufacture votes to win?"

She put a hand on her chest. "Me? No. I don't have that kind of power. But the people who control me do."

Joe went silent for a moment. "You're admitting to me that someone else controls you? Let me guess. Wealthy donors?"

Jessica nodded. "You could say that, but it's worse. So much worse."

"How about you just come out and tell me?"

She bit her lower lip. "You know those men who are always following me?"

"Your security detail?"

"My babysitters." She grimaced. "They work for a powerful cartel. That cartel owns this town, and they own me."

"You seem awfully friendly with gangbangers. Are you sure you're not just one of them?"

"It's all a façade." Her shoulders slumped. "When I ran for mayor, it was an uphill battle. My opponent was a wealthy man and very popular in these parts."

"Because he was Mayor Marquis Davis's son, Arty," Joe said. "From what I heard, Marquis went from middle class to wealthy after becoming mayor. But the city did well under him even if he was making a dishonest living off of it."

"Yes, and I had no hope of overcoming all that money and goodwill." Jessica folded her arms. She was wearing a black dress that showed more cleavage than seemed necessary for a secret nighttime meeting. She seemed to be pushing up her breasts as if making them look a little bigger.

Joe spoke again. "Arty died in a car wreck, didn't he?"

She nodded. Stepped a little closer. "A man approached me and offered to help my campaign. He said he represented powerful interests that could guarantee my victory."

"And you took that offer without hesitation."

"I thought it over. But I was so determined to become the first female mayor of this city, that I agreed to it. Two days later, Arty ran off the road and crashed into a light pole. His blood alcohol level was way above the legal limit." She shivered. "I received a message from the man the next day. It just said, Congratulations, Mayor Herrada."

"You're trying to scare me off, mayor?"

Jessica nodded fervently. "Yes, Joe, I am. These people are dangerous. And by people, I mean cartel. They own this town. They own me, the city council, and the police. The gangs are unified under their flag and there is no room for opposition."

"Call for a federal investigation."

"People have tried and died." She blew out a breath. "I don't know how, but they have people in high places. People in the federal government who cover for them. They're no ordinary cartel."

"I'm not sure I believe you."

Jessica held out her hands as if trying to take his.

"Bitch!" Andrea shouted. "Keep your hands off my husband!"

Joe's hands went up defensively. "I'd prefer you not touch me."

Andrea grinned. "Don't touch my husband, you harlot."

Jessica lowered her hands. "Joe, you need to believe me. I don't want to see anything happen to you or your wife." She sighed. "Look, they want me to annex as much land as possible. That's why this issue has come up for a vote. The cartel already has the fix in at the county level."

"They control the county too?"

"Just the important people who make decisions. That's why annexation was green-lighted." She bit her lower lip. "I'll see if I can exclude just your land from the deal. And if that fails, I'll try to get you grandfathered into the older regulations which means nothing will change for you. How does that sound?"

"It sounds like you're buying me off and trying to scare me off at the same time."

"That's exactly what's happening here." She unzipped the front of her dress, revealing matching lingerie underneath. "And you can have so much more if you want. You're a very desirable man, Joe."

"Zip it up," Joe said in the same commanding tone he used to use with the people under his command.

Jessica looked exasperated. "You're not the least bit tempted?"

"You cannot tempt a man who has it all," he shot back. "Now, zip it up, get in your truck, and go. I'll think about your other offers."

"So, you're not incorruptible."

"Mayor, the last thing in this world that I want is to get into politics. To get elected to public office. I want you to understand that scenario is a complete nightmare to me. All I want is to be left alone and to be left out of annexation. If you can guarantee me that, then I'll drop my campaign so fast your head will spin. Go back to your cartel overlords and tell them that."

"I couldn't possibly tell them that." She smiled. "It's good to know that you're pragmatic."

"Guarantee me no annexation, and we'll call it a day."

Jessica nodded. "I think I can guarantee it. I'll let you know something very soon."

"In the meantime, my campaign signs will keep going up. I won't stop until I have confirmation."

"Understood." She zipped up her dress. Sighed. "You're a sexy man, Joe Donnely. Your wife is very lucky."

"I'm the lucky one, mayor." The camera rotated toward darkness. They were probably far outside of the city. The video ended.

"That whore." Andrea was seething. "She didn't know what kind of a man she was dealing with."

Carver knew what kind of a man Joe was. He was a man who never saw much reason to marry. Who hadn't cared about romance or even pursuing women. He'd seen the men in his elite force go through relationship trauma and would always tell them their first mistake was trusting someone who wasn't a SEAL.

In the years after his retirement, he hadn't changed much. Then Joe had run into Andrea at an event and become a completely changed man. A romantic, of all things. Carver had seen the night and day difference.

It made Carver want to believe there was a perfect match for everyone out there. But he wasn't going to waste time looking for it. Carver got enough pleasure from the physical company of a woman. He didn't need the emotional baggage of love and romance.

Andrea took deep, calming breaths. "I'm sorry, Carver. I just want to tear that woman apart for even trying to seduce my man."

"Joe's a better man than me."

She flinched. Looked up at him. "Oh, God. Did she—"

"I talked with her. She told me the same thing she told Joe, more or less."

Andrea's mouth dropped open. "You slept with her, didn't you?"

Carver decided a lie was better than the truth. "No. But she offered."

"Oh, thank God." She put a hand over her chest. "She's disgusting. A cartel prostitute."

Carver played the next video. It was dark except for a pair of red taillights. The lights seemed to be standing still. There was another light coming from the left of the taillights. Carver enhanced the image by increasing its brightness.

He recognized where it was. Joe was standing on the concealed road leading to the warehouse. The taillights began to move away. The gate had probably opened. Light spilled out of the building.

The rollup door had been lifted. The vehicle the taillights belonged to was revealed. It was Jessica's pickup. She stepped out of it and went inside the building. The light faded as the rollup door was closed.

The video ended.

The date and timestamp on the video showed it was just thirty minutes after Joe's meeting with Jessica. He'd followed her there. That directly connected her to the Emiratis and the warehouse. To the human trafficking operation.

The next few videos were of Joe infiltrating the warehouse. He'd done it all in the same night. So much for the careful and steady approach Carver had thought Joe would use.

Joe waited until Jessica's truck was gone. Then he went in through the gate just like Carver. He sneaked to the side of the building and tested the cast iron gutter. Instead of climbing it, he opted to toss the grappling hook over the lip of the roof.

Joe climbed to the top. He inspected the skylight. He set his backpack on the roof. Opened it and pulled out a small torch. He used it to soften the metal frame. Then he used a suction cup to silently remove the window and set it aside.

He tied a rope to the metal vent pipe and lowered himself onto the giant hoist below. Then he climbed down the ladder to the top of the residential area.

Joe spent a lot of time wandering around above the apartments. He spent time listening to the men talking. The audio quality wasn't that great from above the ceiling. He eventually went down through the paneled ceiling in the utility closet.

He saw the metal door and tested it, but it didn't open. He looked into the hallway, but the men were still up and about, so he didn't leave that room. He eventually climbed back into the ceiling and the video ended.

"Joe, what were you thinking?" Andrea shook her head and looked at Carver. "He never said a thing about this."

"He probably didn't want you to worry." Carver shrugged. "He was being proactive. Trying to find out what he was up against and how true Jessica's assertions were."

Andrea laughed. "Being proactive doesn't usually mean infiltrating a cartel beehive."

"Not to ordinary people," Carver said. "Joe wasn't ordinary."

"No, he wasn't." She found a smile in her sadness. "And I was lucky to have him."

Carver started the next video. It was dark but he could hear a scuffing noise, as if someone was sliding on a rough surface. A spear of light danced around the darkness. It didn't do much except show distant walls and glimpses of steel ceiling beams.

The camera dropped lower. A hand reached out and picked up a fistful of dirt. The dirt fell slowly from the hand. It wasn't dirt. It was sand. The coarse kind of sand that you'd find all over the arid landscape outside.

The flashlight trailed over the sand. It stopped on a dark patch. Joe walked over to it and knelt. The sand was black and crusted. Joe picked up a handful. "Blood," he said. "Old and dried." He dropped the clump.

Joe stood and started walking again. There were large metal and wooden frames stacked on the ground. Some of them looked like they could be used as walls. Others looked like they fit together to form something.

The flashlight angled up. The ceiling was distantly visible. It was hard to make out any details from that distance, but it looked like the ceiling of the warehouse. This room definitely wasn't the cargo bay, and it wasn't the side of the warehouse with apartments.

This was the side of the warehouse beyond the metal door.

CHAPTER 36

Carver wanted to know how Joe got into the restricted area.

He kept watching the video, hoping it would show him. Joe continued walking around the space. The entire floor was covered in sand. There were more metal and wooden frames, wooden boxes, ropes, and other materials lying in organized piles near the concrete walls.

Carver knew from his earlier visit that steel plates covered where the skylight had been previously. That the windows weren't boarded up on this side. They were bricked in. The restricted area was a fortress.

Apparently, it was a fortress with a lot of sand and miscellaneous materials stacked in it. The only thing that pointed to it being used for nefarious purposes was the caked blood in the sand. The Ukrainians had killed something in there.

The question was, what had they killed? An animal? A person? It didn't seem likely it had been a person. The human trafficking side was busy giving citizenship papers and free houses to the migrants. Not killing them.

Maybe they trafficked in endangered animal species. Or dangerous animals.

"What is all that?" Andrea asked after a few moments of silence. "It's bizarre."

"I don't know," Carver said. He kept watching.

The video ended and he started the next one. Joe was in a concrete tunnel. It was dark, but his flashlight provided ample illumination to see everything. A sound echoed down the tunnel. It sounded almost animalistic. Like something wailing.

The flashlight turned off. The screen went black, but the video was still playing. Voices echoed. Two men speaking Arabic. There was shouting. Feet stomping across concrete. The video was still black so Carver couldn't see what was happening.

He heard the faint whisper of sand. Probably Joe running across the sand-covered floor. It continued for a while and then there was the sound of boots scuffing against concrete. There was more shouting in Arabic.

It sounded like the shouts were far away. Echoing in a large space. Flashlights lit the area. They were below the camera. It seemed Joe was climbing. The shouts eventually subsided. The flashlights converged together.

Two men were barely visible in the light beams. They conversed for a moment, then their flashlights turned the other way. They seemed to turn a corner and vanished. Probably into the concrete tunnel Joe had been inside.

"Whew," Joe said. "Close one."

There was more scuffing of boots on concrete. A dim light came on. Probably the light from Joe's night vision goggles. There was a regular flashlight on the side of the headband. A black rope became visible.

There was a gray surface behind it. Probably the cinderblock wall. Something passed in front of the camera. Maybe a ledge that Joe was pulling himself onto. The view rotated and the gray concrete ceiling was visible in the light.

Joe was lying on his back. Looking up at the ceiling. He was breathing heavily. "I'm too damned old for this shit."

Andrea laughed. "Says the man who climbed a two-story warehouse, climbed down to the ground and then back up again after running at full speed. He was in better shape than most kids."

"He still had it," Carver said.

The image shifted again. Joe's hands were pulling up the black rope. It was tied to a narrow metal beam. The image rotated and a hole came into view. It was small. Just big enough for a man to squeeze through.

Joe pushed some equipment through the hole. Then he wriggled through, huffing and puffing. He slid out and onto a concrete ledge on the other side. It was narrow. Just big enough for his backpack to sit on without falling.

Then he looked over the side. The catwalk for the hoist was about twenty feet down. It was on the opposite side of the ladder. Carver knew exactly where it was. He knew why he hadn't seen the hole.

Well, besides the obvious reason that it was dark. He wouldn't have seen it from underneath because of the concrete ledge. The edges of the hole were neat, like it had been bored with a machine.

There was an old metal box next to the hole. A piece of conduit curved from the bottom toward the hole, but the pipe had been cut. It had probably been a subpanel for the hoist. Maybe there'd been a hoist on the other side, but it had been removed.

The hole had been for utilities access. They'd been so thorough in covering the roof and the windows but hadn't bothered with this hole. Maybe they didn't think it was possible for anyone to ever access it.

They hadn't known Joe.

The video ended. Carver started the last one. Joe was packing gear into the back floorboard of his pickup. He was talking, narrating where he'd been and what he'd done.

"Just in case something happens to me, this is a record of what I found in the supposedly abandoned warehouse next to Albert's." Joe kept talking as he walked around the truck to get in. Judging from the scenery, he was parked somewhere on the back side of Albert's place.

The truck was next to what looked like a shed. There was a big pile of large timbers. Old, rusty sheet metal. Carver recognized the location. It was across the road that bordered the back side of Albert's salvage yard.

There were some abandoned houses there. It looked like Joe had parked behind them. It was a good spot to conceal the truck.

Joe kept talking as he climbed into the truck. Carver noted that the dome light didn't come on. It was good to know his friend had been thorough.

The truck started. The headlights remained off. It started moving. Joe had just finished talking about how he'd gotten through the skylight and was talking about the space above the apartment section of the warehouse.

He pulled onto the road. Drove behind Albert's place. The steel-plate fence was visible on the right. A pair of headlights turned onto the road ahead.

"Who the hell is out this time of night?" Joe said.

Andrea smiled. "God, I miss his voice."

The car drove past. It screeched to a halt. Turned around. Came up behind Joe fast. It wasn't a police car. It was a dark sedan. Since Joe's headlights were off, it was hard to see what it was.

Joe turned on his headlights. He kept driving. The car kept following him. He kept going straight, past the turnoff he'd usually take to go to the ranch. He drove into a residential neighborhood and pulled into a driveway.

The car blocked the driveway behind him. Two men got out, dimly lit by a flickering streetlamp.

Joe got out and walked toward them. "Can I help you?"

"What were you doing there?" The man on the left had an American accent. It was too dark to make out his features.

"Doing what where?"

The other man spoke with a Hispanic accent. "Answer the question, homie. What were you doing behind the salvage yard?"

"What are you wearing?" A flashlight blinked on, blinding the camera for a moment. "What the hell? Are those black fatigues?"

"Let's take him to Yusef, " the Hispanic male said. "Get some answers."

The camera moved. The flashlight abruptly spun off into darkness. There was a shout of alarm. A gun fired once. There was a scream.

"He stabbed me!" the Hispanic man said. "He—" his voice cut off with a gurgle.

The camera went lower. A dim light highlighted a Caucasian face. A young guy was staring up at Joe. He was gasping. "You mother...son of a...I knew they wanted to kill you...for a reason."

"Who is they?" Joe said. "Who wants to kill me?"

A final breath rattled from the man's throat and his eyes glazed over.

Joe cursed. "I know this kid. Brent Landry." The camera shifted around as Joe took in his surroundings. A dog barked in the distance, but the neighborhood was dark and quiet. The homes looked rundown. Some of them looked abandoned.

The camera focused on Landry again. A pool of blood was soaking into the cracked concrete driveway beneath him. Joe cursed again. He bent down and something covered the camera. There was a thud. Shoving.

The obstruction shifted, and the camera showed Brent's body in the bed of the pickup. Joe leaned over the other guy. "I'm pretty sure this guy runs with Hugo." Joe turned the man's neck for a look at his tattoos. "Yeah. Same gang." He shoved the body into the pickup bed too.

There was a clank as Joe closed the tailgate. He examined the concrete. He picked up a handgun and a knife. He tossed them into the back of the pickup. He walked to the side of the driveway, picked up handfuls of sand, and dumped them on the blood.

He brushed off his hands. "I don't think anyone lives here. Hopefully the sand will conceal the blood for a while."

Joe walked down to the car. It was still running. Still blocking the driveway. Joe opened the door and looked inside. It was clean. There was a cardboard box in the back. Joe opened the back door. He looked in the box.

There was a large white brick inside. He cut it with his knife. Put a finger in the white powder. Tasted it. "Cocaine. How gauche."

Andrea shook her head. "He just killed two men and he's cracking jokes."

Carver wondered if it made her feel any different about Joe, but he didn't ask.

Joe opened the trunk. There were weapons inside, neatly racked inside a metal box. He looked them over. They were Caracal. The same UAE made weapons the Emiratis were carrying. Mostly CAR816 compact rifles.

There was body armor, suppressors, and boxes of ammunition. Joe whistled. "Enough to supply a small army."

He took the weapons, the body armor, the ammo, and put it in his truck. He removed the license plate, all the documents from the glove compartment and the center armrest. He walked to the abandoned house and tested the front door.

The door jamb was broken. It looked like someone had kicked in the door ages ago. Joe walked through the dark house. There was an old, rotting couch inside. Trash all over the floor. Mold on the walls.

He went through a door and into the garage. There was no power, so he opened the garage door manually. There was an old mattress and other trash lying around. He moved the mattress against the wall.

After a while, he had enough space to park the car in the garage. He walked back to the car. Moved it forward so it wasn't blocking the driveway. He went to his truck and backed it onto the street. Parked it on the shoulder.

He drove the car into the garage. Then he backed his pickup up to the garage. "Why did I put the bodies in my truck?" Joe muttered. "Stupid move, Donnely. Just plain stupid."

Carver had wondered the same thing. He would have pushed them onto the dirt so the blood soaked into the ground and didn't stain the concrete. Joe had probably thought he'd do something else with the bodies. Maybe bury them in the middle of nowhere. Let wildlife do the rest.

Joe unloaded the bodies from the pickup and put them in the trunk of the car. He was wearing gloves, so he didn't wipe anything down. He closed the garage door. He piled trash around the car. Pushed the mattress behind the car so it leaned against the garage door.

Joe kept piling garbage from the house around the car until it looked like just another derelict item from the house. He looked at the weapons and other items he'd taken from the car. "Not sure if I should keep them at my place. Maybe they're safer here."

He moved everything into the backseat of the car and covered the crates with newspapers and old blankets.

Then he left. He walked down to the truck. Got in. Started driving. The video ended.

"Wow." Andrea ran her fingers through her hair. "I can't believe what I just saw."

"I'm sorry you had to see that, Andrea."

She shook her head. "I'm not. My husband was a badass. He took out two armed men who were probably going to kill him." She smiled proudly. "My only regret is he isn't around to clean up this filthy town."

"Guess it's up to us."

She nodded. "Yeah. I wish I could kill two men with my bare hands."

"Technically, he used a knife."

"I prefer a rocket launcher."

Carver grinned. "I'll see what I can find."

She grinned back. "Please do." Her expression turned serious. "What do we do with these videos? Does it make Joe look better or worse?"

"I don't think they make much difference one way or the other," Carver said. "You won't find justice in this town. Probably won't find it further up the food chain, either."

"So, what do we do?"

"We make our own justice." Carver checked his phone. He had several missed texts from Albert. "I've got to go to town."

"Why?"

"Albert's bike rally."

Andrea looked confused. "Why are you going to a bike rally?"

"To see if I can use it to my advantage." Carver grabbed the truck keys and left. He drove back into town and reached the salvage yard. The place was crawling with police.

Albert was standing in front of his gate. There were six police cars parked on the road in front of it. A dozen cops were up in Albert's face. There were at least as many other men standing behind Albert. Probably bikers.

Carver parked across the road. Walked over to the gate.

"You will close and bar this gate." The cop talking looked like one of the mayor's security guards from the festival. "Everyone better leave now, or we'll lock you up."

Carver leaned against one of the cop cars. "Albert has a permit."

The cop blinked and looked away from Albert and toward Carver. He narrowed his eyes. "Stay out of this."

"I don't think I will," Carver said. "Albert has a perpetual permit signed by Mayor Davis."

"The mayor revoked it."

Carver looked at the cop's name badge. "Officer Harper, I'm afraid she lacks that authority."

"What are you, some kind of lawyer?"

Carver shook his head. "Nah. I'm just a guy who can read."

The bikers behind Albert laughed.

Harper's face turned red. He put a hand on the hilt of his handgun. "You'll follow my orders or be arrested for disobeying a police officer."

One of the bikers stepped forward. "We're about tired of your unlawful orders."

Harper bared his teeth. "You're just some random biker who doesn't even live here."

"Want to bet?" The man showed his ID. "I'm a citizen of El Fuerte. I own Rick's bar on the east side."

A Hispanic man stepped forward. "I'm a citizen and a local businessowner too."

"Me too." A woman stepped forward.

Albert walked over to Carver and spoke in a low voice. "I asked the other business owners who supported Joe to help me out. They were happy to come over."

"Good idea," Carver said. "Bottom line is, you have the real law on your side. The cops don't."

The other business owners kept coming forward. Harper wasn't swayed.

He motioned to the other cops present. "We'll just arrest all of you, then."

One the business owners, a big guy who owned a gym shook his head and put a hand on a holstered revolver. "You try, and we'll arrest you for unlawful actions."

Harper laughed. "Yeah? Who do you think the courts will support? Some yahoo with an illegal gun, or the police?"

"This gun is perfectly legal and licensed," the gym owner said. He unsnapped the holster. "And I got it to protect me from tyrants like you."

Harper tugged his gun out. Aimed it. "Drop the weapon."

The other cops pulled guns. Aimed them.

All hell was about to break loose.

CHAPTER 37

The cops looked ready to open fire.

"Down on the ground!" one of them shouted. "Get down now!"

"How about you all lower your weapons before this town is about twelve cops short?" Albert was standing off to the side with Carver. The police hadn't looked over at him. He was holding a pair of Glocks, one in each hand.

Harper's eyes went wide. He spun toward Albert.

Carver backed away just a little. He didn't want to get caught in the crossfire.

Harper didn't seem to know if he should train the gun on Albert or Carver. The other cops looked uncertain. Like they hadn't seen resistance before.

The gym owner pulled his gun. Three of the other business owners drew their own handguns.

The Hispanic business owner spoke. "Looks like a Mexican standoff."

Carver wondered if the cops had enough trigger discipline to avoid a shootout. Because if one person pulled the trigger, they were all going down.

Albert stared down the barrel of Harper's gun. "I'm not afraid of you people. This is our town. Not yours. Not the mayor's. I have a permit for this bike rally and it's going to start, given hell or high water."

Harper worked his jaw back and forth. He backed up. Raised a hand. Lowered his gun and holstered it. "Yeah, you do that. We'll be back with reinforcements."

The other cops holstered their handguns. One of them spat at Albert's feet. They got into their respective cars and drove back into town.

Albert holstered his pistols and sighed in relief. "I thought we were going to have a shootout for sure." He looked at the gym owner. "Thanks, Big George."

Big George grinned and holstered his revolver. "I'm sick of those assholes."

"Me too," the others chimed in.

Carver pursed his lips. "They'll be back like he said, with reinforcements."

"I guess we'll have to be ready then," Albert said.

"How many bikers have arrived?" Carver asked.

"About fifty so far," Albert said. "They're setting up camp in the back area."

One of the female business owners sighed. "We just painted nice big targets on our backs."

"We already have targets, Belinda." Big George sighed. "Plus, wasn't Harper harassing you regularly already?"

She nodded. "He comes in the bakery almost every morning for his free eclairs and coffee."

"Him and his goons expect free lunches at my café," the Hispanic man said. "I tried to refuse one time and they smashed three tables."

"Same," Belinda said. "I told him I couldn't afford to keep giving him free food. That I didn't mind giving him free coffee, but the food was too much. He smashed a display case and said, oops. I guess this place isn't under my protection anymore."

"These cops are mafiosos in blue," Big George said. "We're not going to be free until we get rid of them all."

Murmurs of agreement went up from the others.

"How are we going to do that?" Belinda said. "We can't exactly punch their cards."

Big George snorted. "Yeah. Too bad we're law-abiding citizens."

Albert looked at Carver. "You're a former Navy SEAL like Joe. What do you suggest?"

Carver had been expecting the question. "A couple of crooked cops is one thing. The corruption in this town goes all the way down to the roots. The mayor herself told me that she's controlled by a cartel. That everything she does it at their bidding."

Big George whistled. "I suspected something like that. But you heard it from her own lips?"

Carver nodded. "She told Joe the same thing. She wanted me to relay that message to Andrea, so she'd drop out of the mayoral race."

Belinda looked horrified. "Wait, she told Joe that?"

Carver nodded. "Joe didn't care about politics. He just wanted to stop his property from being annexed."

"How do you know that? Did she tell you?"

"I have firsthand knowledge thanks to a video Joe recorded."

There were gasps all around.

"A video?" Big George was wide-eyed. "You have it with you?"

Carver shook his head. "What's important to understand is that I could show those cops the video and it wouldn't change a thing. Hell, I could probably show it to the attorney general of California and it wouldn't matter."

"He's right," Albert said. "The system is rotten from top to bottom."

"Okay, so back to strategy," another woman said. "What are we going to do now that we pissed them off?"

All eyes turned to Carver.

He knew bloodshed wasn't the answer. At least, not for these people. They were mostly raw civilians. Probably hadn't killed a single person in their entire lives. Probably couldn't pull the trigger if they needed to.

The better answer was psyops. "Call all the TV news stations you can. Ask them to come cover the bike rally live. Go to the store and buy as many high-resolution cameras as you can. Set them up around here and livestream the rally. Shine as bright a light as you can on this place and the roaches will scatter."

"I like that idea," Big George said. "Hell, I already got a bunch of those Brighton Security cameras Joe recommended to me. He said they have their own local battery and storage so they can keep recording even if the power is cut. And the resolution is ultra-high definition."

Carver nodded. "Do that. Get a big crowd of reporters too if you can. And you need to start now. Call in favors with anyone who has a big social media presence."

"I already know a guy," Belinda said. "He goes by Nathan the Lawyer and has millions of followers. He's been making videos about a corrupt mayor up in Illinois. He might be willing to help out with a livestream here."

"Sounds like you've got everything covered," Carver said. "Better get to it right away, though. You'll probably have SWAT and more cops ready to bust down the door in an hour or two."

"Yeah, let's get to it!" Big George ran back inside the gate. "I'll go get those cameras."

The other business owners followed him inside. Albert remained outside. "Did you really find a video with Joe talking to the mayor?"

Carver nodded. "He used a hidden camera. She even tried to seduce him."

Albert whistled. "That woman is a snake."

"Maybe the cartel is forcing her to do everything, but I'm starting to think she actually enjoys it."

Albert laughed without humor. "You're damned right she enjoys it."

A small compact car exited the gate. Big George was driving. His head practically touched the roof. Belinda was the passenger. She rolled down her window. "We'll be back soon."

Albert gave them a thumbs up. "Be careful."

They drove off.

Carver gave Albert a look. "Was that Big George's car?"

Albert nodded. "We all make fun of him for it. He doesn't care." He glanced in the direction of the warehouse. "My nephew never saw that van. Did you find out anything?"

"No. I'm certain they're somewhere in town. Where that is, I don't know."

"I asked my relatives to keep an eye out. This town isn't that big."

"How many relatives do you have in these parts?"

Albert chuckled. "A lot. More nieces and nephews with kids of their own than you can shake a stick at."

Carver wondered what it would be like to have all that family. All those blood relatives walking the Earth. Maybe even living just down the road. He couldn't even imagine it.

He had more to do. A lot more. "Think you and your friends can hold down the fort?"

"I sure hope so." Albert patted his handguns. "I don't want it to come down to these bad boys."

"Are you willing to use them?"

He nodded. "I don't want to, but I will. I can't let these people act like they own us."

"Good." Carver walked over to Joe's pickup. "I'm going to drive around town. Look for that van."

"I'll ask Carlton and Reggie to get their boys together and do the same. Maybe if they get organized, they'll find something."

Carver took out his phone and opened the maps app. He walked back over to Albert. "They'll need to do a grid pattern. Drive nice and slow. A Mercedes Sprinter van should stick out."

Albert nodded. "Yeah, it should."

Carver had another thought. "Monty told me about a young girl whose body was found in town a while back. A suspicious van was seen at the location too."

Albert snapped his fingers. "Yeah, I remember that. It was over near Dan Sullivan's old furniture warehouse. It closed down years ago. Hasn't been in use since, as far as I know."

"You have an address?"

"Yeah. Fifth and Rowan. Can't miss it. It takes up an entire block."

"Thanks." Carver got in the pickup and took off. The cartel or whoever ran the operations in this town had a fondness for abandoned warehouses. Maybe that very same warehouse was being used by them.

There was no good way to avoid the traffic cameras, so he just drove straight through town. He reached the intersection of Fifth and Rowan. There were a lot of boarded up buildings in that section of town.

The warehouse was on the left. It took up an entire city block. The area looked like it had once been a thriving center of mom-and-pop businesses. There was a large billboard rising from behind an old drug store.

It said, *Mayor Jessica Herrada's downtown revitalization zone. Always working for you!*

It didn't look like a lick of work had been done in the area. The area around the police station and the town square had obviously been revitalized. This part of town hadn't been touched.

Carver drove around the warehouse. It had elevated loading bays in the back and a pair of ground-level rollup doors. No sign of a van. But it could be parked inside. And since he'd driven straight here, it was likely anyone inside knew he was outside.

There were no cameras nearby. The lack of revitalization also meant that there had been no reason to put cameras or anything else here. So, there was a chance they didn't know exactly where he was.

He parked next to a rollup door. Got out of the pickup. Tugged up on the door. It creaked and slowly went up. He stepped to the side. Readied his Glock.

If anyone was inside, they didn't react. He looked inside. There was a big, empty receiving zone. There was a stack of broken pallets in one corner. They looked old and weathered.

There was an old couch and some broken furniture against the back wall. The rodents had chewed up the cushions so much that the springs were showing.

It looked empty and unused.

He looked at the dust on the floor. It was undisturbed except for some animal prints. No tire tracks. Nothing to indicate a van had driven in here. He walked the area up and down. He went to the front.

There was an empty showroom with old vinyl tiles. The red paint was peeling off the walls. The drywall was broken in places. There was an old mattress with beer cans and bottles strewn all around it.

Cigarette butts, used drug paraphernalia, and stained magazines were scattered on the floor. It looked like people had partied here. Maybe even lived here. But it didn't look like anyone had been here for a long while.

Carver looked everywhere. There wasn't a basement. The building was single story with a high industrial ceiling in the showroom. There really was nowhere to hide people, much less a van.

It made sense that if this place had been used for trafficking, that it had been abandoned after the big news about the dead girl. Even if the cartel controlled the town, it was still better to keep such things concealed.

Maybe this place had been used by Yusef and gang. Or it might have been a completely different group. Maybe it had never been used at all, and they'd just dumped the body here. It wasn't important.

El Fuerte was full of derelict buildings and houses, especially for a small town. But it still had plenty of life. It was like a tree with a rotten core, but the branches still grew leaves. It still looked green in the spring. But it was dangerously close to toppling over.

Carver left the building. He walked back past the pickup. Along the line of businesses. Not a single one was open. Some looked like they'd closed permanently more recently than others. There was a commercial for sale sign outside one strip of buildings.

Others had for lease signs in the windows. Like most shopping strips, someone else owned the buildings and leased them. When the businesses left, the owner probably couldn't get anyone to replace them.

They'd probably foreclosed on the properties a long time ago and lost their shirts in the process. El Fuerte was going through the same slow death as San Francisco. It was just on a much smaller scale here.

He walked all around what had once been the business district. There was no sign of the van. No other large buildings that might be ideal for keeping Monty and the others. They might not have even bothered keeping them alive.

There was a good bet they'd already been killed. The bodies dumped somewhere in the nature preserve. That's what Carver would have done. No sense in keeping people alive if they're a threat to security.

The police department wouldn't care about Monty's death. The two people from the call center would be reported missing. There would be news reports about them for a while and then they'd eventually be forgotten by everyone except their loved ones.

Then he thought of something else. A better way of finding the van. And he might have free and open access to it very soon.

It had taken him two hours to make his way around the business district. That was plenty of time for the El Fuerte police to get their act together and go back to Albert's. They might also be biding their time, but it seemed unlikely.

Carver drove toward the town square. He parked across the street from the gate leading out of the police station motor pool. There was a lot of activity. A lot of hustle and bustle behind the fence.

He kept watching. Wished he had some coffee and a piece of pie. He was getting hungry. But now wasn't the time to eat.

A little more than half an hour later, the gate opened. A line of police cars exited, followed by a SWAT truck. There was nothing special about it. It looked no different than a standard food truck. The kind with a kitchen built inside.

It was painted black and said *EL FUERTE SPECIAL UNIT* in all caps on the side. It looked like a relic from the eighties or nineties. Which made sense. If a cartel owned the cops, why bother upgrading their equipment to armored cars?

Two unmarked cars trailed out last. Carver recognized the police chief in one. The last one had a long scratch on the hood and the side. That was Monty's unmarked car. Some other guy in plainclothes was driving it.

Someone at the station, probably Chief Lynch, had sent someone to retrieve Monty's car from the restaurant parking lot. The lines connecting the dots became stronger than ever. There was no difference between the cops and the criminals in this town.

This place made Morganville look like Mayberry.

The gate started closing slowly after Monty's car left. Carver got a good look inside. There wasn't a car left. They were going in force to Albert's. Carver hoped Big George and the others were all good and set up by now.

He drove around the building. Parked out front. There was no point in trying to hide. The cameras would see him whether he was driving or on foot. He went inside. Officer Nichols was behind the desk, same as last time.

She blinked and did a doubletake. "Are you late? The convoy just left." She apparently still thought Carver was one of the mayor's men.

"I'm not going with them. I'm tracking something down, but I need to review some camera footage."

She nodded. "Oh, okay. Does it have to do with those assholes at the salvage yard?"

He nodded. "They might have other associates in town. I need to find out where they are."

"Great." She buzzed the door open. "Let me know if I can help. I'm so sick of these people who think Mayor Herrada isn't the best mayor this town has ever seen."

Carver nodded. "Thanks." He went through the door. He went through the lower floor and took the stairs up. As expected, no one was around. No one except the people in the Operations room.

There were four people inside last time, each with their own desk. They were watching the convoy as it traveled toward Albert's. One of the smaller screens had a red square around a vehicle. Joe's truck. Just like last time.

Those four people didn't worry Carver. It was the man behind the door in the back wall that concerned him. That was the guy who probably interfaced directly with the cartel, or whoever was in charge.

And he planned to walk right inside.

CHAPTER 38

Carver went inside.

The people at the desks were talking excitedly.

"Do you think there will be a shootout?" the woman at the end desk said as Carver walked inside. She stiffened and stared at him. "Who are you?"

Carver gave her a dead-eyed look. "Do you always ask so many questions?"

She blinked and her mouth dropped open.

The man at the desk closest to the door spun his chair around to see who she was talking to. "Hey, it's a legitimate question! This is a secure area."

Carver ignored him. He went to the keypad on the back wall and punched in the same combination he'd seen the dark-haired man punch in yesterday. The door clicked open. He looked back at them. "Any other questions?"

The man went pale and shook his head. No one else objected either. Carver went inside. The back room was about the same size as the front. The right wall was covered in large monitors. There was a rack of servers on the left wall along with multiple lithium backup batteries.

The dark-haired man was sitting at a desk. He was also watching the police procession as it headed toward Albert's. He had earbuds in his ears and was humming along with whatever music he was listening to.

Carver stepped left so he'd be out of the man's peripheral vision. Then he walked up behind him. The man must have seen a reflection, because he jumped out of his chair and spun around. He had good reflexes, that was for sure.

Then the man saw the Glock in Carver's hand. Saw the barrel pointing about chest level. His eyes widened.

The man was neatly dressed. It looked like he kept in good shape. But he didn't look like a man who'd trained to fight. Like someone who'd been in a gang and could pull a trigger without hesitation.

Carver pointed to his own ear. "Take those out."

The man removed the earbuds. His tanned face paled. "You're Carver." He spoke with a light accent. It wasn't Mexican, but that was about all Carver could discern.

Carver nodded. "Last time I checked. And you are?"

The man gulped. "Luis. How did you get in here?"

Carver wasn't about to point out the severe shortcomings in their security. They were so overconfident and arrogant, they probably never realized someone might try to just waltz right on into the lion's den.

"I'm asking the questions here, Luis." Carver motioned toward his chair. "Have a seat."

Luis sat down.

"Now, I'm going to ask some simple questions. You're going to answer them truthfully." Carver came closer. "Otherwise, things will get unpleasant."

"Are you going to kill me? Because you know that once you leave, I'm going to tell everyone what happened here. There's nowhere you can hide from us."

"So, you're not afraid to die?"

Luis paled even more. "No."

"Good. I'm glad you have some backbone." Carver sat on the edge of the desk. "There's another possibility. If you answer my questions and tell them, then they might just kill you."

His brow pinched. Like he hadn't considered that possibility.

Carver kept talking. "Or I could just torture you and leave your broken, but still living body for them to find. Just let me know which you prefer."

Luis took a deep breath. Stiffened his spine. "What do you want to know?"

"Where did they take Monty and the others?"

"I don't know what you're talking about. I just watch the monitors and notify them when something or someone of interest is in town."

"So, you're low on the totem pole." Carver had found it was always good to get a little background on the people you interrogated. Sometimes it was helpful. "How did you get this job?"

Luis blinked. Like he wasn't expecting that question after the first one. "I was working operations for them in Los Angeles, and they moved me here."

"So, you've been with the cartel for a while."

"My brother is an enforcer. He said I was too soft for street work and got me a job in the technical side."

"That's good to hear. Glad your brother is looking out for you." Carver holstered the Glock. He didn't think Luis would be much of a threat. But he was still ready just in case. "Now, back to the Mercedes. I'm going to need to see where it went. Pull up the footage from around twelve thirty on the western side of town."

Luis tapped a few keys on the keyboard. A list of files appeared. He scrolled down and opened one with a timestamp of noontime. It showed the road leading into town. The same road the van should have taken.

The video was in segments. The camera had only recorded when it detected movement. It showed several cars had come into town that way, but none of them were vans. Luis picked another video file.

This file was from another road coming into town. There were several cars, but not the van.

Carver sighed. "Are there any locations in town that they'd take a prisoner?"

"There's a warehouse on the northwest side. Right next to that salvage yard."

"It didn't go there." Carver frowned. "Anywhere else?"

He shook his head. "Not that I know of."

Carver nodded at the screen. "Keep looking."

Luis pulled up file after file. There was no sign of the van. He frowned and pulled up a map. The cameras were marked on the map. There were even more of them than Carver's app showed. Some appeared to be inside buildings.

"Are those cameras in houses?"

Luis nodded. "People of interest."

Carver took a picture of the image. Just in case.

Luis clicked on camera markers for intersections on the north side. A screen with several timestamps appeared. He reviewed the files. Still nothing. "Are you sure this van came to town?"

"Positive." Carver couldn't imagine where else they would have gone. Unless they'd driven north into the nature preserve and executed the victims there.

Luis stared at the map for a long time. Then he frowned. Traced the mouse along the southern highway where there were no cameras because it was outside the town. He clicked a camera at an intersection on the east side of town.

The van was the third vehicle recorded. It was headed north. Luis snapped his fingers. "They came in from the south. They didn't come through town for some reason."

"Where did they go?"

Luis checked the subsequent cameras. The van had driven into the northern neighborhoods. The one with all the boarded-up houses. The same area where Joe had hidden Landry's car and his body.

"Why is that neighborhood like that? Everyone just pack up and leave?"

Luis shrugged. "I think a developer was buying up houses so he could demolish them and build apartments. Then the real estate crash hit like thirteen years ago and killed the project. I only know about that because some guy at a bar was talking to me about all the abandoned buildings in town."

"Any chance they could have been going somewhere else besides that neighborhood?"

Luis traced the mouse along the streets. "The area is a loop. There's no outlet on the north side. The road loops north and branches into two other roads, then goes back south to reconnect with the highway."

"So, it's a sure thing it's in there somewhere."

Luis checked later footage. "No signs it ever came out."

Carver nodded. "You've done real good, Luis. I haven't even had to torture you once. I'm going to ask you one more question that will determine if that remains the case."

Luis gulped. "Okay."

"What happened to Joe Donnely?"

Luis looked confused. "I was told to monitor his movements closely. We had his vehicles' license plates tagged in the system, so they'd be flagged whenever they came into town. That started a little over a month ago. Around the time he said he was running for mayor." Luis held out his hands helplessly. "That's all I know."

Carver believed him. "Is the mayor part of the cartel?"

Luis blinked. "The mayor? No, we control her. Although I have to say she seems happy to follow orders."

"I agree." Carver stood. Stretched. "Luis, you've done well. I'm going to leave here and if you pretend that none of this happened, then I think we'll both be happier."

Luis wiped sweat from his forehead. "I agree. It's a good thing the people out front don't know who you are, or we'd both be screwed."

"I wouldn't be screwed, but you would be." Carver walked to the door. Paused. "Don't give me a reason to visit you again, okay? I don't want you tracking Joe's cars anymore." He left before Luis replied.

The people in the operations room watched him go. They looked confused. Maybe a little eager to go ask Luis who in the hell his visitor was.

Carver left the same way he'd come in. He even waved goodbye to Officer Nichols. She smiled a little this time.

He got in the pickup. Turned it around and headed toward the abandoned neighborhoods. There were three residential streets on the northeast side of town. All three were lined with derelict houses.

There was a big sign out front. *New Apartments Coming Soon!* The sign was weather-beaten and rotting. It had been put up a long time ago and left to rot like the neighborhood.

The houses were little shoebox buildings. Rectangles with moldy vinyl siding or rotting plywood. They'd probably been built in the seventies or eighties. Affordable homes built as cheaply as possible.

It was interesting that no one else had tried to buy the land or develop it, especially considering the cost of real estate in California. Maybe it was one of those places that just took decades to recover.

Either way, it had worked out for Joe, and now it was helping the cartel. The van was going to be at one of these houses. It was too tall to park in a standard garage. It would be sitting outside, or maybe parked in a backyard.

It had been a while since Monty had been taken prisoner. Four hours and counting now. He might be long dead. They might have buried him and the others in one of these back yards. But if that was the case, why hadn't the van come back out yet?

Maybe they just parked it here during downtime. Maybe there was another cartel hideout in these parts. He wasn't going to know until he combed the area. There were a few issues to iron out first, though.

He wasn't sneaking up on anyone with Joe's pickup. The exhaust was throaty and loud. That might be fine for showoffs, but it was no good for stealth operations. It was also still daylight. Anyone with a pair of eyes would see him walking around.

Covering three streets alone was also no mean feat. Each road was about a hundred yards long. The three-street area was the acreage of several football fields. In a car, it wasn't that bad. On foot, it was huge.

The best option was to narrow the search parameters. Use logic to pinpoint a more precise area. It boiled down to the objectives of the cartel. Did they want a house that was as hidden as possible, or a house that was positioned more strategically so they could see all incoming traffic?

The most hidden homes would be in the middle of their respective streets. The house in the center of the middle street would be an ideal choice. The house in the center of the last road would be a good second bet.

If they wanted a house with a clear view, they'd choose a corner lot. Probably on one side or the other of the middle road. The road names front to back were Pansy Street, Petunia Street, and Poppy Street. Alliterate street names. Real cute.

Petunia Street was the most likely location to find the right house. There was another neighborhood to the west, so he drove there first. This area was upper middle class. Nice houses. No derelicts.

The houses were mostly similar, but just different enough not to be a cookie cutter neighborhood. He parked on the side of the road in front of a house that was even with Petunia Street in the abandoned neighborhood.

He dug in his bag for a ragged shirt, torn jeans, and a dirty beanie. It was a little warm for a beanie, but it completed his homeless man outfit. It had worked so well in San Francisco, that he'd kept the old clothing.

A cloth facemask completed the outfit. He hadn't seen many people wearing facemasks in these parts, but it probably wouldn't stand out too much if he was spotted. He slid out of the truck and slouched to conceal his height and size.

The houses had fences in their backyards. No soliciting signs in the front yards. But there were power lines running between this house and the next, leaving a space for the utility right of way.

Carver used that space to walk between the fences and past the backyards. He crossed through a dry ditch and entered the unfenced backyard of an abandoned house. He crept along the back of the house and looked around the corner.

This house was on Pansy Street, the road that looped around the neighborhoods. Petunia street, the middle road, was directly across the road from this house. Carver used his monocular to study the corner home.

The windows were broken. The roof was caving in. There were no boards on the windows. No light emanating from inside. It looked like this wasn't the place.

He swept the monocular up and down the road. Looked carefully for signs of life. Something moved at the far end of Pansy Street, right where it curved at the northern end. It wasn't a human. It was furry and walking on all fours.

Carver zoomed in. It was a coyote. It was eating something. He zoomed in further. It looked like it was eating someone's cat. Probably from one of the middle-class houses. Since the coyote looked unconcerned with anything except eating, it was safe to assume that there were no humans in the nearby houses.

He walked north past the next house over, so he was in line with the backyards of the houses on Petunia Street. Then he looked both ways and dashed across the road. He pressed himself up against the back of the first house and made his way along it.

There was a rotting fence in the backyard two houses over. It was leaning heavily inward. There was a drainage ditch separating the backyards of these houses from the ones on Pansy Street.

Aside from the rotting fence, it was a straight shot for a hundred yards, give or take, from the first backyard to the last. The rotting fence was a welcome barrier. It prevented him from being completely exposed.

He studied the backs of the houses on Pansy Street with his monocular. Most of the windows weren't boarded. The developer probably didn't see a reason to waste the resources when demolition was imminent.

There were no signs of life at the houses in this section. He didn't have a clear view of the houses on the other side of Pansy Street, but that was okay. It meant if someone was occupying one, they wouldn't have a clear view of him either.

Hopefully, it would appear a homeless man was just looking for a place to settle in for the night. It was only early evening, but that was the prime time for a homeless person to look for supper and shelter.

Carver continued along the backyards. He reached the rotting fence and looked over it. There was a rusting swing set and monkey bars. Faded plastic children's toys. The sliding glass door had been smashed out a long time ago.

It was dark inside. No sounds. No signs of life. He walked around the fence. Crouched and looked through the rest of the backyards. No van. If it was here, it should be easily visible. Which meant it was probably behind a house on the other side of Pansy Street.

Another fence caught his eye. It was in bad shape just like the one next to him. But there was a green fiberglass roof standing up behind it. It was probably a greenhouse. But it might also be a carport.

It was in the yard next to the corner lot at the other end of Petunia Street. He hustled to the next house. Slid along the back of it. Paused to look inside the smashed sliding glass door. The inside of the house was dark and empty.

He went to the next house. Inspected it from outside the back door. It looked the same. No furniture, nothing inside. Just dusty countertops and broken glass. He was two houses down from the next fence.

Carver reached the corner of the next house. He crouched and went to the back door. Looked inside. Also, dark and quiet. He continued to the corner. The windows on the neighboring house were boarded.

The plywood was slightly weathered, but not enough to indicate it had been there for a decade. The driveway went from the road and continued behind the fence. Carver crept up to the fence. Looked through a hole.

There was an old fiberglass carport back there. A silhouette was visible through the translucent material. It was a high-roof van.

This was the house.

CHAPTER 39

Monty was sore and stiff.

He'd been stuck in this room for hours. His throat was parched, and his stomach was growling. It seemed he'd die of thirst or starvation before they got around to killing him.

Chief Lynch stood across the table from Monty. Stared at him like he wanted to spit in his face. Then finally said something. "You could be nice and comfy. Earning good money. All you had to do was listen to orders."

"I draw the line at sexually abused dead kids, Bart."

Lynch's eyes flared at the insubordination. "You're a worthless waste of space, Ford. Well, at least you were. Now you'll be worth something."

"What's that supposed to mean?"

Lynch bared his teeth. "You'll find out soon enough." He leaned his fists on the table. "I'm going to ask you a few questions. I want honest answers."

Monty bared his teeth back at him. "Good luck with that."

Lynch reached behind his back and pulled a ballpeen hammer from the back of his pants. "You can answer, or you can get your fingers broken one at a time. Your choice."

"Fine," Monty said. "Ask away."

"Where is Brent Landry?"

Monty blinked. "Huh? Isn't he on vacation?"

Lynch nodded as if satisfied with the answer. "How did you find out about the hacked modem?"

"Wait, you're telling me you don't know where Landry is?"

Lynch shook his head. "That's not how this works. Answer or I'll break a finger."

Monty sighed. "I talked with tech support. They figured out what happened. Other than that, they don't know anything except that your boy, Brad, is the one who did the hacking."

Lynch tapped the hammer on the metal table. "I never liked you, Ford. I'd be happy to bash your head in here and now. But that would just make you worthless again." He abruptly smashed the hammer on the metal table.

Monty had already pulled his hands back. He'd been wary of a surprise strike. "Sorry to disappoint you, Bart. I guess we're both despicable human beings."

"I'm actually doing some good in this world, Ford. You, on the other hand, will be forgotten."

"Good?" Monty laughed. "What good are you doing?"

Lynch didn't answer. He turned and opened the door to leave.

"Wait!"

Lynch turned around. "What?"

"Any chance I can get some water or food?"

Lynch bared his teeth again and left.

Monty hadn't expected a positive reaction. But he had wanted the door to remain open long enough for him to get a glimpse of the other side. Unfortunately, there was nothing but more gray cinderblock walls and a corridor.

Where in the hell were they?

Monty had learned one thing for sure. There were no plans to let him live. He and the others were going to die here. He sighed and leaned his head on the table. The klaxon blasted the silence. He looked up at the camera. Wished he could wrap his hands around the neck of whoever was watching him.

He moved his bound hands up to scratch an itch on his forehead and he realized something. They hadn't taken his watch. Probably because it looked like a cheap dollar-store digital timepiece and not a smart watch.

Technically, it was a knockoff. It was cheap. And that was why it didn't look the same as a regular Apple watch. He lowered his hands under the table and leaned back. Bowed his head like he was defeated.

He wriggled his hands in the cuffs until he was able to reach a thumb over and touch the watch screen. The LCD readout vanished. A grainy image of phone apps appeared. He tapped the map app.

The app opened, but the connection to the phone was bad. It took several seconds for it to be populated with information. After nearly a minute, a blue dot appeared on the map. The blue dot was inside the outline of a building.

It took maximum effort to reach finger and thumb to the screen so he could pinch zoom. Finally, he got it to zoom out enough, so a road was visible. The outline of another building was also visible.

It wasn't in satellite mode, so it was just a white outline. The road name wasn't on the map. He had to scroll to the side or zoom out more. Straining his wrists in the cuffs, he was able to slowly pinch zoom a little more.

The road name became visible. He knew exactly where he was. He was in the old police station on the northwest side of town. It wasn't far from the salvage yard. Maybe three blocks west of it and right across the road from an abandoned warehouse.

This area used to be downtown El Fuerte. Then downtown moved further south of the highway when the new town hall was built back in the eighties. Mayor Davis had a new police station built next to town hall and this location had been phased out.

It was a big building, occupying a full city block. There had been plans to redevelop it into apartment lofts, but like a lot of things in this town, those plans had fallen through. And now it might be the place where he died.

CARVER DREW HIS GLOCK.

He attached the suppressor. A section of the old fencing had fallen over in the back yard, leaving a gap for him to fit through. And that's just what he did before easing up to the door. He could see into the carport now. The Mercedes van was there.

This house didn't have a sliding glass door. It had a regular wooden back door. The windows were boarded up. The door itself wasn't locked. He gently twisted the knob. Eased the door open. It scraped loudly on the floor.

If someone was inside, the jig was up. He rammed his shoulder against it and burst into the kitchen. It was empty. No furniture, no dishes, no people. That didn't mean anything. He put his back against the wall.

Slid toward the next room. Cleared the corner. The house was quiet and dark. No lights. No odors. Carver cleared all the rooms and closets. The house was empty. The van was here, but no people.

There was only one reason. He'd been set up. He rushed to the back door. Crouched and looked around. The fence blocked his view, so he made his way to the gap and looked around the corner.

He expected to see a group of heavily armed men running his way, but the yards were just as empty now as they'd been moments ago. That didn't make him feel any better. He went to the van. It was locked.

Was it possible they hid the van here but didn't use the house for anything? There was plenty of room to store it at the warehouse. He couldn't think of a reason why they wouldn't store it there.

Well, there was one good reason. Diversification of safehouses. Putting all your eggs into one basket could be risky. If, for some reason, the FBI or other law enforcement actually did their jobs and raided the warehouse, this van would be safe.

They might have safehouses all over town. Fallback positions in case something went wrong. From that perspective, it made perfect sense, even in a town they owned lock, stock, and barrel.

Carver went back inside the house. Opened the door leading to the garage. The interior was clean. Lined with shelves. The shelves were full of boxes. Boxes of ammunition. Boxes of zip-tie handcuffs. Black hoods, earmuffs, tape, chloroform, and various other supplies.

It was a complete one-stop shop for abducting people. Perfectly tailored for all your kidnapping needs. It reminded Carver of the supplies his team stored in the basement of the safehouse in the tiny Ukrainian town of Dmytrivka.

That had been one of three safehouses used by Scion. Keeping the van and these supplies here made more sense in that context.

A fresh puddle of condensation told him that another car had been in the garage recently. Things began to make more sense. The van was stored in the carport out back, hidden behind the house and from an aerial view.

When they needed to kidnap someone, they parked a regular car in the garage. Geared up. Got in the van and did the deed. They dropped the victims somewhere else then returned the van here. But where did they take their prisoners?

Luis had reviewed the videos from the west side of town. The van had gone undetected on the south side before turning north and coming here. That made the old business district the perfect place to drop off the victims.

But Carver had combed the old furniture warehouse and all the buildings there earlier. He hadn't been inside each and every one of them, but he'd looked through windows. Most of the buildings weren't that large.

There had been no vehicles parked nearby. Nothing to indicate someone had been there anytime recently. He felt relatively certain that Monty and the others hadn't been delivered to any of those buildings.

Carver studied the map app with the marked camera locations. He zoomed out and examined the area as whole. There were two ways the van could have returned from the restaurant. One route looped south of town. The other route approached directly from the west, entering the north side of town near the warehouse.

There were no cameras on the outskirts of the west side. Probably because that was where the warehouse was. Also, probably because there were no traffic lights and very few businesses there. The van hadn't been seen at the warehouse, but what if there was another building being used in that sector?

The van could have entered the northwest side of town and driven three city blocks before hitting the first traffic cam on the north side. He opened the picture he'd taken of Luis's map. Confirmed there were no cameras in the northwest sector.

If they dropped someone there, then taken the outer loop south and around the city that way, they would have avoided cameras until they went due north on the other side of town. He didn't know why they'd take that roundabout route instead of driving straight across the northern highway, but they might have had their reasons.

He zoomed in further on Luis's map. The traffic cams were marked with red icons. The ones that were inside buildings were blue. The ones that were in parking lots were shaded orange.

There was a single camera in the northwestern section of town. It was colored orange. It was in a parking lot. There was a red X across the icon which probably meant it was offline.

Carver scanned the map and found other cameras with the same red X. They might not be offline. They might be restricted, meaning Luis couldn't access them. They might be reserved for someone further up the food chain.

He went back to the map app. Looked at the building with the parking lot camera. It was a large building. Almost as big as the abandoned furniture warehouse. It wasn't labeled with a name.

He opened a web browser and ran a search. *El Fuerte history*. The first result was the El Fuerte Historical Society. It had the complete history of the town, starting with the founding and running all the way to current times.

There was a page about the historic downtown. Apparently, town hall and the police station had been built in the eighties under the reign of Mayor Davis. The original downtown had been further north on the highway.

Davis had commissioned a town hall. Once it was built, he had a new police station built. The old one was decommissioned and marked for redevelopment. There was a picture of the old downtown.

The old police station was a single-story red brick building. It wasn't tall, but it was wide, taking up most of the city block. Carver switched to the map app and looked at the street view. He examined the building from all sides.

There was a fenced area. Probably where the motor pool had been. The main entrance was boarded up. The image taken by the mapping vehicle was a few years old. But it was probably still accurate.

Carver didn't even have to go there to feel certain of one thing. That was the place where they'd taken Monty and the others. It had a drop off zone for prisoners. Jail cells. Concrete walls. Very few windows.

It was the perfect place to hide people. And it was close to the warehouse if they needed extra manpower close at hand.

It was also a secure location. He wasn't going to sneak in there in broad daylight. And it apparently had a camera in the parking lot that watched for unwanted visitors. He'd have to pinpoint the location before doing anything.

Carver had a missed text on his phone. It was from Albert. It said, *Watch this!* A link was below. He clicked the link. Another app opened. A video started playing. It took Carver a moment to realize it was showing the road in front of Albert's place.

Police cars lined the side of the road. A SWAT van was parked there. Armed police and SWAT members were standing across the road. They seemed to be confused. Waiting for orders.

A motorcycle rumbled past and went through the gate and into Albert's. The police didn't try to stop it. They just watched. Chief Lynch was pacing back and forth out front. He looked furious.

A middle-aged black man appeared on the left half of the screen. Probably the man Big Georgie had mentioned, Nate the Lawyer.

Nate laughed. "It's working folks. When you shine the light, bad people are less likely to do bad things. They might be corrupt there in El Fuerte, but they don't want the entire world to know it."

Text at the bottom of the screen said, *Live Stream – 437,241 viewers.* Live chats ran up the side of the screen, new ones appearing every second.

We'll watch them all weekend if we have to!

Keep Albert safe!

Throw the corrupt mayor and all her henchmen in jail!

Nate started talking about the bike rally. He said he was going to start an interview with Albert soon. The camera panned over to show the inside of the gate. There were several news crews there with reporters talking into the cameras.

Carver turned it off. It looked like the psyops route was working just fine. Not even the cartel wanted their foul deeds broadcast to half a million people. The coverage would likely spawn even more coverage.

There was another text from Albert. *They cut off the internet and tried to storm the place. But we held them back. Then Big George took the footage right off the camera's internal memory and sent it to the reporters over a cellular connection. The cops backed off real fast then.*

Carver replied. *How many bikers are there now?*

He pocketed the phone then studied the supplies in the garage. There was a duffel bag already stocked with supplies for any kind of abduction his heart desired. He took it and left the house. Headed back to the truck.

He had another thought on the way there and detoured to the house where Joe had hidden the bodies and the car. The back door was unlocked. He went through the kitchen and into the garage.

The car was still there. Still covered in trash. There was still a faint stench of rot in the garage. Not as bad as it would have been weeks ago. The bodies had probably been eaten up by insects and rodents by now.

He wasn't there to look at corpses. He was there for the other thing Joe had left here. The crate of weapons from the trunk of the car. He found the chest in the back seat just as he'd seen it in Joe's bodycam footage.

Carver inspected the first rifle he laid hands on. It was a CAR816. A compact combat rifle. Made for close quarters combat. There was a custom rail with a slot to hold the suppressor. It was a real nice piece of work and didn't make the rail unnecessarily huge.

The rail was the piece around the barrel. Designed primarily to keep all the heat from the barrel away from the operator's skin. This one was only slightly larger to accommodate the suppressor on the bottom.

The suppressor fit flush with the end of the rail. Carver pushed it in. There was a click and a spring pushed it out. He slid it out of the rail and twisted it one full turn to attach it to the rifle. This suppressor was skinnier than most but a little longer to make up for the diameter.

Carver pulled a magazine from the chest. It was semitransparent so he could see the bullets inside. It was fully loaded—thirty rounds. He rocked it into the mag well. He doublechecked the suppressor to ensure it was fully attached. Everything looked good.

He went into the den and fired a single shot into the wall. The rifle coughed. A bullet smashed through the drywall and zinged off something on the other side. It wasn't silent, but it was damned quiet.

He switched to burst fire. Tested it. It spat three bullets with one trigger pull. He checked the heat from the barrel by holding a hand near the rail. It seemed normal. He tested fully automatic and emptied the magazine.

The last few shots were a little louder. The suppressor was putting off a lot of heat but no signs of warping. The important thing was the gun worked. That was all he needed to know.

It was perfect for his evening plans.

Carver reloaded the magazine from one of the ammo boxes. He took the other six magazines and confirmed they were fully loaded. Thirty rounds in each magazine. That might be enough if he got into a firefight.

Hopefully, it wouldn't come to that.

He left the abduction house and carried his newfound treasures to the pickup truck. He put the kidnapping supplies and the rifle into the passenger floorboard. Started the pickup. He pulled out of the neighborhood and headed south.

Carver took the long way around town to avoid cameras. There was no compelling reason to think Luis wouldn't start tracking him again. No reason to take the chance, anyway.

He circled the south side of town, away from cameras, then cut north on the west side of town. He stopped at a small strip mall. Parked behind it and put on his black fatigues. Then he leaned the seat back and got some shuteye.

He needed to be refreshed for what was to come.

CHAPTER 40

Two clenched his fists.

He stared at the livestream recording events at the salvage yard. A man called Nate the Lawyer kept going on and on about the police teams across the road. It was a real bad look for El Fuerte. A real bad look for his boss.

He turned to Mayor Jessica Herrada. "Carver did this. Textbook psyops against a superior force."

She glared at the screen. "That bastard is smart. Very smart. I think we'll just have to wait it out. I know the cartel won't be pleased, but there's nothing else we can do."

"Agreed." He closed the laptop. "Probably best to have them stop all shipments until after the rally."

Mayor Jessica Herrada slapped a hand on the counter. "I don't like being played. After this is over, we need to deal with Albert. Shut that place down for good. And I want all of Donnely's supporters tagged and taken at the first opportunity."

Two put a hand on her shoulder. "Not a good idea. It's too close to home."

She was seething. "These little people think they can go against me?"

Two was already calm. Getting emotional never solved anything. Especially not when you were up against someone like Carver. "What we have to do is let them think they've won. We might have to sacrifice a few people to make it look real."

Jessica took deep breaths as if trying to calm herself. "I really don't like that idea. I want them to know they've lost. I want them to realize that this is my town, not theirs."

"I know it's unappealing, but we need to get Carver out of here first." Two went to the refrigerator and pulled out two beers. "He's convinced Joe was murdered. He's not going anywhere until he's convinced his friend is avenged."

"And how are we supposed to convince him of that?"

Two grinned. "We find a scapegoat and let Carver have his way with them. The man's a drifter. He'll be gone as soon as he thinks it's over. Then you can do whatever you want." He popped the tops off the beer bottles and held one out to her.

Jessica took the beer. Clinked her bottle against his. "Sounds like a plan." She took a sip. "Who are we throwing to the wolves?"

Two already had the perfect candidate. "Domingo."

She laughed. "You really don't like him, do you?"

He shrugged. "It's just business."

"How are we going to set this up so Carver isn't suspicious?"

Two gave it some thought. "Let's use the detective—what's his name?" He snapped his fingers. "Ford."

"That drunk?"

He nodded. "Yeah. We'll have Lynch tell him Domingo did it. Then we can cut Ford free so he can go tell Carver."

"How do we cut him free without arousing suspicion?"

"Easy. Lynch makes him an offer. Tells him to play ball or else. Ford agrees and we cut him loose. He tells Carver and Carver kills Domingo. Carver is satisfied and leaves town." He made a show of wiping off his hands. "Easy peasy."

"Why don't we say it was Hugo? He's dead already. Problem solved."

"Because someone like Carver won't be satisfied with that. He'll want to kill the perp with his two bare hands." Two nodded in assurance. "Domingo is the better choice. And we can set him up easily."

Jessica's anger faded. She smiled. Stood on her tiptoes and kissed him. "I knew there was a reason I kept you around." Her hand wandered to his crotch. "Maybe two reasons."

Two ran his hand down her back. "Let me take care of this first. Then I'll take care of your appetite."

She laughed. "That's what I love to hear."

MONTY JERKED AWAKE.

They'd moved him, Alice, and Brad into jail cells. He and Brad were sharing a cell. Alice was in a cell with another woman. He only knew that because they shoved her inside on the way to his cell.

He'd counted ten other people being held here. Mostly men. The guards were all dressed in EFPD T-shirts and dark slacks. They were cops. Some he knew on sight. Others he'd never seen before. There were at least five of them.

One of the Arabs had made an appearance earlier. He'd spoken to the cops. The cops pulled everyone from their cells and made them line up against a wall. The Arab had taken each person's picture, then left.

The cops made the prisoners strip down, fold their clothing neatly, and set it on a bench. Then they'd made everyone stand still, arms by their sides, while they inspected them. Mainly, they leered at the women.

One guy groped the women. Sized them up like meat. A feisty Latina slapped him. He punched her in the stomach. She doubled over and lay moaning on the floor.

Monty felt certain they were about to be executed. Instead, one of the cops went from person to person, reading off a long list of crimes. Mostly about subverting democracy, disrespecting their leaders, and spreading propaganda.

If anyone tried to speak out, they'd get a fist to the guts. After the first two guys were nearly knocked out, everyone kept quiet. Once that farce was over, they'd been shoved back into their cells.

The clank of a metal door echoed in the hallway. One of the cops was there. He unlocked the cell door and motioned for Monty to follow him.

Monty stood and followed without argument. Another cop was there. He gripped Monty's arm and yanked him along as if he was resisting arrest. They left the cells and went down the corridor to the interrogation room.

Lynch was there looking smug.

"What is it now?" Monty said. "Are you going to break my fingers after all?"

Lynch was staring at something on his phone. He looked up and grunted. "Well, it looks like you were right."

Monty frowned. "About what?"

"Donnely was murdered."

Monty stiffened. "What? You're admitting it?"

Lynch barked a laugh. "Admitting what? It looks like some hothead decided to take matters into his own hands even though an agreement had already been reached. Donnely was getting out of the mayoral race. The problem was solved."

"It was Hugo, wasn't it?"

Lynch shook his head.

Monty grew suspicious. "Why are you telling me this?"

"Because Brent Landry has been missing for weeks. Do you know how hard it is to find bent detectives?"

"Not too hard."

"Harder than you'd think." Lynch grunted. "The mayor wants you around. She wants the old Monty back. The one who followed orders and took the money."

Monty thought about it. It was better than having his fingers smashed with a hammer. Better than being killed. "She must really be desperate."

Lynch sighed. Stood. "Have it your way, you damned moron."

"No, wait!" Monty held up his cuffed hands. "You'll tell me who killed Joe and then let me back in?"

Lynch waggled a hand. "You can come back in, but why would I tell you who killed Donnely? We can handle that internally."

"Yeah, but I know someone who would take care of the problem happily and for free."

Lynch's forehead furrowed. "Who? That Carver fellow? He's not one of us."

"Yes, but Joe was his friend. You give me the name and I'll make sure he gets it. The killer won't be a problem after that, guaranteed."

Lynch stared blankly at him. Tilted his head like he was considering it. "Let me ask. They might be okay with that. But we want this Carver fellow gone."

"Once Joe's murderer is dead, I think he'll be happy to leave."

"You might be right." Lynch stood. "See? You're still a decent detective. Just take the money and be a well-paid detective too."

"Give me the killer's name, and I'm in." Monty felt a surge of elation. He could be a hero. At least for Carver and Andrea. Help them find the justice they deserved. And then he could go back to being a lovable bent detective again.

But one thing still bugged him. "You don't know where Landry is?"

Lynch shook his head. "Haven't heard from him in over a month."

"You think he's singing to the feds?"

Lynch laughed. "Landry? No way in hell. Something must have happened to him."

"Gosh, I hope not." Monty lied. He hoped Landry was rotting in an unmarked grave. He wished he could shake hands with the killer.

"Okay, I'll go talk to the boss. I'll let you know what she says." Lynch motioned toward the two-way mirror. The door buzzed open, and he left.

Monty breathed a sigh of relief. This was all going to be over soon.

CHAPTER 41

Carver was locked and loaded.

He held the CAR816 at the low and ready and hustled across the road and into the old section of downtown. He found a two-story building. The windows were smashed out, so he simply stepped inside.

He went to the roof. Crawled to the lip. Used the monocular to survey the decommissioned police station across the road. He saw the camera. It was on a pole in front of the building. It was angled to the southwest.

There was another camera on the other side of the pole watching the road to the north and east. After carefully scanning the rest of the area, he confirmed that the motor pool area on the northwest side of the building couldn't be seen by either camera.

He'd have to find a perch to view the back of the building. To make sure there weren't cameras on the side of the building that he couldn't see from here.

Carver noted several broken places in the chain link perimeter around the motor pool. He noted a metal door on the side. Double glass doors on the front.

One break in the fence was out of sight of the cameras. The metal door on the side might be in the field of view for the cameras, but he'd need to look from another angle to be sure.

He left the roof. Went a block south. Circled west and then north until he reached a former bakery on the west side of the decommissioned police station. It was near the building where he'd spotted the person looking for him at Albert's last night.

A broken window let him into the single-story building. The roof access was in a former storage room. A ladder led through a hatch. He climbed up and crawled onto the roof. It was just high enough for him to look over the fence around the motor pool.

There were cameras on the back. They looked old. Real old. Probably from the early eighties. It was doubtful they even functioned. They were right above two large rollup doors. There was probably a repair shop on the other side.

One of the rollup doors wasn't closed all the way. The rubber at the bottom was about three inches off the ground. Either someone had left it that way, or there was something wrong with it. After looking up and down the building, it seemed that was his best infiltration point.

There were no patrols around the building. No signs anyone was inside. These people relied heavily on the appearance that the buildings were vacant. It had worked out well for them so far but it came with its share of disadvantages.

There were few working streetlamps on this side of town. No lights in the parking lot around the old police station. And since there were no thermal cameras on the perimeter, it meant they wouldn't see Carver coming.

He climbed back down inside the old bakery. There were rows of brick ovens and stainless-steel tables. The place had probably once been at the very center of town. A real popular place to visit. Now, like so many places here, it was abandoned and forgotten.

Carver hustled across the street. He put his back against a wall. Examined the nearby buildings to ensure there weren't hidden cameras on them. He didn't pick up anything. No sign of infrared showed up in his monocular.

He reached a building just across the road from the station. Right across the road from a break in the fence. He kept low and dashed across the street. Pulled the fence away from the fence post. Slipped past it.

It was a thirty-yard walk to the rollup door. He didn't run because it would be too noisy. It was dark enough that no one would see him. Since they weren't using external patrols, the coast should be clear.

Once he reached the rollup door, he went prone. Looked under the crack. It was dark on the other side. He used the monocular. No heat signatures appeared on the scope. He gently lifted the door.

It screeched. The sound echoed in the emptiness on the other side. He winced and raised it just high enough for him to crawl under. Then he eased it back down. He looked around the space.

There were car lifts. Toolboxes. Compressors. Stacks of tires. All the fixings for a fully operational mechanic shop. This place was in use. Why didn't they store their van and kidnapping gear here? Why keep it separate?

Maybe for the same reason the human trafficking operation was across the highway. They didn't keep all their eggs in one basket. If one secret operation was discovered, the others could keep going unaffected.

The whole town could be riddled with places like this. Each one serving its own purpose. Each one connected loosely to the other.

There were three police cars inside. They looked new. If anyone discovered this place, maybe they would claim it was used for overflow. A backup mechanic shop for police vehicles.

Carver took cover behind an SUV. He scanned with his monocular and found two exits. One exited outside. The other went further into the police station. That was where he was going next. Once he confirmed no one was coming to investigate the noise the door had made.

He'd give it ten minutes. It only took four before someone entered the shop. They didn't turn on the lights. They used a flashlight. A radio crackled and someone spoke.

"It's in the first car. Back floorboard."

The man clicked the receiver. "Copy that. ETA on transfer?"

"Zero-thirty-two hours," the person on the radio replied.

"Plenty of time for some fun." He chuckled.

Carver used his monocular in night vision. The flashlight was directed toward the cars, so he was able to make out some details.

The man spoke again. "Are we on body disposal tonight?"

A sigh from the radio. "Affirmative."

"You think she'll be one of them?"

"She and the other two are going over tonight. You know they don't return them in one piece."

"Yeah. What a shame. Guess we'd better have our fun before they take them."

The man went to the sedan. Opened the back door. Pulled out a case of beer. The cheap kind in cans. He tore open the side of the carton. Removed a can and popped it open. Took a long gulp and sighed.

He removed a brown paper bag from the car. Pulled out two small boxes. The night vision on the monocular helped him make out the writing. They were condoms and lubrication.

The man spoke on the radio. "You sure there's enough time for all of us?"

"Plenty. Get your ass back here."

"Coming." The man started walking back toward the door.

Carver had used the time to circle back around the SUV. Around the front of the sedan. When the man faced away, Carver put the barrel of the CAR816 to the back of the man's head. "Hi."

The man froze. He dropped the case of beer and the paper bag. They smashed on the floor.

"Tell me about this body disposal," Carver said. "Inquiring minds want to know."

"I don't know what you're talking about."

Carver drew a knife. He pressed the point to the back of the man's neck. Right in the middle of the cervical vertebrae. The part just below the skull. "There's a very specific nerve ending right here. It connects directly to the cerebral cortex. If I cut it, it'll be like you had a stroke. You'll live but be permanently disabled for life."

The man stiffened. "Who the hell are you?"

"You don't know?"

The man hissed a breath between clenched teeth. "You're that Carver guy. The SEAL."

"I am."

The man seemed to believe Carver. "Look, we don't kill anyone, okay? They just send us the bodies and we take them for cremation and disposal."

"Then who killed Joe Donnely?"

"Killed him? I heard it was an accident."

"I don't believe that."

Sweat trickled down the man's temple. "I had nothing to do with it. It was an accident. Please, I've got a wife and kids."

"Yeah? Would your wife approve of the fun you're planning with the condoms and lube?"

"It's not what you think!"

Carver didn't care. "What goes on in the warehouse across the road?"

"They don't tell us anything. They just bring us bodies. You've got to believe me. I'm a good person."

"Where is Monty Ford and the others they kidnapped?"

The man nodded his head slightly toward the door. "They're in the jail cells. I can take you there. Just don't paralyze me."

The threat of paralysis was a lie. Carver would have to shove the knife through the joints in the man's spine to do anything. But most people didn't know that.

"Where do you take the bodies for cremation?"

"Just down the road to the old funeral home."

Carver thought he heard something, but it was just the man's teeth chattering. "What do you do with the ashes?"

"There's an open grave. We keep it covered when it's not in use."

"Who are the people that are being killed?"

"I don't know. I swear it. They just bring them in. Sometimes we hold them here. Sometimes they hold them across the road. It just depends on when the clients arrive."

A door scraped open. Someone entered the same way this guy had. "Dave, where the hell are you? The boys are getting tired of waiting."

"A good person, eh?" Carver slit the man's throat before he could shout. A gurgle was all that escaped.

Carver mimicked the dying man's voice. It wasn't a good job, but it was good enough. "I need a hand carrying the beer." He picked up Dave's flashlight and aimed it toward the voice.

"Really?" the unseen man laughed and walked around the cars. He shielded his eyes. "Come on, man. We've got to hurry before the clients arrive. Nigel is making the girls shower so they're fresh."

"Good." Carver's CAR816 coughed. A red dot appeared in the other man's forehead. He fell backward. Thudded onto the concrete floor. Carver checked Dave's weapons. Caracal. He still didn't understand why this was their weapon of choice.

It didn't make sense to use weapons that were rare in the US. Maybe they weren't using black market suppliers. Maybe they had an official outlet. Or there might be former UAE military folks involved.

It wasn't unheard of for people in military supply to build up a healthy weapons stash before they left the service. Maybe it was something like that. It didn't have to make sense. It didn't even really matter.

Carver left the weapons and hustled to the door the two men had come through. He cracked it open and looked to the other side. There was light from somewhere down a dim corridor. Just enough light for him to see by.

The walls were cinderblock. The floors were old vinyl. There was a distinct odor in the air. Like fear, blood, and human waste all mixed into one. Water was running in the distance. Men were laughing and shouting.

Carver slipped down the hallway like a ghost. He didn't have to be too quiet. The voices were loud enough to drown out someone running with wooden clodhoppers. But there was no need to take chances.

"I'm done waiting," one of the men said. "Besides, it's my turn to go first. I want the blonde."

"We draw straws like we always do," a gruff voice replied.

"I never win the draw! Why can't I go first?"

A third person spoke. "Shut it, Mike." He had a slight Hispanic accent.

"No, you shut it, Pedro!" Mike shouted back.

"Both of you shut it!" the gruff speaker roared. That was probably Nigel.

Carver reached the entrance to the locker room. He peered inside. There was a partition wall blocking the view of the showers. He slid along it while Mike kept arguing his point. He looked around the corner.

These were the jailhouse showers. The ones in open rows where prisoners showered in front of the guards. A tall, blonde girl was huddled under a shower. Next to her was an older Hispanic woman with black hair. Long handcuffs secured them to the tiled column with the shower.

They were surrounded by three men. Three of El Fuerte's finest. The men were laughing and leering at the women. Making obscene gestures.

The women were trying to cover themselves with their hands. The handcuffs restrained them from doing much. The girl looked terrified. Her face was red. Probably from tears, but the water was washing them away. The Hispanic woman looked frightened but furious.

The three men wore casual police uniforms. Black slacks with black t-shirts that had EFPD stitched on them. Those were probably their police cruisers in the garage. One stood in front of the girl. One was pointing at the Hispanic woman. The other was next to him, still squabbling.

The angle was no good. A bullet might go through the one guy and into the girl. One of them also body blocked the other guy. By the time Carver dropped him, the other guy would have time to run behind one of the concrete partitions.

They were also close enough to the women to use them as hostages if Carver tried to get them to surrender.

That was okay. Carver had a better idea. He backed up into the hallway and mimicked Dave's voice again. "Guys, I need some help."

"With what?" Mike said.

"Go help him," Nigel said.

Mike cursed and his feet stomped across the tile. He emerged in the hallway. Carver had taken cover inside a doorway just down the hall. He'd placed the case of beer in the middle of the floor. Put the condoms on top.

"Dave? What the hell?" Mike huffed and walked down the hall. He bent down to pick up the bottle. Carver put a bullet through his temple. Mike fell forward like a rag doll. His forehead smacked the tile. Then he slowly fell over sideways.

Carver yanked his body out of the hallway. There was a streak of blood, but the hallway was dim. No one would see from a distance.

He took the lube out of its box. He emptied the bottle on the floor just outside the showers. Then he went back to the same doorway he'd ambushed Mike from. He mimicked Dave's voice again.

"Mike, stop it! That's not yours! Stop!"

Nigel roared. "God damn it, Mike!" He stormed out of the showers with a head full of steam and turned the corner. His feet slipped out from beneath him so fast, he didn't even have time to register it. His head bounced off the wall. His shoulder hit the floor.

He was stunned for a second. Carver took that second to put a bullet in his head. The suppressor quieted the shot, but the bullet burst out of the back of Nigel's head and whined.

"Yo, what the hell was that?" Pedro said.

Carver had stepped over the puddle of lube. He was against the partition just inside the shower room. He pivoted around the edge. Pedro's eyes flared when he saw Carver. An instant later, a bullet made that his last facial expression ever.

Pedro toppled over backward. The women screamed. The screams echoed. If someone else was here, they'd come running.

CHAPTER 42

Carver put a finger to his lips.

The screams turned to whimpers.

"How many more are there?"

The blonde woman stared at him with wide eyes. "There were five total."

"Five total guards in this entire place?"

She nodded. "It was always the same five men, except when another guy would show up to take people away."

Carver frisked Pedro's body. Didn't find what he was looking for. He went to the hallway. Searched Nigel. Found the handcuff keys.

Carver went back inside. Grabbed towels from a shelf. He gave them to the women. "Don't be afraid. I'm here to help. The five men are dead, okay?"

"D-dead?" The young woman's mouth dropped open. "Really?"

The Hispanic woman narrowed her eyes. Took the towels. Handed one to the young woman. Held out her wrists toward Carver.

Carver unlocked the cuffs. Backed up. "Is Monty Ford here somewhere?"

The blonde girl shook her head. "We were in a holding room together, then they took him somewhere. He said they interrogated him earlier. Maybe they were taking him there again. After they took him they took me and Brad to another place where they were holding everyone else."

The other woman wrapped a towel around herself. "Who are you?"

"No one in particular." Carver looked around. "Where were they holding you? How many of you are there?"

"You're Carver, aren't you?" The blonde woman looked him up and down. "I'm Alice. I met Monty earlier to talk about a hacked modem. He told me about you."

Carver wished Monty hadn't told her about him. "It's best if you don't remember my name. If you forget you ever saw me."

"Uh, it's kind of hard to forget the man who saved your life."

"Those men were going to rape us!" The other woman kicked Pedro's body with her bare foot and winced. "What the hell is this place?"

"What's your name?" Carver asked.

The woman took a deep breath. Shivered. "I'm Melinda Torres."

"Were you kidnapped?"

"Yes!" She started to shake. "My God, it's just hitting me."

"Did they say why you were kidnapped?"

Alice nodded. "They made it a point to tell people why they were there. They told me that I'd helped the wrong side. That I was meddling in things I should have left alone."

"I run a video channel," Melinda said. "I talk about politics."

"You have a particular leaning?" Carver asked.

She shrugged. "Middle of the divide. But that has me posting mostly negative things about politicians in this state."

"You ever receive death threats? Anything like that?"

"Yes, all the time. The comments are mostly positive, but I still get plenty of negative feedback. Especially about the illegal immigration issue. They're just allowing people to pour into the country unvetted. It's making the homelessness issue spiral out of control!"

"Did you ever say anything specifically about Jessica Herrada?"

Melinda nodded. "Yes. I did several pieces on corrupt mayors around the country. I just released my first piece on her two weeks ago." She pulled the towel tighter around her. "I woke up one night and found a man standing by my bed. He had a gun."

"Holy crap!" Alice's mouth dropped open. "That's terrifying!"

"He made me get up, go to my computer, and delete all the videos off my channel. Then I had to delete all my backups, everything." She licked her lips nervously. "His face was covered. He told me that if I did what he said, everything would be okay. But once I was done, he jabbed me with a needle. I woke up here."

"These crooked cops lined us up against a wall and read off a list of offenses," Alice said. "Almost everyone was in there because they'd committed some kind of political crime. They accused some people of trying to overthrow local governments. Of plotting against leaders. I'd say ninety percent of them had never even heard of Jessica Herrada."

"So, people of a particular political persuasion." Carver motioned them to leave the shower. "Do you have clothing anywhere?"

"They took our clothing when they lined us up against the wall," Alice said. "They put us in the cells and gave us buckets to use for toilets."

"It's like a third world jail." Melinda started walking.

"Careful around that corner," Carver said. "There's lube on the floor."

Melinda carefully walked around it. She stared at Nigel's body. Spat on it. "You know what's ironic? They accused us of subverting democracy. They told us that we're the ones trying to steal it."

"They treated us like animals." Alice's step faltered. She stopped and leaned against the wall. "I just knew we were dead. That I'd never see my parents again. Never get to see sunlight again."

Carver held up a hand to slow them down. "How many more prisoners are there?"

"I don't know. Maybe ten?" Alice counted people off on her fingers. "Me, Monty, Melinda, Jeremy, Craig, Lamar, Gregory, Mai Ling, Alejandro, and of course, that asshole, Brad. I think the last two guys are Jorge and Booker."

Melinda looked impressed. "You remembered everyone's names?"

Alice sighed. "Names just stick with me. Especially when the people are being accused of war crimes or whatever."

Carver didn't care about names. "Where are the cells?"

"Down the hall somewhere." Alice shivered. "Names I can remember. Directions, not so much."

"They're that way." Melinda pointed north.

"How long ago did they bring you here?"

"About twenty minutes ago," Alice said. "One of the cops had just taken Monty away. They might have returned him to his cell already."

Melinda looked at the bodies in the hallway. "How do we get out of here?"

"We'll get to that." Carver started walking down the northern hallway. He turned the corner ahead and knew this was the right way because there was a heavy metal door set in the wall on the left. It was propped open.

He went through it and found the holding cells. The place smelled like raw sewage. The corridor was lined with a dozen cells. Each cell was separated by a cinder block wall and had bars in the front.

Carver held up a hand. "Wait here." He walked up a short flight of stairs to another metal door. It was unlocked. He looked inside and found the control room. He hit the green buttons for all the cells.

The doors buzzed and clicked open. He went back downstairs and walked into the corridor. People staggered out of the cells. They were stark naked. Some were covered in stains that looked like feces or blood. Maybe both.

"Come on out." He walked inside past them. "Get out there and wait. Don't go anywhere else until I tell you."

"Who the hell are you?" One man tried to run, but he stumbled, apparently weak from malnutrition.

"I'm here to help you escape. But I can't do that if you run. Just wait outside."

"Carver?" Monty stepped out of the last cell. He looked relatively clean. And he was wearing clothing.

That was interesting. Carver walked down the cells. Ensured everyone was out. "Alice tells me you were taken somewhere. Twice."

"Yes. Lynch wanted to make a deal with me."

"Everyone into the hallway." Carver motioned everyone out of the corridor. "Alice, give me a headcount."

"Okay!" She herded everyone through the door.

Carver stepped out after Monty. Turned to Alice.

"Everyone is accounted for except for Brad and Jeremy."

"I was in the cell with Jeremy." A short black man raised one hand while covering his privates with the other. "They said it was his turn to pay for his crimes."

"Any idea where they took them?" Carver said.

The man who'd tried to run spoke in a weak voice. "There's a tunnel. I heard them talking about it. I don't know where it is though."

"Anyone else know?" Carver looked at the group.

"I heard them talking about tunnels once too," an Asian woman said. She was presumably Mai Ling if Carver had to guess.

"I've been here for four days." A young man, his hands over his privates stepped forward. He was bloody and bruised. "I need to get the hell out of here and let my family know I'm okay. Please, can you get us out of here now?"

"If you try to leave now, they'll see you going. They'll send more people after you and you'll never be safe." Carver patted his rifle. "However, if you can be patient and let me do my job, I'll ensure none of these people survive to hunt you again."

The man's eyes widened. "You can't be with the government. Those people are all crooked. I got arrested by the FBI and the next thing I knew I woke up here."

"Same," another man said. "But it was the ATF that broke down my door and raided my house. They told me my channel about guns was breaking the law."

Others spoke up with similar stories. Some had been taken by police from their cities. Some by federal agents. They were from all over the western states.

A young Asian man staggered forward. "I left Los Angeles because of the crime there. I ran a popular channel about all the problems in the state. I don't even think the people who nabbed me off the street were cops. Just two thugs."

The former prisoners started talking to each other. Sharing stories about their abductions.

Monty tugged on Carver's sleeve. "Chief Lynch was going to tell me who killed Joe. He said one of their people did it even though they weren't supposed to."

That got Carver's attention. "That's the deal you made?"

"Yeah. He was going to tell me and I was going to tell you. I was just waiting on him to come back."

"They were just going to give you this information and let you go?"

Monty nodded. "Well, I had to promise to go back on the take. I figured it was worth the price if I could help you."

"But they didn't tell you?"

He shook his head. "No, but I got the impression it was one of those Arabic men. He kept looking at the two-way mirror in the room. Like he was making sure it was okay to give up the guy."

Carver nodded grimly. He had more reason than ever to go after Yusef, Hassan, and their boys. He held up a hand. "Quiet, everyone."

The hallway fell silent. All eyes turned toward him.

"Melinda and Alice are in charge. They'll take you to the showers. You can clean up and wrap towels around yourselves. There might be spare clothing around here somewhere."

"But, I want to go!" One of the men said.

"Jorge, trust Carver," Monty said. "Do what he says. He's a former Navy SEAL and he knows what he's doing."

"A SEAL?" The Asian man nodded approvingly. "I'd say we're in good hands."

"Yes, good hands!" Mai Ling turned to Melinda. "Where the showers? I stink."

Melinda looked at Carver. Nodded. "We'll follow your lead."

"I need you to move the bodies out of the hallway and into one of the side rooms. There's a body in front of a room where I already stored a body. Put them in there."

The Asian man whistled. "You killed all the crooked cops?"

Carver didn't answer. "There are weapons on the bodies. Take them and barricade yourselves in the showers. I need you to remain in place so you're not accidentally seen. I don't want these people to get a warning that I'm coming."

"So, you're a vigilante," another guy said.

"I'm just a guy doing what needs to be done." Carver shrugged. "And it's best if you forget about me once this is over. Tell anyone who asks that I was masked and that I'm under six feet tall."

"Dude, we'll do whatever you ask." The Asian man gave him a thumbs up. "And I just knew people would take the law into their own hands when the government stopped prosecuting people."

Carver had a feeling this incident was going to be detailed in a video or news report. He just had to make sure he was as anonymous as possible. That was the problem with helping people. They'd remember everything about you.

The group made its way into the hallway. The men dragged Nigel's body out of the hallway and pulled it into the room where Mike's body already was. They took the weapons from the dead men and went into the shower room.

Monty stayed with him. "What now?"

"I'm going to find the tunnel. Maybe it leads to the warehouse."

"And then what?"

"Then, I send a few souls to the afterlife." He pointed to the showers. "You need to stay here."

"But I can help!"

Carver thought it over. "You can come with me to the tunnel. Watch my back from there. But if I tell you to stay somewhere, you stay. And keep quiet."

Monty nodded. "Anything you say, boss."

Carver looked at the map app. The cells and shower were in the middle of the building. If there was a tunnel, it would make the most sense to have it on the north side right across the road from the warehouse.

He walked to the northern side, Monty close behind him. The former administrative offices were there. Most of them still had names stenciled on the doors. The place smelled dry and musty. There was another odor too. An earthy scent.

The odor emanated from behind a door next to an office. Behind the door was a narrow storage closet. The floor was gone. In its place was a dirt slope descending into darkness. Carver turned on his tactical flashlight and walked down the slope.

Monty blew out a breath. Carver gave him a warning look and Monty stifled whatever he was about to say.

It took them a moment to reach the bottom, probably twenty to thirty feet underground. It was far below the building's foundation and the parking lot above. Far below the street as well. The tunnel was about seven feet tall and ten feet wide.

Just enough room for two people to walk side-by-side. Heavy wooden timbers buttressed the tunnel every few feet, narrowing the tunnel by about a foot on each side. It looked sturdy enough to avoid a cave-in unless an earthquake struck.

The tunnel passed right under the highway. If it was any closer to the surface, the road probably would have caved in. It certainly provided a covert way to move prisoners across the road without being seen.

Carver thought back to the second truck that had arrived at the warehouse. About the conversation he'd overheard. No one had specifically mentioned the cargo, but it had been different than the migrants.

Yusef had been upset that the truck was delivering to the wrong place. The driver had been complaining about running out of supplies. Probably food and water for the prisoners. A supply chain issue.

Speaking of which, Carver could see exactly how things worked. People were marked for abduction. A kidnapping team took a vehicle like that Mercedes Sprinter van and abducted the marks.

They were taken to a safehouse. Possibly kept prisoner there while more abductees were delivered. Once there were enough, they were packed onto a delivery truck and brought to the former police station.

Monty and the others had been brought straight to the police station since they'd been abducted nearby. People from further away were grouped in remote safehouses before being brought in.

There might be waystations where they were delivered until a larger truck came by and collected them. The logistics were carefully plotted out. It was an elegant system. Not unlike the ones Carver had seen in other countries.

Political dissidents were noisy problems that politicians hated. It wasn't possible to kill them in most countries, at least not without causing a major incident. And some dissidents were too popular to be killed without martyring them.

Then there were the everyday citizens. The news reporters, the citizen journalists, the people running social media channels who talked politics and caused headaches for politicians. They were much easier to get rid of without causing backlash.

El Fuerte was a clearinghouse for dissidents. But they weren't simply being killed. There seemed to be another element in this enterprise. And Carver had a pretty good idea what was happening.

The CAR816 was slung over his back. He rotated it around to the front. Checked the magazine. Twenty-five bullets left. That should do if everything went according to plan. He had plenty of backup bullets if it devolved into a shooting match.

He pulled out his Glock. Attached the suppressor. Gave it to Monty. "Don't shoot unless I tell you to."

Monty nodded.

Carver turned his flashlight on low. Just enough light to make his way through the tunnel without walking into a beam.

It was a long walk. Maybe a hundred yards from one end of the tunnel to the other. He slowed as a dim light appeared from ahead. He holstered his flashlight and put the rifle against his shoulder. Looked through the sight.

Voices echoed from ahead. They were subdued. Almost whispers. People talking so they wouldn't be overheard.

The ground sloped upward. A cold white light shone down from above. He crept up toward the exit. Stopped and listened. Someone was crying. A man. Someone else was telling him to shut up in harsh whispers.

He held up a fist. Looked back to make sure Monty understood that meant for him to stop. Monty stopped and knelt, Glock at the ready.

Carver crouched. Poked his head above ground. There was a room with black cinderblock walls. LED lights overhead. A tall iron cage on the right side of the room. A metal door on the other side.

There were two men in the cage. One was curled up in the back corner sobbing. The other man was young and heavyset. He had a long, thick beard. They were clothed in orange jumpsuits.

No one else was in the room. Carver motioned Monty to join him. Monty hurried up the slope and waited behind Carver.

Carver emerged from the hole. Put a finger to his lips. The bearded man flinched. His eyes widened. He looked confused.

Facing the metal door across the room, Carver backed up to the cell. "What's the situation?"

The bearded man answered. "They brought us here maybe half an hour ago. We were supposed to be taken out but there was a delay."

"Taken to where?"

"Whatever is on the other side of that door."

"How many men?"

"Two men escorted us through the tunnel."

"Who are you?" the bearded man asked.

Monty emerged from the hole. "You're Jeremy, right?"

The bearded man nodded. "Yeah. How did you get out?"

"Carver got us out. We're here for you now."

The other man, presumably Brad, stopped crying. He crawled over to the others. "We're saved? We're saved?" He said it loud enough to wake the dead.

"Quiet you damned idiot!" Jeremy hissed.

Someone on the other side of the door shouted. There was a loud click, and the door began to open.

CHAPTER 43

Carver was already halfway to the hole.

He shoved Monty ahead of him. The pair tumbled down the dirt ramp and into darkness just as the door opened and several people talking all at once entered. They were speaking English, though it was hard to make out what they were saying due to heavy accents.

"I paid good money and I want to see him!" a man was saying.

"There he is," a familiar voice said. It was Yusef. "They are yours. Do what you want."

"Who's the other man?"

"A bonus," Yusef said. "Two for the price of one."

"I'll take it!" The man spoke in a northeastern accent.

Yusef replied calmly. "As I said, Senator, you can do what you want with them."

Jeremy spoke. "Well, Senator Johnson, I knew you were corrupt. Didn't realize you were an absolute criminal too."

"Hello, Jeremy." Senator Johnson sounded terribly pleased. "I used some campaign slush funds to set this up. At first I thought I'd just have you vanished, but then I found out about this and decided it would be so much more fun to kill you myself."

"That man is a senator?" Brad said.

"A state senator from Massachusetts. Crooked bastard." Jeremy laughed without humor. "He tried to get my channel taken offline, but I was out of reach in Indiana."

"You should have just minded your own business, Jeremy." Johnson tutted. "Anyway, you're mine now."

"And this other guy you don't even know?" Jeremy said.

"I can't say no to two for the price of one," the senator said in a lighthearted voice.

"You're a real piece of work, asshole."

Yusef spoke. "Are you ready to begin?"

"Absolutely," the senator said. "But I'm enjoying the look on his face right now. Let me relish this moment."

"As you wish," Yusef said.

Carver had his back to one of the support timbers. He had a narrow view of the area above. Three figures walked past the tunnel exit. They were approaching the cage.

"Have you ever killed anyone before, Senator?" Jeremy asked. "Do you have the balls for it?"

"How do you think I became the most powerful senator in the state, boy?" Johnson laughed. "Where do you think Annabeth Riley vanished to?"

"You're filth. You'd better hope I don't get to you before you can kill me."

"Won't be a problem, boy." Johnson kept gloating. It sounded like he was enjoying it immensely.

He was close to the cage from the sound of it. Carver considered the options. He didn't know the number of men. There might just be the three of them. There might be a fourth near the door. He could take down the three if they were all together, but if they were in front of the cage, the bullets might pass clean through them and into the prisoners.

Carver pulled a slender rod from his thigh pocket. He held up a fist so Monty would stay in place, then crept up to the hole. He extended the mirror at the end of the rod just over the top. Rotated it toward the door. The man who'd driven the van used to kidnap Monty and the others stood there.

He was holding a CAR816 down at an angle. It would take him a second to bring the gun up to aim and fire. He wouldn't have a chance if Carver popped up and shot him.

Carver rotated the mirror the other way. He saw Yusef, a middle-aged Caucasian, and the passenger from the van standing directly in front of the cage. Senator Johnson was leering at Jeremy. Telling him how painful his death would be.

A radio crackled. Yusef answered and spoke in Arabic. An urgent voice replied. Shouting could be heard in the background.

"What is it?" Johnson said.

"Our other clients arrived and don't want to wait. I'm very sorry, but I need to talk to them. You can start now, or you can wait until they're finished."

"I'll start now," Johnson said.

"Do you want this to be sporting or like fish in a barrel?"

Johnson was silent while he decided. "I want to hunt him, but I don't want him to have a chance to fight back."

Jeremy laughed. "Coward!"

"We will leave his hands bound, but his feet free. The maze has already been set up. We will give him a short head start and then you can go after him."

"Sounds great," Johnson said. "Let's get this show on the road."

"Very well," Yusef replied. "I will leave you here and go talk to the other clients. Abbad here and his partner, Nasir, will take you and your prey to the starting position."

Jeremy laughed again. "I'm going to strangle you with my feet, senator."

"Gag him," Yusef said.

There was a muffled roar as Abbad presumably stuffed a gag into Jeremy's mouth. Brad started crying again. Yusef turned and walked toward the door. Carver ducked back down the slope and crouched in darkness.

"Nasir, come help," Abbad said.

A moment later, the man by the door walked past. Carver climbed to the top. The men were facing away from him. One was unlocking the door. Carver aimed. The CAR816 coughed and Abbad's brains exploded from the other side of his head.

Nasir was working the key in the lock. He flinched when he saw the spatter. He flinched again when a bullet burst from the front of his skull.

Johnson was staring at his phone. He blinked in confusion and looked up when Carver dashed out of the hole and walked toward him, rifle aimed at his head.

"What the hell?"

"Down on the floor," Carver said.

Johnson dropped his phone then collapsed to his stomach a second later.

Jeremy said something, but the gag muffled it.

Monty ran out of the hole and stood next to him. "Holy shit, Carver." He was shaking. "I didn't know what you were waiting for."

"The perfect moment." Carver unlocked the cage. He cut the plasticuffs off Brad's and Jeremy's wrists.

Jeremy pulled the gag from his mouth. He kicked the senator hard in the ribs. "Piece of shit!"

Johnson curled up and groaned.

Carver took his Glock from Monty. Handed it to Jeremy. Finish him off now if you want. We don't have time to gloat.

Jeremy kicked the senator in the head. "I want to kill you, but I don't want even your blood on my hands."

Monty held out his hand. "May I?"

Jeremy handed him the gun. Monty popped a bullet into Johnson's head without pause. The senator's body convulsed and went still.

"Damn, that was fast." Jeremy shook his head. "Aren't you a cop?"

"Turns out I'm not a good cop." Monty shrugged and turned to Carver. "What now?"

"The men in the police station are down. The prisoners are in the shower. You two take Brad over there. Make sure to announce yourselves, because they're armed."

"What are you going to do?" Monty asked.

"One of these men murdered Joe. I'm going to clean house."

"I can help," Monty said.

Carver shook his head. "Not unless you want to be the bait."

"I am mostly useless." Monty looked down. "But I don't want you to go in alone."

"I work better that way."

"There's a keycard to the door," Jeremy said. He frisked the dead men. Pulled a card from Abbad's pocket. "I don't know what's on the other side of that door, but it can't be good."

"There's only one way to find out." Carver took the keycard. He went to the door and slid it along the door jamb. This card would probably unlock the other metal door. The one in the room with the TV.

He opened the door. There was a long concrete tunnel on the other side. It was the same tunnel Joe had been in. The sounds he'd heard hadn't been animals. It had been people waiting for their executions.

The hallway was dimly lit. Just enough to see the outlines. Carver hurried down it. Yusef wasn't far ahead. Maybe he could catch him. He reached the end of the tunnel without ever seeing the other man. Apparently, Yusef had been hurrying to get to the other clients.

Beyond the tunnel exit was a series of metal walls. They were the same frames that Joe had seen piled on the ground. Now they'd been erected into a maze. The floor was covered in about a foot of sand.

The sand had been raked, smoothing it out evenly. It was coarse and gravelly. The exact same kind of sandy soil that was present all over the land outside. There were indentations in the sand. Probably Yusef's footprints.

The area was lit by rings of LED lights overhead. Carver looked up and around and realized exactly what this part of the warehouse had been converted into. It was an arena. It could be arranged into multiple configurations, depending on the tastes of the clients.

Johnson had wanted to hunt Jeremey in the maze. Corner him and kill him, probably with a firearm. The Ukrainians had done the same but with bows and arrows. Probably even knives, judging from the amount of blood on them.

The sand soaked up the blood. The bodies were taken to the old police station, transferred to the old funeral home, and cremated. The ashes and ground up bones were dumped into an open grave.

The dead cops had been in a hurry to rape the women. They'd said they were going to be transferred soon. They were probably scheduled for the clients Yusef was going to talk to.

There were no other doors in the vicinity. Which meant Yusef was navigating the maze to get to the metal door on the other side. The footprints went into the maze, supporting that theory.

Carver hurried into the maze opening. Turned left. It branched in two directions. The footprints went left. Carver followed them. He picked up the pace. Paused at the next branch. Followed the footprints.

The maze walls were set close together, giving the corridors a claustrophobic feel. It was designed to make the prey feel even more trapped than they already were. If they took a wrong turn and got cornered, there was nowhere to go. No way around the hunter.

An angry voice emanated from ahead. Carver peered around the wall. Saw the path forked in three directions. Yusef stomped around one corner. He looked frustrated. Probably because he'd taken the wrong path.

Carver wondered if it would be worth questioning him. He quickly decided it was too risky. At least for any extended questioning. He waited for the other man to get close to the fork in the path. Not too close, but just close enough.

He popped around the corner, rifle aimed. "Halt."

Yusef's mouth dropped open. He froze like a deer in the headlights.

"Hands up," Carver said.

Yusef threw his hands up. "You're Carver."

"Who killed Joe?"

Yusef's eye twitched. "It was an accident."

"I know that's a lie. I want to know who did it and how."

"It was not us."

"Someone else said different."

"It's a lie. We did nothing."

The man was lying. He was going to keep lying. And his hand was inching toward the radio at his waist. Carver pulled the trigger. Ventilated Yusef's skull. Yusef collapsed. His blood soaked into the sand.

Carver studied the fork in the path. Yusef had helped him narrow it down to two directions. He looked up at the ceiling. Saw the partition wall that separated the arena from the residential side. Going right would take him closer.

He chose the right path. It spiraled into a dead end. He backtracked and took the last path. It forked two more times before leading him to the metal door. Carver used the keycard. The magnetic latch released.

He opened the door quietly. The TV room was on the other side. No one was there. Hassan was probably with the clients. If the number of Emiratis was still the same, it meant he was only one of two left, plus the clients.

Carver looked into the hallway. He heard voices from behind the double doors. He hurried down the carpeted hallway. Cleared the game room on the left. Cleared the kitchen across the hall.

The other doors were shut. He opened them one at a time. Cleared them. He suspected the other clients were getting dressed and ready for their hunt. They were probably in the locker room with Hassan and the other Emiratis.

Carver went to the double doors. He used the keycard to unlock them. He eased one open. Looked into the hallway on the other side. It was empty but there was activity in the room to the left. The locker room.

Hassan was talking. "We are pleased you came back so soon. I am sorry for the delay."

A man replied in a Ukrainian accent. "We were bored. And we have plenty of American money thanks to the billions your government is sending us."

"They aren't our government," Hassan said with a laugh. "But they are making us all rich, yes?"

"Yes!" The Ukrainian roared.

There was a roar of cheers as he and his men started singing what sounded like The American national anthem, but in their native language.

Carver switched from single shot to burst mode. Then he changed his mind and set it to fully automatic. He looked around the corner. The Ukrainians were drinking vodka from their own bottles. Hassan and one other Emirati were watching them, their backs to the doorway.

With Nasir, Abbad, and Yusef down, Hassan and this other guy were the last two Emiratis standing.

Everyone was conveniently gathered in one place. Carver stepped around the corner. He aimed about chest high. Pulled the trigger, released. Pulled the trigger, released. Bullets caught Hassan and his friend in the backs. They threw up their hands and went down face first on the hard tiled floor.

The lead Ukrainian dropped his bottle. It smashed, sending glass and liquid everywhere. He and the others were all in towels, like they'd freshly showered. There were no weapons in sight. They were unarmed and helpless.

"Who are you?" the lead man said. "What do you want? You want money? We have more than you can imagine."

"Oh, I'm just here for the thrill," Carver said. "I know this isn't very sporting, but it's actually fair when you think about it." He opened fire. Bullets ripped through flesh. Men screamed. Blood sprayed.

Within seconds, they were corpses bleeding out on the tiles. The blood slowly circled toward a drain, meaning cleanup would be slightly less messy.

The suppressor was smoking hot. The bullets had smashed into the tiled walls, and the screams of the men would have alerted anyone living in this place. But it seemed Carver was the only one left standing.

He looked at the dead men's faces. The lead Ukrainian guy was familiar. Real familiar. Carver remembered him from a news story maybe a month ago. He was on television begging the US government for more money.

It seemed clear that money wasn't all being used for military purposes. That would be absolutely no surprise to most people. Any kind of foreign aid inevitably made someone on the other end rich. Only a small percentage made it to the people it was supposed to help.

Carver checked for pulses. Made sure everyone was dead. Then he started clearing the rest of the residential area. The room at the end of the hallway got his attention. It was a large apartment with its own shower. Probably Yusef's room.

There was a desk with a laptop. The laptop was on and a calendar was open on it. The calendar had names and dates. He zoomed out to view entire years and saw that the calendar had started about three years prior.

It had been mostly empty for the first few months. After that, every day was filled with names. There were names in red, and names in green. He figured out that the green names were the prisoners. The red names were the hunters.

He skipped forward to the current year. Looked through the last few weeks. The calendar events had names and details about the events. There were links in the notes. He clicked a link. A video opened in another screen.

The video showed two women running through a maze. A group of men were after them. Carver skipped ahead. He saw the end results and closed the video. He'd seen plenty like that and worse, but it still made him sick to his stomach.

That was what the Ukrainians had been ready to do to Alice and Melinda.

Carver opened a web browser and logged into an encrypted cloud service. He began uploading the calendar to it. The videos were stored on a large external hard drive. He started uploading them too.

The internet connection was fast, but it would still take some time. That was okay. He had plenty of time now.

There was a second calendar. This one was color coded blue. It detailed all the migrant arrivals and their destinations. Links to another website tracked them to ensure they were going where they'd agreed to go.

If migrants didn't do as agreed, a local enforcer was sent to track them down. To scare them into adhering to the agreement. If they didn't, they'd be terminated.

Carver didn't see any indication that this organization was tied to Enigma. There was an organization mentioned several times in other documents he found—the Immigration Rights Coalition.

He skimmed through everything. It was a treasure trove of incriminating evidence. He counted over twenty US politicians who'd paid to play in the arena. Many were local politicians, but some were federal.

Carver sent Leon a text. *Check the encrypted cloud.* Carver was done. He'd killed the people who killed Joe. Hunting down the others involved in this scheme wasn't something he cared about.

Leon enjoyed playing vigilante. He could pursue this if interested. Carver's part was done.

While the data was uploading, Carver went back through the maze and took the tunnel to the former police station. He went to the shower room.

"It's Carver. I'm back."

Monty poked his head around the corner. Sighed in relief. "It's him!" He came into the hallway. "I was starting to get worried. You've been gone for over an hour."

"I had a few things to do."

Carver went into the shower room. Brad, Jeremy, and the others were inside. Jeremy tucked a gun into his waistband and approached. "What happened?"

"I don't know. There are a lot of dead bodies over there. Guess someone had an accident with a gun."

Jeremy laughed. "Man, I hate it when that happens."

Melinda strode over. "Maybe it was a gang war. Who knows?"

"Yeah, who knows?" Monty said. "So, it's safe to go there?"

Carver nodded. "There's a laptop with everything you need to know. Videos too. But I wouldn't watch them unless you have a strong stomach."

Melinda shuddered. "My God. They recorded everything?"

"Yeah." Carver removed the suppressor from the CAR816 and checked the barrel to see if the heat had warped it.

"We had a visitor while you were gone," Monty said. He motioned Carver to follow him to the room where they'd stashed the dead cops. He turned on the lights. There was a new body on the floor. Chief Lynch.

Carver turned to Monty. "What happened?"

"He came back to tell me the name, I guess." Monty shook his head. "He slipped in the lube in the hallway. I came out and put a gun to his head."

"Did he tell you the name?"

Monty looked chagrined. "Yeah. He said it was some cartel hitman named Domingo."

Carver worked his jaw back and forth. "Where is this Domingo person?"

"I don't know. Somewhere around town. I'm sure he would have given me more information under other circumstances, but he said he'd only tell me if I let him go." Monty sighed. "I just couldn't let that happen. He would have returned with an army of cops."

"Agreed." Carver didn't regret taking out the trash, but it looked like he wasn't done here after all.

"So, what now?" Monty said.

Carver went back into the hallway with the others. He was going to have to hunt down Domingo if he wanted to finish this. For now, he'd point these people towards the evidence. Let them do what they wanted with it.

Carver turned to the others. "One of the cops told me they were disposing of bodies in an old funeral home. That there was an open grave. I suspect you'll find a lot of evidence there, but I don't know who you could give it to."

"We need to expose this operation," Jeremy said. "The world needs to know about it."

"Be my guest," Carver said. "Just leave me out of it, okay? I was never here."

Melinda put a hand on his arm. "You were never here."

Jeremy pursed his lips. Nodded. "Yeah, they'd throw you in jail for doing the right thing."

The others in the room agreed one by one. Someone would probably talk eventually. Someone who wanted fame or money. That was just the way things were. But that was about the best Carver could hope for.

He went back through the tunnel and the maze to Yusef's room. Monty and Jeremy followed him. The upload to the cloud was complete. Jeremy sat down and skimmed over the calendar. His eyes filled with tears.

"I just knew it."

"What?" Monty said.

"They got Foo-Foo and Bradimus Rex."

Monty frowned. "Who?"

"Streamer friends of mine. Foo-Foo was a twenty-three year old woman. She started in video games and got political last year. Started covering sexual harassment." He pointed to an open calendar item from four months ago. "She vanished around this time. And it looks like one of the politicians she was calling out for sexual harassment paid to have her taken." His face paled. He stood and ran to the corner. Vomited.

"My God." Monty's eyes welled up. "We've got to expose this to the world."

Jeremy turned around. Tears poured down his cheeks. "We're going to nail these bastards to the wall!"

Carver left them to it. His only concern was justice for Joe. According to Chief Lynch, the killer was a cartel hitman named Domingo. He pulled Monty aside. "Tell me more about this deal Lynch offered you."

"He said he'd give me the killer's name as long as I promised to go back to being a crooked cop on the take." Monty shrugged. "It was pretty cut and dry, although I have to admit I was really surprised at the offer."

Carver understood the offer. "It was a setup."

"I considered that, too, but a part of me believed him."

"They knew you'd tell me the moment you were free." Carver envisioned their plan clear as day. "They wanted to lure me away from the warehouse. They wanted to focus me on a single target. Domingo was bait."

"You think they'd wait for you to make a move on Domingo and spring a trap?"

Carver nodded. "Either that or give up Domingo as a sacrifice in the hope that I'd be satisfied with killing Joe's supposed killer and leave town. Then they could keep operating like usual."

Monty gave him a look. "You shut them down, but the mayor is still in power. Don't you think Joe would want you to get her out of power too?"

"No." Carver brushed off his hands. "I'm done with this town. What happens next is up to you."

"Just like that?" Monty said.

Carver nodded. "Just like that."

Monty sighed. Held out his hand. "Well, Carver, thanks."

Carver shook his hand. "Good luck."

It was time to leave.

CHAPTER 44

Carver left the warehouse by the rollup door.

He walked across the parking lot and left by the front gate. The police were gone from Albert's place. Apparently, they'd decided against acting overtly while they were being livestreamed. But that didn't mean it was over.

The entire reason the police had been trying to stop the rally was because of the warehouse. Maybe once Jeremy, Monty and the others exposed what had been happening in that place, the local police would be too busy defending themselves from prosecution to worry about Albert anymore.

They also didn't know that their chief was dead along with five other crooked cops. It sounded like they were all on the cartel payroll, so they might simply scatter like roaches once they saw the writing on the wall.

Carver didn't go to Albert's. He walked across the road. Hooked right around the old police station. Found the pickup truck sitting where he'd left it. He was tired. It was late. Time to get some shuteye.

He circled north to avoid cameras and headed to the ranch. He kept thinking about the horrors in the warehouse. It wasn't the first time he'd seen an operation like that. But it was certainly one of the most extensive.

Authoritarians often locked up their opposition. Let them rot in jail or made sure they died there. When they wanted to kill the opposition, they just did it. They didn't turn it into blood sport. This operation had gone above and beyond that.

Carver wasn't sure sleeping at the ranch was safe. If the mayor got wind of what had happened at the warehouse, she might send some people to pay him a visit. And that also made him wonder if Andrea would ever be safe there.

They'd have to beef up security. Add more cameras. That tickled something in his memory. Something recent. Something Big George had said about cameras. Carver hadn't given it much thought at the time, but thinking about security brought it back.

Big George had said he was getting the same cameras Joe had recommended. Cameras with local storage and power.

Carver gunned the engine. Got the truck up to a hundred miles per hour. He slowed down once he hit the gravel road leading to the ranch. Moments later, he skidded onto the driveway. Threw the pickup in park. Jumped out and ran into the stable.

He looked around and found the cameras hidden in the rafters. He climbed on top of a stall. The horse inside watched him with big brown eyes. It whickered like asking him a question.

Carver got his hands on a camera. There was a slot in the back of it. Something protruded slightly from the plastic housing. He pushed it in. It clicked and popped out. It was a memory stick. He checked the other camera. Pulled the memory stick out of it.

Then he ran into the house. He went straight to Joe's office. Plugged the memory stick into the laptop. There were two videos on it. He played the first one.

Joe was standing inside the stall with Sunshine. The horse was jittery. He was trying to calm it down. Then he got that look Carver had seen plenty of times before. Joe was suspicious. Looking around.

Joe went to the stable door. Picked up his rifle. He slid the large stable door open and stepped outside. He vanished around the corner. A moment later, a figure dressed in black hurried inside, carrying something close by his side. He wore a ski mask to conceal his identity.

His body concealed whatever it was. The man walked beneath the camera and out of sight. Carver knew there was an empty horse stall there. The man had hidden inside of it.

There was no activity for a minute and the video ended.

Carver played the second video. Joe had just reentered the stable. He set his rifle down. He went into the horse stall and started talking to the horse.

"Calm down, boy. Nothing's out there." He patted the horse's neck. "We're going for a ride, okay? It's going to be fun."

Sunshine whickered. Bobbed his head.

"Yeah, I knew you'd like that." Joe led the horse out of the stall and into the open area. Sunshine's nostrils flared. He twisted away from Joe, then back around. Joe was off balance. Distracted. Trying to calm the horse.

The figure appeared from the stall. He lifted what looked like a mini-sledge hammer with something u-shaped attached to the front of it. A horseshoe.

The man swung the hammer at the back of Joe's head. Joe seemed to sense it at the last moment. He spun around. The horseshoe hammer struck him in the forehead. He went down hard.

The man knelt. Put fingers to Joe's neck. He motioned toward the door. Another person ran inside, also dressed in black. Also wearing a ski mask.

The second person spoke. "He's alive?"

The other figure nodded.

"Good." The person yanked off the ski mask. They slapped Joe with a gloved hand. "Look at me, Joe. I want to be the last thing you see, okay?"

Joe groaned. He was barely conscious, but he was alive. His eyes fluttered open. He looked up into the other person's face. His lips peeled back in a snarl.

"Oh, you see me, don't you?" The second person took the hammer from the other person. Raised it. "You refused the wrong person, Joe."

"See you in hell," Joe said in a low groan. He tried to move, but it was obvious that the first blow had done some damage.

The other person laughed. Raised the hammer. Slammed it down on his face. They raised it to strike again, but the first person stopped them. Shook their head.

The second person snarled at them. "Let me go!"

"If you hit him again, there's no way it'll look like an accident."

The second person reluctantly let go of the hammer and released it to their companion. "Make sure Hernandez handles this. We have an understanding."

The other person removed their ski mask. It was a man with a short buzz cut. He took the hammer. Nodded. "Affirmative. Let's go. The cameras will be back online in one minute."

They hurried out. Sunshine lowered his head. Sniffed Joe. Whickered gently. He licked Joe's face. Like trying to get a response. But Joe was dead.

And Carver knew who had killed him.

His fists clenched. The men in the warehouse had nothing to do with it. Domingo had nothing to do with it. This had been personal. But Joe had been too public a figure to dispose of with the warehouse. So, a plausible accident had been arranged.

The perpetrators welded a horseshoe to a small sledgehammer. Then they waited for him to be distracted by the horse and killed him. The man who'd swung the initial blow looked like former military. Not just that, but former special forces.

Carver didn't know him. But he resembled the description the watcher had given him. He was the watcher called Two. The one who'd followed him to the warehouse last night.

The person who'd gloated and delivered the second blow was someone Carver knew all too well. The person he'd initially thought might be behind Joe's death.

Mayor Jessica Herrada.

Justice was going to be served tonight. It might be risky rushing in, but it was now or never. Once Jeremy and the others brought the warehouse into the light, the mayor would be on high alert. She might not even stick around town.

He ran outside. Went into the garage and grabbed two ladders. Tossed them into the back of the pickup. He was going to need them where he was going.

Carver hopped into the truck. Yanked it into reverse and onto the gravel. He spun the front end around and gunned it back toward town. He cut west across the northside of town when he reached it.

The map showed him the route to the wealthy neighborhood. He wasn't interested in that. He was going to the nature preserve bordering the back wall. The mansion with Jessica's apartment was fifty yards east of there.

Carver cut down a small road that took him into the preserve. It was an extension of the national forest to the north, but there wasn't much forest to it. It was mostly scrub brush and rocks with a dam further west.

He parked in the lot near the trail head. He was still in the same black fatigues. Had blood spattered on his hands and face. That was okay. He was going to get more blood on him before this was over.

Carver pulled the two ladders from the pickup bed and started the short hike to his destination. He reached the border wall around the rich subdivision five minutes later.

The stone wall was high. Maybe twenty feet. It probably cost a large fortune to build. He took one of the ladders from the truck. Leaned it against the wall. Extended it until it reached the top of the wall.

He hefted the second ladder in one hand. Climbed the first ladder. Put the second one on the other side and released the extension locks. It extended to the ground. He lowered the top half to lock the extension latches in place.

The top was about a foot wide. Just enough for him to lay on. He remained there for a moment, looking through his monocular for cameras. There were none that he could see. Covering the entire perimeter was probably just too much to ask for.

It was dark but he could see the silhouette of the fence around the target mansion. It was made of iron bars with sharp prongs on the top. It would be tougher to breach but not impossible. He wasn't going to use the ladders for it. He needed them in place for a quick exfil in case things went wrong.

There was a back gate on the fence, but it was solid iron. A metal plate protected the latch from a slim jim. It might also be connected to an alarm. It was safer to go up and over.

He hurried through the darkness, using the monocular to pick his way through the cactuses and boulders. There was no grass on the other side of the fence. Just more spiny succulents. Militarized landscaping at its finest.

Carver considered using the grappling hook, but it would be easier to climb the iron fence. He gripped the bars and tugged on them. The fence didn't wobble in the slightest. It was solid. Solid enough to hold his weight, at least.

The fence was only ten feet tall, but the sharp prongs on top would be the problem. A problem for most people, anyway. They were no problem for someone with experience.

Carver muscled himself up by gripping the bars. He slung the backpack onto the prongs. He pulled himself up onto the backpack. The tough material protected him from being skewered.

Facing the ground on the other side, he gripped the bars. Swung his feet up and over his head, controlling the flip with his arms. Once he was upright, he dropped to the ground and grabbed the backpack by the strap.

He pulled the CAR816 from the backpack. Pulled the suppressor from inside the rail. Attached it to the end of the barrel. Stealth was key here.

Carver scanned the back of the mansion. There was light coming through the windows on the lower level in the middle of the house. That was where the grand staircase was. Where any guards would be.

There was light seeping through the curtains on the second floor in the south wing. Jessica's apartment was on the first floor of the south wing. There was no light coming from inside that section. Probably because it wasn't in use. Probably because Jessica actually lived in the mansion and not that apartment.

Everything had been a lie. Carver wasn't surprised. He'd suspected it, but it hadn't seemed important at the time. Now it was a little more important. Mainly because he'd changed his mind about what he wanted to do.

He closed his eyes and remembered the layout. He counted the number of guards inside. Just two. A third was at the front gate. There was another at the entrance to the subdivision, but he wouldn't have to deal with him.

It was also possible that Two would be inside. In fact, it was highly likely. Two wouldn't be with the other guards. If anything, he'd be close to Jessica. Maybe in the same bed.

Carver noted the camera locations on the house. There were also floodlights with motion sensors. Once he stepped within range of them, they'd light up the back yard. That would be sure to trigger a response.

There was a single camera over the back entrance. There were three floodlights. He circled wide along the fence. The floodlight on the corner was pointing into the back yard. The sensor wouldn't see him coming from a diagonal approach.

There were two more lights on the south side. They weren't angled toward the corner. He kept low and walked toward the corner of the house, keeping to the side of the motion sensor. He reached the house and pressed himself against the wall.

The sensor was pointing outward. It wouldn't detect him this close to the house. He slid along the wall beneath the other floodlights. There was a lovely Juliet balcony on the second floor. Perfect for his needs.

He pulled out the grappling hook. Tossed it upward. It caught on the railing with a slight clink. He tugged on it to make sure it was firm. There was no wall to brace against since the balcony hung out about four feet off the house.

Carver pulled himself up hand-over-hand to the railing. He pulled himself over the top and took a moment to make sure he hadn't triggered any alarms. Because he most likely would trigger an alarm with his next move.

There were French doors leading inside. They were nice iron doors. He used his slim jim to work into the latch. Unfortunately, there was a deadbolt. This wasn't going to work. At least not without making some noise.

There were windows on either side of the doors. They were vinyl windows, painted to match the black iron. He worked the slim jim into the south window. Used friction to work the lock loose. It took some time, but it was quieter than kicking open the French doors.

Within fifteen minutes, he was inside, standing in a hallway. Going north would take him to the grand staircase he'd seen when he'd entered through the front door. There was light coming from beneath a door at the south end of the hallway.

Carver crept down the hall. The fancy rug masked his footsteps. He reached for the door. Tested the handle. It was unlocked. He cracked open the door and saw what he'd hoped to see. Jessica was in bed.

She was propped up on pillows, asleep with an open book on her lap. The room was huge. Probably as big as the apartment on the bottom floor. The ceiling was vaulted. Stained wooden beams ran up from the sides and corners into a beam along the peak of the ceiling.

Two wasn't there. Carver quietly made his way into the room. Cleared the bathroom and the large walk-in closet to be sure. Jessica was alone.

Carver pulled some items from his backpack. They were from the duffel bag he'd taken from the kidnapper's safehouse. It would be poetic justice to use them now. He dampened a rag with chloroform and quietly made his way across the room.

He put the cloth over Jessica's mouth. Her eyelids opened. Her eyes flashed with surprise. And then she slumped unconscious. That would probably hold her for a while, but he gave her a small dose of a sedative from a syringe to be sure.

Carver went into the hallway and looked over the railing at the center staircase. He heard a conversation coming from the kitchen below. Two voices. Both guards were in there.

He considered his options. Stealth was probably the smartest option. Probably the most forgiving option. But he wasn't in a forgiving mood. He crept down the stairs. Went to the kitchen. Saw the two guards from before inside drinking beer and eating.

It was tempting to pop in and say something. Let them know exactly what was about to happen. But that would be dumb. He aimed. Practiced the shots. When he felt ready, he aimed again, pulled the trigger. Aimed slightly left and pulled the trigger again.

The gun coughed twice. Two headshots. Two less assholes in the world. And a much easier way out of the house.

Carver hunted along the bottom floor and found a small closet with the camera monitors and the wi-fi router. They were cheaper cameras without local storage. He unplugged the wi-fi. It seemed fair, all things considered.

The alarm panel was also there. He took a moment to disable it. Then it was time to go. Time to get Jessica to her final destination.

He was on his way up the stairs when the front door opened. A man stepped inside. He was Caucasian. Buzzed hair. About six feet tall. Wearing black fatigues. He looked like he was getting ready to go on a mission.

The man was Two.

Carver continued upstairs, hoping Two didn't look up. Hoping he didn't make a detour into the kitchen. He ducked into the first room on the right. Crouched in the darkness.

Two jogged up the stairs. He strode purposefully toward Jessica's bedroom. It looked like he had one thing on his mind.

Carver let him go past. He counted to ten, then came out of hiding and went to the bedroom. Two was sitting on the side of the bed. Stroking Jessica's hair. Talking softly to her.

"Did you fall asleep reading again?" Two kissed her forehead. "Wake up, sleepyhead."

It was just embarrassing listening to him talk like that. It reminded him of the way Joe talked to Andrea. How they talked to each other. Like they didn't care if anyone was watching.

Carver stepped into the room, rifle trained on Two's back. "Don't tell me you actually love that woman."

Two stiffened.

"Don't follow through with your first impulse," Carver said. "You're not fast enough."

Two put his hands up. Stood and turned slowly. He looked calm. Unconcerned. "Why are you here?"

"Your plan was smart. A sledgehammer with a horseshoe was a real nice touch. And cutting the wi-fi was sneaky. But you didn't account for the same thing I didn't."

"What's that?"

"Most cameras don't come with local storage and battery backup. These did. I just wished I'd realized that sooner." Carver shrugged. "Live and learn, I guess."

"I don't believe you."

"I'm here with a rifle pointed at your head. What's not to believe?"

"You're bluffing. You're trying to get an admission of guilt. You really think I killed Joe?"

Carver shook his head. "No. You delivered the stunning blow. Your girlfriend is the one who killed him."

Two blinked. That was the only sign he realized the jig was up. "What do you intend to do with us?"

"For starters, drop all your weapons. That includes the knife on your right thigh, the gun holstered on your lower back, and the gun under your jacket."

Two dropped the weapons one by one. "Why not just shoot me?"

"I should. I really should. But that's too quick and I'm real unhappy about what you did to my friend."

"I did it for her." Two nodded at Jessica. "I'd do anything for her."

"That's nice."

Two's eyes narrowed. "Your friend died like a dog. You should have seen the look on his face right when I hit him."

"Thanks."

Two looked confused. "For what?"

"For making sure I don't make this easy for you." Carver leaned the rifle against the wall. "By the way, after I kill you, I'm going to cut off your manhood and feed it to your girlfriend."

Two charged straight at him. It would have caught most people by surprise. But it was a textbook move. Lunge when the enemy is not expecting it. Close the gap when the other person has a long-range weapon like a rifle.

Carver let him come. Two went straight for the midriff. Like he was going to wrestle Carver to the ground. That was a mistake.

Two's shoulder rammed into Carver's stomach. Carver had already planted his feet. He clasped his hands together and brought them down hard on the other man's exposed back. Breath exploded from Two's lungs.

His grip faltered. Carver rammed his elbows on the other man's back. Two lost his grip. Staggered back. Carver didn't like using his fists. The risk of breaking a hand on someone's hard head was the main factor.

In this case, he was willing to make an exception. He delivered an uppercut to Two's jaw. Two's feet left the floor for a second. He crashed onto his back. Blood poured from a cut in his lip.

Carver gripped the front of his shirt. Yanked him off the floor. He spun them around. Slammed Two against the wall. Gripped his neck. Slammed him into the wall again, leaving an imprint of his body in the drywall.

He released Two. The other man staggered drunkenly. Went down in a heap. Carver knelt on his chest. Two wheezed. His arms flailed weakly, trying to dislodge the weight.

"You deserve worse. A lot worse." Carver leaned closer. Drew his survival knife. Stabbed it into Two's groin.

Two screamed in pain.

Carver twisted the knife. He let Two scream himself hoarse. Then he removed his knee from his chest.

Two stared up at him, gasping. He tried to say something, but didn't have the breath for it.

Carver grinned. "You should see the look on your face." Then he put a hand around Two's neck and squeezed until he felt something break. Two's eyes turned glassy. Carver felt for a pulse. Made sure there wasn't one.

His gloves were soaked with blood. He went into the bathroom and rinsed them off in the sink. The material was thin and grippy. It dried quickly with the hair dryer. He put them back on and went to the bed.

Jessica was sleeping peacefully. Carver kind of wished she could have seen what happened. Since that wasn't a possibility, he took the promised souvenir from Two and put it in a small plastic trash bag he pulled out of the bathroom trashcan.

He lifted the mayor's unconscious form off the bed. He slung her over his shoulder like a sack of rice. He returned downstairs, listening in case the third guard decided to abandon his post at the gate and come inside.

He went across the lush, green grass of the back yard. The floodlights blinked on when he exited the back door. But there was no one in the house to notice. No working cameras to record his departure.

Carver unlatched the gate in the back of the fence. He swung it open and went through. Then he hustled with his cargo to the stone wall. This would be a little trickier. Jessica was probably around a hundred and forty pounds.

She wasn't heavy for a woman of her height, but it would make scaling the wall a little harder. Tossing her over was an option, but that might kill her if she landed wrong. It wasn't time for her to die just yet.

He climbed the ladder, angling slightly sideways to keep her legs from getting caught on the ladder. He went down the other ladder and laid her on the ground. Then he climbed back up, retrieved the ladder from the other side.

He laid both ladders on the ground on their sides so they'd be easy to pick up. He slung Jessica over his shoulder, knelt slightly and picked up the ladders. With the backpack, two ladders, and an unconscious woman on his shoulder, he started the hike back to the truck.

CHAPTER 45

Carver knocked on Andrea's bedroom door.

There was no answer, so he knocked again, louder. "Andrea?"

"Huh?" There was the sound of her fumbling with the door handle then the door opened. She stared at him groggily. "Carver? What's going on?"

"I'll explain on the way."

"On the way to where?"

"To town." He nodded toward her closet. "Get dressed."

She blinked out of her grogginess. "Okay. Give me a second." She came out of her room a moment later in jeans and a T-shirt, her long hair thrown back in a ponytail. "What's this about, Carver?"

"You'll see. Let's go." They went outside, climbed in the truck, and drove to town.

Andrea watched him curiously as he drove but didn't ask questions. She probably knew better, thanks to being married to Joe.

Carver drove to the warehouse and parked near the rollup door on the side.

Andrea gave him a confused look but followed him inside. They went back through the apartments and through the metal door. Most of the maze walls were gone, leaving the center of the arena open.

There was one wall standing. They walked to the other side and Andrea gasped. "My God! What is this?"

Monty, Alice, Albert, and all the former prisoners were gathered around the wall looking at it.

Mayor Jessica Herrada glared at them. She was chained to the wall, shackles on her arms and ankles, spread-eagled on the metal surface.

Andrea grabbed Carver's arm. "Carver, what in the hell is going on?"

"Watch this." He gave her his phone. Played the video he'd copied to it. The video of Joe's final moments.

Andrea's eyes grew wider and wider as she watched it unfold. She let out a scream of pain and agony that echoed through the arena when she saw the final blow. She shrieked and rushed Jessica, pummeling her with her fists.

Monty stepped forward. Handed Carver the sledgehammer with the horseshoe welded onto it. They'd found it in what could only be described as an armory. It was in the same area as the locker room and showers.

The armory had everything from guns to swords. It had a large medieval weapons selection. Maces, morning stars, halberds, pikes, and so forth. The sledgehammer was actually a small warhammer. The horseshoe had been recently welded to it.

It underscored that the mayor had known about all the operations in this town and that Two was her lover and right-hand man. She wasn't just a puppet of the cartel.

Carver turned to Andrea. Held the hammer out to her. She stared at it silently for a moment. Took it. She hefted it. Took a practice swing.

Jessica watched her nervously, face growing increasingly worried.

Andrea turned the horseshoe side facing away from her. Then she savagely swung it right into Jessica's knee.

The mayor screamed in pain. "You idiots don't know what you're doing! She groaned. Tears streamed down her face. "I run this town! I run the cartel! If you don't let me go, you'll be hunted to the ends of the earth!"

Andrea swung the hammer. Slammed the mayor's knee again. Bones crunched. An agonized scream tore from Jessica's throat. Andrea bared her teeth. Swung again and connected with the mayor's other knee.

Monty watched in fascination. Carver felt grim satisfaction. He wasn't usually one for a slow, agonizing death, but this woman deserved it.

"Stop for a second." Carver grabbed the hammer before Andrea swung it again. He gripped Jessica's jaw. Turned her head toward him. "What do you mean, you run the cartel?"

Jessica moaned. Spat in his face. "I'm the sister of Pedro Herrada. The head of the Sons of Blood. I was sent here to oversee border operations." She shivered violently. "You kill me, and he'll unleash hell on this town."

Carver stepped back. Turned to the others. "It's your town. What's your decision?"

Albert raised a hand in front of him. Held out his thumb. Turned it down. Monty did the same. The other prisoners turned their thumbs down. Some of them walked to Jessica. Spat in her face.

Some slapped her. Kicked her.

Melinda punched her in the stomach. "Puta!" She hit her again.

Then they backed off. Looked to Andrea.

Andrea was shaking. She was sweating. Adrenalin was probably pumping through her veins. She looked at Carver. "I don't know if I can do it. I've never taken a life."

"For Joe," Albert said.

Carver nodded. "For Joe."

Jessica glared at her. "Do it, bitch! Do it! You don't have it in you, do you?"

Andrea took a deep, calming breath. She stared the other woman in the eyes. "The worst part is, you'll never understand what you took from me. What you took from this world."

Jessica scowled at her. "I did what I needed to do."

"No. You didn't need to do what you did. You did it out of spite and hatred." Andrea wiped tears from her cheeks. "I know this won't bring Joe back. I know it won't make me feel better."

Jessica spat at her. "I knew you didn't have it in you."

Andrea smiled through her tears. "Just because I know these things doesn't mean you get to keep on breathing."

She swung the hammer overhead.

Jessica's eyes went wide. "No!" she screamed.

Andrea brought the hammer down in a full overhead arc. She swung it down on the mayor's head. There was a loud crack. Blood poured from Jessica's scalp. Flowed down her face. Her eyes crossed and she convulsed.

Mayor Jessica Herrada made a terrible croaking noise. A final agonized scream tore from her throat. And then she went still.

Carver checked her pulse. It grew slower, and slower, and stopped.

Andrea doubled over and vomited. She dropped the hammer. Fell to her knees. A low, keening wail of absolute pain fled from her body.

Carver knelt next to her. Hugged her. "Andrea, I'm sorry."

She hugged him tightly. Cried into his blood shirt until she was exhausted. He helped her up. Let her hold on as long as she wanted.

Joe's killer was dead, but the pain Andrea felt would last for a long time.

There were tears in the others' eyes. Albert was sobbing. Monty was looking pensively at the dead mayor. Melinda and the others were hugging each other. Wetting the sand with their tears.

Their nightmare was over. For now.

Monty broke the silence. "How do we handle this?"

"What do you mean?" Jeremy looked confused. "We have tons of evidence tying this to powerful people. Let's expose them. Put everything out there for the public to see."

"Will it be enough to overcome the propaganda machine?" Monty said. "Or will this get buried as another conspiracy theory?"

Jeremy looked at Carver. "What would you do?"

"Collect the bodies. Take them to the funeral home. Cremate them and dump them in the open grave. Then take the evidence and pretend nothing ever happened."

"Huh?" Jeremy looked perplexed. "Are you serious?"

"Serious as a heart attack." Carver shrugged. "I don't want to be associated with this. I want to be forgotten. I've got enough powerful people who want me dead already. No need to add to the list. If you go public, you'll be marking yourselves for execution. Simple as that."

"No." Melinda shook her head. "They tried to silence us. We need to put the world on blast and show everyone what they've been doing. Show how they've been silencing the opposition. This cannot stand!"

"Your choice," Carver said. "But there are plenty more gangbangers in this town. Plenty more crooked cops. The cartel has no problem sending people over the border, so they could easily send a kill squad after the people who ended the mayor."

Melinda was looking at her phone. They'd found a stash with dozens of phones and other belongings that had been taken from the prisoners. Her mouth dropped open slightly. "Pedro Herrada runs the largest cartel in South America. He united the several Brazilian cartels with others in Colombia and Venezuela."

Carver pulled up the search on his phone and entered a name. He cross-referenced it with Pedro Herrada. The results showed a definitive link. Brilhante Tintas, Brilliant Paints in English, was connected to the Filhos de Sangue—Sons of Blood.

The same cartel that had been active in Morganville. The same cartel that had owned Paola and kept Jasper Whittaker in business.

They weren't connected to Enigma, the shadow organization that owned Portland and San Francisco. At least, not as far as he could tell. They might be competitors, or they might simply ignore each other.

Whatever the case might be, they were both cancers on society. Cancer could be cut out but unless it was exterminated, it would always come back stronger than ever. That might happen here.

Carver wasn't a doctor. He was a butcher, plain and simple. And he wasn't sticking around to help the locals with the sudden power vacuum. That was up to them to fill.

Andrea finally spoke. "I think Carver is right."

All eyes turned to her.

Monty raised an eyebrow. "You mean about covering this up?"

She nodded. "We've punished most of the wrongdoers."

Jeremy chuckled. "Um, yeah. They're dead."

"And if we release all of this evidence, we should do it anonymously. Make sure it can never be traced back to us."

Carver saw where she was going with this. "Joe must have told you about psyops."

She managed a smile. "Yes, he did. And since we can't expect help from the state or federal government, we have to handle these matters ourselves. Unless we want the cartel hunting down everyone responsible and killing them one by one." She turned to Jeremy. "Because that's exactly what will happen."

Jeremy pressed his lips into a thin line. "I mean, it's a risk we take as journalists."

"And where did that risk get you?" Andrea waved a hand around the arena. "Almost butchered by the same senator you exposed in your videos."

"We're not really journalists," Melinda said. "We're online commentators at best. We take mainstream news, break it down and show how they're gaslighting the population. I should know. I've watched your videos before."

Jeremy nodded. "True. I'm not actually out there investigating or anything."

"But you're pissing off powerful people. People who have become rich on the government teat." Andrea pointed to the mayor's body. "And Pedro Herrada is going to come for whoever killed his sister. So why don't we play the same game these assholes have been playing?"

Monty grinned. "Kidnap them and put them in the arena?"

Jeremy laughed. "I wish."

"As much as I'd like to, I simply don't have the time, the money, or the inclination to do all that work." Andrea folded her arms over her chest. "But we can collect the bodies, cremate them, and clean up. We make these people simply vanish. Create a mystery. And we anonymously release the evidence."

Jeremy nodded. "Okay, but if I show up among the living again, won't that tell them that I escaped somehow?"

"I sincerely doubt most people in the organization know who's on the schedule. We'll simply delete the entries with our names."

Monty shook his head. "No, leave them. Change the dates to make it look like they were going to be taken next. And add some names."

"I looked up the names of those Ukrainians," Jeremy said. "They were high-ranking military officials in the army. I used the fingerprints of one of them and found a crypto account with almost a billion dollars in it."

"They've been taking aid from the US and giving it to themselves instead of buying weapons or food." Melinda shook her head. "God, what a mess."

Alice moved to the front of the group. "Can you move that crypto somewhere else?"

"Probably, but I'm not about to transfer anything to my bank account." Jeremy shook his head. "The IRS would be all over me in a heartbeat, not to mention it would link me to the Ukrainians."

"I know who can handle it," Carver said. "And I agree with Andrea. So, let's take a vote and get on with it."

Melinda stared at him. "You're a man of few words, aren't you?"

Carver shrugged.

The vote was unanimous. Melinda and Jeremy were the ones Carver thought might vote against it, but they were the first to raise their hands. Brad was the last one to raise his hand. He looked like a man who was almost too ashamed to even vote.

Monty clapped his hands with excitement. "I love this plan. I just hope we can pull it off."

Carver checked the time. "We need to get to the mansion right away. Before the bodies there are discovered."

"We'll collect all the smartphones and fingers required to open them." Jeremy shuddered. "That's one sentence I never imagined I'd be saying."

"Put the severed fingers on ice," Carver said. "And make sure you label which phone go with which finger."

"Oh, god." Alice's face turned a shade of green. "I'm going to be sick."

"It gets easier after you chop off the first couple of fingers." Carver patted her shoulder. "You're going to be okay."

Melinda gave Carver a look. "You're weird."

Carver, Albert, and Monty took the tunnel across the street. The body of the first guard was still in the garage. Carver frisked the body and found the keys to the police SUV. He unholstered his Glock and attached the suppressor.

"You going to shoot anyone that's there?" Monty asked.

Carver nodded. "The guard at the front gate is working directly for the mayor. No doubt."

"Okay." Monty got in the back seat.

Albert took shotgun. "I never thought things would end like this." Albert tutted. "And I'm missing the bike rally."

"Yeah, but which is more fun?" Monty said.

"This, of course." Albert laughed. "Man, the look on the mayor's face right before Andrea smashed it." He sighed. "Good times. Good times."

"Did you see the way her eyes crossed?" Monty said. "I wish I could've taken a picture of that and put it on her billboards."

"Foul, evil woman." Albert's face soured. "I don't believe in killing, but those people deserved it and more."

Carver let them talk it out. They were probably trying to cope with the extreme violence they'd witnessed. He had no doubt that Andrea would relive killing Jessica every time she closed her eyes for a long time.

He reached Paradise Acres and pulled up to the guard house. The guard came outside, a grin on his face. He probably thought one of his buddies was in the car. The windows were tinted, so he couldn't see inside.

The guard rapped on the car window. "You got me some fresh rape videos?"

Carver rolled down the window. The guard barely had a chance to look surprised before a bullet took a shortcut through his brain. He dropped.

"You hear that?" Albert said. "The man was wanting a rape video!"

Carver got out of the car. He hefted the body and put it in the back of the SUV. It was a Chevy Suburban, so there was plenty of space in the back. He went into the gatehouse and opened the gate.

He hopped back in. Drove to the mansion. The man at the gate also looked pleased to see the SUV. Apparently, the dirty cop who drove this car was known for delivering videos of the events in the arena.

Carver waited until the guard was at the window, then lowered it and put him down with a single shot to the skull. He loaded that body into the SUV.

"My God." Albert shook his head. "I don't know how you're so calm about it."

"They're inhuman," Monty said. "They deserve it."

Carver parked in front of the mansion. They went inside and collected the two bodies downstairs then Two's body from upstairs. He used an oxidizer to clean up the blood. Monty searched the rooms and found Jessica's laptop. It was password locked, but he said he'd try to get it hacked.

Once the place was clean, they left. Carver stopped at the main gatehouse to delete the camera footage. It looked like it was stored locally and not in the cloud, so that made things easier.

Monty knew which funeral home the cartel had been using and gave Carver directions. It was an old building on a lot overgrown with weeds and scrub brush. They drove around the back where there was a loading zone for coffins.

No one was in the building. Monty turned on the lights and revealed four large metal boxes. They were eight feet tall with mechanical controls on the side. There were printed instructions next to the first machine.

"I know how to operate them," Albert said. "My cousin used to own a funeral home."

Carver nodded. "Good."

Albert set about warming up the machines.

"How long does it take to reduce a body to ashes?" Monty asked.

"Depends on the size." The SUV was backed up to the delivery door, so Albert opened it and pointed to one of the girthier bodies. "That one might take a couple of hours or more."

Monty stared into the darkness outside. "I wonder how many different people's ashes are in the unmarked grave." He turned to Carver. "Their families need to know what happened to them."

"We'll make sure of it when all the information is leaked," Carver said. "Just make sure the cartel members' ashes are scattered somewhere else."

"Oh, I already got a spot picked out for them," Albert said. "In the county landfill."

Monty laughed. "Oh, that's amazing."

"Yeah. No one is going to know where they vanished to."

"I like it," Carver said. He unloaded the bodies and put them in heavy cardboard boxes and on special gurneys that were used in the cremation process.

"It's okay if we leave you here alone?" Monty asked Albert.

Albert nodded. "I ain't afraid of the dead."

That was good, Carver thought. Because this place was about to be full of bodies.

CHAPTER 46

It was done.

All the bodies were at the crematorium. It'd take a full day or more to cremate them all. All the smartphones had been gathered along with the digits to unlock them. Everyone was exhausted, but spirits were high.

Melinda, Jeremy, Alice, and others had examined all the phones. Discarded the ones with nothing useful. Put the valuable ones in another pile.

Carver had been in contact with Leon. Leon was absolutely shocked by the arena operation. Carver had told him his plan and Leon had been ecstatic.

He'd provided Carver with multiple crypto addresses. Carver took the phones with access to the funds and began moving them to Leon's secret accounts. He also had offshore accounts for any fiat currencies that the phones had access to.

By the end of it, Leon's coffers were full. Almost nine hundred million dollars. He was going to use that to fund a full out war against Enigma, the Sons of Blood, and any other organization he discovered.

He would also handle the anonymous release of all the evidence and the location of the ashes of the victims. It was going wide so no one could stop it. Not even the powerful elite who controlled Enigma.

He would also add more names to the calendar. Make it look like they'd been targeting the political opposition. That might trigger investigations that would uncover the people who were helping the cartel.

He would also send funds to the survivors to help them recover and to fund their efforts to keep their video channels going.

Carver had a final meeting with the former prisoners. He made sure they had their stories straight. That they'd been vacationing, hiking, or otherwise out of touch for the time they'd been gone.

That would explain their absences. There was to be no mention that they'd been kidnapped and rescued. He beat new truths into their heads.

This had never happened.

There was no one named Carver.

Then he left.

Andrea walked him outside the warehouse to Joe's pickup. "Carver, you can have the pickup if you want it."

"It's nice, but it's a marked vehicle." He shook his head. "I'll just take a bus."

"What about the Dodge Power Wagon? I'm sure Joe would love to know that you have it."

He thought it over. Nodded. "I won't be registering it though."

"That's okay." She hugged him. "I think Joe would be ecstatic about how you handled things."

"Joe's not the ecstatic type."

She teared up. "You're right. He'd be silently proud of you. Buy you a beer and slap your back."

"Yeah." Carver nodded. He stared into the distance. "But I'd rather have my friend back."

"Me too." She wiped away a tear. "I spoke with Captain Hernandez. He said they'll return the body tomorrow so we can arrange a funeral. Are you sure you won't stick around for that?"

"I already paid my respects." Carver put a hand on her shoulder. "Joe would understand."

She smiled. "He hated funerals. Called them a waste of time. He told me I could just dump his body somewhere convenient."

"Sounds like Joe." Carver tried to smile, but his face felt heavy. "Okay. I'll take the pickup back and get the Power Wagon. If it doesn't work, I'll borrow that sedan in the garage."

"Whatever you want, Carver." Andrea stood on tiptoe and kissed his cheek. "Goodbye."

"Goodybye, Andrea." He walked to the pickup. Got in. Drove away.

He didn't like what he was feeling. His guts felt twisted and leaden. It wasn't just because of Joe's death. It was because of what he and Andrea had. And what was taken from them. They'd had true happiness.

"It must have been something else," he muttered. And it was something Carver didn't want. The greater the happiness, the deeper the sorrow. Deep down, he knew that was why he hadn't tried harder with Paola.

Their time together had been good. Better than he wanted to admit. And it had stung when she left. But that sting had subsided into a faint itch that reared its head every now and again. As much as he wanted to see her again, he couldn't let that happen.

Because he didn't want to find happiness and risk losing it all. He didn't want to ever feel that kind of pain. That just wasn't the kind of person he was. He was better off alone. Better off doing his own thing.

The best he could hope for was contentment. A cold beer on a hot beach. Or maybe camping in the mountains and living off the land. Carver would never find love because he wasn't looking for it.

And that was fine. Just fine.

— • —

EPILOGUE

Leon finished downloading the files from the mayor's computer. The original laptop was going to be wiped and destroyed. The files from the phones, this laptop, and the laptop at the warehouse were going to be collected, collated, and arranged.

He wasn't onsite but operating remotely. Monty, one of the locals, was giving him remote access to devices so he could organize everything. Most of the files were already uploaded to a storage cloud account that he'd created.

He was forming ideas. Deciding how to release everything for maximum impact. The censorship machines were going to swing into full operation once everything hit the internet. The propaganda was going to be off the charts.

It was clear from the evidence that the Sons of Blood weren't part of Enigma, but they were doing business with them. The human trafficking for citizenship scheme was an Enigma program.

It was designed to help them get their people into power. To further help them destabilize local governments. Their end goal wasn't clear, but Leon could see where it was heading.

His facial identification program was checking all the images and matching them to people. It was doubtful that he could identify any Enigma personnel in these files, but it was worth trying.

The analysis had already identified many of the people who'd participated in the arena. Two powerful federal senators were among those who'd hunted down political opposition and even people they didn't like in the arena.

Leon flipped to the results screen and looked at the new images. One of them made his heart skip a beat. He opened the image. The image had been flagged and linked to other images. But it hadn't identified the person in the picture.

It didn't need to. Leon knew who she was. He immediately took a picture and sent it via encrypted text to Carver. Then he combed through the folder the image had come from.

The folder was titled *Loose Ends*. It was from Jessica Herrada's laptop. There were dozens of pictures of various people. Some of them had red X's across the images. Probably people that had been found.

The image Leon had sent Carver didn't have that red X. But there was an accompanying file indicating that the target had been located. That resources had been dispatched to capture the target.

The target was to be brought to El Fuerte where Jessica could dispose of them in the arena. If the timeline was accurate, the team sent after the target was already on location. It might be too late to stop the kidnapping.

"Shit," Leon muttered. He looked at the picture again. Carver was not going to like this.

The cartel knew Paola's location.

BOOKS BY JOHN CORWIN

Books by John Corwin
Want more? Never miss an update by joining my email list and following me on social media!
Join my Facebook group at https://www.facebook.com/groups/overworldconclave
Join my email list: www.johncorwin.net
Fan page: https://www.facebook.com/johncorwinauthor

PSYCHOLOGICAL THRILLERS
The Family Business
AMOS CARVER THRILLERS
Dead Before Dawn
Dead List
Dead and Buried
Dead Man Walking
Dead By The Dozen
Dead Run
Dead Weather Days
Dead to Rights
Dead but not Forgotten
CHRONICLES OF CAIN
To Kill a Unicorn
Enter Oblivion
Throne of Lies
At The Forest of Madness
The Dead Never Die
Shadow of Cthulhu
Cabal of Chaos
Monster Squad

Gates of Yog-Sothoth

Shadow Over Tokyo

Into the Multiverse

THE OVERWORLD CHRONICLES

Sweet Blood of Mine

Dark Light of Mine

Fallen Angel of Mine

Dread Nemesis of Mine

Twisted Sister of Mine

Dearest Mother of Mine

Infernal Father of Mine

Sinister Seraphim of Mine

Wicked War of Mine

Dire Destiny of Ours

Aetherial Annihilation

Baleful Betrayal

Ominous Odyssey

Insidious Insurrection

Utopia Undone

Overworld Apocalypse

Apocryphan Rising

Soul Storm

Devil's Due

Overworld Ascension

Assignment Zero (An Elyssa Short Story)

OVERWORLD UNDERGROUND

Soul Seer

Demonicus

Infernal Blade

OVERWORLD ARCANUM

Conrad Edison and the Living Curse

Conrad Edison and the Anchored World

Conrad Edison and the Broken Relic

Conrad Edison and the Infernal Design

Conrad Edison and the First Power

STAND ALONE NOVELS

Mars Rising

ENJOYED THE BOOK?

JOIN MY READER GROUP ON FACEBOOK
HTTPS://WWW.FACEBOOK.COM/GROUPS/OVERWORLDCONCLAVE

Printed in Dunstable, United Kingdom